Tyrone put his son down and looked around the room. Mia saw that his Polo was unbuttoned. He wore a white tee, but the undershirt did little to hide his rippling physique.

Tyrone has large pectorals that Mia definitely didn't remember. His arms were also bigger, with defined muscles in his forearms and swollen biceps. And Tyrone used to have a pencil neck that met the rest of his body with no flair. His traps and shoulders had serious bulges now.

And it wasn't overdone. He looked nice. He was damned fine.

Tyrone had a strong jaw line. He was a bit more bronze now, and the darker skin tone accentuated his beautiful hazel eyes. His moustache and goatee were gone as well as his afro. Tyrone sported a crew cut that would have made the Marines proud. His edge-up was flawless. Overall, he was without a blemish.

He looked into Mia's eyes and smiled and she couldn't help but smile back.

"You look good," he said. "You gotta dress like that for work?"

Mia nodded, still a little speechless.

FIXIN' TYRONE

KEITH WALKER

Genesis Press, Inc.

INDIGO LOVE STORIES

An imprint of Genesis Press, Inc.
Publishing Company

Genesis Press, Inc.
P.O. Box 101
Columbus, MS 39703

ISBN: 13 DIGIT : 978-1-58571-365-3
ISBN: 10 DIGIT : 1-58571-365-1
Manufactured in the United States of America

First Edition

Visit us at www.genesis-press.com
or call at 1-888-Indigo-1-4-0

DEDICATION

This book is for anyone who believes
in the possibility of love.

ACKNOWLEDGMENTS

I would like to thank my mom, my sister and my brother. I would also like to thank the staff at the hospital who read my rough drafts and encouraged me along the way. I'm sure I won't remember all of you, and I apologize ahead of time to those I forget, but I must acknowledge Brandy, Vicki, Theda, Erica, Regina, Letty, Alesia, Lynda, Maricela, Crystal, Shonya, Amy, Charlene, Andrea, Kristen, Naike, Emma and Judd. Special thanks to Uncle Steve, Kierra, Vollie, and Jason and a big shout-out to the heart of Fort Worth's poetry scene: Janean Livingston, Mike Guinn, Susan Vogel-Taylor and Anthony Douglas. Anthony encouraged me to write a book for women, and we wouldn't have *Fixin' Tyrone* if not for him. My biggest thanks goes, of course, to Rachel Walker. Thanks for sitting down (even when you were tired and sleepy) and listening to every scene of every chapter of every book I've ever written. Your critiques are always crucial, and I couldn't have done it without you. Thanks to everyone who bought my book. Hope you have as much fun reading it as I did writing it.

Keith Thomas Walker

CHAPTER 1
THE ERIC INCIDENT

This went against so many of Mia's rules.

She'd been dating Eric for only two months. It wasn't necessarily too soon to have sex with him; her rules for sex were based on the quality of dates rather than calendar time, but this particular position was generally taboo for newbies. This was more of a fifth or sixth episode type of thing. Yet on only their *first* sexual encounter, Eric had her bent, exposed and vulnerable.

Yes, *vulnerable.*

A case could be made that all intimate maneuvers put women in positions of inferiority, but Mia knew better. At least with missionary you could *look* at him. You could see his eyes, his expressions, and if you worked it just right, you could see that he wasn't in very much control at all. Mia has seen eyes cross, tears of joy, inarticulate babbling, and even *drool.* But doggy style is different.

Some women view it as just another facet of their sexual repertoire. Some even *prefer* it to regular sex, but for Mia, this was something special; something almost *sacred.* With missionary you can fool yourself into believing a meshing of souls is occurring as the sweat on your bellies mingles, but with doggy style, there's no holding, no kissing. When you're on your knees, there's only raw sex. You're reminded that men are dogs and you might start to wonder if this makes you his bitch.

Any man who thought he was going to simply fold Mia into whatever position he pleased during their first episode of intimacy had another think coming.

Yet there they were.

And this wasn't something you could just *roll* into; it took conscious body placement; willingness on both sides. And Mia had no idea what was going on back there. Eric could be smiling. He could be laughing. He could be rolling his eyes in boredom, or he could have one hand in the air like he was at the rodeo. He could be texting his friends or throwing up gang signs.

Westsiiide!

Even if your man is serious about the encounter, doggy style is not the position for new, gentle lovers who want to develop a spiritual bond. But it felt good. Mia gripped the mattress and lowered her head and moaned into the sheets. Eric wasn't just back there pounding senselessly. As implausible as it was, Mia felt he was actually *making love* to her. He was like an erotic masseur. Hands were here. There. He rubbed her shoulders. Traced a finger down her spine. He caressed her back, and then her sides. His hands slid across her ribs and settled on her hips. He fondled her ass and then was back to her neck again.

Giving herself to a new partner normally made Mia awkward and unsure of her movements, but there was no hesitance with Eric. She didn't even feel like she was with a new lover. He touched every spot she wanted touched. He knew when she wanted more or slower or faster. He was as smooth as a ride in a limousine. He was good.

Too good?

Experienced?

A ho?

Mia forced the thoughts from her head.

Why do you always go there? Does there always have to be something wrong? Why not just enjoy the here and now?

So she did.

Mia wasn't always an audible lovemaker, but since they were already so far past her normal pace of things, what did it matter? She moaned, and this seemed to invigorate Eric. He moaned, too, and their noise together was almost enough to drown out Jagged Edge, but no one drowns out Jagged Edge. On a CD player near the bed, the lead singer crooned about how he felt like he'd walked right out of heaven after losing his girl.

Mia felt like she was walking right *into* heaven. It was much too soon to entertain such thoughts, but sometimes—sometimes it felt so good, and the music was just right, and the motions were so pleasing—sometimes it's okay to let your heart wander just a little.

Pipe layers like Eric are few and far between.

He slammed in deep, reaching depths unexplored in *years*, and Mia cried out in pleasure. *This* is what she had been waiting for. This made up for Richard's pygmy penis, Roland's stanky drawers, and Colin's premature ejaculations. Mia didn't care anymore about this going against her normal pace, and she didn't care what faces

Eric might be making—or *whatever else* he might be doing back there.

If he *did* scream *Westsiiiide!* Mia would twist her fingers, cock her head, and holler out with him—it was *that* good. And the girls at the beauty shop would definitely hear about him tomorrow. Mia would get her unkempt sex-hair fixed with a smile, and she might even get a pedicure if she could straighten out her toes by then.

They climaxed together.

Mia's legs trembled and she sank slowly until she lay prostrate. Eric followed her down, still inside, and he lay on top of her. His body was warm, and it felt good to feel him all over. He breathed against the back of her head. He lifted her hair and kissed her on the neck. He kissed behind her ear and she hummed. Eric knew where all of her buttons were. He sucked her earlobe and told her she was beautiful. He told her he didn't think he'd ever felt as good as he did right then. He seemed poised to tell her he loved her, and Mia was almost ready to believe him if he did.

It was that good.

After a few minutes of snuggling and spooning, he asked her if she wanted to take a shower.

"Do you have to work tomorrow?"

"No. I try not to work on Saturdays," she said.

"But last week—"

"I know. I had to catch up on a few things. That's not the norm."

"So, do you have to leave, or can you stay tonight?"

"My sister's watching the kids," Mia said, looking forward to spending the twilight hours with him for the first time. "What about you?" It was after ten, but Eric worked at the post office and kept odd hours. In the two months they'd been dating, Eric had shifts that started as early as 2:00 a.m. and as late as 11:00 p.m.

"No, I'm off tonight," he said.

Mia smiled.

Eric ran water for their shower. Mia stood next to the sink and studied the floral design on the shower curtain rather than her own reflection. As with many women, Mia was not 100 percent pleased with her figure, and she felt exposed in those bright lights. She stood five feet, nine inches tall and was thin in the waist with shapely hips. She was dark-skinned, the color of cherry wood, with large eyes and full lips. At only 129 pounds, she knew she was *fine*. She needed only to wear tight jeans to the market to be reminded of this, but her breasts were only an A cup.

Some men considered this a failing. Having never stood nude before him, Mia wasn't sure which end of the spectrum Eric was on, but he cleared up any confusion with an unrestrained ogle.

He eyed her with a smile like a child on Christmas.

"You look *real* good, Miss Clemmons."

"You're making me nervous."

"Why?"

"The way you're looking at me," she said, but smiled, her hands unconsciously meeting between her legs.

He held his hands to his sides. "You're not the only one naked."

"Yeah," she said, taking in his full physique unabashedly. Eric wasn't necessarily the most handsome man she'd been with, but she couldn't find any blatant flaws. He was completely bald. That wasn't Mia's thing, but he was also clean shaven and she did like that. The only hair on his head was his thin eyebrows. He reminded her of Tyson Beckford before he went scruffy.

Eric had almost a hundred pounds on her, but he was six feet, two inches tall. He had broad shoulders and a nice chest. His pecs actually had definition. So many men his size had those downward pointing nipples that gave the impression of man boobs, but Eric's upper body was nice.

He didn't have a rippling six-pack, but his stomach was flat, and the further down she gazed, the more impressed Mia was. Small men are quick to remind you that length and width come second to the way you work it—Mia has been with a few who actually proved that adage right—but with Eric she would have the best of both worlds. And as fine as he was, Mia didn't feel she was extremely lucky to have a stud like Eric naked in his bathroom. On the contrary, she felt she *deserved* a man like this.

Mia was thirty-two years old, professional, and college-educated. She had two children with two different fathers, but any man who considered her babies a hindrance was welcome to lose her number. Mia knew she was attractive; she never needed makeup to enhance her beauty. Finding a man was never a problem for her. Finding one who wasn't married, unemployed, uneducated, an ex con, a pimp, a gigolo, a hustler or a player was the hard part. That had proved more difficult than finding the Holy Grail.

But Eric had a government job, drove a Beamer, had his own home, and (this is going to blow your freaking mind) he had *no* children. Not a one. He had never been married and, unless Mia totally misread the previous hour's activities, he was not gay. Eric watched the *news*! That may be no big deal to some, but Mia had dated guys who didn't know the difference between *Enron* and *Exxon*. They could rattle on and on about how Kobe shot the lights out last night but couldn't find China on a globe if their life depended on it.

"The water's hot," Eric said.

"I know this is going to sound cliché," Mia said, "but I don't usually do this."

"What? Take showers? I couldn't tell. You smell like an autumn breeze."

She rolled her eyes. "Yeah, *okay*, but I'm talking about you, and me, in the shower *together*."

"Why?"

"'Cause we're still new. I mean, we made love. That was good—"

"That *was* good."

"Yes, that was good, but I'm still not totally comfortable around you." She smiled and blushed, but he didn't notice.

"So . . . you don't want to take a shower?"

"Yes, I'm going to take a shower. I just want you to know that I don't usually do this with a guy I've only—"

"You've got a great body," he said.

"Thanks, but—"

"Come here."

They showered together. Eric's two-bedroom flat wasn't the most spacious, but his bathroom was larger than most, and the tub easily accommodated them without any awkward squeezes. All squeezes were soft and sensual.

He lathered up a mesh sponge and washed her back. From behind he soaped up her breasts and belly, but when he went down further, it was almost too much for Mia to bear. She turned to face him and found the space between them compromised.

"Wow," she said, looking down. She felt like a kid at the candy shop. *Is that for me?* She took the sponge from him and rubbed his chest and stomach.

"You're beautiful," he said.

Mia looked up at him and he kissed her, slowly. She dropped the sponge and caressed his throbbing member. Any doubts about Eric's strength were vanquished when he grabbed her buttocks and hoisted her into the air. Mia wrapped her legs around his waist and he smoothly entered her again.

You're moving too fast. This is not good.

The warnings were blaring, but Mia was finding it harder and harder to listen to her inner voice. The bathroom filled with steam, and she imagined they were making love in a hot spring. Eric was more vocal this time, which allowed her to be more vocal. His thrusts were slow, but hard; rough, yet passionate.

He turned and leaned her against the back tiles and they stared into each others' eyes. He sucked her neck and she nibbled his ear. Her breaths became heavy and pained, and, when he climaxed this time, they were very wet and very close; breast to breast, belly to belly, cheek to cheek, soul to soul.

CHAPTER 2
A TO Z AND THEN SOME

Eric made margaritas at midnight. They ate leftover pizza at one, and lay in bed and talked until just past 2:30 a.m. They slept together, spooned with visions of plum drops dancing in their heads perhaps, and might have lived happily ever after, but the damned margaritas did them in. Mia woke in the wee hours of the morning with a need to go to the bathroom. She sat up in bed and stepped on Eric's discarded britches on her way off the bed.

And something rattled under her foot.

She yanked her leg up with a start. Still half-sleep, Mia believed some poisonous reptile had slithered into the house. But when she looked down, even in the scant light she saw that it was only his pants crumpled there. She lowered her foot again cautiously until her big toe came in contact with the buzzing again. What she felt made her arms grow cold. Her heart sank like lead in her chest.

Mia tried to allay her fears: *Why does it have to be that?* she wondered. *Why do you always think the worst?* Eric having his cell phone on vibrate didn't mean he was a player. Maybe he was a gentleman. Maybe he wanted to give her his undivided attention that evening.

That was a possibility, a wonderfully charming one at that, but it wasn't going to fly with Mia. Not tonight. She didn't know Eric well enough. No one was making a business call this early, and if he was on call at work he wouldn't have the phone on vibrate. Mia didn't think it was one of his homeboys, either.

What if it's an emergency? If someone got arrested, they would call at any time.

That was her optimistic side talking, but Mia had been through too much bullshit with too many shiesty Negroes to allow herself to be blindsided yet again.

The phone stopped vibrating.

Mia looked back and saw that Eric was sleeping soundly, snoring a little, in fact. Watching him slumber, the pain tugged at her heart again. He was perfect. Dammit, why did it have to be like this with him? Why couldn't she meet just *one* honest man? Was that so much to ask?

You don't know what's going on, she reminded herself. *It could be legit.* And maybe that was true, but Mia would be damned if she wasn't going to find out. And not tomorrow or next week, either. She wasn't going to wait until she had so much of her time and heart invested; losing him would feel like losing an arm or leg. No, she would know this very minute.

Mia daintily slipped out of bed. She crouched over the pants on the balls of her feet. With the stealth of a ninja, she wriggled the phone from Eric's pocket and tip-toed to the bathroom without making any noises louder than her hurried breaths. She locked the door behind her, flipped on the lights, and sat on the toilet wearing only her bra and panties.

The light was bright in there, and sitting with the phone in her trembling hands, Mia felt naked, exposed as the dirty sneak she was. Her heart thumped like techno music. Her mouth was dry. What if he woke up and went straight for his phone?

He had his way with me, Mia told herself. Because he had her in *that* position, she had every right to know *everything* about him. But that wasn't true. This was a clear invasion of privacy and she knew it.

She looked at the phone's display. It read SIX MISSED CALLS.

Damn, six? Was it the same person or six different sluts? The only way to find out was to push the button glowing under the word LIST. The phone would display the missed calls, the phone numbers, and the names Eric saved them under. The only problem was that once Mia pushed that little green button, there was no going back. If the missed calls proved to be legitimate, she would not be able to change the display to read SIX MISSED CALLS again. She might be able to sneak the phone back into his pants, but Eric would know she looked through it.

Mia paused with her thumb on the button. Was it worth it? Eric was a good man. He treated her good, made *good* love to her. He had a car and a job. Lord, a car *and* a job, and a *house,* too. What would he do when he found out she'd been on his cell phone? Mia felt they had a connection, but men don't like women who invade their privacy. Even some honest men would rather be alone than with a jealous woman.

And that was just it; Mia *wasn't* a jealous woman. She'd never stalked a man. Never called more than twice if he wasn't answering.

That's why you've been hurt so many times, she told herself, and that was painfully true. So many guys. So many lies. Mia *never* cheated on a man. She broke up with plenty, but she was always honest with them. She always tried to spare feelings.

Mia made a decision and planned her excuse: *I'm sorry, baby; I just can't take this kind of chance no more. I've been hurt too many times—too many men cheated on me. I wanna be with you, and I wanna trust you—but I just couldn't sleep 'til I knew who was calling you all night. I know it's wrong, but I gotta protect myself sometimes, you know? Look, if you don't want to be with me anymore, I understand, but I just want you to know that I'm sorry and I only did it because I like you so much . . .*

Her speech ready, Mia held her breath and pushed.

All of the calls came from the same person, but pushing the button still didn't tell her who. According to the phone, the caller's name was simply "*D.*"

Damn. Mia's frustration was now with herself. All of that fret, all of that sneaking, and she still didn't have the information she wanted. *D* could be a first or last name. *D* could be male or female. *D* could be the supervisor at the post office. *D* could be his dad, for all she knew.

Call the number—but that was out of the question. It was bad enough she was going to have to explain to Eric why she was a *freaked-out schizoid*. She'd be damned if she'd have to explain herself to one of his relatives, too. She felt like crying. This was—

The phone began to vibrate in her hand. Mia stared at it in shock. It was *D* again. *Seven calls!* Answering it was out of the question, but her traitor thumb pushed the green button anyway. *What are you doing? You're an idiot!* But the deed was done.

The house was deathly silent, and Mia thought Eric would hear her very heartbeats through the bathroom door. She held her breath and brought the phone to her ear, saying nothing. She waited for what felt like an eternity, and the caller finally spoke.

"Hello?" It was a female's voice, and though this was the terrible thing Mia expected, she actually felt relief for the time being.

I knew it! But she still didn't know anything.

"Hello?" the voice said again. It was a *rough*-sounding voice, not rough-*raspy*, but rough-*mean*. The voice sounded like someone *country;* someone who made grits and babies and kicked ass for a living.

"Uh, hello?" Mia whispered.

"Who *dis*?" the caller wanted to know.

"Um. Listen, I'm sorry." Mia thought fast. "Eric's asleep. I heard this phone vibrating. I was half-sleep too—I thought it was mine. I didn't mean to answer his phone."

"Who is you, *bitch*?" the caller spat. There was acid in that voice. Mia knew then that she had been right all along.

"Who are *you?*" Mia asked.

"*Bitch,* you the one answering my *husband's* phone!"

Husband? That's wrong. Just plain, old wrong. Mia's face went slack as if tranquilized.

"Eric said he wasn't married."

"Who is this? *Candy?*"

"No," Mia said. This was terrible and getting worse.

"*Sheila?*"

"No."

"*Brenda?*"

"No—look, I don't know who you are or who those people are—"

"I told you, *I'm* his wife. If dis *Candy,* ho, I already told you to leave my man alone. With yo *trifling ass.* You need to quit playin'."

"Listen," Mia said. "My name is Mi—um, Meesha. I didn't know Eric was married. God. I shoulda known, though. *I shoulda known.*"

"What? You a *new one?*"

A new one?

"Okay, I'm really confused right now," Mia said. "I didn't know he was married. There are no women's clothes over here. No family pictures. If, if he has a lot of girlfriends, I definitely didn't know that, either. How many . . . I mean, *God,* this is *sick.*"

"He ain't got no *girlfriends!*" the caller said. "He got a *wife,* and dat's *me.* All them other bitches ain't shit."

Mia's head spun. Her world was falling out from under her. She held onto the sink for support. "Maybe we're talking about a different guy." She hoped against hope.

"Naw, we talkin bout the same *sorry bastard*. Tall, dark and handsome, that's why *you* want him. Work at the Post Office, got a black BMW, license plate F7R PU9. You got his phone, don't you? Ain't you been looking through it? Seen all them numbers in there? Everybody got a letter. He go from *A* to *Z,* girl. I don't know how he remember all that, but he do.

"That's a *playa's* phone, baby. *Z* is his mama. *W* is work. A couple of them other letters *really is* his home- boys and stuff, but the rest of them is hos—*bitches just like you!* That's why you can't hardly catch him, 'cause you start callin' them numbers and you don't know who it is. What you think all them letters was for?"

Mia found it hard to catch a breath. Her eyes welled with tears and she couldn't see straight anymore. Hot air fumed from her nostrils.

"I didn't look through his phone," she said finally. "I told you; I just answered it."

"What am I? Am I still *D*? He change that shit up a lot. I been *D*, *E*, *F*, damned near all them letters."

"Yeah, you're still *D*."

"Well, call *F* and *Q*, if you don't believe me. *Q is* dat bitch Candy. She know about everybody and still be messing with him."

Mia just listened and breathed. Somewhere down the line she pissed off God. That had to be it. Her mother wanted her to be a teacher, but she majored in business instead. She didn't honor her mother and father, so God cursed her.

"You there?" D wanted to know.

"Yeah."

"What, you *cryin?*"

Mia sniffled and realized she was.

"You didn't know *nothing?*" D asked.

"I just met him two months ago," Mia admitted. "I thought he was too good to be true, but, *whoo,* I never thought it was this bad."

D calmed a bit. "I feel you girl. He slick. He roll up on you at the grocery store? That's where he meet most of 'em."

"Yeah," Mia sighed.

"Watch this," the caller said, "'*Hi. I don't usually walk up to strangers,*' you know, he be tryin to play all shy and shit, '*but I can tell by your purchases that we've got a lot in common.*' He said somethin' like that and then started talking 'bout the shit you had in yo basket? Right?"

Damn. That was almost verbatim.

"Yeah," Mia admitted.

"He tell you he work nights sometimes?"

"This is *awful.*"

"Yeah, he hit you with the *standard.* He don't *never* work no nights. He used to try to tell me that shit, but I go up there lookin' for his ass. I was finna go lookin' fo' him tonight since he don't wanna answer his phone, but I ain't got nobody to watch the baby."

Mia just shook her head.

"Are you at the house or the apartment?" D wanted to know.

"He has a house *and* an apartment?"

"Yeah, he slick, girl."

"He doesn't live with you?" Mia asked. A slight glimmer of hope shone for a moment. Maybe D was just a disgruntled ex.

"Yeah he stay with me, sometimes. We separated, but we got *fo'* kids. He ain't tryin to get put on no child support."

Mia coughed. "F-*four* kids?"

"Oh yeah, he like to say he ain't got no kids, too. He good, girl. Go look in the living room. He got three pictures in there; one got all three of them. Two of 'em got just the oldest boys. He ain't got no pictures of the baby yet, 'cause she new . . ."

"He said those were his nieces and nephews."

"Like I say, he good, Meesha."

Mia had been caught off-guard by a few players, but nothing like this. All of the information D had given her was impossibly horrific, and begged one question.

"Why do *you* still wanna be with him?"

But that was obvious. "What you talking bout? He my *husband*," D said, then asked, "You said y'all at the *house*, right?"

"Yes. Why?" Mia asked.

"I'm on my way over there," D said.

Whoa, stop the train. "Why do you want to come over *here*?" Mia squealed.

"What you mean, *why*? I told you, he my *husband*." She pronounced *husband* as if it had a couple of extra u's and no s. *Huuubbin.*

"I know, but—"

"What you finna do when you get off the phone? Go in there and tell him all this shit? He ain't gon' do nothing but deny it. He told Candy I was just some bitch he broke up with who want him back."

Mia still hadn't ruled that possibility out, but she wasn't going to be another Candy. Even if Eric *wasn't* still married to this woman, he was still a player, and he had more drama than she wanted in her life.

"Why do you want to come over here *now*?" Mia asked again.

"I'ma confront him. He can't lie if we both standin' right there."

Mia shook her head. "I don't think that's a good idea. I don't wanna be around that. You're gonna be all loud and screaming." Mia was black herself, and she didn't like to label people, especially derogatively, but D was coming off a little *ghetto*. She sounded like the kind of girl who might be involved in one of those "Hood Fights" videos on YouTube. That thought made Mia fear for her own safety.

"I'm not gon' get loud!" D said loudly.

"What about your baby?"

"She 'sleep. I'll bring her with me."

"Look, if you want to fight me, or whatever, I don't want your man. I'm just gonna leave."

"Where he at?"

"He's in there sleep."

"Good," D said. "He sleep hard. It's like four-thirty now. I can make it there by five. I'm already dressed."

Already dressed? The hair stood on Mia's arms.

"No, naw. I'm just—I'm just going to leave. I don't want any trouble."

"What you think gon' happen?" D asked. "You want this nigga to keep gettin' away with this? See, it's bitches, scuse me, I don't mean to call you no bitch. I'm just upset." D took a moment to compose herself. "*Girl*, it's women like *us* that gotta stick together. You know what I'm saying? Niggas like Eric, they keep doin this shit 'cause we keep lettin' them. He don't care if you leave. He hit it already, right?"

Mia didn't like admitting to adultery. "Well, I mean, we . . ."

"Yeah, it's cool, girl. I know. See, he already done got what he wanted. He don't want *you*. He don't wanna be with *you*. He just wanted what he got. You can leave— that ain't shit to him. He got mo hos. What we need to do is *confront* his ass. He been lyin to me for a long time, and I want to look him right in the eye while both us standin' there and see what he got to say then. He *need* to be caught. Ain't you tired of triflin' niggas doin' this shit to you?"

And, that was the kicker. Mia *was* tired as hell of *trifling-ass* niggas doing this kind of shit to her. Eric needed to be taught a lesson, but the lady on the other end of the phone was seriously nutty.

D said she was on her way and Mia agreed to wait for her. Before they got off the phone, Mia had one last question: "Um, D? That's not your name, right? *D*?"

"Naw, girl," the woman said. "My name *Shareefa*."

Shareefa? Wow. No way was Mia going to stick around to see what Shareefa looked like. Oh, hells no.

Mia checked the time on Eric's phone. It was a quarter after four. She would be out of there in no more than five minutes.

He shoulda just turned it off, she thought. *This never would have happened.* But at the same time Mia was glad it was all out in the open. This would be devastating if she didn't find out for another month or two.

To quash any doubts, Mia took a few seconds to look through the phone as Shareefa suggested. And either his *wife* was right, or Eric was a secret agent.

And Eric wasn't no secret agent.

There were no names in the contact list; only letters, from A to Z. There were more than fifty contacts, so there were also an AA, BB, and so on. Mia didn't even consider dialing any of the numbers. She still couldn't believe any of this, but she required no more confirmation.

She sat on the toilet for another minute, still more upset than angry. She wondered if there should be any repercussions. Eric's wife, or whatever she was, was on her way, but Mia thought maybe she should pay him back, too. They only dated a short while, but she really liked him. It was much too soon to believe he might be *the one,* but when you're single with two kids, you're always looking for *the one.* Mia didn't need a man financially, but she didn't need her feelings kicked around, either.

She knew her girlfriends would tell her men are dogs and this type of thing is to be expected, but Mia wasn't a man-basher like the rest of her clique. She knew she would one day meet one who wasn't full of shit. It would have been nice if Eric was that one, but he really didn't need to be. He just needed to be honest. He needed to stop hurting women.

She dropped the phone between her legs and it slid into the toilet water with no splash. That felt good, but Mia knew she wouldn't feel significantly better until she got home, with her family.

She crept back into the bedroom and dressed in darkness, watching him sleep. Eric snored lightly, but it wasn't offensive. It wasn't something she couldn't get used to if they lived together.

The hell? Damn, girl. Mia gritted her teeth and forced the thoughts from her mind. It was over. She knew it was, but there was a part of her that still wanted him; wanted to know if this *Shareefa* lady really was Eric's wife, and if so, maybe he could explain how they were divorced but she won't let it go.

But the kids? The phone?

Mia slipped into her heels and crept quietly from the room. Before leaving, she checked the pictures hanging in the living room above the mantle. The largest one was of three beautiful children. A girl and two boys smiled back at her. She knew she probably shouldn't risk turning on a light, but her curiosity got the best of her.

With the lamps shining brightly, Mia wondered how she missed the resemblance before. It was possible for an uncle to have *some* similarities, but the oldest boy was Eric's spitting image. Even the girl's eyes and nose were like transparencies of her father's.

All doubt gone, the anger finally rose in Mia. She wanted to throw the picture frame into the glass coffee table. She wanted to take it to the bedroom and smash Eric's face with it. At least she could get a knife from the kitchen and slash his tires on the way out, but there was no need for that. Mia was thirty-two years old. She wore slacks and skirt suits to work.

That pretty Beamer sitting on flats was a delicious image, but Mia knew she wouldn't do it. She had two kids. She was a professional woman, and professional women did not slash tires when they were scorned.

Mia held her head high and left, like a lady. She even closed his front door behind herself on the way out. Taking the high road never felt so bad, but she had only to think about her children to know she was doing the right thing. Anything she couldn't do in front of them was probably not a good idea.

The high road came to an abrupt end when Mia tripped on one of the many bricks lining Eric's driveway. "*Dammit!*" she hissed, and bent to rub her offended foot. The toe was fine, but her new shoes had a fresh scuff. *Why is all this happening to me*, she wondered, looking around for whatever she tripped on. There were hundreds of bricks planted in his sidewalk and driveway, and only *one* of them was loose, and Mia just happened to run into that one.

From a crouched position, she wiggled the block free from the ground. It was an Acme brick. Mia looked up and Eric's beamer seemed to grin at her.

"This has got to be a sign," she whispered into the night.

No, it's not. Don't do it.

God gave me this brick.

You're too old for that.

But it came loose for me.

You'll be sorry. And she probably would, but there was no way fate was going to give her a brick and expect her not to use it. Mia shut up the scaredy-cat voice in her head and walked to the front of Eric's car. If you're going to break out a window, it might as well be the most important one, right? She reared back like Nolan Ryan in his heyday, got as much momentum as her triceps could muster, and chucked that brick harder than anything she'd thrown in years.

And damn if it didn't bounce right off.

That's a sign.

Yeah, whatever, Mia thought. She inched in for a closer inspection and saw there was a small chip at the point of impact. It would break. She just needed a more feasible instrument.

The tire iron from her trunk worked just fine.

On the way home the local radio station had the nerve to play the same stupid Jagged Edge song Mia listened to when she and Eric were in the throes of passion.

Walked right into heaven, my ass. She put in a CD more appropriate for her mood. Lil' Kim knew exactly just how she felt.

Wanna bumble with the bee, huh?

BZZZT! Throw a hex on yo whole family!

CHAPTER 3

THERAPY

Nestled almost right in the middle of Lancaster Avenue, Overbrook Meadows's longest thoroughfare, was Claire's Beauty Palace; truly a diamond in the rough. Just two years after its grand opening, the salon was a certified financial triumph; owner Ernestine Pollard wouldn't have it any other way. She brought decades of experience to the venture. Ernestine already owned two other successful beauty shops in the city and was in the process of acquiring a defunct home-style restaurant within the next month or so.

At sixty-one, Ernestine was a notable role model and mentor to minority entrepreneurs all over the city. The last time she lost money on a deal, the schools were still segregated—and not all of her deals were good ones. Claire's, for example, was located smack dab in arguably the worst neighborhood in Overbrook Meadows.

Mia grew up nearby, so she was used to the vagrants, hooligans, and gangbangers in the area. She would never cruise Lancaster after dark, but Saturday mornings were a different story. If you needed your hair twisted, permed, braided or weaved so flawlessly you'll start thinking you really do have Indian in your family, Claire's was definitely the place to go.

Ernestine devoted most of her time to this, her favorite salon, so you could meet the living legend herself behind the register on most days. Today she wore a purple blouse and black slacks with a wig she called the Halle Berry. Ernestine was the color of coffee with no cream. A large, confident woman, she exuded maternal instincts, and had already developed a close bond with all of her employees and most of her customers. A lot of the girls at the salon called her *Mama*, and Mia was no exception.

And as with her other shops, Mama Ernestine employed a cast of lively characters at Claire's. These divas could lay the most natural tracks you've ever seen and give better advice than your marriage counselor at the same time.

Vasantha was a beautiful, twenty-two-year-old Latina. She was very talkative, with a body fine enough to get in a music video if that was her thing. She had pencil-thin eyebrows and bronze skin that made her look like Cleopatra.

Gayle, at forty-three, was a bit older and a bit wiser, too. She was full-figured, as sweet as a box of Godiva's and attractive without a lot of makeup. Gayle was also a hopeless romantic and aspiring poetess. Unless they've heard one of her slam pieces, most people didn't realize what a strong woman she was.

Vicki, also known as Delite, never met a man she couldn't manipulate. Brown-skinned and stacked like Buffy the Body, Vicki drove a brand new Infinity M35, though her part-time job at Claire's was her only taxable income.

And not to be outdone by the many Asian-owned nail shops in the area, Ernestine hired her very own Vietnamese manicurist. Nancy wasn't a hard-core nail lady like her counterparts—meaning she had no thick accent and she conjugated her verbs perfectly—but she could sand a crusty heel with the best of them.

Nancy was actually a business major at Mia's alma mater, Texas Lutheran University. She airbrushed her favorite customer's fingernails and giggled at a quagmire right out of a romance novel.

"So, you used a tire iron?" Nancy clarified. She had large teeth and a big smile that always put Mia in a good mood.

"You should have broke *all* his windows," Vasantha noted. "I ever catch my boyfriend cheating on me, I'm going to cut his thingy off like that girl, Jon Benet."

"Wow," Mia said. She reclined in her chair as Vasantha put the finishing touches on her shoulder-length flip. Vasantha wore tight jeans and a tight tee shirt. She smelled like cinnamon. "There's like, so much wrong with what you just said," Mia continued.

"Jon Benet is that little girl who got killed by her parents, fool!" Natiesha shouted from the waiting area some fifteen feet away. Natiesha was a regular at Claire's. Today she came to get her braids taken down. Mia thought her pink and fuchsia extensions never should have been put in. Natiesha was known for her big mouth, and she never missed an opportunity to dispense her questionable wisdom.

"No, not her, then," Vasantha said, her hands full of Mia's locks. "Who's the one who cut off her boyfriend's thingy?"

"That's *Lorena Bobbitt*," Nancy said.

"Yeah, her," Vasantha said. "I'd cut off his dick like that Lorena Bobbitt chick, and then I'd *kill him* like Jon Benet."

"Oh, that's awful," Ernestine called from the register.

"Yeah, that's pretty sick," Mia agreed.

Claire's was predictably packed this afternoon. There were ten girls in styling chairs already and five more waiting to have their hairdos stacked. Almost everyone had an opinion about the Eric incident.

"No, what's sick is him cheating on you. With *all of those girls*?" Vasantha shook her head. "No, honey. He *need* to have his thingy cut off. You did good with that window."

"What'd you say you call him? *Secret Agent Double-O Player*?" Gayle laughed. She was applying the prettiest cornrows Mia had ever seen on a brooding stallion named Janice. Janice was tall and light-skinned, and built like Alicia Keys with bigger breasts. Mia didn't idolize many women, but she often wondered if she would have the same problems with men if she was built like Janice.

"Girl, I've never seen anything like it," Mia mused. "He called me this morning, too."

"For real?" Nancy gasped.

"Yeah. I think I got two messages on my phone already."

"What the hell is he calling you for?" Gayle wondered.

"I don't know," Mia said. "I hope he doesn't want me to pay for his windshield."

"Ooh, girl," Janice said. "He prolly do. Are you gonna call him back?"

"Maybe," Mia said. "I really don't want to, but on the message he says he can explain *everything.*"

"That's bullshit," Gayle said, and Mia knew she was probably right.

"I had a boyfriend like that," Vasantha offered. "Every time I look in his phone, he had like four Joses, six Jesses, and he didn't even know nobody named *Jesse!*"

"You shouldn't have been looking through his phone," Natiesha noted.

"Aw, forget that," Vasantha said. "You *gotta* look through they phone. If Mia didn't look, she never woulda knew what he was doing."

"Hell, yeah," Gayle agreed. "You *better* look through his phone."

"I usually *don't* look through their phones," Mia clarified. "I just happened to step on it when I got up, and it was vibrating. I still almost didn't look."

"I don't look through my man's phone," Janice said.

"Girl, ain't nobody gon' cheat on you," Gayle said. "We talkin' bout *regular* women like *us,* or like me for sure. I know I *have to* look through they phone."

"No you don't. You're pretty," Mia said.

"I know I'm *pretty,*" Gayle said. "But it's not even about that nowadays. Look at you, Mia. You look good. You know you do. Got a house and a good job and everything. But it *still* happened to you."

"You *are* pretty," Nancy chipped in.

"I just got caught slippin'," Mia said. "But this nigga was slick. He showed me pictures of his kids and everything. He said they were his nieces and nephews. I didn't even see the resemblance 'til afterwards."

"After what?" Janice asked.

"After*wards*," Mia said.

Nancy smiled.

"That's 'cause you wanted some," Natiesha blurted.

"Mmm, hmm," Janice nodded. "You had yo blinders on, girl. How long was it since you got some?"

"Before Eric?" Mia closed her eyes and thought for a second. "Damn, that must have been, no. Yeah, that was Colin."

"*Colin*? That was four months ago!" Vasantha calculated.

"He really doesn't count, though," Mia said.

"That was the five-minute man?" Gayle asked.

"*More like a* two-*minute man*," Vasantha and Mia said at the same time and laughed.

"So was it *good*, girl?" Janice wanted to know. "You at least get yo rocks off before his wife called?"

Ernestine shook her head.

"That's not funny," Mia said. She grinned and stared at the mirror, but her stylist wasn't working anymore.

"Well?" Vasantha asked. Gayle stopped braiding Janice's hair, too. It seemed like everyone was waiting for an answer.

"It was so good," Mia reminisced. "It was so good, even *after* his wife called I started trying to convince myself she was lying about who she was."

"Damn. That *musta* been good," Janice said.

"Was her clothes over there?" Vasantha asked. "If it wasn't none of her clothes over there, she might have been lying."

"Did you see any kids' toys?" Nancy wanted to know.

"Did he have a *big dick*?" Gayle asked.

"Oh, my," Ernestine said, and everyone laughed.

Mia laughed, too. When she composed herself, all the ladies were still looking at her.

"What?"

"His *dick*," Vasantha reminded. "Was it big or what, girl?"

Mia looked around for a point of reference but could find none. "You ever been bowling?" she asked.

"Shut—*up!*" Gayle squealed.

"Stop lying," Vasantha said with a grin.

Nancy just stared up in confusion.

"Damn, girl, you tugging my hair," Mia said. "Okay, it's not as big as the *whole* pin, but you know that fat head they got above the stripes?"

"Shut—*up!*" Gayle exclaimed.

Mia laughed and Nancy's mouth hung open.

"You *sure* that was his wife?" Vasantha asked. "I wouldn't cut off no wee-wee if it was *that* big!"

The whole place howled.

"I'm kidding, I'm kidding!" Mia cut through the noise. "It was only about eight inches . . . *limp.*"

The room again erupted in cackles and catcalls. A couple of the women thought Mia should call *Special Agent Double-O Player* back to see what his explanation was, but there was wisdom dispensed also. It came from the most likely source.

"You're a beautiful woman, Mia," Ernestine said. "You're beautiful *and* you're smart *and* you're successful. You don't have to share your man with *nobody*, no matter how big his wee-wee is!"

Everyone laughed again, but Mia knew the words were heartfelt.

"And you too old to be bustin' out windows, child," the elder went on. "You should be ashamed of yourself."

And Mia did feel a little embarrassed for the first time. She took solace in the matriarch's words and left the beauty shop, as always, a fresh, vibrant, and confident woman.

CHAPTER 4

THUG LOVE

When she got home, Mia was not upset to find her sister's car missing from the driveway. Crystal usually kicked it with the kids on Saturday afternoons. They would be back in a couple of hours, and Mia was happy to have a little time to herself.

Crystal was only twenty-one. She was rambunctious, indecisive, and at times immature—basically all things that came with that confounding age. She was Mia's little sister by way of the same mother, but they had different fathers. Any curiosity about why an intelligent, successful woman like Mia burdened herself with two children from two different unmarried gentlemen could be traced back to their mother, Sophia Clemmons.

Sophia was a lover of life, though life didn't seem to love her back by the end of it. Mia's mom never looked before she leapt, practiced what she preached or learned from her mistakes. A few of her kids, Mia in particular, inherited a lot of these characteristics. Sophia had four children in all, and each child had a different daddy. Even still, when she succumbed to lung cancer six years ago, Sophia met her maker with no regrets.

Que sera, sera, she was fond of saying. *Whatever will be, will be.*

That motto would have been fine and dandy if Sophia had no dependents, but Crystal was only fifteen at the time of their mother's death. Mia was fresh out of college and she had both of her own children by then, but she took her little sister in with open arms. And to the surprise of everyone, especially Mia, Crystal began to show her worth right away.

Back then Mia was a new face at Prospect Investment Firm—not only new, but also a minority *and* a female. She had to make sure her butt was present at every power lunch and late-afternoon meeting, and with Crystal at home to watch over her children, everything worked out perfectly.

Mia was now the manager of the securities and loans department. She was on pace to make vice president one day, and she knew much of her success wouldn't have been possible without her little sister playing nanny at home.

But Mia's life was a bit more settled now, and Crystal wasn't a child anymore. She was twenty-one, old enough to go to school and get started on her own career in Mia's opinion, but Crystal had no such ambitions. She took an occasional course at the local community college, and so far wanted nothing more than to live under her sister's roof.

Crystal picked Mia's kids up from school and was a faithful babysitter, and in return she enjoyed a fairy-tale life of free room and board and sometimes even an allowance. Mia was close to it, but so far she hasn't felt the need to push her eaglet from the nest.

Inside, Mia dropped her purse on the couch and found a few dishes in the kitchen to wash. She checked her answering machine, and, according to the display, she had four new messages. She played them as she wiped a few stubborn stains from her countertops. The first three were insignificant, but the last one piqued her interest. It was Eric again. Mia thought he of all people should understand why she wasn't calling him back, but he seemed to be getting more persistent:

Mia, this is Eric. I—I really wish you would return my calls. I don't know what happened last night. Well, I know you talked to Shareefa, but I don't know what she told you. I know it was kooky, whatever it was. If you'll call me, I can explain everything. I am not married to that woman. I can tell you that right now. Whatever else she told you is a lie. This isn't the first time she's done this. Just call me back, I can explain. I promise. I thought we had a good connection, Mia. Don't let it go because of this. All right? Okay, um, bye.

That was interesting. Mia wanted to return the call just to hear what he had to say, but she reminded herself who she was dealing with here. This was *Double-O Player*. He *might* have an elaborate explanation for the phone, the wife, and the kids, but that only meant he was an accomplished, *seasoned* liar. Mia was curious, but didn't think she'd ever believe another word Eric said.

Calling him back was put on the back burner anyway. Mia heard her front door open, followed by the excited clamoring of two adorable babies, ages seven and nine.

Many people will say that their child is the *most beautiful ever*. They'll bombard even the most casual acquaintance with photos, and even hire an agent to get their pride and joy in commercials.

Mia has never done any of those things, but she knew—with no uncertainty—that her two kids were the most precious, the most beautiful, and the most intelligent children in the whole world.

Tyrone Christopher Story was the older sibling. Everyone called him TC. He was in the third grade and was a fan of math and puzzles. TC had fair skin like his father. He also had thick hair that didn't kink much when he grew it out, but Mia kept it trimmed short. She was well aware of how cute light-skinned boys look with a bushy mane, but Mia thought that was usually more of the parent's vanity than anything else.

Mica Lynn Clemmons (*Mica* pronounced to rhyme with her mother's name) was simply gorgeous; her mom's spitting image. Unlike TC, Mica's skin was dark. She also inherited her mother's full lips and small nose. Mica had her father's large eyes, and that was sad because her father was dead—had been since before her birth.

He was a skinny punk named Calvin Mitchell. Eight years ago, Mia loved him more than she loved herself, but Calvin only cared about his homeboys and his money. He took six bullets over a dope sack that turned out to be walnut pieces cut to look like crack, and Mia never forgave herself for falling for the thug. She never forgave Calvin for choosing the streets over his daughter.

In an interesting twist, the kids had what some called "opposite personalities." Nine-year-old TC was more likely to jump into his mother's bed during a thunderstorm, and seven-year-old Mica liked to catch frogs in the backyard and bring them into the house. They both enjoyed flying kites, playing video games and exploring shadowy creeks, and Mia loved them more than anything she'd ever seen on this planet.

TC rushed in with his latest *Goosebumps* paperback. Mia never forced the series on him and was glad he had such an interest in reading.

"Hey, Mama!" He wrapped both arms around her for a big bear hug.

"Hey, lil' man. What you got there?"

"It's a *Goosebumps*! Aunt Crystal took us to the library."

"You haven't read that one before?" Mia asked.

"I don't think so." TC studied the cover art, then looked back to his mother. "Did I read this one before?"

"I don't know," Mia said. "It looks a little familiar."

"I don't think so. Maybe a long time ago. I'll read it again anyway. I like *Goosebumps*."

Mia smiled. "Where's your sister?"

"She's outside with Aunt Crystal. They're getting something out of the car."

"And you didn't help them?"

"I was going to . . ." TC looked away shyly. "You want me to?"

"You're the man of the house," Mia reminded. "Of course I want you to help. What did she get?"

"Just some stuff," TC said. "We went to a garage sale."

Mia sighed. "I told her to stop bringing that junk to my house."

"It's not junk," TC defended. "She got me some Hot Wheels. And this other thing for herself. It's kind of big. I don't know what it does. Something about feet."

"Where are the toys she bought you? Don't tell me you've got a lady bringing them in for you?" Mia fixed a look on the boy.

"Uh," he gave her a sly smile. "Outside. I'll go get them." He rushed out and Mia followed to see what Crystal was trying to bring in this time. The girl had a thing for junk.

And it was junk.

"What are you going to do with that?" Mia asked from the front door.

Crystal held the plastic contraption with both hands and bumped the car door closed with her ample hip. "Girl, yo hair looks good," she said.

"Don't try to butter me up," Mia said.

Mica had a dolly in one hand and a Slurpee in the other, but she still threw both arms around her mother. "Hi, Mommy. Your hair's pretty."

"You heard your aunt say that."

Mica smiled and Mia was lost in her eyes for a moment.

"No. I didn't hear her. I thought it up by myself."

"What is that thing?" Mia asked as Crystal scooted by.

"It's a foot massager," she said without stopping. "Don't worry. I'll keep it in my room. You'll never see it."

"Where you gonna put it? It won't fit under the bed. You've got too much junk in there already, Crystal. Stop giving those rednecks your money."

Crystal kept walking, and Mia followed her inside, not for the first time a little envious of her little's sister's physique. Crystal wore stretchy Capris today with a blouse that stopped an inch above her belly button. She and Mia were different on many levels, but their physical contrasts were the most obvious.

Mia considered herself *fine*, but Crystal was on another level. Black men love women with full hips and thighs and a nice ass. On Mia, these proportions were *thick*. On Crystal, they were *phat*. Crystal could win a bubble butt contest wearing slacks. She was also taller, light-skinned, and her 38C boobs put Mia's 36As to shame.

When they were younger, Crystal had big teeth, and Mia could at least tease her about her *gator mouth*, but Crystal grew into her features. Now Mia could only make fun of her sister's *big butt*, but they both knew Mia would kill to have one just like it.

"Mama, my daddy's getting out of jail."

The words made Mia forget about the foot massager. She looked down at her son, who beamed a toothy grin. She didn't understand why he was so damned happy about someone who could have been in his life for the last six years but *chose* otherwise.

And, yes, a convict will tell you anything you listen to, but Mia knew better. They *chose* to do whatever they did, ergo, they *chose* to go to prison.

"Who told you that? Aunt Crystal?"

"Nope, I sure didn't," Crystal walked back into the room on the defensive. "He found out from that letter Tyrone sent. The one *you* gave him. Don't even try to blame me."

Mia remembered the letter. She got it in the mail just three days ago. Tyrone sent her one also, but it was sitting, still unopened, on her bedroom dresser. She knew Tyrone was getting out of prison, had dreaded it for six months, but it wasn't fair for her to transfer those emotions to TC. She sat on the couch and her little ones plopped down on either side of her, hip to hip.

"Yeah, he's getting out Monday," Mia said.

"*This* Monday," TC stressed.

"Yes, *this* Monday," Mia said. She rubbed the top of his head. "You excited about seeing your daddy?"

Crystal sat on a love seat and listened quietly.

"Yes," TC said. "I'm going to ask him to take me to Six Flags!"

"Six Flags? Monday's a school day," Mia reminded. "And when people get out of jail, they usually don't have a lot of money right away. You might have to wait a while before he can take you to Six Flags." Mia's heart skipped a beat at just the thought of an ex-convict like Tyrone alone with her baby, but she didn't show it.

"Well," TC considered things. "Where *can* he take me?"

"How about we go to the park?"

"You're gonna come, too?"

"Well, I might. Do you remember your daddy? You were only three when he went away."

"Um, I remember him a little."

Mia smirked. "What does he look like?"

"He, um," TC shrugged. "He look like me!"

Mia smiled. "Who told you that?"

He looked around. "*Everybody*?"

"Everybody like *who*?"

He put his head down. "Aunt Crystal?"

Mia gave her sister a look and Crystal cocked her head and twisted her neck.

"Girl, you know Tyrone look just like that boy."

The kids giggled.

"Yeah. He does look a lot like you," Mia went on. "So, you're not going to be scared when you see him?"

"Nope."

"What are you going to tell him?" Mia wondered.

"Hmm . . ." TC put a finger to his lips. "The first thing I'm going to say is *where you been?*"

Mia and Crystal laughed, but the kids didn't find too much humor in it. Mica tugged at her mother's arm.

"What, baby?"

"When TC's daddy get here, is he going to take *me* to the park with him?"

Mica's voice was so sweet and innocent, Mia's heart melted like butter.

"Would you like that?" she asked.

"Yes," Mica said. "I wish my daddy wasn't dead."

"Oh, baby." Mia wrapped her arms around the cutie. TC grabbed his mother's waist from the other side and put his head on her chest.

"I love you, Mom," he said.

Not to be outdone, Crystal wiped her eyes and rushed forward. "*Awww.* Group hug!" She grabbed onto the whole bunch.

Mia buried her face in Mica's hair and no one saw her tears.

They ate spaghetti for dinner that evening. They didn't always eat as a family; Mia's work kept her away from the dining table at least three nights a week, so whenever all four of them were together, it was a happy time. Mica spilled a glass of lemonade all over her first plate, and they didn't tell TC he had a tomato sauce moustache until the dishes were all clean and put away.

Afterwards they put in a movie and laughed at Alvin, Simon, and Theodore as if they hadn't seen the chipmunks in a theatre just six months ago. Even Crystal stuck around, which was surprising because she had a new boyfriend and what he had in his britches had been the only thing on her mind for the last few weeks. After the movie Mia made the kids root beer floats and read them a few chapters from TC's *Goosebumps* as they snuggled on the couch and sipped quietly.

She let them stay up a little later because it was Saturday night, but by 11:00 p.m. they were bathed, with sparkling teeth and heavy lids that made the Sandman's job a little easier. Each was fast asleep within twenty minutes of their head touching the pillow.

After she tucked them in, Mia found Crystal in the living room. She lounged with her little sister on the leather sofa and told her about the creep she almost spent the whole evening with yesterday.

"Has he called since then?" Crystal asked.

"Yeah. He left me two, no, three messages today. He left one on the answering machine while you were gone."

"I wish I woulda been here," Crystal said. "I woulda told him something."

"It was so *unreal*," Mia said. "I've been with players before, but this guy was right out of a mystery magazine. I looked at his phone, girl, and all I saw was *letters*. He didn't have *one* name in there."

"How he keep up with all that?" Crystal wondered.

"That's what his wife said," Mia snickered.

"You sure that was his wife?" Crystal pondered. "You know it's some shiesty bitches out there who'll do some shit like that."

"I know," Mia said. "At first I was like, yeah, she's telling the truth, but he left that message and now I don't know. I mean, I know something's up with him, but she may *not* be telling the whole truth."

"*Dang.* What if you busted out his windshields for nothin'?" Crystal pondered.

"I only broke *one windshield.*" Mia said. "And he's still lying. Even if that's not his wife, he still had pictures of his kids in there. He didn't have no reason to lie about them."

"What if them wasn't his kids?" Crystal said, playing the devil's advocate.

"I saw the pictures. They looked just like him—not like a close relative, either. One of them boys looks *exactly* like him. The girl looked like him, too."

Crystal hummed. "That don't even sound like you, Mia. I didn't know you be checkin' they phones."

"I don't," Mia said. "When I stepped on it, if it wasn't buzzing, I never woulda knew about this. And I still almost didn't check it. But, girl, it was like *four* in the morning. I kept thinking about how good he was and how mad I was gonna be if I found out he was full of shit."

Crystal smiled.

"I'm talkin' *good,*" Mia said. "I haven't had it like that in two years."

"*Damn.*"

"This was our first time, too, but it didn't feel like it. He kissed my neck and whispered in my ears. Then he sucked my earlobes."

"*Oooh,*" Crystal squirmed in the couch. "How come I can't get no nigga to suck my ears? They do that when they tryin to get some. Once you give it up, all that snuggling stops."

"I know," Mia said. "That's me, too, but Eric was different."

"So, if that *wasn't* his wife and those *might not* be his kids, you prolly bust his windshield for nothing."

Mia shook her head. "He still had that secret agent phone—don't forget. And those *were* his kids. I'm not a genealogist, but I know when that's somebody's kids."

"You positive?"

"I'm positive."

"Well, forget him then."

"Easier said than done."

"It was that good?"

"It wasn't just the sex," Mia admitted. "We went out five times. He took me to a nice restaurant; one where you have to get a reservation, girl. And he was interesting. He didn't ask me a bunch of stupid questions. He was a good listener. He really knew how to treat a woman. I thought it was going somewhere."

"Maybe it still is," Crystal said. "You gotta at least call him to see what he says."

"Yeah," Mia said. "I might."

"What you got to lose?" Crystal asked. "What else you got going? Oh, I forgot yo baby's daddy getting out Monday. You could go out with Tyrone."

Mia rolled her eyes. "I'll go out with Eric *and* his wife before I go out with *Tyrone*."

Crystal laughed, but she knew her big sister was dead serious.

Before she went to bed, Mia plucked her prison letter from the bedroom dresser and sliced it open with one of her neatly manicured nails. She wasn't really interested in what he had to say—Tyrone always spat the same shit—but since she was probably going to see him Monday, she might as well read it.

Looking at his handwriting made her reminisce.

When Tyrone first got locked up, Mia really did miss him. For a while they shared deep correspondences, but eventually she moved on. Tyrone stayed stuck. Mia didn't know what it was about prison that made men think they had so much game, but she stopped putting stock in Tyrone's words a long time ago. His promises about what he was going to do when he got out and how much better their life was going to be together stopped sounding good five years ago.

Raising two babies by herself while pursing a higher education turned Mia's compassion into resentment. Every time she looked into TC's eyes, watched him crawl around in diapers and later walk, her pain grew deeper and her loathing for Tyrone grew red hot. But she got over it. Today she was lukewarm. Actually she was ice cold. Tyrone was getting out, and that was fine, but the only thing he had to offer was child support. Mia only wrote him back four times in the last two years, but he still didn't get the picture.

Hey, girl.

I just want to say what's up. Let you know what going on in my life. I told you this a couple months ago, but in case you didn't get my letters I want to let you know I'm getting out next week. I'll hit Overbrook Monday the 29th. I sent a letter to TC, too, to let him know. I can't wait to see my little boy. I can't wait to see you ether.

Thanks for the pictures you sent me while I was locked up. And thanks for the letters you wrote. I know you are buzy. You got a job and you don't have time to write me as much as I want, but you did write me sometimes. I appreciate that.

I know you say you moved on with your life, and that's good. It's good that you got a nice job and a house, too. I'm not mad at you. I just wish you would take me sereously when I say I want to do right by you. I want to do right by TC, too. I want to raise my son. Not just visit him sometimes when it's my turn to see him. I want to raise him like my daddy didn't do for me. I want to live with y'all and be his daddy and your husband.

You told me that you don't love me no more, and I know how you feel. I know I hurt you and make your life hard when you had to raise TC all by your self. I respect you as a woman for that. You a strong woman Mia but you still not married. I think there's a reason for that. I remember you loved me and we had good times together. If you remember the good times and maybe try to forgive me we can have a life together again. You, me, TC and Mica. I will raise her like she my own daghter if you let me.

Anyway, I'll be back home Monday. See you soon.

Love
Tyrone

Mia folded the letter and slid it back into the envelope. Six years later and he was still saying the same thing. *I wanna be TC's daddy. I'll take care of y'all. I'll raise Mica like she's my own. Blah, blah, blah.*

Mia wasn't cold-hearted. She didn't think Tyrone was *purposely* lying about his intentions, but he *was* lying. When you're locked up, you've got nothing but time to ponder all sorts of things: what you'd do different, where you made mistakes and how you're going to make it all better once you get out.

But once they hit the free world, niggas like Tyrone only stuck to the script for about a month or so before old habits and old friends had them right back in the revolving door. Mia had no doubt in her mind Tyrone would be back in prison within five years of his release. She had seen it too many times. There's no rehabilitation. The best Mia could hope for was that Tyrone would develop a positive relationship with TC before he messed up again.

And it wasn't that she had anything against him as an individual; on the contrary, Mia really liked Tyrone. It was what he *was* that she couldn't stand. She couldn't understand what she saw in him to begin with, but whatever it was lingered a couple of years after he got locked up. She had *another* baby by *another* thug, and he wasn't around today either.

Thugs.

That obsession was in her past, but Mia remembered when she couldn't wait to get a roughneck in her bed.

She met Tyrone when she was twenty. Well, she didn't meet him for the first time then, but Mia *re-met* Tyrone when she was twenty. They went to high school together, but were only casual associates then. Tyrone played basketball and dabbled in track, but his leanings towards thuggish behavior were already evident. He wore his pants below the waist, kept his hair long, and hung with the bad kids who smoked weed behind the gym.

In those days, Tyrone tried to stick anything that moved, but Mia was a good girl and their circles never crossed. She kept her nose in the books, avoided weekend parties, and could care less about delinquents like Tyrone, who struggled to make passing grades even in their electives.

Tyrone graduated a year ahead of her, and Mia completely forgot about him until they met again during her freshman year at Texas Lutheran. Mia was downtown with a few girlfriends waiting in line for movie tickets. When the light-skinned hooligan approached them, it took Mia a few moments to figure out who he was.

"Hey, didn't you used to go to Poly High?" Tyrone had asked.

Mia looked the boy up and down, took in his baggy jeans, tattooed forearms, and fluffed-out Afro with no recognition. "I don't believe I know you."

"Damn, girl. Look at you—talkin' all *proper*. I'm *Tyrone*. We was in the same health class. I wasn't there a lot of them days, but I remember you. Your name's Mia, right?"

Mia was flattered that this boy she didn't even know remembered her name, and something else struck her as her girlfriends huddled and giggled in the background: Tyrone was *fine*. He had nice little muscles on those yellow arms, a dashing smile, and intense hazel eyes. Mia liked his jewelry. He looked *dangerous*, and he had a swagger. After a whole year of dating nothing but collegiate types, Tyrone had something about him that was altogether different and definitely alluring.

Mia gave him her phone number that day, and she still remembered how her friends reacted once he walked off.

"You're not really gonna go out with him, are you?"

"I don't know. I might," Mia said.

"He looks like he sells drugs," one of them said.

"He looks like he beats up on his girlfriend," another noted.

"Is he a rapper?" the third wanted to know, and Mia was hooked from that moment on.

Tyrone called her that same night and came to pick her up for their first date the very next day. When Tyrone rolled up to her dorm in his old-school Cutlass with candy flakes and chrome rims, the security guards tried to kick him off the campus. Mia had to rush downstairs to tell them he was here with her.

When she got into the car with him, Tyrone turned his system all the way up out of spite. Thumping bass from Tupac's "No More Pain" rattled all of the windows in her dorm. A few students peeked out of their blinds to see who was out there, and Mia never felt so special.

Tyrone took her to a park (of all places), bought her a snow cone, pushed her on the swing, and they got busy in the back seat of his car before he dropped her off. Mia liked to look back on that day and say they *made love*, but deep inside she knew there was no lovemaking involved. They *had sex*. Like animals. And she loved every minute of it.

From the moment he walked up to her in front of that movie theatre, Mia couldn't get enough of Tyrone. She loved his hair, his eyes, his thin goatee, and his tattoos. He picked her up after classes almost every day and showed her things she'd never seen before. Mia never wanted to go back to her dorm by the ten o'clock curfew.

One day she didn't.

Infatuated with her whirlwind romance, Mia dropped out of school towards the end of her freshman year. She regretted it right away, but Tyrone was the only thing she really cared about. She didn't go back for two semesters.

When she did get back in school, Mia found out she was pregnant with TC, but by then her relationship with Tyrone was on a downward slide. Mia wanted to spend more time with him, but Tyrone was stuck in the streets. He sold drugs and stayed out all night sometimes doing God-knew-what. He only picked her up from school once, maybe twice a week.

Mia figured he was seeing other women, but she never caught him red-handed. To make matters worse, Tyrone started going to jail around this time. He did four months on his first bid and got six the second trip. He was in jail when TC was born. By the time he got popped for the big one that would send him to prison, Tyrone and Mia were already broken up.

Mia had a new boyfriend by then, and Calvin Mitchell would be the one to cure her of her *thug-love* tendencies. This one left Mia with a big belly full of Mica and another broken heart. Mia was eight months pregnant when she attended Calvin's funeral. A month later she had two bastard kids by two no-good bastards. But she also had her college degree and her mother's tendency to never look back.

Mia never dated anyone remotely similar to Tyrone after that. In the six years since he'd been gone, Mia learned to forgive, but she would never forget what thug love got her. The hell with *swagger*. Mia wanted a man with a 401K, his own house, and no drama.

This new attitude led some to view her as stuck up, but Mia saw it differently. She was poised, confident, and independent. She was a good mother, a strong woman who didn't need a man to help provide for her and her kids.

Anyone who had a problem with that could kiss her ass.

She balled Tyrone's letter into a tight wad and sent it flying into a small wastebasket with one shot.

CHAPTER 5
DOUBLE-0 PLAYER

Mica sat at the dining room table with spoon in hand, but when Mia passed through, she saw that the utensil was dry.

"What's going on?" she asked.

"Nothin'," Mica said, her eyes low.

"Why aren't you eating?"

"I *was* eating."

"Don't lie. You haven't put your spoon in there yet."

"I don't like oatmeal," Mica said. The girl was more finicky than a vegan.

"I'll eat hers," TC said, always a trooper.

"No, Mica's going to eat her own oatmeal," Mia said. "You guys didn't get any toast? Where's Crystal?"

"She's in the bathroom," TC reported.

Mia went to the kitchen and put two slices of bread in the toaster. "We're leaving in fifteen minutes," she told Mica on her way back through the dining room. "And you're eating that oatmeal before we go."

"But I don't like it," Mica whined.

"Don't let me come back in there and see that spoon still clean," Mia said without stopping.

Monday mornings were a bit of a hassle. Most of the time Crystal woke up early enough to help get the kids ready, but there was always something. Today Mica was sleepy and a bit fussy, but she would eat, hopefully without getting tears involved.

Back in her own room, Mia selected pearl earrings from her jewelry box. She went to her bathroom to put them on and look over her outfit in the mirror. Today she wore a black skirt suit. The skirt had just enough stretch to accentuate her hips and butt. The jacket was one of her favorites. It had a Peter Pan collar with three buttons down the middle.

Mia checked her locks and applied a little gel to a few out of place hairs. She looked good. Mia tried to dress to the nines every day, but she took extra care to look her best on Mondays. Her appearance affected her whole attitude, and how she felt today might carry through the week.

And she *felt* good.

Back in her room she slipped into a pair of dress pumps and snatched her briefcase from the bed. She made it back to the dining room with seven minutes to spare. Mica's spoon was soiled, but not much was missing from her bowl.

"Okay, so what's the deal with your breakfast?" Mia took a seat across from the pouting princess and winked at her son. TC smiled and winked back.

"I don't like these apples in here," Mica said. She held up a half-eaten piece of toast. "I ate this."

"You need energy. Oatmeal's good for you."

"Can't we—"

"Eat a spoonful before you say anything else," Mia suggested.

Mica did as she was told. "Can't we go to 7-11 on the way?"

"You'd rather have a taquito?" Mia asked.

"I li—"

"Eat a spoonful before you answer."

Mica did so. "I like taquitos."

"How'd you do on your test last week?" Mia asked.

"I got—"

"Eat a spoonful."

She did. "I got a 94."

TC giggled.

"What?" Mica asked him.

"You're eating your oatmeal!" he said.

Mica gave her mom a look.

"Keep eating," Mia said.

She got up and went to the living room, where Crystal was lounging on the sofa wearing pajama bottoms and a tank top.

"Must be nice," Mia observed.

"Don't start," Crystal said. "I got an 11:30 today."

"Which class?"

"Humanities." Crystal managed to say it with a straight face.

"You still undecided?" Mia asked.

"Yeah, but I'm going to have to take this anyway, whatever I major in. Might as well get it out the way. I gotta take religion and college algebra, too. Those classes are hard."

"You're only taking *one* class this semester?"

Crystal rolled her eyes. "Yes, Miss *Magna cum Laude*, I'm taking *one* class. Next semester I might take two. Don't look at me like that. I be busy, girl."

"Doing what?" Mia wondered.

"I gotta, uh. I pick up the kids from school. Help them with their homework. Sometimes I fix 'em dinner . . ."

"All of that stuff happens after 3:00," Mia noted. "Between eight and one you can take four classes. And don't use my kids as an excuse. I'll hire a nanny and you can have all the free time you want."

"Naw, I'm fine. I was thinking about going to cu, cuh." She looked puzzled. "What's that school you go to where you learn to cook, like a chef?"

"That's *culinary*," Mia said with a grin. "You're lucky you're twenty-one. Don't think you can be thirty-something with all these frivolous ambitions."

"Ooh good—I got ten years!" Crystal said and rolled onto her stomach. "Wake me up when you're *forty*."

Mia threw a pillow and caught her in the back of the head. "You oughta be ashamed of yourself." She scooped her purse from the sofa and opened the front door. "Come on y'all. Time to go! Put your dishes in the sink. Aunt Crystal says she'll get them for you."

"Bitch," Crystal called from the couch.

The kids rushed in and Mia admired them for a second. TC wore a white golf shirt. It was tucked in neatly, and his khakis were without a wrinkle. He sported a black, braided belt that was one of Mia's favorites. Mica wore a white blouse also. It was tucked into her navy blue, pleated skirt. They both wore white tennis. These were the colors mandated by the school's uniform policy, but Mia didn't think they could have looked better in anything else.

"You guys look great. Aunt Crystal did your hair?" she asked Mica.

"*Thank you!*" Crystal shouted.

"Yes, but I picked out the barrettes," Mica said. She had four perfect ponytails. TC's short hair always looked nice and well-groomed. He could smooth it out with his bare hands.

"You look good, too, Mama," TC said.

"Where are your backpacks?" Mia asked, and they rushed off in separate directions to retrieve them.

"You gonna be home for dinner?" Crystal asked.

"I don't know. I'll call."

Mia drove a Lexus GX 470, a four-door sports utility vehicle. It was black, her favorite color. The kids piled in, and she set off for their elementary school no more than half a mile away.

"My daddy's coming home today," TC called from the back seat when they got around the corner.

"Yes," Mia said. "You're excited, huh?"

"Yeah."

Mia watched TC beaming in the rearview mirror.

"I thought about him last night," he went on.

"I thought about him, too," Mia said.

"You miss TC's daddy?" Mica pondered.

Wow. Mia hesitated. "Not like, well, I think about him sometimes."

"Was he cool?" TC wanted to know.

"Cool like what?"

"Like 50 Cent," TC said. "Or Lil' Scrappy."

No more BET for you, Mia thought. "Well," she said, "if you think those guys are cool, then yes, your father is cool."

"Does he have a gold necklace?" TC wondered.

"He did when we were together," Mia said. "But that was eight years ago. He might not still have it now."

"I hope he does," TC said. He rattled on about his father for the rest of the way, and Mia hoped Mica wasn't starting to feel left out. If she said she wished her daddy was alive again, Mia would have to go to work with her mascara running.

But she didn't. Mia pulled up in front of the school and they jumped out, almost running by the time they hit the sidewalk. Mia didn't think she'd ever been that eager to get started on her times tables. She watched them until they disappeared through the main entrance.

Prospect Investment Firm was one of the world's largest discount brokers. According to last year's figures, it served seven million individual and institutional clients and had over $1.2 trillion in assets from three hundred cities across the United States.

The Prospect building was one of the tallest in downtown Overbrook Meadows. It was already a historical landmark. Mia was the manager of the securities and loans department. She arrived at her corner office ten minutes early this morning, but still considered herself late.

Mia's responsibilities at Prospect included quality control over loan setup, trade management communications, accrual calculations, billing, and other system and database maintenance. She was expected to motivate and drive team members to meet and exceed business performance metrics and drivers. Mia also had to develop and implement process improvements and procedures to support and meet departmental and corporate goals and objectives. To simplify, she busted her ass every day, signed off on six-figure deals, and did her best to bring in as many millions as she could each year.

Mia was a fastidious boss, but also compassionate. She was overbearing at times, but still nurturing. She was at the top of her game, and there was no glass on her ceiling. She made almost a hundred thousand a year, but her goal was half a million. And best of all, she loved what she did.

Miss Tenery walked in before Mia had a chance to sit down. Mia's secretary was Caucasian, tall, and slightly emaciated. When they first met, Mia was sure the woman was bulimic, but after three years of working with her, she realized Miss Tenery simply preferred to look that way.

Miss Tenery had a strong jawline and pointy noise. She wore thick-rimmed glasses, no makeup, and kept her hair pulled back in a bun on most days. She reminded Mia of Miss Hathaway from the *Beverly Hillbillies.*

"Good morning, Miss Clemmons. Enjoy your weekend?"

Mia gave up asking her secretary to call her by her first name a long time ago. Prudes like Tenery even referred to children as Mr. or Miss.

"It was nice," Mia said. "How 'bout you? It was your anniversary, right? Have fun?"

"Well, there's not much to enjoy at my age," the woman said. "We had a nice dinner."

Mia thought that was a bit sad, considering her secretary was only forty.

"So, what's going on?" Mia asked. "You've got that look in your eyes."

"Oh, just the usual," Miss Tenery said, looking down her nose at a ledger she toted. "You've got a nine o'clock with Mr. Burgess—that's sure to be hell. Mr. Manitou wants to meet before noon, so I penciled him in at eleven. And we've got that new hire. Did you want to orient her bef—"

"After lunch," Mia said.

"One o'clock?"

"That's fine."

"You've got the meeting with the big boys at three, and . . ."

"I need to get out of here by five today," Mia said, thinking about Tyrone.

"The CMBS director wanted to see you."

"Can he wait 'til tomorrow?"

"I guess he's going to have to," Miss Tenery said and scribbled on her pad. "Oh, and you have this message from an, Eric, *Mauldin*? I'm not sure what this one is about." She handed Mia a slip of paper.

Mia took the note and stared at it with a confused expression. "When did he call?"

"His message was on the voice mail when I got in," the secretary said. "Is there a problem?"

"No," Mia said. "It's okay." She slid the memo under a stack of papers on her desk.

"Very good," Miss Tenery said. "Would you like some coffee?"

"Thanks," Mia said. "One cream and one sugar."

"There are donuts in the break room."

"Any éclairs?" Mia asked. Her face lit up.

"Vanilla cream?"

"Ooh, yeah, if they've got one. No sugar in the coffee if you bring an éclair."

"Yes, ma'am," the thin woman said and stepped out of the office.

When she was gone, Mia retrieved the WHILE YOU WERE OUT memo and studied it again. There was only one notation on it other than Eric's name.

Please call me.

Mia wondered why he was being so persistent, but she didn't have time to return his call 'til after lunch.

"Hello?"

"Eric, this is Mia. I got your message."

He sighed. "Thanks for calling. I thought you weren't ever going to call back."

"How did you get my work number?"

"You—I'm sorry?"

Mia waited.

"You told me you worked at Prospect."

"I never gave you my number here."

"I know, I—I'm sorry. Is there a problem?"

"How'd you get the number?" Mia asked.

"I looked it up in the phone book. I mean, it took thirty minutes to get somebody on the line who could transfer me to *your* department. It was a little hard, but I found you. Thanks for calling me back."

"Okay," Mia said. "So what do you want to tell me?"

"Can we meet somewhere and talk?"

"I don't want to see you, Eric. I talked to your wife."

"*Shareefa is not my wife*," he almost shouted. "What did she tell you? Listen, Mia, I really want to see to you in person."

"Eric, there's nothing you have to tell me that you can't say right now. You've got five minutes."

"That's—fine. Okay. Let's start from the beginning. You answered my phone Friday night, right?"

"Yes, Eric. I answered your phone. I also dropped it in the toilet. If you—"

"No, don't worry about that. But when you answered it, it was Shareefa. I don't know what she told you, but she showed up at my house later thinking you were still there. So whatever she told you was enough to make you want to leave."

"She said she was your wife and you have four kids together."

"*What?* That's a lie, Mia. I don't have any kids. And me and Shareefa were never married. I was engaged to her for a while, about two years ago. But we broke up. She's *nuts*, always going through my phone, checking up on me. After she moved out of my house, she—she wouldn't let it go. She's harassed two of my girlfriends since then, and if you break up with me, you'll be the third one who did because of her."

"She said you're a player, Eric. She said I could look through your phone and see that you didn't have any contact names; just letters. I looked and it was true."

"Mia, you've got to believe me. Shareefa was the reason I started that stupid system in the first place. She would never leave my phone alone. This was before we broke up. I got so mad one time, I just changed the names of all my contacts so she wouldn't be able to harass my friends anymore. I did that *for her*, and now she's saying I did it so I can be a player? This is crazy. Did you ask her if it was like that when we met? Did she tell you I had a restraining order against her?"

Mia wasn't buying it. "If you broke up with her, why is the phone still like that?"

"Mia, don't buy into that. She's a *liar*. When I changed all my contacts, I had to memorize them, and I guess it was just easier to keep it like that once we broke up. I figured it would come in handy if I ever ran across another jealous woman like her."

"You've got four kids."

"Mia, I don't have *any* kids. Couldn't if I wanted to; low sperm count. They would have to make them in a lab, and I'm not paying that much money for that. Well, I haven't. Maybe if—"

"I saw the pictures, Eric. In your living room; those pictures *you* showed me. Shareefa says those are your and her kids."

Eric actually started laughing. "Mia, I'm telling you, you can't believe *anything* that woman says about me. Those are my *nephews* and my *niece*. I told you that."

"They look *exactly* like you, Eric. You can't tell me that oldest boy isn't your son."

He chuckled again. "Mia, I keep the pictures up in the living room because I love them. They're like my *god*-children, since I can't have my own, but they are definitely not my kids. I know—given everything you've already heard—this is going to be hard to believe, but I've got a twin brother. Seriously. Those are his kids."

"Bullshit."

"Mia, I give you my word. I have pictures of him, videos—us, together. I have school pictures. Third grade, fourth grade, anything you want. I can show you. I'd bring *him* to show you if I could, but he's in Iraq. She told you they were *my* kids? Man, that's a new one. That's *crazy*. *My* kids? I hope you don't believe that."

"I don't know what to believe," Mia said, and that was the God-honest truth.

"Well, if you still believe her, will you at least meet me so I can show you my brother's pictures? She's a liar, Mia; an evil, *evil* woman. Please believe me. I thought we had something special."

"I gotta go, Eric. Five minutes is up."

"Are you going to meet me? Can we have dinner tonight?"

"I don't know," Mia said.

"Well, tell me you believe me, at least. I'll bring a copy of the restraining order if you want to see it."

"I'll call you later."

"Tonight?"

"We'll see," Mia said.

"Okay. Talk to you later. And, once again, I'm sorry about all of this. Hopefully this is just a little hump we can get over."

Mia hung up and looked around her office for the candid cameras. There were none, which meant this was all real. Unbelievably, ridiculously, and *preposterously* real.

She sighed heavily and left her office to find the new hire.

Crystal called the office to let her know Tyrone had been calling, but Mia didn't have time to call her sister back until the drive home.

"Hello?"

"Crystal, it's me."

"Oh, what's up, girl. You off already?"

"Yeah. Tyrone's been calling?"

"He called twice already; once when we first got home and again around four-thirty."

"What'd he say?" Mia asked.

"He said he wanted to come see TC. He got a deep voice. He sound like he look good."

Mia shook her head. "I'm already on 35. I'll be home by five-thirty. What are the kids doing?"

"Mica's playing a video game. TC's bouncing off the walls."

"He knows Tyrone's been calling."

"He answered the phone the first time," Crystal said.

Again Mia felt that sting of uncertainty. "You let them talk?"

"Not really. I think Tyrone said who he was and TC said hi. They might have talked for a minute. TC came and gave me the phone."

"What'd he say after that?"

"He just told me he wanted to come over."

"No, I mean TC."

"He was happy. Girl, what's wrong with you?"

"I don't know," Mia said.

"You mad 'cause Tyrone talked to TC?"

Mia knew it was wrong to feel that way, but couldn't help it. "That's wrong, ain't it?"

"Yeah, Mia. Just 'cause *you* don't like him, don't mean you should ruin it for TC. That's his daddy, the only one he got."

"That's *deep*, Crystal. Your wisdom surprises me sometimes."

Crystal chuckled. "Girl, I be watching *Montel.*"

Mia laughed too. "Hey, where did Tyrone call from?"

"I don't know."

"Can you get the number off the caller ID?"

"Yeah," Crystal said. "It's, um, 8-1-7, 5-5-5-"

"Three-four-eight-six?"

"Yeah. How you know?"

"That's his mother's number," Mia said. "It hasn't changed in ten years."

"I don't even remember my *last* boyfriend's phone number," Crystal said. "You've got a *bionic* memory!"

Mia chuckled. "Tell TC I'll be home in a minute and Tyrone can come over then."

"All right," Crystal said and hung up.

Mia took a few deep breaths before calling TC's father. She dreaded this moment for the last six years but knew it had to be done. Tyrone's mother answered on the first ring.

"Hello. Mrs. Story? This is Mia."

"Mia? *Mia?* Good Lord, girl. I haven't heard from you in ages."

"Yes, ma'am. It has been a while. How's everything been going?"

"Oh, fine, baby. I hear you did real good for yourself . . ."

"Thanks," Mia said. "I've done all right."

"You're calling for Tyrone. He hasn't stopped talking about you since he got home. Hold on, baby, let me get him for you. *Tyrone!*"

Mia wondered why old people didn't take the phone away from their mouths when they yelled. She waited a few seconds, and then heard a voice that sent a little tremor down the small of her back. And Crystal was right. His voice was a lot deeper.

"Hello? Mia?"

"Hi, Tyrone. Welcome back."

"*Man*, it feels good to be back. How you been doing, Mia?"

"Fine."

"I called you today," he said, "talked to TC."

"Yeah. Crystal told me."

"He sounds good," Tyrone said. "Like he's doing good. He sounds smart, too. You raised him right, I can tell."

"Thanks."

"Are you home yet? I want to come see y'all."

"I'll be home in five minutes," Mia said. "You can come see *TC*."

"I wanna see you too, Mia."

"Tyrone, I told you—"

"Yeah, I got your letter. I still wanna see you, though. Is that all right?"

"I'm almost home," Mia said. "It'll take you about twenty minutes, so you can leave now if you want."

"All right. I'm on my way. I can't wait to see y'all. Mica, too. I miss you," Tyrone said.

"All right, we'll see you when you get there." Mia disconnected with an odd feeling in her gut. She was nervous, but she didn't know why. She called Eric just so she could talk about something different.

"Hello?"

"Eric, this is Mia."

"Hey. Thanks for calling back. What are you doing? You're off work."

"Yeah. I'm on my way home."

"Cool. So, uh, were you taking me up on my offer? You wanna have dinner tonight?"

"Yeah. I've been thinking about what you said. I feel stupid. I mean, if everything you've told me is true, I'm an idiot."

"No, you're not. That girl is convincing. If I were in your situation, I probably would have believed her, too. What time can you get out?"

"Probably not until seven-thirty."

"That's great. Do you want to go to T'afia?"

"No. I don't feel like getting dressed up. There's a Chile's close to me on Altamesa."

"That's cool. Can I pick you up?"

"No," Mia said. "I'll meet you there."

"When are you going to let me pick you up, like a traditional date?" Eric wondered.

"I don't know," Mia said. "Bring those pictures and we'll go from there."

"You want me to bring the pictures?" he asked. "I thought you believed me."

"Do you not want to bring the pictures?"

"It's not a problem, it's just—"

"You're making me wonder if this dinner is a good idea," Mia said.

"Don't say that. I'll bring the pictures. Everything's cool. Seven-thirty, right?"

"I'll call you if something changes."

"Okay. I look forward to seeing you."

"Bye, Eric." Mia hung up and drove the rest of the way home in silence. She wondered if she shouldn't postpone one or both of her scheduled encounters, but figured it was best to get them over with—the Eric situation in particular. She couldn't go one more day without getting to the bottom of that one.

CHAPTER 6

DADDY'S HOME

When she got home, TC met her at the front door.

"Mama, I talked to my daddy today!"

"Yeah, I heard. I talked to him, too."

"Is he coming?" The boy was so anxious. Mia smiled down at him. Out of his school clothes, TC wore denim shorts, a white T-shirt and leather sandals. He was getting taller. He didn't look so big this time last year. Mia checked her watch.

"Yes, he's coming. Should be here in about ten minutes."

"Cool!" TC spun, his legs already pumping, but Mia grabbed the back of his T-shirt and halted his forward progress.

"Where are you going?"

"I'm gonna tell Mica!"

"No, *I'll* tell Mica," Mia said. "Where's Crystal?"

"In her room, on the computer."

"You go tell your aunt, and *I'll* talk to your sister."

"Okay!" TC yelled and sprinted off in that direction. Mia went to her daughter's room and found Mica lying on the floor on her stomach. She had a video game controller in her hands, and her eyes were riveted to the television screen no more than five feet away. Mia sat on her bed and watched from behind. Shrek and Fiona were scampering through their swamp collecting snail eyeballs for some reason. Mica controlled the male ogre rather than his portly wife.

"How's it going?" Mia asked.

"Fine," Mica said without looking up.

"How was school?"

"It was okay."

"Just okay?"

"Yeah."

"You know TC's dad is coming over, right?"

"Yeah, I know. TC keep talking about it. He won't shut up."

"Is he getting on your nerves?"

Mica pushed "Pause" and looked back at her mother. "A little."

Mia patted the bed.

Mica sat next to her and stared down at her hands. "I'm in trouble?"

"For what?"

"I said TC got on my nerves."

Mia smiled. "TC's daddy is coming over, and your daddy's in heaven. So I can understand why you're a little upset. Everything you're feeling is fine. You're just a little girl and you didn't do anything wrong. Your daddy should be here too, but he's not. It's okay to be upset."

"It's not fair," Mica agreed.

Mia looked up at the ceiling. "No, it's not, but we have to get through this. Your daddy's been gone for a long time. You knew TC's dad was going to get out sooner or later. We've got to keep moving on. Me and you, we're *Clemmons* women. Clemmons women don't cry when things don't go our way. Even though you're sad, you have to keep your chin up."

Mica lifted her head a little. "Why did my daddy have to die?" she pondered.

Mia fought back tears, knowing she had to lead by example. "Mica, when I met your dad, I really loved him. He was tall, dark, and handsome. He had eyes just like yours. Every time I look at you, I still see him a little. He treated me good, most of the time, but he wasn't a good person. He did bad things. I'll have to explain it to you when you're a little older, but no matter what he did, he didn't deserve to die. Nobody ever deserves that.

"But that's where being a strong woman comes in. Even if something happens to us that's totally unfair, we still have to keep marching on. One day Mommy will get married and you'll have a new father. And I'll make sure he's a good person this time. Deal?"

Mica smiled. "Deal. Are you going to marry TC's daddy?"

Mia grinned. "No, but I'll make sure I get one you like. I won't even marry him unless you say you like him. Okay?"

"Okay," Mica said. "Can I go in there when TC's daddy gets here?"

"Yes. This is your house, too. Come on, let's go in the living room and we can wait for him together."

"Okay!"

Mia hoped she'd have time to change clothes, but Tyrone came a little earlier than expected. She was sitting on the couch with Mica when the doorbell rang. TC rushed from his aunt's room and ran straight to the door. Crystal followed him out wearing the same pajama bottoms and tank top she had on this morning.

"I thought you had a class today," Mia said.

"It got cancelled."

"You picked the kids up like that? You didn't feel compelled to change clothes *all day*?"

"I was—"

But Crystal's explanation got cut off by the entrance of a man Mia still recognized, though there were a multitude of physical differences.

"Hey, TC! You got big, boy!" Tyrone stepped in and scooped his son up for a full-body hug, and Mia stared, unaware that her mouth was open.

It was the same Tyrone, but the six-year stint inside changed him in many ways. He wore a pair of jeans that were starched to crisp perfection. His K-Swiss sneakers were dazzling white, probably brand new. He wore a solid blue Polo shirt that was short-sleeved with no patterns.

Mia stared at his arms, which had the same tattoos she remembered, but she also noticed a few new ones. He now had a length of barbed wire above his left bicep. In the same area on his right arm, Mia saw the letters *TC* tattooed in Old English lettering.

Tyrone put his son down and looked around the room. Mia saw that his Polo was unbuttoned. He wore a white tee, but the undershirt did little to hide his rippling physique. Tyrone had large pectorals Mia definitely didn't remember. His arms were also bigger, with defined muscles in his forearms and swollen biceps. And Tyrone used to have a pencil neck that met with the rest of his body with no flair. His traps and shoulders had serious bulges now.

And it wasn't overdone. He looked nice. He was damned fine.

Tyrone had a strong jawline. He was a bit more bronze now, and the darker skin tone accentuated his beautiful hazel eyes. His moustache and goatee were gone, as well as his afro. Tyrone sported a crew cut that would have made the Marines proud. His edge-up was flawless. Overall, he was without a blemish.

He looked into Mia's eyes and smiled, and she couldn't help but smile back.

"You look good," he said. "You gotta dress like that for work?"

Mia nodded, still a little speechless.

Tyrone dropped to his knees and stared at his son at eye level.

Mia looked over at Crystal and she was looking back at Mia. Crystal's eyes were big. She looked at Tyrone then back to Mia and mouthed the word *Damn!*

Indeed, Mia thought.

"You gettin' big, boy," Tyrone said. He reached out and held the boy's shoulders. "You gettin' old, too. How old are you? Nine already?"

TC looked to the ground nervously. "I'll be ten in—"

"I already know," Tyrone said with a big smile. "September twenty-sixth!"

TC looked up at him and smiled back. "How'd you know that?"

"I'm yo daddy," Tyrone said, then pulled him in for a hug. "I'm yo daddy. I know everything about you."

Mia still had Mica in her lap. It was odd to see TC disappear in those massive arms. Mia thought that hug was going to make her uncomfortable, but she actually felt good as she watched the embrace.

Tyrone stood and looked down at his son with his eyes glistening. A tear rolled down his cheek and he wiped it away nonchalantly.

"I know you're a little nervous, but you don't have to feel weird around me," he told TC. "I'm your daddy, but I wanna be your friend, too. I wanna have fun with you. We can do anything you want."

TC's face lit up. "You wanna see my Hot Wheels?"

Tyrone grinned. "Yeah, man. I want to see whatever you got to show me."

"C'mon," TC yelled, already racing towards his room.

Tyrone looked to Mia with uncertainty. TC stopped when he realized no one was following him.

"Mama, can Daddy come in my room?"

Mia nodded. "Sure. He can go."

"Come on!" TC yelled, on the run again.

Tyrone stopped at the couch and looked down at Mica. "And who is this beautiful little girl?"

Mica turned towards her mother's breasts.

"Go ahead, tell him your name," Mia encouraged.

She looked back to Tyrone hesitantly. "I'm Mica," she said softly.

"I know," Tyrone said. "Your name is Mica Lynn Clemmons. I know a lot about you, too."

Mica smiled and looked back to her mother, a little surprised.

Tyrone stuck out a hand for her to shake. "I'm Tyrone. Nice to meet you."

"Go ahead," Mia said when her daughter made no move to reciprocate. She watched Mica's tiny hand get swallowed up by Tyrone's, and again Mia didn't feel awkward like she thought she would.

"Daddy, you comin?" TC called.

"I'm gonna go play with TC," Tyrone said to Mica. "You wanna come? Is it all right if she comes, Mia?"

Mia nodded and Mica bounced from her lap. She took Tyrone's hand and led him out of the room.

"I'll show you his room."

Mia watched them go, and for the life of her she couldn't understand why she didn't have any of the uneasiness she expected. Tyrone looked back at her and winked, and that brought it all back into perspective.

This nigga ain't slick, she thought. *I wanna be TC's daddy. I'll raise Mica like's she my own.* That shit wasn't happening.

Crystal couldn't wait for them to leave. "*Girl*," she said in a hushed voice.

"I know. He looks good," Mia said, also whispering.

"You didn't say he was *fine*," she hissed. "He *fine*, girl! Look better than anything you brought home since *I* been living here."

"Thanks a lot," Mia whispered. "And you haven't seen Eric yet. He's fine, too."

"You talking bout Secret Ag–"

"I don't think he's a player," Mia said. "I talked to him today."

"What'd he say?" Crystal asked.

"I'll tell you later, but he explained everything. I'm going out with him tonight."

"What about his kids?"

"They're not his," Mia said. "We'll talk later. Can you look after them for a minute? I want to change clothes."

"Okay, but you better know what you're doing. You bust his window out. It could be a set-up."

"It's not a set-up," Mia said. "I'll talk to you when this fool leaves."

Tyrone didn't leave for an hour. After TC showed him around his room, Mica took him to her room and they sat on the floor and played a video game. Mia watched from the doorway after she changed. Seeing the three of them together made her feel good for a minute, but she kept reminding herself that this was all part of Tyrone's ultimate scheme.

But still, she couldn't stay mad at him. And for what it was worth, he did have a good rapport with TC and Mica.

When Tyrone said he had to leave, the kids started to fuss, but Mia sent them to the dining room to eat a dinner Crystal had ready for them. They bid their adieus and Tyrone said he would come back later in the week, most likely on Friday, to visit with them again. He hugged them both, and they scampered off, leaving Tyrone and Mia in the living room alone.

He started to say something, but Mia led him outside first. Tyrone took a few steps down the sidewalk, then turned to face her. She saw that he'd brought his mother's car, and it squatted in her driveway like a hippo at a football game. The '88 Bonneville was long and ugly and so out of place in her neighborhood that Mia wondered if someone might think she was being robbed.

"You did good, Mia," he said. "You got a nice house. *Real* nice. I never thought you were gonna be so successful."

Yeah, I bet you didn't, she thought, but said nothing. She wore jeans and a sweater now, and socks with no shoes.

"And you look good, too," Tyrone went on. "You still got your figure. You're as fine as you were when I walked up to you at that movie theatre. You remember? When you were downtown with your friends from college."

Of course Mia remembered that day. It would be ingrained in her psyche forever.

"You look nice too, Tyrone. I see you've been working out. Got some new tats. What's that one on your right arm?"

He smiled. He raised his sleeve and Mia's legs felt weak for a second. With his arm bent, that bicep swelled like a grapefruit.

"This is for TC. I wanted to have him with me. I got this when I was on my second year. I was gonna get another one with Mica's name over here." He pointed to a spot under the TC tattoo.

"I don't know why you would do that," Mia said. "She's not your daughter."

"I know," Tyrone said, still smiling. "I just wanted it for when I got out. I told you I want to raise—"

"Yes, Tyrone. I got your letter. You want to raise Mica like she's your daughter, but I don't need you to do that. She's fine. You and TC can have your relationship and whatever, but Mica's not your child."

"I know she's not," Tyrone said, his smile faltering for the first time. "But I was hoping that if you and me—"

"Let's get this straight right now," Mia said. "There is no and will be no 'you and me.' What we had was good, but that was a long time ago, Tyrone. We weren't even going together by the time you went to prison. I don't know why you picked me to have this fixation with, but you need to let it go. It's over, has been for damned near a decade."

Tyrone's smile went away entirely. He nodded. "What about my son?"

"You can see him. I don't have a problem with that, just call. Once you get a job we can have a visitation schedule."

"I don't want a *visitation schedule*," he said. "I want to live with him and raise him."

He looked pretty upset, but Mia stuck to her guns. "Tyrone, you'd have to live with *me* to live with *him*, and you're *not* going to live with me. We're through. Been through."

He nodded again and seemed to accept this.

"All right," he said. "Well, can I at least have a hug before I go? I haven't seen you in a long time."

Mia thought about it for a second and softened. "Okay." She took a step forward. Tyrone met her halfway and threw his arms around her. Mia reciprocated, and for a moment it felt good to have him close again, but that changed quickly. Tyrone's arms slid down her back, and before she knew it he had her ass in his hands, *both hands*; one hand per cheek.

Mia pushed off quickly, but Tyrone was already backing away. His big smile was back, and he held his arms out in a *Who me?* gesture.

"Don't ever do that again."

"I'm sorry," Tyrone said, laughing now. "I'm sorry. I haven't touched a woman in six years, Mia. I didn't mean to do that, but, *damn*, it felt good."

"You'd better leave."

"All right," he said. "But I want to say something right here." He looked to the sky. "Before God and all his angels, I'm going to say this: I want to be with you, Mia. I want to *marry* you, and I'm not going to stop feeling like this 'til you got a ring on your finger, either mine's or someone else's."

Mia didn't know what to say. "Call before you come by this weekend," she managed. Her heart thudded like she had a kicker box in her chest.

Tyrone turned and walked to his mother's bucket. "I'm serious," he called over his shoulder. "And quit looking like that. You woulda hit me in the face if you didn't like it."

He got in and the muffler sounded like it was going to explode when he started the car. Mia stood on her porch and watched until he was out of sight. She went back inside and leaned with her back on the door, her chest rising and falling. For the life of her, she couldn't understand why she was smiling.

"How long are you going to be gone?"

The sisters faced each other in the two-car garage. Mia stood between her Lexus and Crystal's champagne Tahoe. Crystal stood on the steps leading to the kitchen.

"I don't know. Nine, nine-thirty. In time to put the kids to bed. You got something to do?"

"I'm supposed to go over Sydney's house," Crystal said.

"To do what?"

"Nothing. Just kick it." She grinned.

"All y'all seem to do is *kick it*. When are you gonna bring him by so I can meet him?"

"He been by here before."

That was news to Mia. "When?"

"He comes by after classes sometimes, and we go eat lunch."

"Why don't you bring him this weekend," Mia offered. "Why are you hiding him? He got a hunchback?"

"Naw," Crystal laughed. "You gonna like him. He finna get a contract."

"A *contract*? Doing what?—And please don't say *rappin'*."

"What's wrong with rappin'?"

Mia rolled her eyes and opened her car door.

"You should change clothes," Crystal noted. Mia wore the same sweater and jeans she put on when Tyrone came by. The sweater reeked of Soccer Mom. The jeans were comfortable but didn't hug her thighs like her typical date outfits.

"What's wrong with what I have on?"

"Nothin, if you ain't tryin to get none."

"I'm *not* trying to get none," Mia said.

"Still thinkin about Tyrone, huh?" Crystal smiled and licked her lips.

"No, I am not thinking about Tyrone. Why would I be?"

"He practically proposed to you," Crystal said.

"A lot of guys have proposed to me," Mia reminded her. "And most of them had a job, had never been to prison, and didn't drive '88 Bonnevilles with bad mufflers. They had a ring, too."

"Yeah, but he looked *good*," Crystal reminisced.

"You'd sleep with a handsome hobo," Mia predicted.

Crystal opened the door, and TC and Mica could be heard clamoring inside.

"You liked it when he grabbed yo booty," Crystal teased.

"I don't know what part of my story gave you that impression," Mia said, a little surprised by her sister's take on things.

"You woulda hit him in the face if you didn't like it," Crystal said and disappeared inside the house.

That was odd. Mia never even told her Tyrone said the very same thing.

Eric wore dark slacks, black, square-toed Stacy Adams shoes, a white button-down, and an unbuttoned black sports coat. He stood and pulled Mia's chair out for her.

"I thought we weren't getting dressed up," she said as she sat down.

Eric sat across from her. "I'm sorry. You've had so many bad impressions of me already, I just want to make sure all the rest of them are positive. You look great, by the way. You look good in anything you have on." He grinned, but Mia didn't smile back.

"You don't know how happy I am," he went on. "I thought I'd never see you again."

"Where are the pictures?" she asked.

"Wow, straight to the chase, huh?"

"Well, they *are* important."

A red-headed girl approached their table. She wore a white blouse with black pants. "How you guys doing? I'm Sarah. I'll be taking your orders tonight. Would you like to start off with our boneless buffalo wings?"

"Mmm, I'm not sure." Eric picked up his menu and Mia did the same. "Do you want an appetizer?" he asked her.

"No. I just want dinner," Mia said. "I could order right now, actually."

"Okay, and what would you like?"

"The Cajun chicken pasta," Mia said. "Bleu cheese on the salad."

Eric looked at her over his menu. "You have to be home soon?"

"Crystal's going out tonight. I can only stay a couple of hours."

Eric ordered the same thing she was having and sent the waitress away with their menus.

"So, where are the pictures?" Mia asked again once their waitress was gone.

"I have them." Eric reached and produced a blue notebook from the seat next to him. "You still think I'm lying, don't you? You can't see, for half a second, how I might be telling the truth?" He placed the folder on the table before him, and Mia looked down at it.

"Sure I can see how you might be telling the truth," she said, then looked into his eyes. "I wouldn't be here if I didn't. But you've got to admit this whole thing is pretty hard to swallow. You have a perfect explanation for everything. This twin brother of yours is pretty convenient."

"You're right," he said. "I would have told you about him on our first date if I thought she would use his kids to hurt me. But we really haven't talked about our families a lot. I don't know much about your mother and brothers . . ."

"But you know they exist," Mia said and looked down to the folder again.

"Well, my brother exists, too," Eric said and opened the folder. His index finger trembled a little as he did so, Mia thought. But it might not have. There *was* a flickering candle on their table.

Eric produced three photographs. He handed each of them to her, and Mia studied them with a feeling of tremendous guilt rising within her. The twin brother was a spitting image. He and Eric had the same haircuts, the same features, and even the same clothes in one of them.

"His name is Anthony. We're both thirty-four, and we're identical. That one is us when we were seven, at Coney Island. The other one is when we tried out for football. We went to Skyline, in Dallas. Here's our most recent one. Christmas, two years ago at Mom's."

He then handed her court documents.

"This is the restraining order I filed against Shareefa. See, here's me as the complainant, and there's Shareefa's name."

He reached over the table and pointed to the areas of interest. Mia wasn't an expert in legal jargon, but the restraining order appeared to be legit. Eric even had a six-page affidavit where he described his ex-fiancé as abusive, obsessive, and neurotic. There were at least ten instances of stalking noted. According to the affidavit, Shareefa Tamara Jones had done everything from harassing Eric's mom to slicing his tires. The court order was finalized just two months ago.

"She never could accept that we weren't together anymore. She has showed up at my job, gone through my mail . . ."

Eric's voice started to fade out. Mia put the restraining order down and studied the pictures again, two of them in particular.

"These two. You say you were seven in this one, and this one was when you were in high school?"

"The football one? Yeah. We were freshmen."

Mia flipped the pictures over. "These look new. They aren't the originals, are they?"

"No," Eric said. "Those were in my mother's photo album. When I went to visit last Christmas, I got her to make a copy of them for me. I tried to get the originals, but she wouldn't give them up. Had them for years." He narrowed his eyes. "Why? Is there a problem?"

"You only have these three pictures?" Mia asked.

"Well, I have more pictures of him at home, with his wife and kids. I've got some of him in his uniform, too. Why? What's wrong?"

Nothing, Mia thought, *except the only pictures you have of the two of you together look brand new. And there are websites on the internet that specialize in fake celebrity nudes. If someone could fabricate a picture of Jennifer Anniston in the midst of a sticky gangbang, then you could have pictures of a secret twin brother.*

But how far-fetched was that? Mia wondered. Was she so paranoid she was going to *make* his story a lie no matter what evidence he provided?

"Nothing," Mia said. She gathered his papers and photographs and handed them back to him. "I'm sorry. You shouldn't have had to do that." She rubbed her face. "I hope you don't think I'm some *crazy* or something."

Eric smiled. "Mia, I understand exactly how you felt. I've been dealing with Shareefa for a long time. She can definitely make you feel crazy. She broke my windshield that night, after you left, and I still don't—"

Mia nearly choked on her water. She put a hand to her face. "*Ugk*, I—I'm sorry. *Excuse me?*"

"You all right?"

She nodded, her eyes watering.

"Um, Shareefa, she broke my windshield after you left. She swore up and down she didn't do it, but she's done it twice already. Are you sure you're okay?"

Mia cleared her throat and managed to get a breath of air down. "I'm sorry," she said, and took another sip of water.

Eric smiled. "I thought I was going to lose you again," he joked.

"Eric," she said, "Shareefa didn't break your windshield. You didn't call the police on her, did you?"

"No," he said. His brow furrowed. "I was tired and didn't feel like staying up to wait for them. Plus I didn't want my deductible to go up again. I just cursed her out and bought another one. Why do you think Shareefa didn't break my windshield?"

Mia took a deep breath. "Well, remember what I did to your phone?" she asked. "When I was still mad at you . . ."

He shook his head. "I don't believe it."

"I'm sorry," Mia said. She grabbed her purse and produced a checkbook. "I want to pay for it. The phone, too."

"*You* broke my windshield?"

"Yes, Eric. I'm sorry. I—I don't know what came over me. How much was it?" She started writing the check.

"Stop," Eric said. "Look at me. *How* did you break my windshield?"

"Well, I threw a brick at first, then I used my tire iron."

"*You* broke my windshield?"

"Yes, Eric. *I* broke your windshield. Do you need me to get it in the newspapers or what?"

He smiled. "You must really like me."

"I must have really *hated* you," Mia corrected. "But I was out of line. I can't believe I did that. No one can."

"I don't want your money," Eric decided.

"You're taking it," Mia said. "I'm a grown woman. I pay for my mistakes. How much was it? The phone, too." Her pen hovered over the checkbook.

Eric leaned back in his chair. "You know, when Shareefa said, '*I don't know. Maybe yo other bitch broke it!*' I wouldn't have believed her in a million years."

Mia smiled. "I hope you didn't let that bitch call me a bitch."

Eric finally gave her a price, and Mia wrote a check for her damages. The food came shortly afterwards, and they actually had a nice time together. Eric told her about his whole family, every cousin it seemed, and Mia shared a bit of her lineage, too. She also told him about TC's father coming home from prison. Eric was a bit concerned at first, but Mia assured him the jobless, convicted felon had no chance of a late-round comeback. She did not tell him about the ass-grabbing incident, though, and certainly not about Tyrone's lofty declaration of love.

Standing next to Mia's car later on, Eric hugged her and kissed her good night, and it was good, but also a little different.

CHAPTER 7
GAME FOR DAYS

After such a tumultuous start, Mia thought her whole week would be off-kilter, but it turned out pretty nice. With her questions resolved about the player—who turned out not to be a player—she was able to exhibit her trademark confidence.

Tyrone called almost every day to inquire about his son, but his true intentions were clear. He always wanted to chat longer after they were done discussing TC.

"So, uh, what you doing?"

"I'm cooking, Tyrone. I'll call you later. Maybe we could set something up for the weekend."

"What you cooking?"

"I'm busy, Tyrone."

"All right. I just want to see my boy."

"Okay, but I'm working late the next two days."

"You can call me when you get through eating if you want. I'll be woke."

Mia was pretty sure Tyrone only wanted to see his son half as much as he wanted to see her, but she only felt comfortable with monitored visits, so that was unavoidable. She allowed him to on Thursday, and Tyrone showed up at 5:30 sharp, as dashing as ever, with gifts in hand. The gifts were actually from Family Dollar. It said so on the bag he toted them in, but the kids fussed over the trinkets as if they'd come from Bloomingdale's.

Tyrone sat on the couch with TC on one side and Mica on the other. Mia sat across from them on the love seat. Today Tyrone had on khaki Dickies with a blue golf shirt. The shirt had no designs except for the Polo insignia on the left breast. He was still strikingly handsome, even though he had fresh stubble under his nose and on his chin. He wore a goatee when they were dating, and it looked like he was growing it out again.

He had two gifts for his son: The first was a cheap version of the Hungry Hippo game. The second was a Hot Wheels car Tyrone said was a 1970 Chevelle SS.

"I'm going to bring you a different car every time I see you," he promised. "You're going to have the biggest collection in Overbrook."

"What if you bring me one I already have?" TC asked.

"I'll just take it back and get you another one," Tyrone said. "If you think you got *this* one, let me know. I'll take it back right now."

"No, I don't have a Chevelle. I got four Camaros and three Corvettes. I think I have a Charger, but no Chevelle."

Mica's gift was a figurine from the Bratz toy line. The doll was dark-skinned with full lips, just like Mica.

"Don't think I forgot about you, lil' Mama." Tyrone handed it to her, and Mica glowed like it was her birthday.

Mia watched them, wondering if Crystal hadn't picked up the wrong kids from school. Mica and TC were known to balk at dollar-store toys that required neither assembly nor batteries, but they fussed over Tyrone's presents like they were orphans.

"I wanna get you a case to keep all your cars in," he told his son. "I saw one at Wal-Mart. It was big, built like a suitcase, kinda. It had a plastic front, so you can see all your cars, and each one fit into a little slot."

"I have something like that," TC said. "It's small, though. Like a lunch box."

"How many cars does it hold?" Tyrone asked.

"Um, I don't know. Maybe twenty."

"I'ma get you a bigger one," Tyrone said. "One you'll be able to keep *all* your cars in."

"Cool."

"Let me see what you got again so I can make sure I don't bring the wrong one next time."

"Okay. Come on!"

The three of them scampered off, without asking her permission this time, and Mia was left in the living room alone. Tyrone looked over his shoulder and shot her a wink as they passed. Mia rolled her eyes at him and got up to see what her sister was doing.

Crystal was on her computer updating her MySpace page.

"Tyrone still here?"

Mia nodded. "In there with the kids."

"He look good today," Crystal said.

"How you know?"

"I peeked out there when he was giving them they toys."

"Didn't even see you."

"That's 'cause you was staring all up in his face," Crystal said.

Mia sighed. "I don't know why you keep doing that."

"I don't know why you keep denying it. You know you like that boy."

"What is it about Tyrone that makes you think I want him?"

"He's—"

"*Fine*," Mia cut her off. "You're stuck on that. Yeah, he's cute." She looked around to make sure no one was coming. "He's got a nice body. Every brother coming out of the pen looks like that. Tyrone ain't special."

"He's TC's daddy."

"So? TC's *nine*. We've been doing just fine without his daddy."

"He *wants* to raise his son, though. A lot of niggas ain't trying to do that. He wants to raise Mica, too. You *know* a lot of niggas ain't trying to raise *another* man's kid."

"Of course I know. I'm thirty-two and single. But just 'cause Tyrone wants to do it doesn't automatically make him the man for the job."

"What do you have against him?" Crystal wanted to know.

"He's a *thug*, Crystal. That's the end right there. I don't date *thugs*, and he's a thug. He's a hoodlum, an ex-con, a jobless convicted felon who stays with his mama."

"But what if he wanna do right? You'll date him if he change?"

"Tyrone can't do right."

"No, for real," Crystal said. "What if he really wants to do right? Would you take him then?"

There was no need in considering that. "Tyrone's not gonna do right. Even if he wanted to, he wouldn't be able to get a good job with a felony on his record. Anyway, I got a boyfriend who's already doing right."

"Yeah," Crystal said. "He's boring, though."

"You mean *stable*?"

"Whatever."

"Speaking of boyfriends, when I am going to meet yours?"

Crystal grinned. "You wanna see him tomorr—wait, he goes to the studio on Friday. You can meet him Saturday if you want."

"Saturday's cool. I'm going out with Eric that night, though. Do you mind watching the kids?"

"Can Sydney stay over while you're gone?"

"Overnight?"

"Naw, just for a couple hours. Why? You planning on staying *overnight* with Eric?"

"I might," Mia said with a slight smile.

"I'ma tell *Tyrone*."

"Speaking of, I'd better go check on them," Mia said. "He might be in there teaching my babies gang signs!"

Tyrone was not teaching the babies gang signs. In her son's room, they were playing some type of game that involved cars, dolls, and a few stuffed animals. On his hands and knees, Tyrone looked as much like a kid as TC and Mica. Mia backed out of the doorway without them noticing her.

At seven-thirty, it was time for the kids to eat. Tyrone hugged and kissed them both, and Mia walked him out-side—keeping her distance in case he tried to goose her again.

Tyrone took a step off her porch then turned to face her. "You look good, Mia."

She wore baggy canvas shorts and a loose-fitting T-shirt. She didn't think she looked in any way remarkable, but Tyrone stared at her like she was dressed for the ball.

"You look good, too, Tyrone. I see you're trying to grow your beard out."

He smiled and rubbed his chin. "Actually, I'm gonna keep it smooth. They won't let you grow a moustache in the pen. I didn't like it at first, but after a while I thought I looked pretty good with a clean face. What do you think?"

"It's fine," Mia said. "Either way."

"Which way do you like the most?"

"I'm not that concerned with it," she said. "I guess you look better without it."

"I'ma shave then."

Mia shrugged.

"Oh, I forgot something." Tyrone reached into his pocket and produced three $20 bills. "Here. I was meaning to give you this."

Mia looked at the money but didn't reach for it. "What's that for?"

He shrugged. "I figure I should help you out a little bit if I can."

"You mean *child support*?"

"Yeah. I guess. I don't really want to call it that, though. I don't wanna be put on no child support."

"Do you have a job?"

"I been doing a little work with my uncle. He gave me a hundred dollars today. I bought them toys with some, gave my mom thirty. The rest is yours."

"I don't want that," Mia said.

"Why not?"

"'Cause you just got out Monday. I'm sure you need it."

"I put my son's needs in front of mine."

Unexpectedly, his words made Mia feel warm all over.

"That's nice, Tyrone. It really is; but I can't take your last."

"Why?"

"I don't need it."

"Take it," he urged, "I'm gon' do right by you and my boy."

"All right," Mia said, and reluctantly reached for the money. But instead of releasing it, Tyrone grabbed her hand and held on to it. His touch sent a jolt of electricity up her arm.

"I wanted to ask you something," he said.

"Let go of my hand, Tyrone."

"Am I hurting you? Dang, Mia, why you trippin' with me like this? You actin' like I got a disease or somethin'. I can't even *touch* you now?"

"Okay," she said and did not pull her hand away.

"I was wondering if we can, *me and you*, if we can go out this weekend. My uncle says he'll let me use his car. I know you don't wanna go in my mom's." He looked over to the hoopty in Mia's driveway and chuckled. "We can go in that if you want to, but we might get stuck on the side of the road somewhere."

Mia wasn't smiling. "Tyrone, I can't go out with you."

"Why not?"

"I have a boyfriend."

He flipped her hand over. "I don't see no ring on yo finger. Can't you go out with that lame next week?"

Mia smiled and drew her hand back. "You got some nerve."

"What you mean?"

"You assume my boyfriend's a lame. Why? 'Cause he doesn't sell dope? Never been to jail? That make him lame?"

Tyrone grinned. "I don't know nothin' about all that. I don't know nothin about him. I say he lame, 'cause he got a good woman like you and don't know what to do with her."

"You don't know what you're talking about."

"Does TC like him?"

"My boyfriend?"

"Yeah."

"What does that have to do with anything?"

"I'm just askin' if my son likes him. The kids will let you know if yo man ain't no good."

"He hasn't met them," Mia said, not sure why she was sharing so much.

Tyrone nodded. "Yep. Just like I figured. You don't want to take him around yo kids 'cause it's somethin wrong with him. You *know* it's something wrong with him."

"My dinner's getting cold," Mia said.

"Cool. That's cool. What about this?" He still had the sixty dollars in his palm.

"Are you going to give it to me, or do you just want to hold my hand?"

"I would love to hold your hand, and every other part of you." Tyrone's eyes were so enticing, Mia thought she would get lost in them. He held out the money, and she took it without incident. He turned and walked away.

"What about *next* Saturday?" he called over his shoulder.

"I'll still have a boyfriend then."

"I'll give it about a month," he said and opened the car door. He stared at her over the hood of the Bonneville. "He ain't right. You'll see it by then."

"What makes you so sure?" Mia asked.

"'Cause *I'm* the one you're supposed to be with. That's why after all this time I been gone, you still ain't married.

You can *settle* for somebody else, but you know I'm right."

Mia stood on the porch and watched until he pulled off. That Bonneville was just as raggedy as his game. Tyrone was definitely full of shit, but when she got back in, TC told her he had the best dad in the world. Mica was pretty enamored with the ex-con also.

CHAPTER 8
TREAT HER LIKE A LADY

Saturday was a great day.

Mia made it to Claire's at ten in the morning, and once again her man problems were quite the buzz. Everyone was glad she had gotten to the bottom of the Eric quagmire, but a few ladies, Vasantha in particular, still thought Eric was a master player.

"This could be his *ultimate* alibi," she said. "The *twin brother*. He only use that one when he *know* he caught and can't think of no way out. And he's in the *war*? You better watch it, girl. Till you *meet* his brother, I say he ain't got one."

As for the pictures, Vasantha said they were Photoshopped, but she was the only one who felt this way. Nearly everyone else was inclined to believe Eric's side of the story. Mia was glad for that, because she was still feeling tremors from their one night of passion.

As Vasantha gave her auburn highlights, and Nancy applied gloss to her French manicure, Mia told her girl-friends about TC's father coming home. She also told them about his declaration of love before God and all the angels.

"Are you gon' give him some?" Gayle wanted to know.

"Of course I'm not," Mia said, but something in her eyes made a couple of the girls think otherwise.

And to Mia's surprise, most of the women thought Tyrone *was* sincere about his claims. Mia agreed that prison does change *some* men, but she didn't think Tyrone had that Malcolm X-type experience. Either way, her girlfriends were more interested in his *outer* transformation anyway.

Mia told them Tyrone was built like Evander Holyfield in his prime. His eyes were hazel, the color of a wheat field. She said Tyrone's skin was bronze like an Aztec warrior's and smooth like melted chocolate. Mia told them that when he grabbed her butt, a flash of lightning bolted from her heart, shot down her belly, and settled between her legs.

The overall consensus was that she should definitely jump his bones.

"Ooh, fresh out of prison, with all that *stamina* built up in him." Vasantha actually had her eyes closed. "Girl, you *better* give him some before somebody else throw it at him. He want you. He want you *bad*."

"Stop pulling my hair!"

Mama Ernestine would be the only one with sound advice. Today she wore a lavender blouse, black slacks, and a wig she called the "Lil' Kim." Before Mia left the beauty shop, the matriarch took her hands and lectured as only a mother could:

"That Eric sounds like a good man. Y'all had your problem, but you got over it. If he ain't cheatin', he might be the one you've been looking for. The other one, your baby's father, he sounds like trouble. You a smart woman, Mia. You deserve the best, and I think you know Tyrone ain't it."

Mia left the beauty shop, as always, a fresh, vibrant, and confident woman.

When she got home, the kids were in their aunt's room, crowded around the computer.

"What's going on?"

"TC was showing me this game," Crystal said. "Did you know they're already using computers at school?"

"Yeah," Mia said. She went and put a hand on her son's shoulder. "They've been doing that since last year."

Mica wrapped an arm around her waist. "Hey, Mama."

"Your hair looks good," Crystal said. "You still let that Mexican do it for you?"

"Yeah. Vasantha's the best one there."

"I wanna do hair when I grow up," Mica said.

"No you don't," Mia said with a frown.

"That's wrong," Crystal said. "You should let her do hair if she wants to."

Mia looked down at her pint-sized princess. Today Mica had six ponytails with white bows. She wore a pair of denim overalls that she hated; Crystal thought they looked really cute on her, and Mia did, too.

"Baby, if you want to do hair, you have to go to college and get your masters first. You'll be the most *overqualified* hairdresser in the city."

Mica smiled. Crystal smiled, too, and Mia shot her a sneer.

"Go put your shoes on," she said. "We gotta go."

"Where we going?" TC asked.

"To the museum. I told you last Friday."

"TC got a bad memory," Mica informed. "He's got marbles in the head."

"*You've* got marbles in *your* head," TC said.

"No, *you* do!"

"Get your shoes!"

They took off, arguing all the way. Crystal turned the computer off and then looked her sister up and down. Today Mia wore a green printed plaid skirt with black leather boots that were almost knee high. She had a white long-sleeved blouse with a green scoop neck vest over it.

"You look too good to be hanging out with the kids."

"I can't help it." Mia smiled and did a model twirl. "Eric says I look good in anything I have on."

"You're just going to the museum?"

"We're going to the Omni, too. They've got this show on dolphins, and—"

"Dolphins?"

"TC likes dolphins. What's wrong with that?"

"Nothing," Crystal said, but she had a look on her face.

"Anyways, I think the feature this weekend is Ramses the Great."

"Ooh. That's a good one. I like mummies."

"You like mummies, but TC can't like dolphins?"

Crystal rolled her eyes, and Mia went to gather the kiddos.

The Overbrook Museum of Science and History was a place of fond memories for Mia. It was one of few educational venues her mother took her to when she was a child. Mia knew the layout like the back of her hand, but she let TC and Mica explore freely, losing themselves in the many winding corridors lined with priceless artifacts.

They went to the Omni first, and this was truly a theatre like no other. All of the seats were tilted upwards, towards the domed ceiling. The feature presentation played all around you, even on the walls. It was like a 3-D experience without the glasses, and Mia loved watching her babies jump every time a dolphin swam close to the cameras.

The trio left the show excited, energetic, and eager to learn. They toured the dusty trails of the Wild Wild West and made fun of a life-size Neanderthal. The T-Rex was scary, but they thought Genghis Khan was cool. They even read from a replica of Anne Frank's diary. The mummy exhibit had ended one week earlier, but no one complained.

TC and Mica were still pretty hyper three hours in, so Mia took them to the children's area, where they could do anything from electronic finger painting to making their own television show. Mia took a well-needed seat on one of the benches, and watched her little ones interact with other children their age. The kids were so animated, she'd swear Crystal gave them cookies for lunch.

When a nice-looking gentleman approached and said, "Excuse me," Mia moved her purse, thinking he wanted to sit down. He did take the seat, but he continued to look at her.

"Hi, I'm Matt."

"Hi," Mia said.

"Which one is yours?" he asked.

Mia pointed out TC, but couldn't immediately find Mica's ponytails in the crowd. "I have a little girl here too, somewhere," she told the stranger.

"That little ball of fire is mine," Matt said, pointing to a red-headed boy who looked either five or six.

"He's cute," Mia said, still looking for Mica.

"Yeah. He's all I got. Just me and him since my wife passed."

"That's sad." Mia gave the man a good look this time. He was white, around her age, with brown hair and no moustache or beard. He wore wire-rimmed glasses, and had a prominent Anglo-Saxon nose and a friendly smile. Mia didn't think he was hitting on her; some people are just friendly chatters, but Matt cleared up any doubt.

"You have a beautiful son, but that comes of no surprise because his mother is beautiful as well."

"Thank you," Mia said.

"I would love to have your children over one afternoon for a play date with my son, Jeff," the stranger went on.

"Well, maybe th—"

"*And* if they're busy that day, then we can ditch the kids and have a nice dinner with just me and you. What do you say?"

Mia couldn't hide her surprise.

"You have a pretty smile," he said.

"Thanks. Your name is *Matt*, right?"

"You remembered! Great. But you're not going to go out with me, are you?"

"Well, you seem like a really nice guy . . ."

"Is it because I'm white? Tell me that's it, because the alternative is I'm either unattractive or I have body odor."

Mia laughed. "How about *this* alternative: I have a boyfriend."

"Ahh." Matt nodded. "The boyfriend strikes again, eh? Of course. Well, do you mind if I sit here for a minute or two? If I get up now everyone will know I got shot down by the prettiest lady in the museum."

"Wow, Matt. You sure know how to make a girl feel good. You can stay as long as you want."

"Great," he said. "Any chance you cheat on your boyfriend?"

"No," Mia said with a smile.

"Can't fault a guy for asking."

"No, I guess there's no harm in asking."

Mia was as chipper as the kids when they left the museum.

But when she got home, she was a little irked her sister's car was not in the driveway. Mia was pressed for time, but managed to prepare a wholesome tuna casserole dinner in only forty minutes. She was getting dressed for her date with Eric when Crystal rushed into her room, catching Mia in only her bra and panties.

"What is it, girl? I'm in a hurry."

"Hey, you said you wanted to meet Sydney today, right?"

"Oh yeah. I forgot. Well, I'm going to have to meet him another time. I'm on my way out the door. I fixed dinner. Can you serve the kids for me?"

"Okay. But you can still meet Sydney today."

"I said I don't have time."

"He's already here," Crystal said. She stood in the doorway grinning, with her hands behind her back. She wore a pair of denim Capris that would only fit over her ass if she tugged on them while lying down. Her little pink T-shirt was just as tight. She was busting out in so many places, you didn't know whether to ogle her breasts, hips, or those shapely thighs. Mia didn't even bother chastising her because this was typical attire for Crystal whenever a boy was around.

"He's *here*? Where?"

"In the living room."

Mia sighed. "Okay. I'll go say, 'Hi,' when I get dressed."

"Okay," Crystal said. "I'll keep him company 'til then."

"I bet you will."

"You said he can stay while you're gone, right?"

"Not all night."

"I know. Just till ten, or eleven . . . twelve . . ."

"*Ten*," Mia said. "And that's *only* if I like him."

"You'll like him," Crystal promised.

"All right. Get out of here so I can get dressed."

"Your booty's getting a little bigger," Crystal noted before she walked out. Mia didn't think that was the case, but she checked in her bathroom mirror anyway.

It wasn't.

For her evening with Eric, Mia wore a dark blue dress that was both sexy and comfortable. She felt like she was walking through a field of silk. The gown was sheer chiffon, with an empire waist of smooth satin. The pleats were soft and flowing like a moonlit beach.

She stepped into her favorite Manolo sandals and clasped a diamond-studded tennis bracelet around her wrist. The bracelet matched her earrings, and her earrings matched her pendant. She spritzed Burberry on her neck and chest, and the transformation was complete.

Mia stood before her full-length mirror, put a hand on her hip, and cocked her head to the side. *Damn*, she looked good. Eric would be putty in her hands. Tyrone would say she looked like a princess, but Mia didn't know why that thought crossed her mind.

She passed through the dining room on the way out. The kids were seated and eating and arguing as usual. She broke them up and gave them each a kiss good bye. Everything was going perfectly until Mia got to the living room where Crystal and her new boyfriend waited. Before Sydney even had a chance to open his mouth, Mia decided she didn't care for the boy.

Not at all.

First off, Sydney slouched on Mia's $2,300 sofa like he was at home. He had one hand in his lap—*palm down*—and the other one—*oh, no he didn't*—on Crystal's thigh. And he had *gold* and *platinum* and *diamonds* everywhere. All of that bling would cost $50,000 or more if it was real, but from halfway across the room Mia could see most of it, if not all, was cheap and tawdry.

So right away she knew he was a liar. And he was boorish, horny, and disrespectful.

"Dang, Crystal. This yo sister? Y'all *both* look good!"
We'll add stupid to that list.

Before she spoke, Mia took a moment to remind herself that she was not Crystal's mother. Crystal was twenty-one, old enough to make her own choices about whom she chose to be with. Mia reminded herself that she too had an unhealthy obsession with thug-types when she was Crystal's age. Mia considered these things in just half a second. She walked into the room without missing a beat, and there was a nice, big smile on her face. No one could tell she felt like vomiting.

"Hi. I'm Mia." She stuck out her hand, figuring he'd at least straighten up in the seat to shake it.

"What's up, girl. I'm Sydney. They call me *Detroit*."

He shook her hand without standing up, a major faux pas as far as Mia was concerned, but she didn't feel like giving him an etiquette lesson. She didn't want to talk to him at all and really didn't even want him in the house, but Crystal sat next to him smiling ear to ear.

Sydney, a.k.a. "Detroit," was dark-skinned with low eyes and short hair. He had big diamonds in his ears, bracelet, and necklace, but, surprisingly, none in his mouth.

"I hear you're a rapper," Mia said, her smile still painted on.

"Yeah," Sydney said. "I got a demo out to some people right now, but I'm already in the studio working on my second album. Gotta stay on the grind, you know? I got my demo in the car. You wanna hear it?" He leaned forward, about to get up for the first time.

"No," Mia said. "I really don't listen to a lot of rap. You can leave it with Crystal. I'll check it out when I get back."

"Cool," Sydney said. "*Righteous.*"

Righteous? Where did this clown think he was? New York, 1965?

"Right," Mia said. "Righteous. Well, I have to go. It was nice meeting you."

"Yeah. You, too. You got a pretty house. It's *nice.*"

The way he said *nice* made Mia think that in addition to rap, Sydney might do a few cat-burglaries on the side.

"Crystal, can you walk me outside?"

Crystal did as she was told.

Mia took a few steps towards her beautifully land-scaped lawn, then turned and stared at her sister.

"Okay. What's wrong with him?" Crystal asked.

"I didn't say anything was wrong with him."

"I see that look. You don't like him. You don't like *nobody* I go with."

Mia sighed. "Tell me what *you* like about him."

Crystal shrugged. "He's cool. He can rap. He wrote a poem for me. It was *romantic*." Crystal beamed, but Mia was still waiting to hear the good part.

"He's *fine*. He got a nice car," Crystal went on.

Mia looked over at the Cutlass sitting on the street. It didn't even have a paint job. Someone had sanded it down and left a gray primer, but Lord knows how long ago that was. The bucket was sitting on chrome, twenty-inch rims, however, and Mia guessed that was what caught her sister's eye.

"He's gonna get it painted," Crystal said. "It looks good on the inside."

"He didn't stand up when he shook my hand," Mia said.

"Everybody ain't all proper like you."

"When I walked in, he had one hand on his *dick* and the other on your thigh."

"He wasn't rubbin' on me or nothin'. We was just sitting there. What's wrong with that?"

"He's got on more fake jewelry than TC had when he dressed up like a pirate last Halloween."

"How you know it's not real?"

Mia shook her head in exasperation.

Crystal's face fell. She crossed her arms and poked out her lip.

"So he can't stay for a while? You want him to leave?"

"Yes, I want him to leave," Mia said. "I want him away from my house and away from my children and as far away from you as possible. But I'm not gonna run your life. I don't like him. That's my opinion. You feel differently, so you're going to have to figure him out on your own. I bumped my head with Tyrone *and* Mica's daddy. I can tell you right now you're bumping your head with that fool, but that's something you're going to have to see for yourself. If I tell you to stop seeing him, you'll just want him more."

Crystal's smile was back. "So he can stay?"

"Yes, but tell him to keep his hands to himself. Don't let him walk around my house. I don't want him hanging around my kids. If they come in the living room with y'all, send them to their room.

"*Seriously*. I'm going to ask the kids when I get home. And if anything comes up missing, I'll hire some big, ugly niggas to beat him with metal pipes."

"*Dang*," Crystal said. "You're going a little overboard, aren't you?"

"For *his* sake, I hope I am," Mia said. "But I'm serious."

"All right. You look nice tonight, by the way. Where's Eric taking you?"

Thinking about Eric distracted Mia from the hate she was developing for Crystal's boyfriend. She smiled. "I don't know. He said it was a surprise."

Mia's magical evening began when Eric answered his door. He wore a dark-blue three-piece suit with a vest. The pants and coat were pinstriped, his collar shirt was solid black, and his tie was blue with black stripes. There was a black handkerchief neatly folded in his breast pocket, and he wore a black fedora with a small, blue feather in the band.

As awed as Mia was, Eric was equally taken aback.

"Miss Clemmons, you are the most beautiful woman I've ever seen."

"You look very handsome yourself," Mia said. "I know *that* didn't come from the Men's Wearhouse."

Eric chuckled. "No. It didn't. But you shouldn't be so critical. I shop at the Wearhouse all the time, and they have a lot of nice—"

"Shut up and kiss me," Mia said.

"I'd be much obliged." Eric removed his hat and pulled her close.

Crystal's boyfriend could learn a lot from this guy, Mia thought, but then their lips mingled and she forgot what she was thinking about.

"Where are you taking me?" she asked.

"It's a surprise."

"You're going to have to tell me sooner or later. I don't do blindfolds."

"That's okay. By the time we get there, you'll be surprised anyway."

And he was right.

When Eric got on the interstate, Mia thought he was headed towards one of the fancy restaurants downtown, but he kept going. He passed through Crowley, Forest Hill, and a few more suburbs. When he left the city limits, Mia shot him a few glances, but Eric just smiled.

They were headed towards the fair city of Arlington. Mia didn't think there was anything there that would warrant all this secrecy, and she was right. Eric stayed on the freeway and soon that city was in the rearview mirror as well.

By the time they got to Dallas, Mia had stopped trying to guess. She thought they might shoot past this metropolis also, but Eric merged to the right lane and took an exit. Ten minutes later they pulled up to a lavish building known as the Ritz Carlton, and Mia had to put a hand over her mouth to stop from squealing.

Eric looked over at her and grinned. "Surprise."

"This place is amazing," she said.

"You've been here?"

"No, but I had a girlfriend who was going to have her wedding here. We researched it on the internet. I still remember a lot of the pictures."

"Well, let's go make some *real* memories," Eric said. He got out, gave the valet his keys, and then he went to open Mia's door for her. He helped her out of the car, kissed her again, and they walked in arm-in-arm.

The hotel's foyer was as exquisite as Mia remembered from the internet, but Eric was right; everything was more beautiful in person. There were marble floors, chandeliers, and expensive vases with floral arrangements so exotic they looked otherworldly. There were gold and brass motifs and a bar made of honey-colored onyx. Everything glowed. Mia felt like Cinderella as she traipsed down the hallway.

Eric lead her into the dining area, where a handsome maitre d' seated them in a booth next to a huge window that overlooked the Dallas skyline. Everything on the menu looked superb. Mia had honey, soy-glazed wild salmon, tempura herbs, and miso-clam broth. Eric had prime-cut rib eye with cauliflower, twice-baked potatoes, and crispy asparagus.

They drank wine and enjoyed themselves for more than an hour after their waiter took their plates away. Mia thought things couldn't get better, but Eric had one more surprise for her. When they left the dining room, he took her to the elevators instead of the exit. They went up eighteen floors and stepped out into an elegant hallway.

"Don't tell me you got a room, too," Mia said.

Eric produced a key from his coat. "I wouldn't take you to a mere *room*, my dear. I have a *luxury suite*."

Nothing Mia had ever experienced could compare her for the romance of that evening. They laughed, and talked, and danced, and held each other close. But as the evening slipped into the twilight hours, Mia began to feel guilty. She had a problem. It wasn't something she had any control over, but it could potentially turn their enchanted evening into a frustrating nightmare.

They sat on the king-size bed kissing and cuddling. When their caresses turned to heavy petting, she decided to drop the bomb before things got out of hand.

"I have to tell you something."

"What's wrong?" Eric asked, his smile as big as a fat kid with a box of honey buns.

"My monthly visitor is here," Mia said. "I'm sorry. I would have told you, but I didn't know you were getting a room—I mean, a *luxury suite*. That's the problem with surprises sometimes . . ."

Eric's smile faltered only a little. "Well," he said, and paused.

Mia thought he was going to say, '*Well, there are other things you could do*,' which would have cost him a shot at her goodies for at least a month, but instead he hit her with an oldie, but goodie, a la Jermaine Stewart.

"Well, we don't have to take our clothes off to have a good time."

"Oh no?" Mia said.

"We could dance and party, all night," Eric said.

"And drink some cherry wine?" Mia mused.

"*Uh huh*," Eric sang, and then he kissed her. He kissed her so tenderly, so softly, Mia wasn't sure if their lips touched.

CHAPTER 9

MIA IN DEMAND

Mia was neck-deep in papers and files and figures. She had a pencil in her mouth, a pen on her ear, and a tension headache stomping on the back of her eyeballs. And it was only 11:00 a.m. Her phone rang, and Mia snatched it up angrily.

"What is it?" she growled.

Fortunately Miss Tenery was used to this sometimes hostile work environment.

"That *Eric* fellow is holding on line four," she reported.

Mia rubbed her forehead. "Oh, I don't have time for that."

"Shall I say you're out?"

Mia sighed. She hadn't returned any of his calls this week. "No, I'd better take it."

"Very good," Miss Tenery, said and there was a click on the line.

"Hello. Eric?"

"Mia. What's going on? Good to hear your voice. Glad you're not dead."

"It hasn't been that long."

"I haven't seen you in *three* weeks," he said. "The last time I had a chance to kiss those pretty lips was a—"

"At the Ritz," Mia said. "I remember. I'll never forget."

"So why the silent treatment?"

"Eric, you know it's not like that. I told you we had that Comsec account coming up. We have that new girl here, too. It's been crazy. By the time we show her how to do everything, we could have been done twice already. Mr. Manitou's been riding my ass—"

"I know you're busy at work," Eric said. "But you don't call when you get home, either. I haven't seen you two weekends in a row."

"Eric, I worked the last two Saturdays, and I'm so tired on Sundays that I don't feel like doing anything but being with the kids. It's not you, though. Don't take it personal. I'm off tomorrow. Maybe we could do something then."

"Okay. So three weeks later I finally get a date? I take you to the Ritz, get a luxury suite. We can't even do anything 'cause you're on your period, but that's okay. *Three* weeks later you finally have time for me? You know, we haven't been intimate since that first time. You remember—that night you broke my windshield. But all right, Mia. I'll take your crumbs. What do you want to do tomorrow?"

Mia exhaled hot fumes from her nostrils. "Eric, I'd better get off the phone before one of us says something we'll regret."

"Huh? What's wrong now? You can't call me when you get home. You can't talk to me at work. You seemed to have had a lot of time for me a month ago."

"Eric, work was different then, and it'll be different a month from now. This is the way my life is. I'm sorry I haven't called you as much lately, but I usually don't leave here until six or seven. I barely get home in time to have a late dinner with the kids, read to 'em and tuck 'em in. I have to get up at six, so by the time the kids are in bed, I'm ready to pass out, too. Yes, maybe I should have called you last night, but we're not in high school. I figured you could go a day or two without hearing from me."

"I don't think it's immature for me to want more than what you're offering."

"Okay, Eric. I get it. I will call you more often. But right now I've got a stack of papers on my desk. I've got a headache already and it's not even lunchtime. Nothing I say right now is going to sound good, so why don't you just let me call you when I get off. It's Friday. We can stay up all night, fall asleep with the phones on our ears if you want."

"Don't patronize me."

"I'm sorry."

"When are you going to let me meet your kids?" Eric asked. "We've been dating for two months."

"How about this," Mia offered. "We can *all* go out tomorrow."

"Really?"

"Sure. I usually spend Saturdays with them, but it would be nice if you were there, too. They've been asking about you. I think they're ready to meet you."

"That's awesome," Eric said. "Hey, I'm sorry about getting an attitude. I just miss you is all."

"I miss you, too, Eric. We cool? I gotta go."

"Okay, *Miss Busy*. We cool. But, can I ask you something?"

"Sure."

"That guy, TC's father, is he still coming by?"

Mia found that question odd. "Um, yes. I started letting him pick TC up last week. He's coming to get him today, as a matter of fact. Why?"

"So, you been seeing that nigga more than me?"

"You're not serious."

"No. I guess not."

"Good. Gotta go."

"All right. Bye, Mia," Eric said and hung up.

Mia hung up too and stared at the phone for a second. Eric was tripping, but she knew she had a lot to do with it. This was an ongoing problem, and not just with this boyfriend. Mia was so focused on her dream that sometimes she didn't consider how it affected others. Some men could go a few days without talking to their woman, but Eric wasn't one of those guys. Now she knew. She would try to be more attentive to his needs, but there was no ring on her finger, so the dream still came first.

Mia wondered why Eric had asked her about Tyrone. While it was true she saw TC's father more than her boyfriend lately, Mia didn't see why that was a problem. She never spoke positively about Tyrone to Eric, and she certainly never said anything that would make Eric think she liked the hoodlum. She hoped these weren't signs that Eric was going to be insecure and whiny. Mia hated those types.

Miss Tenery marched into her office a few minutes later. "You haven't made plans for lunch yet, have you?"

Mia looked up at the clock. "No, why?"

"Mr. Manitou is expecting you at Kapparis at noon."

"*Kapparis*? Who picked that? Why couldn't we just do lunch here with a couple of sandwiches?"

"I'm not sure," Miss Tenery said. "I believe Mr. Manitou *wanted* to meet there."

"That man is weird."

"Most Africans are," the secretary said, and then turned beet red. "Um, I'm sorry, I mean to say—"

Mia shook her head. "That's not cool. You really need to work on that negativity."

Miss Tenery was very embarrassed. "I'm sorry . . ."

"I guess I'd better get ready to go," Mia said. "Do you have the reports?"

"Yes ma'am," Miss Tenery said, happy to leave the room.

Mr. Manitou was a senior analyst for Prospect Investments. Mia didn't know which African country he was from, but she knew his family was wealthy. He was very dark-skinned with short, salt-and-pepper-colored hair, although he was only forty. Mr. Manitou was a stickler for details. He carried himself with an air of superiority Mia wished more black men possessed, but kids in America aren't taught about African kings and queens. Mr. Manitou had firsthand experience.

He stood and pulled Mia's chair out for her as she approached his table. She couldn't get used to this sort of pampering, no matter how many times it happened.

"Thank you, sir. You're very polite."

"It is my pleasure," Mr. Manitou said. He spoke with a rich accent Mia found charming.

Mr. Manitou wore a beige suit with a white collar shirt and a trendy tie. He was dark-skinned and exceptionally handsome. He reminded her of R&B singer Tyrese. He had large, rough hands, but his nails were manicured. Mr. Manitou was a nice enough guy, but too much of a hard-ass for Mia's tastes. She was a hard worker herself, but didn't think this guy ever stopped to smell the roses.

Eager to start and be done with their meeting, Mia popped her briefcase open, pushed her menu to the side, and dropped three large file folders on the table.

"I think you're going to like these projections," she said. "The Comsec account is going to make us look real good in the next quarter."

Mr. Manitou smiled. "Too much work. You look stressed. Let us eat first."

"Well, we have a lot to do," Mia said. "I thought we could get through the quarterly stuff before lunch gets here. We can look at the accrual calculations while we eat, and—"

"No, put it away," Mr. Manitou said. "You should calm your nerves. We'll talk about work after we eat. Okay?"

That was actually *not* okay. Doing it his way would stretch this one-hour lunch into two, but technically Mr. Manitou was her superior, so Mia returned the folders to her briefcase and picked up her menu.

"Okay. What's good? Have you been here before?" she asked.

The analyst studied his own menu. "What would you like for an appetizer?" he asked.

Mia couldn't hide her frustration. "Mr. Manitou, I don't believe we'll have time to go over all of this if we get an appetizer. It's gonna be hard enough with just lunch."

Mr. Manitou shook his head and smiled. "Mia, you must *relax*. Forget about work for now. Pretend your briefcase isn't even there. The food will not taste the same on a stressed palate."

"I've never heard that before."

"It is true."

"So, you're not concerned that we may not have time to go over these projections?"

"If we do not finish, I will come by your office Monday or sometime next week. 'Tis no rush."

"Okay," Mia said. She was a little perplexed, but this was Mr. Manitou's meeting. He could conduct it in whatever manner he wished, as far as she was concerned.

"I've only been here once," she told him. "I don't know what I would order for an appetizer. I'm not even sure I can eat an appetizer *and* a lunch, but if you get one I'll take a few bites."

Mr. Manitou smiled. "Great. I was thinking about the funghi ripieni."

"You have a nice accent."

"I speak five languages."

"I'm impressed," Mia said. "I'll be more impressed when you tell me what *funghi ripieni* means."

"You said it very nicely yourself."

"I was just mimicking you."

"That's great. Mimicking is the most basic form of learning."

He sounded like a wise griot. Mia loved listening to him talk.

"Funghi ripieni is mushrooms stuffed with crabmeat and fresh herbs," he said.

"That sounds good. I think I will have a few of those."

"And your main course?"

"Mmm. I don't know. You seem to know what you're doing. What would you suggest?"

Mr. Manitou looked over the menu. "Would you like a pasta or chicken? Or maybe steak, or perhaps fish?"

"Something with chicken," Mia said and closed her menu.

"Do you like the breast?" he asked.

"Sure."

Mr. Manitou summoned their waiter.

"You guys ready to order?"

"Yes. We are going to start with the funghi ripieni. The lady is having pollo portobello, and I will have the bistecca alla griglia this afternoon." He looked over at Mia. "Would you like a red wine?"

She was startled. "Um, I have to go back to work. Don't *you?*"

Mr. Manitou smiled. "Yes. Of course you're right. I'll have tea."

"Tea's fine with me, too," Mia said. She gave her co-worker a queer look, and when the waiter walked away she asked, "You want to get *drunk* at our business lunch?"

He laughed. "Mia, you are truly an American woman. All work. But that is good. That is what attracts me to you."

For the first time Mia started to get an inkling of what was going on.

"I'm afraid I haven't been entirely honest with you," he said. "Mia, you are a very beautiful woman. I've watched your progress in the company, and I must say I am very proud of the work you have done. I brought you here today to tell you I've become enamored with you. I would like to see you more often, outside of work."

Mia listened, growing more shocked with every word. She knew she was attractive, but never had so many potential suitors accosted her in such a short period of time. And if she were the gold-digging type, this one would be considered the *jackpot.* Mr. Manitou made six figures every year—not counting the investments his *old* money brought in. Eric's sixty-thousand paled in comparison.

"Well," she said finally. "Don't think I'm not flattered. Actually, I'm *floored.* I never thought you had these feelings for me. But to be honest, I have a boyfriend."

"I see," the analyst said. "Are you engaged to be married?"

"No," Mia said. "We've only been dating for two months."

"Well, surely your ties to him are not so rigid . . ."

"Not really, but I am faithful to him." She smiled, hoping to be as inoffensive as possible.

"Well," he said, "I'm glad I asked you this away from the office. I would hate to be sued for sexual harassment."

Mia giggled. "I'm not that type of girl," she said. "We're both grown. If you tell me you like me—here or at the office—I'm not going to use it against you. You're an important man to our company. I look up to you. In truth, I'm honored. You could have any woman you want, and you chose me. That makes me feel special."

"You are wrong," he said with a smile. "If I cannot have *you*, then I cannot have *any* woman I choose."

"Touché."

The waiter brought their appetizer and disappeared again.

"I suppose I'll have to eat all three courses by myself," Mr. Manitou said.

"Are you crazy? This has been the nicest part of my day," Mia said. "And these things look good. I'm not going anywhere."

Her date smiled, and they dove into the stuffed mushrooms.

They were delicious, as was the rest of their meal.

Mia got off a little after six. She was five minutes from home when Tyrone called her cell phone.

"Hello?"

"Hey, this Tyrone."

"What's wrong?"

"Why you have to assume something's *wrong*?"

"Okay. What's going on?"

"It's somethin' wrong," he said.

"What's wrong?"

"My car broke down."

"TC's still with you?"

"Yeah. He cool."

"Where are you?"

"I'm right over here by yo house. I was finna drop him off when the muffler fell off. We over here off McCart and Woodway."

"Oh. You are close."

"Yeah. It's only like a half mile. We could walk to yo house from here."

Mia didn't know if he was serious, but *her* baby wasn't walking half a mile. "No, I'll come get you. Did you call Crystal?"

"Naw. I called you first. You home already?"

"I'm on my way. I just exited McCart. I'll be there in about three minutes."

"Cool," Tyrone said. "Hey, TC wanna hollar at you."

"Put him on." She waited only a few seconds.

"Hi, Mama!"

"Hey, lil' man. What's going on?"

"Daddy's car broke down."

"I heard. You doing okay?"

"Yeah. We had fun."

"Really? What'd y'all do?"

"He took me to see Grandma. Did you know I had a grandma?"

"Mmm, yeah. I did. Was she nice?"

"Yeah. She gave me *five dollars!*"

"Wow. That *was* nice. You gonna put it in your piggy bank?"

"Nope. I already spent it. Daddy says kids my age shouldn't save money. He said—"

There was a momentary rustling.

"Hu—hey! Mia?"

"Tyrone?"

"Hey, girl. Don't listen to him. He don't know what he talking 'bout."

"I was just thinking that sounds like something you'd say."

"All right. He was in the store talking bout, 'Mama say I have to save my money.' I made him spend it, though. You mad, huh?"

"No, Tyrone. I'm not mad. I see your car."

"Cool," he said, but she had already disconnected.

Tyrone was right about the damage. Mia pulled up behind his mother's Bonneville, and she could see the muffler hanging down to the street. She honked her horn, and TC bounced out as happy as ever. Tyrone got out, too, and he was as handsome as ever. He wore blue Dickey pants and a blue T-shirt; nothing fancy, but it didn't take much to make him look good. He was clean-cut, neat, and breathtakingly muscular.

Eric was fine, too, but he was a bigger guy. He had more of a sturdy, lumberjack type of body. Tyrone was leaner and more cut. Mia didn't have to see him topless to know he had more definition in his chest than Eric, and Tyrone probably had a six-pack too.

He opened the back door and helped TC in, then took the front seat next to Mia. He shook his head. "I'm sorry about that. I knew that muffler was gon' fall out sooner or later. Shoulda got it fixed before I put my lil' soldier in there."

Mia nodded. She was thinking the exact same thing.

"Dang, Mia. You look good."

"Thanks," she said without looking at him.

"I mean, I know you prolly dress like this every day, but I don't never see no women dressed like you."

Today Mia wore a blue pantsuit with a baby blue blouse. Tyrone was the first person to compliment her outfit that day, but she didn't show how good it made her feel.

"Mama!" TC called from the back, "Daddy wants to take me to *Six Flags* Sunday!"

"Really," Mia said and turned onto her street.

"You're dropping him off first?" Tyrone asked.

"Yeah. We're right here," Mia said. "Plus, your neighborhood gets a little rowdy this late."

"No, it doesn't."

"What, did it get better over the last ten years?"

Tyrone chuckled. "Naw. You right. It got a little worse."

Mia pulled to a stop in front of her house and sent TC on his way. When Crystal opened the door for him, Mia rolled down her window.

"Tyrone's car broke down! I'm going to take him home!"

Crystal smiled an evil little smile and waved but didn't say anything. Mia looked over at her passenger, and Tyrone had the same wicked smile.

"What?" she said.

"I didn't say nothin'."

"Yeah, but you got that look on your face. I don't know what you're thinking, but forget it." She put the car into gear and headed towards the south side of town.

"You make that face all you want," Tyrone said. "But I know it ain't you."

"What are you talking about?"

"You, lookin' all mean. You ain't gotta wear that face for me. I *know* you. Don't forget."

"Yeah. You know me. I know you, too, that's why I got this face on."

"What that mean?"

"It means if I smile at you, you'll think I'm giving in, and the next thing I know you'll be grabbing my ass again."

Tyrone laughed. "I'm not gon' grab yo ass just 'cause you smile at me."

"Why'd you do it the last time?"

"I told you. I was fresh out. I ain't seen no female I wanted more than you, and you was looking good. That was just somethin I *had* to do. I was thinkin' about touching you for six years."

"So you cool now?" Mia was skeptical.

"I still want you. You know that. But I ain't doin' that bad now. I'm not gon' touch you if you don't want me to."

"You musta got you some then," Mia said, but she really didn't want to hear his response.

Tyrone smiled. "No. I haven't. I know most niggas come out the pen wanna jump on whatever they can, but I want *you*, Mia. I can wait."

"You can wait? Tyrone, that's silly. What are you waiting for?"

"I told you, I give that boyfriend you got a month. It's been three weeks. Y'all broke up yet?"

"Nope."

"Well, I still got another week."

"You got high hopes."

"Mia, can you honestly say you don't want to be with me at all?"

"I have a boyfriend."

"You didn't say you don't want me."

"Okay. I don't want you."

"You lying now."

"How you figure?"

"I know how much you loved me. You can't make that go away just 'cause you want it to."

"Oh, you raise a baby by *yourself* for nine years and see if your feelings about things don't change."

"I said I was sorry about that. I'ma make it up to you."

Mia frowned.

"Say, let me ask you something," Tyrone said. "Why you call my son TC?"

The question caught her off guard. "Why do you ask? What's wrong with TC?"

"Nothing," he said. "Except his name is *Tyrone*. Like mine. Why you don't call him Tyrone?"

"You know why."

"How am I supposed to know?"

Mia sighed. "You were in jail. I had this brand new baby, but he had your name. I wasn't finna keep calling out your name. I didn't want to think about you, so I called him TC."

"That's what I figured."

"You got a problem with it?"

"No, ma'am. Don't get mad."

"I'm not mad."

"So, what about Six Flags?" he asked. "You gon' let me take him?"

"Tyrone, that's a big place. You're not going to want to follow him around all day. And you won't be able to ride anything 'cause he's too small to get on all the cool stuff. He's too small to sit on some bench waiting on you, too."

"I wouldn't sit my son on no bench."

"Maybe not, but still . . ."

"Why don't you come with me, then? You and Mica."

"I don't know, Tyrone."

"C'mon, girl. He been asking me since I got out. He wanna go bad."

"Why Sunday? That's not enough notice."

"Just say yes. I'll pay for it. Yo ticket, too."

"You're gonna buy *four* tickets to Six Flags, *plus* the food *and* games?"

Tyrone nodded. "I know you're just asking, 'cause you think I'ma say I can't afford it. But, yeah. I'll pay for all that stuff."

"*This* Sunday?"

"Yeah. We can go tomorrow if you want."

"No. Sunday's better," Mia said, thinking of Eric.

"So we gon' go."

She considered it for a minute and couldn't think of a reason not to. "I guess so."

"Damn, can you ever smile?"

"You think you've given me something to smile about?"

"I love you," Tyrone said.

Mia didn't smile. "No, you don't."

"Don't tell me what I feel. I *know* I love you."

She looked away.

"I know I love you, 'cause I been out the pen for a month," Tyrone said. "And all them hoodrat bitches keep tellin' me how good I look. They want me bad, but I don't wanna hit none of them. I only want you. And I'm horny as hell. Tell me that ain't love."

She did smile then.

"You got such a pretty smile. I want you to smile at me more."

"We'll see," she said.

They drove in silence for a while and soon arrived at his mother's house. There were hoodlums about, but not the level of degradation Mia expected. But then again, it was only seven o'clock.

"What are you going to do about your car?" she asked.

"Me and my uncle gonna get it tonight, hook some chains on it and bring it over here. It just needs a new muffler. I'll have that bad boy fixed by tomorrow afternoon."

"Good," Mia said.

"I'm having a lot of fun with my boy," Tyrone said. "Thanks for lettin' me kick it with him by myself."

"It's all right."

"Are we gonna go early Sunday, or do you want to wait 'til later on when it starts to cool down?"

"I'll let you know tomorrow."

"All right, well, thanks for the ride," Tyrone said. When he leaned in to kiss her good night, Mia leaned in, too; it just felt right, but she caught herself the moment their lips touched. She pulled back quickly as if she'd been shocked. Tyrone's lips were still puckered. They were red and full and soft. He reminded her of LL Cool J.

He opened his eyes. "What's wrong?"

"Tyrone, I got a boyfriend."

"You was finna kiss me."

"That was an accident. I don't know what just happened."

"That's fate, girl," he said as he got out of the car. "That ain't nothin but fate."

CHAPTER 10

WHEN IT RAINS

Mia drove away with her pulse racing. That was crazy. She couldn't even begin to understand what just happened. Unfortunately, an even worse tragedy occurred to distract her from the Tyrone quagmire. Her cell phone rang, and it was Crystal.

"What's up?"

"You on yo way home?" Crystal asked.

"Yeah," Mia said. "Why?"

"Girl, don't trip. Everybody's fine."

"What's wrong?" Mia asked, tendrils of fear already tickling the back of her mind.

"Somebody just threw a brick through the living room window," Crystal said, but that didn't make sense.

"What?"

"Somebody just threw a brick through the window in the living room."

Hearing it twice didn't help. "What are you talking about? Are you serious?"

"Yes, Mia. There's a brick on the floor. Glass is everywhere. The kids were in Mica's room, but if they were in here, somebody could have got hurt."

Hearing about the kids made a hard, cold lump form in the pit of Mia's stomach. Her head swam and there didn't seem to be enough air in the car anymore.

"Are they all right? Where's TC? Nobody got cut, did they?"

"No," Crystal said. "No one was in there when it happened. We just heard a loud crash. When we came in here, we saw this stuff everywhere. The curtain fell down—"

"Who did it?" Mia shrieked.

"I don't know. Nobody's out there . . ."

Mia heard someone crying in the background. The sound squeezed her heart like a cold vice. "Who is that?"

"That's Mica. Be quiet, girl, it's okay."

"What's wrong? Is she cut? You don't have her in the glass, do you?"

"Mia, calm down. Nobody's hurt. She's just scared. The sound of the glass breaking scared her, and when she saw the mess, she started crying. She's all right, though."

"Where's TC?"

"He's right here. He's fine, too."

"Who threw a brick through my window, Crystal?"

"*I don't know.* Why you asking me like that?"

"If that damned nigga you brought over there—"

"Sydney wouldn't throw a brick in our window. Sydney love me. Why you blaming me anyway? It could just be something random."

"No, I don't think so," Mia said. "Did you call the police?"

"For what?"

"You're supposed to call the police if someone attacks your house, Crystal! I leave you with my kids and you don' know what to do? We might not be the only ones. Have you been outside? Any other houses damaged on our street?"

"No. I didn't go out there. It *just* happened. I would have to walk through that glass, and Mica was crying. I— I'll check now if—"

"No. Stay in there with the kids. I'll be there in ten minutes."

"You okay, girl? You not gon' wreck or nothing, are you? We're all right. Don't worry about us. You don't need to speed."

Mia took a deep breath and let it out. "Okay. I—I just. You don't have any idea who it could have been?"

"No," Crystal said. "But it wasn't nobody *I* know. I know that much."

"Is there a note on it?"

"What you talkin' bout?"

"A note. On the brick. Did they put anything on the brick?"

"It's just a brick, Mia. Why would they put a note on it?"

"Never mind. Tell the kids I'll be there right away."

"Okay. You don't know who did it either?"

"I have an idea," Mia said, and disconnected.

She banged her fist hard on the steering wheel.

"Shit!"

This was ludicrous. She lived in a good neighborhood, didn't start trouble with people. She didn't go to the club, didn't have catty girlfriends, and wasn't sleeping with anyone's man—*or was she?* There were over two hundred contacts in her cell phone, but only one name came to mind. Mia dialed the number. After only two rings, he answered.

"Hello?"

"Eric, this is Mia."

"Hey, Mia. Just got off?"

"Yeah. Um, how's it going? Anything . . . weird happen today?"

"What do you mean?"

"Look," she sighed, "I'm not trying to accuse you of anything. I'm just really stressed out and don't know where else to look." She took another breath and let it out slowly.

"What's wrong?" Eric asked in the interim.

"Someone just threw a brick through my window, at home," Mia said. "Again, I'm *not* accusing you. I know you didn't do it, but maybe that girl, Shareefa. Do you think she might do something like this?"

There was a long pause.

"Hello? You still there?"

When he finally spoke, Eric sounded deflated. "Mia. I'm sorry."

Her heart did not beat for a few seconds. "Sorry for what, Eric?"

"Someone broke a window at my house, too," he said. "I got home at five and there was this big hole in my window. There's a brick in here, too. I kinda thought it was Shareefa, 'cause I had an argument with her yesterday, but I didn't think—Mia, if she had anything to do with your window getting broke, I don't know what I'd do."

Mia shook her head. Her eyes were blurred. She blinked hard and realized she was crying. "What do you mean '*if*?'" she spat. "If your window got broken too, then you *know* it was her. This is," her head started to swim again, "this doesn't make sense. Why, how, how would—"

"Mia, calm down. If it was her, we can put her in jail. She can't do this."

"What do you mean she *can't?* She *did*, Eric. My kids were at home! How the hell does she, what—Eric, does she know where I live?"

He sighed. "Mia, I didn't think she did, but—"

"What do you mean, '*but?*' Either she does or she doesn't! What the hell kind of shit am I involved in?"

"Mia, calm down."

"*Don't tell me to calm down!* Did you not hear me? My kids were at home. *They could have been hurt!*"

"She wasn't trying to hurt anyone."

"Stop defending her! How does she know where I live, Eric?"

There was another long pause.

"*Eric?*"

"She followed Candy around for a while," he said softly.

"Candy? Who the hell is Candy?"

"That's the girlfriend I had. Before you. She broke up with me because of Shareefa. Shareefa, she, she did something like this to her."

Mia thought she might have to pull over. "What? What are you—are you saying she's done this before?"

"Yes," Eric said. "But this doesn't have to come between us, Mia. We can—"

"Why is she not in jail?"

"It's not that easy."

"The hell it ain't! Someone throws a brick through your window, and they're supposed to go to jail."

"I tried," Eric said. "Trust me, I tried. But there was nothing I could do. Everything she did to Candy, we never had a witness. It was all circumstantial. We knew it was her, but that wasn't enough to get her locked up. She didn't do that stuff without thinking about it first. She was smart."

Everything she did to Candy?

"*Smart?* So, what are you saying, Eric? Crystal didn't see her at my house either. So she gets away again?"

"Mia, we have to stick together. We can go to the police—"

"Did you see her break *your* window today?"

"No. I told you I didn't. But—"

"Eric, then what you're saying is she gets away with it again."

"I didn't say that, Mia!" Eric screamed, finally a little rattled himself. "She's messed up in the head! What am I supposed to do?"

"This is ridiculous."

"Yes! It is. But we can stick together. She doesn't have to win."

"She doesn't, Eric? She knows where I live. She attacked me at my home and could have hurt my children. And there's nothing we can do about it. Why doesn't she win, Eric? Tell me why she doesn't win?"

"Because she wants us to break up, Mia. She wants to ruin my life. If we break up, *then* she wins, but it doesn't have to be like that."

"So, what am I supposed to wait for?" Mia asked. "Should I keep letting her attack me until I have enough *proof* to stop her? I'm not fighting some crazy lady, Eric. I don't need this."

"Don't say that, Mia."

"I gotta go, I'm at home."

"Mia, don't say that. Tell me you're not leaving me."

"Eric—"

"*Please, Mia.* Just, *please* tell me you're not leaving me. Don't let her do this again. It's not fair."

"Eric, I have to call the police. I have to look at my house. My daughter's standing in the doorway crying. Goodbye."

"Mia, pl—" He started to say something else, but the line went dead.

The next couple of hours were somewhat of a blur for Mia. From outside she assessed the damage to her home: There was a huge hole in her main front window, and her

Manchester curtains hung at a 45-degree angle. Once inside, her first mission was to calm the kids, but they were actually more excited than frightened by the time she showed up.

Crystal had called the police when they got off the phone earlier, and two officers arrived five minutes after Mia walked in. In Tyrone's neighborhood, it might have taken days for a unit to respond to a mere vandalism call, but there were no homes under $200,000 on Mia's street. Plus Crystal told them someone was attacking a house full of children.

And it turned out Eric was right. The police took all of Mia's information. They even jotted notes about her possible suspect. But frankly there was nothing they could do just because she was *pretty sure* Shareefa was involved. Mia might be able to win a civil suit with this kind of circumstantial evidence, but it wasn't even enough for them to bring Eric's ex-girlfriend in for questioning.

After the police left, Crystal got the kids started on dinner, and then she and Mia cleaned up the mess. Mia told her about the conversation she had with Eric, and Crystal asked if she would stay with him. Mia said she didn't know. Crystal thought it would be silly to risk her home, property, and possibly her *life* just so she could go out with some stupid boy.

But Mia didn't want to talk about it. She wanted to find a way to cover the hole in her window. They found a piece of cardboard big enough to tape over the jagged orifice until she could call a glass repair shop tomorrow.

They vacuumed the whole room twice but still kept finding stray shards here and there.

Mia used a Phillips screwdriver, the only tool she had any skill with, to fix the curtain rod, and she remounted her drapes. When they were done, there was no evidence of the vandalism from inside. That went a long way in making everyone feel better, but Mia wouldn't feel completely comfortable until she was sure it wouldn't happen again.

Before she put the kids to bed, Mia cuddled with them on the sofa and explained how bad things sometimes happen to good people. TC somehow steered the conversation to religion, and Mia then had to explain why God *allowed* bad things to happen to good people, which she was no good at.

Afterwards, Mica thought they should probably say their prayers that night, and Mia thought that was a wonderful idea. The three of them got on their knees in the living room and thanked God for the good people, prayed for the bad ones, and were grateful no one was injured when the brick came in. Mia promised there would be no more bricks in their living room, and they marched off to their bedrooms in good spirits.

When they were gone, Mia sat alone on her sofa and considered things; mainly how she never wanted to have these kinds of talks with the kids and what she could do to avoid them in the future. Crystal came in and sat next to her.

"Can I plug the phone back up?" she asked.

Mia had her disconnect the line when the police where there because Eric would not stop calling. "Yeah. What time is it?"

"It's ten-thirty."

"He's still up," Mia said. "He's gonna call as soon as you plug it in. I've got nineteen missed calls on my cell already."

"Dang," Crystal said. "So, you're gonna call him?"

"I guess. Why do you care?"

"'Cause I'm finna call Sydney. I don't want Eric to keep calling while I'm on the phone."

"All right," Mia said. "I'll call him."

"Decided what you're going to tell him?"

"Not yet."

"You better do the right thing. You don't want that bitch showing up at your job."

Jeez. That was sickeningly true. "Leave me alone," Mia said.

"Don't get an attitude with me, 'cause yo man—"

"Crystal, leave me alone," Mia said again, and her little sister left without further comment.

Mia fished her cell phone from her pocket, but didn't dial the number for another forty minutes.

"Mia?"

"It's me, Eric."

"My God. I was worried about you. No one's answering your phone."

"I disconnected it."

"Why?"

"Because you wouldn't stop calling."

"I wasn't calling to harass you. I just wanted to know you were all right."

"I know, Eric. But I was busy. I couldn't talk, and you didn't seem to understand that."

"I'm sorry. I guess I can be kind of persistent."

"Kind of," Mia agreed.

"So, is everything all right?"

"Yeah. I fixed my curtain. I put a piece of cardboard over the hole. I was mainly upset because my kids were here. She could have hurt somebody."

"I know," Eric said. "I feel really bad about that, Mia. You don't know how bad I feel. I've been trying to get in touch with her, but she's not answering her phone. Did you call the police?"

"They couldn't do anything, just like you said. There were no witnesses. They said they wouldn't arrest her just because we *think* she did it."

"Yeah. I've been through that. Mia, I don't know how I'm going to make this up to you, but you've got to let me."

Mia didn't respond.

"Mia, you don't blame *me* for this, do you?"

"No, Eric. It's not your fault. You don't have any control over what that woman does. You got your restraining order, you've called the police on her, that's about all you can do. She's crazy, bu—"

"She's sick."

"Yeah, but it's not your fault. It just happens. There are a lot of crazy people out there. Sooner or later, everyone's going to meet one."

"You're taking this pretty well," he noticed. "You were freaking out when I talked to you earlier."

"That was just heat-of-the-moment stress," Mia said. "I usually handle things better than that. I'm sorry I cursed at you."

"Mia, you don't have to apologize for anything. Everything you did and said was within reason. Hey, I fixed my window today. I was wondering if you'll let me come and fix yours."

"You fixed your window already?"

"Yeah. I started on it after you hung up on me."

"*You*, what do you mean? You fixed it yourself?"

"Yeah. I used to work for this remodeling company. I can lay tiles, tape, and bed sheetrock, all kinds of stuff. I would like to come and fix your window, if you'll let me. I have extra supplies. It won't take that long, no more than an hour. I really want to do that for you."

"I don't know, Eric."

"Mia, please. I'm begging you: Please let me fix your window."

"Okay," she said. Mia really didn't need his handyman services, but decided she should at least break up with him in person. Eric was a good guy. He deserved that.

He showed up at 10:00 a.m. sharp. Mia had Crystal take the kids away before he arrived. She didn't think things would get ugly, but breakups always had the potential for ugliness.

Mia answered the door wearing jeans and a white golf shirt. She had on her most comfortable bunny slippers, and her eyes were pink and puffy from crying. She wore a white bandana on her head; it was tied from the back, so only the top of her hair was exposed. Eric still thought she looked amazing. He embraced her, and she endured it rather than feel comforted by his touch. Eric sensed something was wrong, but believed her when Mia said she didn't get enough sleep last night.

She sat on the sofa and watched him work. Eric wore jeans and a tee shirt, and he was fine. He had a nice, round butt, a big, strong back, and powerful arms. Mia knew that a part of her still wanted to be wrapped up in those arms, but there were other things to consider, things more important than her personal happiness.

Eric made small talk as he worked, but by the time he had the new glass set and weather-sealed, he was starting to look worried. He took his tools to the car then came back to talk to Mia. She stood in her doorway, waiting with her arms crossed.

"Well," he said, wiping his hands on his pants, "I'm done."

"It looks good," Mia said.

Eric shrugged. "I want to apologize again for what she did."

"You don't have to keep apologizing for her."

"I know, but I feel like I should. This is all my fault, in a way."

That's the kicker, Mia thought. *In a way, it is your fault.* "Don't blame yourself," she said.

"I, uh, I notice your kids aren't here," he said.

Mia nodded. "They went downtown with Crystal."

"Today was the day I was supposed to finally meet them," Eric went on. "It seems odd that they're not here. It doesn't feel like we're all still going out today . . ."

Mia nodded. "That's right, Eric. We're not going to go out today."

He hoped against hope. "Did something come up, or do you . . ."

"I can't see you anymore," Mia said bluntly. Her nose filled with moisture.

Eric's eyes quickly welled and a lone tear snaked down his cheek. "Mia, don't do this." He grabbed her hand, and she didn't immediately pull it away.

She shook her head. "I don't have a choice, Eric. You're a good guy—a *wonderful* guy—but I can't risk this."

"Mia, don't you see? If you leave me, she wins." He was fully crying now. Mia sniffled and realized she was, too.

"Eric," she said, "you're right. If we break up, she wins. But I can't stay with you just so she doesn't win. I've got more to think about than that. You said she follows you and your girlfriends around. That's crazy."

"I know, Mia. But it's not me."

"I know, but can't you see why it doesn't matter? If she's slick enough to stay above the law, then what am I supposed to do? Look over my shoulder every day? Worry about my kids going to school? Worry about her burning down my house? Eric, I like you. I like you a lot, but we've only been dating three months. It took my whole life to get to this point."

"So I'm not worth it?" There was a hitch in his throat.

"Don't say that."

"I wanna know the truth. All this *stuff* comes before me?"

"My kids come before you, Eric. Yes. They do."

"She's not gonna hurt your kids."

"How do I know that? How do *you* know that?"

"Mia, she just wants to scare you."

Mia took her hand back. "Well, she did. I've got enough stress at work. I'm not going to take on more problems purposely. And I'm not going to put my family in harm's way over any man."

"You're talking like you don't even care about me."

"I do, Eric, but what are my options? Your girlfriend Candy, she came to the same conclusion, didn't she?"

"Candy didn't love me."

"So what are you saying? I would take this risk if I cared enough about you? Is that the way you see it? I can't do it, Eric. I can't think of one reason why I should go through this."

"Because I love you," he said, and it was the first time he ever told her that.

"That's not enough," Mia said and backed into her house.

"I thought you were stronger than that," Eric said, his lips quivering, tears streaming down his face.

"Oh, I am strong," Mia said. "You're everything I want in a man, but I'm letting you go."

"It's not fair," he moaned, and Mia thought those were her sentiments exactly.

Mia closed the door, then went to her room and cried into her fluffiest pillow.

CHAPTER 11
TYRONE'S BIG ADVENTURE

Mia didn't make it to her Saturday morning appointment at the salon. After Eric left, she languished for what felt like hours. At one point, she heard a noise in the hallway. When she looked up from her pillow, Mica was standing in the doorway on the verge of tears herself. Nothing had happened to her, but the sight of her mother crying always affected the cutie.

Mia got up and held the little girl close to her heart. The embrace was comforting, therapeutic. The longer Mia held on, the better she felt, and soon the pain receded like ocean tides. Mia put an end to her pity party and enjoyed a nice day at home with the kids. They played Scrabble, had a checkers tournament, and decorated gingerbread cookies. Mia pushed them on the swings in the back yard, and even climbed halfway up her pecan tree with them.

Tyrone called towards the end of the day to confirm they were still going to Six Flags tomorrow. Although her heart told her to cancel, Mia didn't renege. It wasn't expected to be very warm, so they decided to go midday. Tyrone would come to her house at three, and Mia would drive them all in her Lexus.

When she got up Sunday morning, the first thing Mia did was call Claire's. Unlike most of the city's salons, Ernestine kept her shop open seven days a week. Mia didn't think she'd be able to get an appointment, but things were pretty slow. They penciled her in for noon. Mia walked through the doors at 11:52 a.m.

Claire's was always a great place, but there were drawbacks to going on Sunday. First of all, this was the Lord's Day, so all of the die-hard Christians weren't in attendance. Ernestine wasn't there and neither was Vasantha. Mama Ernestine's words of wisdom would be sorely missed, and Vasantha was the best hairdresser in the building in Mia's opinion. Nancy didn't work on Sundays either, so Mia had to let her nails go one more week.

Gayle was on the clock, however, and Mia was happy to sit in her chair. Gayle was deep, insightful, and soothing—just what the doctor ordered. She washed Mia's hair, but it was more than that. Her large hands not only lathered in shampoo, but they massaged the stress away as well.

"Has he called back?" Gayle asked.

"Yeah. Just once," Mia said. "I had a message on my phone this morning."

"What'd he say?"

"The same thing: I'm letting Shareefa win by breaking up with him. He still sounds pretty bad."

"Are you gonna call him back?"

"No," Mia said. "Why? Do you think I should?"

"I would," Gayle said. "But I don't have kids. Plus I'm not built like you. My options are a little limited."

"Don't say that. You know you look good."

Gayle was naturally beautiful. She rarely wore makeup, and didn't really need it on the occasions she did. She *was* overweight, but nowhere near sloppy. She dressed nice and had a big butt and big breasts. And any man who really got to know Gayle would probably never leave her.

"I know I'm *pretty*," Gayle said, "but most of the guys I hook up with are assholes. They think just because I'm a big girl, I've got low self-esteem, too. Once they see I don't take too much shit, they move around, try to find somebody easier to handle. Some girls will put up with anything just so they can say they got a man."

"There are guys out there who will treat you right," Mia said.

"Yeah," Gayle said. "I run into one, maybe two a year. But it's hard to keep 'em. There are too many skinny girls like you running around this city. If he really is a good man, he'll probably get scooped up by one of them."

"Are you seeing someone now?"

"I'm boning a guy right now," Gayle said. "But it's only *sex*. He ain't about shit. Don't wanna do nothing. That's another thing; most guys around here are sorry. That's why I say I'd prolly work it out with somebody like Eric. He sounds like a keeper."

"I know," Mia said. "It's hard. What would you do about his ex?"

"I'd kick that bitch's ass," Gayle said matter-of-factly. "Let me find out some bitch is following me around.

Breaking *my* windows? Oh, hell naw. I'd make Eric show me where she stay and beat that ho up in her own front yard. Bet she won't throw no more bricks after that."

"I haven't had a fight since the second grade," Mia admitted.

"I'm not saying *you* should fight her. I'm saying that's probably what *I* would do. You, naw, Mia, that's not you. And like I said, if I had kids at home, I'd let it go, like you did. Don't start trouble with somebody who knows where your kids sleep. Especially if you already know they crazy."

Mia already felt that way, but it was good to hear it again. "I'ma miss him, though," she said.

"Sounds like he was romantic."

"When he took me to the Ritz, I felt like I was a princess at the ball," Mia said. "He did everything for me. I don't think I've ever been pampered like that. He didn't even trip when I told him we couldn't have sex."

"You just slept with him that one time, huh?" Gayle asked.

"Yeah."

"That's been damned near a month ago, ain't it?"

"It's getting close," Mia admitted.

"And you're going out with Tyrone today?"

"I'm not *going out* with Tyrone," Mia said. "He's taking my son to Six Flags and I'm going *with them*. Mica, too. This is not a date."

"Whatever. You *are* gonna be with him, though. Walking around the park all day. Holding hands and stuff. Ain't you getting a little hot for him yet?"

"I'm not *hot* for him. It might be nice to get in bed with him, but there's too many strings attached to that. It's not even worth it. And we're not *holding hands!* He doesn't have anything I want, Gayle. It's gonna be hard enough when he finds out his prophecy has been fulfilled."

"What prophecy?"

"He kept telling me Eric and I were going to break up. He said we would break up within a month."

"Tyrone said that?"

Mia rolled her eyes. "Yeah."

"When?"

"About three weeks ago."

Gayle cocked her eyebrow.

"Don't even start. It doesn't mean anything."

But maybe it did. "Girl, that could be *fate.*"

"Please don't say that. I don't believe any higher power wants me to be with *Tyrone.*"

"You don't think *God* wants a father to raise his own son?"

Mia sneered. "Have you been talking to Tyrone or something? You sound just like him."

"I'm just saying," Gayle went on, "that *is* his son. I don't think it'll hurt nothing if you give him a shot."

"Are you serious?"

"He ain't *that* bad, is he?"

"He chose the streets over me and his baby," Mia reminded. "If he had stayed with me, who knows where we would be right now. But he wanted to go to the pen. Now he's got a record. No car. Some bullshit job, no future."

"But you make a lot of money, Mia. You don't need him to bring much in, do you?"

"I don't *need* his money at all, Gayle. But I do need a man with a good career, his own car and house. I'm not babysitting a grown-ass man. I'm already doing that with Crystal, and that's enough."

"But what if he gets all that stuff? A job and car . . . You'll go out with him then?"

"He'd still be irresponsible. He'd still be a thug, and I don't date thugs."

"But they know how to lay pipe *real good*," Gayle squealed.

"Oh, trust me, I know."

"So what's next, then?" the hairdresser wanted to know. "You dating somebody else, or you gonna go on another one of your droughts?"

"I don't have *droughts*."

"Girl, you be going four, five months without talking to *no* man. That's a drought."

"That's not a drought."

"Whatever. You got somebody else or not?"

"Not really," Mia said. "This millionaire asked me out last week."

"Shut—up."

"No, I'm serious. It's a guy I work with. He's African."

"*African?* Africans got some big dicks."

"I'm pretty sure there are some Africans out there with three-inch dicks."

"Maybe two or three on the whole continent. The rest of them are packing. What does your African look like? I know he fine."

"He is fine, girl. He's also charming and sophisticated. He took me out to lunch last week and ordered our meal in Italian. He speaks five languages."

"You already went out with him?"

"Not really. We were supposed to be having a business lunch, but he started flirting with me as soon as I sat down. He told me, 'Put those folders away. You work too hard,' or something like that. He's got a thick accent. It's cute."

"Damn, Mia. You got good luck with men this month."

"I don't know if you can call it *luck*. The one guy I want to be with has a crazy girlfriend. I can't even see him anymore. I've got my baby's father hounding me. He's fine and all, but he's a loser. I can't count the guy from work. He's got it going on, but he probably doesn't want to go out with me anymore because I shot him down. He's a proud man."

"Your hand still looks better than mine," Gayle said.

"Oh, and this white guy asked me out a couple weeks ago," Mia said.

"All right, bitch, that's enough."

Mia got her hair trimmed and flipped to perfection. She wished Mama Ernestine was there to throw her two cents in, but the talk with Gayle helped put a lot of things in perspective. Mia left the beauty shop, as always, a fresh, vibrant, and confident woman.

When she got home, the kids were already dressed and excited. Mia had only thirty minutes to get ready herself, but she was only going out with Tyrone, so it didn't matter what she wore. She pulled out a Nike sports suit she bought online but never tried on. The pants were black polyester and spandex. The top was pink and black, long-sleeved with a zipper down the middle.

When she put the pants on, they felt a little tight. A look in the mirror confirmed her lady lumps might be too enticing for a day with Tyrone, but Mia decided to wear the outfit anyway. She looked nice, ready for a volleyball game or track meet, though she'd only be standing in long lines all day. She put on pink and black low-top Pumas and was ready for her date—*day. It's not a date*, she reminded herself, *just another day.*

Back in the living room, Crystal had her ready to change clothes.

"Girl, yo booty look big in them pants."

"No it doesn't," Mia said. "I checked. They're not that tight."

"What are they? *Spandex?*"

"Mostly polyester."

Crystal walked up to her and pulled on the fabric. "I thought you didn't want Tyrone to grab yo booty."

"He's not gonna grab my booty."

"Girl, *I* wanna grab yo booty. You got a tight, *round* ass."

"I'm changing," Mia said.

"Naw, girl. I'm just kidding. It looks good. Plus the shirt covers most of it."

But it didn't.

"Dizamn!" Tyrone held a balled fist over his mouth to block the expletive, but Mica and TC heard it and giggled. Everyone but Crystal was in the living room. They were on their way out the front door when Mia realized she forgot her purse. It was when she turned her back and headed to her room that Tyrone let out his cat call.

Mia looked back and gave him a mean look for cursing in front of the kids, but he was already apologizing.

"I'm sorry, Mia. I didn't mean to do that." He still had his fist over his mouth, chuckling now.

"I'm changing clothes," Mia said, but she was smiling too.

"Naw, girl! *Don't!*" Tyrone almost yelled, then said, "I mean, don't change. It's fine. You look *fine*. Plus we running late, come on. Get yo purse. Let's go."

"What's wrong with your outfit, Mommy?" Mica asked.

"Nothing," Mia said, a hand over her butt.

"Nothing," Tyrone agreed. "It's perfect. It looks good, don't it, TC?"

"It looks good, Mama. Let's go! Let's go!"

"Let's go!" Mica said.

"Yeah, let's go!" Tyrone yelled. He picked Mica up over his head and she giggled.

"You ready to ride the *Shockwave?*" he asked her.

"Yeah! What's that?"

Today Tyrone had on tan, canvas shorts. Mia hadn't seen his bare legs in years, and of course they were sexy. *Couldn't there be some part of him that didn't look good?* she wondered.

Tyrone wore footies and white low-tops. He had a sparse amount of hair on his bronze legs, but Mia liked that, too. His calf muscles were developed, like he'd spent the last six years running track rather than in the pen.

Tyrone had on two white T-shirts; the one on top was bigger and a little longer. He was freshly shaven, and his haircut looked new. His edge-up was sharp and crisp. His hazel eyes seem to glow as he smiled down at Mica. And he had new bling, but it was tasteful; just one silver link necklace. Mia thought gold looked better against his skin tone, but the silver looked nice, too.

In her room, Mia grabbed her purse and started looking for a different bottom to put on, but Tyrone wasn't having it. He opened the front door and the kids rushed out.

"C'mon, Mia!" he called from the doorway. "You ain't got time to change clothes!"

So she didn't.

They piled into her SUV *as is* and hit the road. Tyrone was still grinning ear to ear. Mia rolled her eyes at him.

"You better not try anything," she said.

"I won't," he promised with a hand over his chest. "Scout's honor."

"What do you know about the scouts?" she asked him.

"I know a little bit about everything," he said and mouthed a kiss. If nothing else, Tyrone was very persistent.

Mia wondered how long she could keep her problem with Eric a secret, but it started to unravel before they even hit the freeway, thanks to TC.

"Daddy, somebody threw a brick in our house!" he shouted from the back seat. Mia adjusted the rearview mirror so she could give him the eye, but the damage was done.

"Somebody threw a brick in yo house?" Tyrone asked.

"It was nothing," Mia said.

"They broke our window," TC said.

"What?" Tyrone said.

"It was *nothing*," Mia said again. "Everything's fixed now. No problem. It's over."

"All right, but who did it?" Tyrone asked. He looked really concerned.

"It was a bad person," Mica informed. "We prayed for them."

"That's good," Tyrone said, then looked to Mia again. "Who threw a rock in yo window?"

"It was nothing."

"Yes, it was something," Tyrone said, getting a little agitated. "How somebody gon' throw a brick through yo window? Where was yo punk as—I mean, where was yo boyfriend? Bet nobody won't throw no bricks if *I* was living there."

That actually made Mia feel good, even though it came from *Tyrone*.

"We're not together anymore," she said. "It had something to do with the brick, but I can't talk about it now."

"Y'all broke up?" Tyrone lit up like a Christmas tree. "I told you! I knew it! Didn't I tell you?"

"Yes, Tyrone. You told me. Now drop it. I don't want to talk about it right now."

"What you mean you don't want to talk about it? We *gotta* talk about this. This is—"

"*This is* something I don't want to talk about right now," she said again and shot a glance towards the kids.

"Oh," Tyrone said. "Okay. But the first ride they get on, me and you gon' talk." His smile was warm and comforting.

"All right, Tyrone. We'll talk then," Mia said, and she was smiling, too.

Tyrone paid at the admissions gate like he said he would. The two adult tickets cost $47 each. The kids could get in for $35 a piece. And that was just the beginning of the gouging. As soon as they walked in, a hyper, redheaded girl ran up to the foursome.

"Hey, you guys want me to take your picture?"

"Yeah," Tyrone said. "We want a picture!" He grabbed Mia's shoulder and pulled her close to him. He smelled like Cool Water.

"C'mon, y'all. Get close." He positioned the kids for a nice family photo.

"All right, everybody. Say cheese!" the teenager said.

"CHEESE!" everyone said, even Mia.

"How do we get the picture?" Tyrone asked Mia after the shot was taken.

"Before you leave, you can go to the gift shop and buy a keychain with the picture in it," Mia said. "I think they sell mugs, too."

"I want a mug!" Mica yelled.

"I want a keychain!" TC piped in.

"And so it begins," Mia said and rolled her eyes.

"Naw, it's all good," Tyrone said. "I'ma hook y'all up. C'mon! Let's get you on one of them roller coasters so me and yo mama can talk!"

But Tyrone and Mia didn't get a chance to talk at the first attraction. The Mini Mine Train required an adult passenger, so all four of them buckled up for the ride. Mia and Mica shared a seat in the middle of the train, and Tyrone and TC took the spot behind them.

"You ever been on this before?" Tyrone ask TC.

"Yeah, it's fun."

"Is it scary?"

"A little bit."

An attendant pushed one of the buttons behind his booth and the small train began to roll down the tracks.

"Hold on," TC warned.

"For what?" Tyrone asked.

The cart clanked on what sounded like unstable tracks and then suddenly they took a steep drop and were engulfed in darkness. The ride was only two minutes long, but there was a lot of excitement packed in. The train shot out into daylight, made a quick right, then dipped back down into a darkened tunnel. At one point, it made a left that seemed to never end, as if they were sliding down a twisty straw.

The climax came when the cart began a slow, rickety ascent. They went up so high they were level with the branches of nearby trees. Everyone knew what was coming, but that knowledge left them ill prepared for the high-speed plunge back into darkness.

Mica and TC shrieked, but above them Mia heard Tyrone yelp like a little girl, and that was almost the best part of her day. When the train came to a squeaky stop back at the station, Mia turned in her seat and grinned at her son's father. Tyrone was still wide-eyed, but he smiled back at her.

"You all right back there, hoss?" she asked him.

"You know that was scary. Y'all wasn't scared?" he asked.

"That was a *children's ride*, Tyrone," Mia said.

"*I* thought it was scary," he said. "I been gone six years. Doin sixty-five on the highway scares me!"

This cracked Mia up, and the kids as well.

The adults finally had a chance to talk when Mica and TC got in line for a twirling teacup ride. Mia sat on a nearby bench, and Tyrone took a seat next to her. He stretched out his left arm on the back of the bench and had the nerve to throw the right one behind Mia's shoulders.

"Um, you need to move your arm," she said.

"Oh, my bad." He moved it and stared into her eyes. "You look good," he said. "Got yo hair done today?"

"Yeah."

"It's, um, *stunning*," he said. "Where'd you go?"

"Cut the small talk," Mia said. "Go ahead and say what you want to say."

"All right. So why yo boyfriend throw a brick in yo window?"

"He didn't. His ex-girlfriend did."

"Why she do that?"

"'Cause she wants him back, why else?"

"So he was cheatin' on you with her? That's why you broke up with him?"

"No. He wasn't cheating on me."

"How you know?"

Mia hadn't considered that. "Anyway, I broke up with him because that crazy bitch was following me around. That's the *only* reason I broke up with him."

Tyrone nodded, then smiled. "So, you see how I was right, though? Everything happened just like I wanted it to."

"You wanted a brick in my window?"

"Naw. Quit playin'. You know what I'm talkin' 'bout."

"Yeah. We broke up. Just like you said. Your prophecy has been fulfilled, oh great one."

Tyrone didn't say anything. She looked over at him and he was cheesing, flashing all thirty-two.

"That doesn't mean anything," Mia said.

"How come it don't?"

"'Cause I'm still not going out with you, Tyrone."

"Why not?"

"'Cause you're not the type of guy I go out with. You are not my type. My ex-boyfriend was perfect. You're nothing like him."

"Damn, you just gon' put me out like that? What make him so much better than me?"

"Well," Mia counted on her fingers. "He had his own car."

"Nah." Tyrone shook his head. "I ain't got one of those."

"He had his own house."

"Nope, ain't got one of them either."

"He had a good job."

"I got an *all right* job."

"Working for your uncle?"

"He got his own shop. Made me manager."

"How many people you got under you?"

"Huh?"

"Who do you tell what to do?"

"Um, that one dude who sweeps," Tyrone said.

"My ex-boyfriend has money in the bank, you know, '*Shawty, what you drank?*' "

"Next," Tyrone said.

"And he was romantic," Mia said.

"Okay." Tyrone lit up. "I got him on that one. I'm romantic as hell!"

"Wow, spoken like a true poet," Mia said.

"Naw, for real. I *am* romantic."

"Tell me something you would do for your girl on a romantic date."

Tyrone thought about it for a second. "You mean *now*, or if I had some money?"

"If you could afford anything you wanted."

He twisted his lips in a sneer, and even that looked good. "All right. When I show up at her door, I'd have *flowers.*"

"What kind of flowers?"

"Uh, roses. White ones," Tyrone said.

Mia smiled. "What would you be wearing?"

He grinned. "You know, some G shit. Long-sleeved, blue Polo; button-down, straight out the cleaners. I'd have on me some Fubu jeans, like a light blue, lighter than the shirt. Have 'em long so I can roll 'em up a little at the bottom. They'd be starched down, too. Got my Polo boots on, ya know, looking fly."

Mia thought about Eric's three-piece suit. "Shirt tucked or untucked?" she asked.

"Prolly *un*-tucked," Tyrone said. "Straight out the cleaners, it look tight like that."

"Where would you take her?"

"Hold on. First, I got a limousine rented. That's gon' be parked on the street waiting for her."

"A limo?"

"Yeah. A white one."

"Then what?"

"Then I'd take her to one of them *fancy* restaurants."

"Which one?" Mia asked.

"I don't know. One of 'em."

"You'd take her to a fancy restaurant with jeans on and your shirt untucked."

"Yeah," Tyrone said. "We'd fall up in that bitch like 50 Cent and them. You know them rap niggas don't never get dressed up when they go to fancy places. What that T.I. say in that song? '*Up in Benihana's see me slang in dem chairs.*' "

"Wow," Mia said. "That *is* romantic."

"I'm just trippin'," Tyrone said. "I would treat her like a lady."

And Mia believed him.

"So, you gon' let me take you out?" he asked.

Mia smiled, but shook her head. "Seriously, Tyrone, I can't go out with you."

"Why not?"

"I just broke up with my boyfriend *yesterday*. You don't wanna be my rebound, do you?"

"Well, at least your reason has changed," he noticed.

"What reason?" she asked, but the kid's ride was done then. They rushed forward, as happy as hobos on Thanksgiving.

"Did you see me?" Mica asked.

"Yeah, we saw y'all," Mia said.

"Did you see *me*?" TC asked.

"What did we do?" Mica asked.

"What do you mean?"

"You *didn't* see us! Y'all weren't even watching!" TC deduced.

"They were kissing," Mica guessed.

"We were not kissing!" Mia said.

"Why didn't you see what we did then?" TC wanted to know. "When we went sideways, me and Mica put our hands up in the air."

"Were y'all kissing?" Mica asked Tyrone, and the bastard just grinned. Mia hit him on his arm.

"What are you grinning about?"

"I knew it!" TC said. He held his finger in the air as if he'd just cracked the Lindbergh case.

"We were not kissing," Mia said again. "You'd better tell them we weren't kissing."

"Y'all want cotton candy?" Tyrone asked. He stood from the bench and pointed at a nearby vendor.

"Yeah!" the kids said in unison.

"Tyrone," Mia said.

"C'mon, y'all, let's go," he said. His smile was infectious.

"I want a pink one," Mica said.

"I want pink, too," TC said. "I mean *blue*!"

"Tyrone!" Mia said.

He turned then. "C'mon, Mama. We finna get some candy. Don't be mad. We can kiss some more later."

"I knew it!" TC yelled again.

Mia wouldn't let the kids have cotton candy until after lunch, so they went to Gator McGee's Mountain Grill and had swamp burgers and chicken tenders. Tyrone insisted that he pay there, too, but Mia slid her Visa before he had a chance. Afterwards TC took them to the carnival grounds where, despite eleven attempts, Tyrone was never able to shoot a ten-inch basketball through an eleven-inch hoop.

The kids tried to throw darts at balloons and toss rings onto bottles, but they too came up short each time. Huge panda bears and cuddly Smurfs stayed on the racks as $5 bill after $5 bill yielded no fruit. Mia knew a bad business move when she saw one, so she directed them away from the carnies towards Looney Toons USA.

With only four hours till closing, the kids challenged themselves to get on thirty more rides, and they gave it a damned good shot. They got on sixteen more coasters, and an adult rider was required at most of them.

With all the time spent standing in such close quarters, Mia kept expecting Tyrone to accidentally brush a hand across her backside, but it never happened. Every time she looked back at him, he was enjoying a joke with the kids or simply staring at her, almost in awe, as if he couldn't believe his great fortune. By the time a voice announced over the loud speakers that the park was closing, Mia was ready to ask Tyrone what the hell his deal was, but of course she didn't.

The kids had to be in bed by ten, so Mia stopped at McDonald's on the way home. She let them eat in the car, which was such a big no-no it was outlawed in the driver's manual, but they were unusually neat nibblers tonight. TC tattled on Mica for dropping *one* French fry, and that was an all-time low.

When they got home, Tyrone helped get the children inside. He wasn't really needed, but there was something Mia wanted to ask him all day, so she let him in. Tyrone hugged Mica good night and planted a kiss on her cheek, and Mica hugged him back. Mica didn't even hug Crystal back half the time, but she threw her arms over Tyrone's neck like she did with her mom. Tyrone gave TC a hug, too, then Mia shooed them off to their rooms.

"Thanks for letting me take them out," Tyrone said. He was cheerful, but visibly tired.

"I'll walk you to your car," Mia said.

Outside, the moon was big and beautiful. There were a lot of bright stars in the sky. Mia reached into the house and turned off her porch light, but she could still see Tyrone clearly on the sidewalk. He had his hands in his pockets and his arms close to his body. A cool breeze rattled the leaves on Mia's pecan trees.

"So, where'd you get the money?" she asked him.

"Oh yeah, thanks for reminding me." He reached into his front pocket and came out with a fold of twenties. "I wanted to give you this."

"What's that?"

"Two hundred," Tyrone said. He took a step forward and held the money out for her.

"Where'd you get that?" Mia asked. "You already spent about two hundred today."

"You ain't gon' take it? What's wrong?" But he knew. "Mia, I got this from work. *Honest* work. I told you I work at my uncle's shop. He's teaching me a lot. I'm doing good there."

"Fixing cars?"

"Yeah. I asked him for five hundred dollars. You know, like an advance. Told him he could take it out my checks. He knew I was taking y'all to Six Flags. He helps me out. He wants me to do right."

"So you blew four hundred dollars in one day?"

"I'm *giving* you two hundred dollars. This ain't blowing it. And I didn't blow the other two at the park, either. Every dollar I spent was worth it."

She took the money from him. "Are you trying to impress me? Throwing all this money around?"

Tyrone shook his head. "How am I supposed to impress you with *four hundred dollars*? You got like *ten* bedrooms in your house, a *Lexus*, a *Tahoe*. I'm broke. I can't impress you, Mia. I want you to know I'm serious about my kids, though. I'd do anything for them."

His words were so heartfelt, Mia didn't remind him that Mica wasn't his child.

"I'd do anything for you, too, Mia."

She smiled. "Tyrone, I don' think—"

"Can I have a hug?" he asked.

Of course. "Yeah, I been waiting for you to make that move."

"What move? We had a nice day. I had a good time with you. I miss you. I want to hold you. I'm not trying to be slick. I'll tell you what I want."

"And you want to do *what* with your hands if I hug you?"

"I already told you," Tyrone said. "I won't touch you nowhere you don't want me to."

It went against everything she believed in, but Mia was finding it harder and harder to resist his charms. What harm can one little hug do? *Plenty*—but she did it anyway.

Tyrone stepped forward, and he was not smiling now. His eyes were set and serious. He put his arms around Mia's waist and pulled her close to him. Her breasts pressed against his chiseled torso. His hands were big and warm. They slid to the small of her back, but stopped there, came back up to her sides, and then his vice-like arms consumed her.

Mia closed her eyes and wrapped her arms around his cobra-shaped back. Tyrone's body was hard, and smooth. She traced her fingers down his spine. His muscles flexed like a stallion in stride.

She felt his lips on her forehead, then her temple. He kissed her cheek, then the top of her ear. He kissed her cheek again. His breath was hot, but sweet. He nuzzled the corner of her mouth, and Mia turned away.

"Why not?" he whispered, but Mia couldn't respond. His right hand came up. He brushed her cheek gently with his fingertips, then ran his fingers through her hair. He pushed her face towards his, and Mia did not resist this time.

He kissed her top lip, gently, then sucked on the bottom. He licked her bottom lip, then pecked the top one softly. Mia kissed him back and something like a cymbal crashed in her chest. She felt his hands slide down the small of her back once more, but again they stopped. She knew what he wanted. Tyrone had always been a *butt man*. But this was *wrong*.

Twenty-four hours ago, she was physically *sick*, she was so distraught over the loss of Eric. Now she was in Tyrone's arms. *Tyrone*, of all people, but everything felt so nice, and so right. Tomorrow she might hate herself, but tonight, for this moment at least, she needed to feel something *different.*

"Go ahead," she whispered, and Tyrone didn't need to be told twice. He squeezed her buttocks with both hands and pulled her hips forward. He caressed her, fondled her, then gripped more tightly. Mia's pelvis was pressed to his, and felt him hardening against her. And she felt lightning; a dull explosion of electricity pulsated between her legs.

She pushed away then.

Her chest rose, then hitched. She lowered her head and exhaled. Tyrone backed away, his face marred with unfulfilled ecstasy for a moment, but then his eyes softened. There was a noticeable bulge in his shorts. Mia looked away coyly.

Tyrone turned away from her. "The kids still up?" he asked over his shoulder.

"Yeah," Mia said. *Any old excuse will do.*

He took a jerky step towards his mother's car.

"I guess I better get going," he said.

"Okay," Mia said.

He took a few more steps into the darkness, then turned, his hands meeting over his crotch. His skin seemed to glow in the moonlight. His eyes glistened. "My, my grandmama's having a family reunion in a couple of weeks," he said. "I was wondering if you and the kids could go with me."

"All right," Mia said, glad he hadn't asked her for anything more; she would have agreed to anything.

"All right," he said. "Cool. So, I guess I'm gonna go."

Mia didn't respond. She watched him get into the car, and it started with no racket this time. Apparently there *was* more than one thing Tyrone could do with his hands. He drove off without further words, and Mia was happy to find the kids were in their rooms when she got in, rather than in the living room giggling through the peep-hole.

CHAPTER 12
BREAKDOWN

Crystal woke her up at 1:30 a.m. Mia looked first to her alarm clock and then to her sister, who only wore boxing shorts and a tank top.

"What? What are you doing?"

"Eric's on the phone," Crystal said. She had the cordless in her hand.

"What?"

"It's *Eric*. He says it's important."

"Crystal, is something wrong with my clock, or is it really *one-thirty*?"

"It's one-thirty," Crystal confirmed. "I told him you was sleep. He said it's important, and I had to wake you up."

"I'm not getting up for that," Mia said and rolled over.

Crystal woke her up again at 1:52 a.m.

"Mia?"

"Crystal, are you crazy or what? You *know* I work tomorrow."

"I know, Mia, but he's here."

"Who's here?"

"Eric."

Mia unwillingly fought to shake the sleep off. "*Where?*"

"He's outside, at the front door."

She sat up with a start. "Eric is *here?*"

"Yeah. I told him you was sleep, but he came over here anyway. He says he needs to talk to you."

"You're kidding."

"No, he's on the porch."

"You opened the door?"

"No. I talked to him through the door. He said, '*I'm here, so you have to wake her up now.*'"

Mia threw her feet over the bed and slipped into her slippers. She looked at her clock again. 1:53 a.m. The alarm would go off in four hours. She shook her head at Crystal and stood on unwilling legs. She grabbed a robe she kept on the closet door.

"I can't believe this," she said. "What are you doing up so late anyway?"

"I was talking to Sydney," Crystal said.

"What the hell is *he* doing up so late?"

"He still at the studio. You going out there?"

"Hell, no. Are you crazy? Did he say what he wanted?"

"No. I thought it was something about that bitch who broke yo window. That's the only reason I woke you up the first time. He just keeps saying I gotta wake you up, it's important."

"I don't believe this shit." Mia kept a gun in the house. She thought about retrieving it, but couldn't really see Eric as a threat. He was one of the sweetest men she had ever known, in fact. If he had come this late, it had to be important.

"Do you want me to get my bat?" Crystal asked.

"No," Mia said. "Something must be wrong." She laced up her robe and grabbed a baseball cap from her dresser. This would be the roughest Eric had ever seen her, but he was the one showing up uninvited at two in the morning. If he was expecting a fashion show, he had another think coming.

"I don't think you should open the door," Crystal said.

"Why not?"

"I got a bad feeling."

Mia frowned. "A bad feeling like what? Am I going to get shot or stabbed?"

"That's not funny."

"Crystal, I can't even count how many times I've lived through your bad feelings."

"One day it's gonna be the real thing," Crystal promised.

"Well, thanks, sis. You can go to my funeral and tell everyone, '*I told her, but she didn't listen.*'"

"I will, too, watch."

Mia stepped past her and crept cautiously through her shadowy home. She would never admit it, but Crystal's creepy premonitions spooked the hell out of her. The fact that Crystal was wrong 100 percent of the time did little to allay her fears.

In the living room, Mia squinted through the peephole in her door. And there he was. Eric wore jeans and a T-shirt. His shirt was faded and soiled, and if she didn't know better, Mia would guess it was the same one he had on when he fixed her window two days ago. The jeans looked the same, too, come to think of it. Eric's eyes were soft and pained. His features were set in a mask of unrelenting sorrow. He wasn't crying, but his shoulders hitched like he was having dry heaves.

"He looks pretty bad," Mia whispered.

"He looks *crazy*," Crystal clarified.

Mia jumped a little. She knew her sister followed her into the room, but she didn't know how close Crystal was. "Girl, get off me." Mia shot a soft elbow into her gut.

"You goin' out there?" Crystal asked in a hushed voice.

"I don't know," Mia whispered back. "I guess so."

"He looks crazy," Crystal reiterated.

"I know, but I don't want him out there all morning."

"Why don't you call the police?"

"For what? He's not doing anything."

"They can still take him for being crazy," Crystal informed her.

"Eric, what are you doing here?" Mia yelled through the door. She watched through the peephole. His face lit up at the sound of her voice.

"Muh, Mia? Mia, is that you?"

"It's me, Eric. What are you doing here?"

"I need to talk to you." He moved his face up to the door and talked into the peephole as if it were an intercom. This move distorted his features to carnival-mirror proportions, and Mia had to back away.

"Eric, it's two o'clock in the morning. I'm asleep. We're going to have to talk tomorrow."

"I need to talk to you *now*," he groaned. Even speaking through the door, Mia could hear a pained quality to his voice.

"Okay, Eric. What do you want to tell me? Hurry. I'm going back to bed."

"I want to talk to you *in person*, Mia. I need to see your face."

Crystal slapped her sister hard on the shoulder. "Don't go out there!" she hissed.

"*Ouch*, girl! Stop hitting me," Mia whispered. "I don't want to go out there," she yelled at Eric. "It's too late. I don't have any clothes on. It's gonna have to wait 'til tomorrow."

"It's an *emergency*," he pleaded. "It won't take more than a minute. I promise."

Crystal hit her again.

"Girl, stop hitting me!"

"You better not go out there," Crystal whispered.

"I'm *not* going out there. I'm just going to open the door."

"*Why?*"

"So I can see what he wants and he can leave."

"Why don't you just call the police?"

"Quit being so scared," Mia said and unlocked her dead bolt. Crystal started to say something else, but Mia cut her off. "All right, Eric. Here I come." She pushed Crystal into a corner behind the door. "I'm going to leave the door open. If something happens, you come out there."

Crystal nodded, but she didn't look like she'd be any help in a crisis.

Mia opened the door slowly. The first thing she realized was that her peephole needed to be cleaned. Eric looked much worse than she thought. His white T-shirt was not merely dingy; it was filthy. The neck area was stretched and loose, and there were dried stains all over. Mia couldn't tell if the maroon-colored blotches were ketchup or blood. The foggy, yellow discolorations might have been beer or urine.

Eric was like a caged animal. His eyes were wide and wild. He stared at Mia, but seemed to look *through* her. His dark-brown skin was ashen, and Mia could smell the alcohol on him from four feet away.

"Mia," he said. His hand went up, and he took a staggering step forward. For a brief moment Mia felt like she was in a zombie flick.

"Stop, Eric." She held up one thin arm as if she could stop him with her delicate hand alone, but he did stop. Her heart was stuck in her throat. Her mouth was dry. *Crystal was right.* "You're scaring me," she managed.

As pitiful as he already looked, that statement distorted Eric's features further.

"Mia, no. Don't—don't be afraid of me. I would never hurt you."

His words did little to quell her fear. Mia still held the doorknob with moist fingers. "What are you doing here?" she asked.

"I came to give you this," he said, reaching into his front pocket.

Mia knew he was reaching for a weapon. A dozen exit strategies ran through her mind, none of which were guaranteed, but he didn't pull out a knife or a gun. Instead, Eric produced a jewelry box. Mia hoped he wasn't going to do what it looked like, but he opened it, then dropped to his knees on her walkway. He lowered his head and held the box up for her as if it was a sacrifice.

Mia saw that there was a ring inside, a *big* ring at that, but she looked past the offering. Eric was crying again. His bald head bobbed up and down like a fishing float.

"Eric, get up."

"M—Mia, I—I know I haven't known you very, very long, but—"

"Eric."

He looked up at her. His eyes were wet and bloodshot. "Please don't leave me."

Mia couldn't have been more hurt if she watched a big guy with a club bash a bag full of kittens. She let go of the door and stepped down onto her sidewalk.

"*Whatchoo doing?*" Crystal breathed, but Mia ignored her.

She walked up to Eric and closed the jewelry box. From his knees he stared up at her. His mouth was open. His lower lip trembled.

"Mia, I want to marry you," he said.

She shook her head and stood next to him. He was sweating. Mia wiped the top of his head with her small hand, and he turned towards her, burying his face in her robe.

"Eric, you don't want to marry me," she said, stroking him tenderly.

His whole body trembled, and he sobbed uncontrollably. His head was warm, and his breaths were hot. She felt the heat all the way to her belly.

"I—I duh—do," he managed. "I do, Mia."

"No, you don't," she said.

"*I don't want to lose you.*"

"Eric, this isn't you."

"*I nuh—need you.*"

"Eric."

He looked up to her. She put her hand on his cheek, and stroked his eyebrow with her thumb. "Eric, I don't want to remember you like this," she said.

"*Buh, but is, it's not fair,*" he moaned. He buried his face in her stomach again.

"We're not together anymore," Mia said. "What we had was good, but it's over now. You need to go home, Eric."

He shook his head. "I can—can't live without you."

Mia bit her bottom lip and shook her head slowly. "Look at me, Eric." He didn't immediately respond. "Eric, look at me."

"Mia, you don't understand how bad I feel."

"I do, Eric. I do." She stroked his head again. "But it's over. We're not going to get married." His didn't react to that, so she said it again. "We're *not* getting back together. We had a good time together, Eric, but you shouldn't have come here tonight. When I think about you, I want to remember the good things—how you treated me, the restaurants you took me to. I want to think about nights like the Ritz Carlton. I don't want to have *this* memory in my head. All I have left is your memory, Eric. Don't spoil that."

That seemed to get through. His features melted from apologetic to embarrassed. He buried his face in her robe again, sniffled, and then said, "I'm sorry."

"Eric, you were a strong black man," Mia said. "You still are," she corrected herself. "Now get up before Crystal calls the police." She didn't think it would work, but the pouting prince pulled his face from her stomach and looked up to her. Mia smiled down at him. "Get up," she said and winked.

Eric slowly made it to his feet. Once upright, Mia had to crane her neck to look up at his face.

"Wow. I almost forgot how tall you are."

He smiled and looked away nervously. He wiped his nose with the back of his hand. "I feel like a fool."

Mia reached up and wiped a spot of moisture from his cheek. "I ain't gon' lie, bruh. You *do* kinda look like a fool."

He chuckled. "Don't sugarcoat it. Tell me *exactly* how you feel."

"And you're dirty, too," Mia said. "I wasn't gonna say anything, but if you insist . . ." She grinned. "You gonna be okay?"

"Yeah," he said, and rubbed his eyes with a meaty paw. "I'm sorry, Mia. I shouldn't have done that. I haven't slept much since yesterday."

Mia smiled. "Oh, you're missing sleep, too?" She looked at an imaginary watch on her wrist.

Eric smiled too and then looked at the box in his hand. He quickly shoved it into his pocket.

"You must think I'm an idiot."

Mia sighed. "No, Eric. I don't think that." She looked back to the house. Crystal stood in the doorway with a confused expression.

Eric looked up and saw her too. "*Oh, God.* This *is* bad." He chuckled and then took a deep breath and straightened himself. "I'd better go."

Mia nodded.

"What time is it?" he asked.

"It was two when I came out here."

"Is today *Monday?*"

"How much have you had to drink?"

"Just a couple of pints . . . You—you never believed me about my twin brother, did you? Is that why you said no? He's stationed in Afghanistan now. You can talk to him—on the phone. He's got a webcam . . ."

"I did believe you," Mia said. "I do believe you, but it's not about that. You know that's not our problem."

He nodded. "Yeah."

"You be careful," Mia said and took a step away from him. Eric nodded, then turned and walked slowly to his BMW, which was parked on the curb. Mia waited until he was gone before she went back inside.

"What'd he say?" Crystal asked when she closed the door.

"He asked me to marry him," Mia confided.

"*Ewww.* What'd you say?"

Mia gave her sister a dumb look. "I said *yes*, Crystal. Didn't you see how happy he was?"

"You don't have to get an attitude."

"I'm sorry. I'm tired. I had a long day."

"Can Sydney come over tomorrow when I get out of school?" Crystal asked.

"I guess so."

"Did Tyrone grab yo booty today?" Crystal inquired.

The memory of it gave Mia a wicked smile. "He did," she said. "He grabbed it, and rubbed it, and squeezed it . . ."

Her sister lit up. "*Bitch*! You liked it?"

"I must have," Mia mused. "I'm the one who told him to do it."

"*Uh, uhn!*" Crystal grabbed her arm. "Sit down. Tell me *everything*!"

"It's too late," Mia said. "We have to talk tomorrow." She staggered off towards her room.

"Did y'all kiss?" Crystal called after her.

"A little," Mia teased.

"*Ooh*, did y'all *do it*?"

"*No!*" Mia said adamantly. "I am not sleeping with *Tyrone*." But even she didn't believe that.

CHAPTER 13

A NIGHT AT MILLE FLEURS

Miss Tenery walked into Mia's office at 10:30 a.m. "Mr. Manitou would like to speak with you."

Mia looked up from the papers on her desk. There were no lights flashing on her phone. "Did he say what extension he was at?"

"Oh, no. He's here," Miss Tenery said. "In *person*," she clarified.

"Oh." Mia sat up in her chair. "You sent him the CME stuff?"

"Yes, ma'am. I'm not sure what this is in regards to."

Mia pursed her lips. "All right. Send him in."

"Very well." The secretary nodded and left the room

Mr. Manitou worked three floors up. It was odd that he would stop by Mia's office. She didn't owe him any reports. Even if she had missed a deadline, she didn't think he would come down to chastise her personally.

The door swung open again, and the senior analyst strolled in as proud and handsome as ever. He wore a wheat-colored suit with a white shirt. His smile was warm and inviting. Mia stood to shake his hand.

"Mr. Manitou."

"How are you, Mia?" He grabbed her hand and cupped his left hand over it. "It is very good to see you again."

"Thank you," Mia said and smiled. "You got the CME files last week?"

He let go and took a seat in an executive chair across from her desk.

"I have been out of the office, Mia. I saw your files this morning, but I have not looked at them yet. I am sure they will be in order. Your work is always exceptional."

"Thanks," Mia said. "Have you been out of town?"

"Yes." Mr. Manitou grinned. "And thankfully it was not business this time. I went home to visit my family in South Africa." He was in a good mood, which made Mia relax a little.

"Is it nice this time of year?" she asked.

His eyes rolled back in ecstasy. "Ah, Mia, it is a very beautiful place. I am from a city called Saldanha, just north of Cape Town. We have the most beautiful beach you've ever seen. The most pristine waters."

"It sounds wonderful."

"It is. Have you not been to Africa?"

"No," Mia said. "It's something I want to do, but it keeps getting put on the back burner. Like so many other things . . ."

"That is a shame," he said. "You must remember that there is more to life than work, work, work. One day we will all die. You should do things you enjoy *now*, while you are young."

"You're right," Mia said. "I wish I could just decide to go to Africa, then do it."

"I would have invited you," Mr. Manitou said, "but I did not want to offend. I certainly would not like to cause problems for you and your boyfriend."

"Oh."

"That is the reason I have come to your office, Mia." He leaned forward in the chair. "I want you to know that what happened at our lunch last time was totally out of character for me. I feel the need to apologize once more—"

"You don't have to apologize," Mia said. "That was two weeks ago."

"Yes, I understand. But during my time on vacation, I thought about you often."

Mia raised an eyebrow.

"I cannot feel comfortable," he went on, "until I'm sure you harbor no bad feelings towards me."

Mia shook her head. "Mr. Manitou, trust me. I have no bad feelings towards you. I told you, I was flattered. You are an attractive and charming man. Any woman you're interested in should consider herself lucky."

"As with you, Mia," the analyst said. "Your boyfriend is also a fortunate man, indeed."

Mia knew she could have left it at that. All she had to do was agree that her boyfriend *was* lucky. Mr. Manitou never would have known differently. He would have continued his apology, left her office, and their work relationship would have gone on as usual. But she chose to divulge instead. And why not? She wasn't going with Eric anymore, and even though she kissed Tyrone a couple weeks ago, that certainly didn't make him her boyfriend.

As a matter of fact, Tyrone had been asking her out regularly since that fateful kiss, and she shot him down each time. He was free to see TC, but what happened after Six Flags was a fluke.

"He, um, he's not my boyfriend anymore," she said.

Mr. Manitou's eyes grew wide. "What is this?"

"You heard me," she said. "I broke up with my boyfriend. Two weeks ago. It was right after you asked me out, actually."

"Ah." He leaned back and crossed his legs. "I am very sorry to hear that," he said, but he didn't look very sorry at all.

"It's okay," Mia said. "It happens."

"Yes, well I hope it was not a *bad* breakup," he said. "I would hate to see you upset."

This was all a game, and Mia knew the rules well. He didn't care if she was upset or not. He wanted to know if she would go out with him or if a grieving period was required.

"It's okay," Mia said. "I only went out with him for a couple of months. It's not like we were married."

Mr. Manitou smiled at this. "So, you are single then? There is no one else?"

Mia thought about Tyrone again, but there was really no comparison. Mr. Manitou was a senior analyst at a trillion-dollar-a-year investment firm. Tyrone was a grease monkey at his uncle's auto shop. Mr. Manitou had money in the bank; *millions*, at that. Tyrone had, well, he had a shiny new necklace. And Mr. Manitou took awesome trips to places like South Africa. Tyrone went to cool places like the Texas Department of Corrections. Mia didn't even know why she was considering it.

"There's no one else," she said.

"Well, would you say 'yes' if I asked you out again? If not, I would look like a bigger fool than I did at our lunch."

"Mr. Manitou, yo—"

"Please, call me Babatunde."

Mr. Manitou's way easier, Mia thought. "*Babatunde,* did I say that right?"

"Yes. It is fine." He smiled eagerly.

"Babatunde, you didn't make a fool out of yourself at our lunch. I already told you that. And as to whether I would say 'yes' if you asked me out again, that's something you have to find out on your own. It takes all the fun out of it if you already know what I'm going to say. Asking people out is risky. Is it worth it?"

"It is most definitely worth it," he said.

Mia smiled.

"So, Miss Clemmons, would you do me the honor of having dinner with me?"

"I'd be delighted," Mia said.

"Great!" Mr. Manitou clasped his hand together. "When shall we go?"

"I'm not sure. I have to check my schedule."

"Are you free tonight?" he asked.

"Tonight?"

"Yes. I have a reservation at Mille Fleurs for 7:00 p.m. Can you join me?"

Mille Fleurs was the hottest French restaurant in the city. Mia was definitely interested, but there were other things to consider.

"You have a reservation, with whom?" she asked.

"What do you mean? I would like to go with *you*."

"You said you already have a reservation. Who were you *planning on* going with?"

Mr. Manitou smiled. "Ah. I understand. No, Mia, it is not what you think. I made the reservation for *myself*. I was not planning on taking anyone with me."

"You were going to the best French restaurant in town *by yourself?*"

"Yes," he said immediately. "Is that such a strange thing?"

"It is kind of odd," Mia admitted. "Most people would rather stay home if they were alone."

"That is not how I am," he said. "I love French cuisine. If I choose to eat it, I will eat it. If I eat it with friends, it is good. If I eat it alone, it is still good. But I will eat what I wish whenever I wish. I will not deprive myself of a nice meal simply because I have no date."

That actually made a lot of sense. Mia wished she could be so independent. She wondered if Crystal had plans for the evening.

"I think I can go," she said. "Are you going back upstairs? Could I call you back and let you know in about five minutes?"

"Yes," Mr. Manitou said and stood. "I am on my way there right now."

"All right," Mia said. "Thanks for stopping by."

"No, thank *you* for having me," he said and stepped out of the office.

Mia called her sister when he was gone.

"Hello?"

"Crystal. What are you doing?"

"Nothing, just watching TV."

"Did you go to school today?"

"Huh?"

"Did you—girl, you heard what I said."

"I wasn't feeling well."

Mia sighed and shook her head. "Look, I need you to watch the kids for a little bit tonight."

"You going out?"

"Yeah, just for a couple of hours."

"You're going out with *Eric*?"

"*No!* Why would you even say that?"

"Tyrone?"

"Quit being silly."

"Who?"

"Don't worry about it. It's a new guy."

"*Mia, Mia.*"

"What?"

"Nothin'. You've had a good month as far as men . . ."

"Yeah? That's what Gayle said."

"Who's Gayle?"

"One of the girls at Claire's. Anyway, I gotta go. I need to get out of here before five."

Mia called Mr. Manitou back to confirm their date for the night. He wanted her address so he could pick her up, but as a rule Mia never let new guys come to her house. She told him she'd meet him at the restaurant at seven, and Mr. Manitou grudgingly agreed. He thought it very unusual that she didn't want to ride with him, Mia said it was probably just an American thing.

She left the office at 5:00 p.m. sharp. Tyrone called her on the way home.

"Hello?"

"Hey, girl."

"What's up?"

"I was wondering if I can come pick up TC today."

"That's fine. Where you taking him?"

"Nowhere. I was gonna bring him over here. Mama wants to kick it with him for a while. Plus, he likes playing with Kilo. How come you ain't got no dog?"

"I don't know. I'm thinking about getting one. How come your dog's named *Kilo*?"

"That's tight, huh?"

"That's not what I was thinking," Mia said.

"They named him when I was locked up," Tyrone said. "I would have named him something pretty."

"Like *Dopesack*?" Mia teased.

"Naw, funny lady. Say, can you come with us? Mama wants to see you, too."

"I haven't seen her in so long. How's she doing?"

"She's fine," Tyrone said. "'Cept she got that sugar. They was talking 'bout cutting off her leg last year, but she pulled through. I'm glad. I woulda been messed up if I got out and she didn't have no leg."

"That's sad," Mia said.

"So, you're coming with us?" Tyrone asked. "We can bring Mica, too."

"Sorry, I have something to do."

"Like what?"

"What do you mean '*What*?' That's not your business, Tyrone."

"It's like that?"

"Of course it's like that. What are you thinking?"

"I just thought since we—"

"Okay, that thing that happened after Six Flags. Tyrone, that was nice. I won't say I didn't like it, 'cause I did. But that didn't make you my boyfriend."

"I know that. I just thought you was gonna give me a chance at least."

"Tyrone, I seriously don't think we should go out. We did that. It didn't work. Remember?"

"I was a kid then. I was young and stupid. I jacked it up. I know that. You know I'm not the same person I was then."

"You *seem* more mature," Mia admitted.

"So why you stallin' me out like this?"

"I'm just not sure about you."

"I'm going to quit askin' you. You know that, right? It's gon' get to a point when I don't even ask you no more."

Mia knew she probably could have nipped it in the bud right then. All she had to say was, *Well, don't ask me anymore*, and that would have been it.

"What time are you coming?" she asked.

"At six," he said.

"I'll have TC ready."

"All right. Bye."

The plan was perfect. Mia would get home at five-thirty. That gave her thirty minutes to get TC ready and find an outfit for her date with Manitou. She would take off her work clothes and put on shorts and a T-shirt, so when Tyrone arrived, she would look stay-at-home-casual. When he left at six, she would still have thirty minutes to change.

The plan was perfect, but it fell through when Tyrone arrived twenty minutes late. Mia had no choice but to get dressed early, and Tyrone had no choice but to see her in the elegant gown. She knew there would be a reaction, but didn't get the one she expected. She had him fitted for anger, maybe a little indignation, but Tyrone looked downright miserable.

Mia wore a black V-neck dress with her favorite patent leather sandals. The dress was shimmering silk and long-sleeved. A satin belt encircled the waist and tied in the front. The gown wasn't tight, but it was form-fitting around the bust and hips. From the back it clung to her butt like a Band-Aid, and it must have reminded Tyrone of the pants she wore to Six Flags. Why he was even in her room, Mia had no idea.

"So, this why you can't go say 'Hi,' to my mama? You finna go shake that thang in some *other* nigga's face?"

Mia was staring into the mirror mounted on her bedroom dresser, putting on her earrings. Tyrone stood in her doorway, looking a little scruffy around the chin, Mia thought. He wore black Dickies, a black T-shirt, and a look of frustration.

TC's room was in the opposite direction. No way did Tyrone make it to her room by accident.

"What are you doing in my room?" she asked. Mia was fully dressed, but Tyrone would not have free range of her home. Who did he think he was?

"I say, you finna shake that thang in some other nigga's face, ain't you?"

Mia's face fell slack, then a sneer rose in the corner of her mouth. "I don't owe you an explanation for anything I do," she said, then, "Where's TC?" Mia didn't want things to get ugly, but she would not be disrespected in her own house.

"He's in the living room with Mica."

"What are you doing in my room?"

"I was gon' ask you again if you would go with us, but now I see why you can't go. You look nice, Mia. You—"

"You can't come in my room," she said.

"Why not? You got clothes on, what's—"

"It's *my* room, Tyrone. You don't have any business in here. You need to stay in the front room or the kid's room."

"Why you talkin' to me like that? Like I'm some burglar or somethin'?"

"I didn't say that."

"That's the way you making me feel. Talkin' 'bout I can go here, but not here, like you don't trust me or somethin'. You actin' like you don't even know me."

Mia softened a bit. "I just don't like you barging in my room, charging me up about my personal life."

Tyrone rubbed his chin and looked her up and down. "So, you finna go out with somebody, huh? That's why you all prettied up."

"What did I just say?"

"I'm not chargin' you up. I'm just askin', *politely.*"

Mia sighed. "What difference does it make?"

"Why won't you go out with *me*?"

"Tyrone, I told you—"

"Yeah, you told me you don't know about me. You not sure. In the meantime, you havin' all yo little fun. This a new nigga or the same one?"

"Tyrone—"

"What make them niggas so much better than me?" His face twisted up. "That's what I really want to know. What, they throw a lot of money at you? Get you some *filet mignon? Caviar?* That what make them better than me?"

Mia couldn't even get upset, because Tyrone was on the verge of tears.

"Have fun," he said, then turned and stormed down the hallway.

Mia reached out. She almost called out to him, but she put the hand over her mouth instead and fought off a wave of her own tears.

The incident with Tyrone should have been reason enough to stay home, but there were certain things Mia never did. She never cheated on a man, never slept with her girlfriend's man, and she never stood one up, either. She pulled up to the valet parking at Mille Fleurs at 7:02. Babatunde Manitou met her at the entrance.

He wore a black suit, with a white shirt and a black tie. Mia thought he looked like a member of the Nation of Islam. After the argument with Tyrone, she wasn't really in the mood for romance, but her date gave it his all. Mr. Manitou greeted her with two dozen roses. Mia cradled them as he led her to his table. She wondered if she looked like Miss America. She wondered how long Tyrone would stay mad at her.

Everything at Mille Fleurs was top-notch, all the way. Their waiter wore a tuxedo and spoke with a French accent that wasn't too cheesy. And the setting was incredible. Beautiful works of art were mounted in equally beautiful frames with intricate designs. Chandeliers provided romantic lighting.

Even the menu was high-class. It came in a leather cover, had a lot of calligraphy and no prices. And once again Mr. Manitou wowed Mia with his linguistic skills. He ordered *bifteck avec pommes frites* for himself and *poisson du jour* for Mia. His meal turned out to be a rib-eye with French fries. Mia got fresh fish, the catch of the day prepared according to the chef's whim.

Everything was perfect. Mia couldn't have asked for more. But still, she wasn't happy. She hated how even miles away Tyrone was still able to ruin her date, but halfway through their meal Mr. Manitou decided to ruin it himself.

"You are not eating much," he said. "Is something troubling you?"

Mia sighed. "I'm sorry. I don't mean to be distracted. I have things on my mind."

"It is probably work. You do not go very long without thinking about the office."

Mia smiled.

"Is it something you would like to talk to me about?" he asked.

"No," she said. "It's nothing, really." She looked into his eyes. "I'm thinking about you now. Just you."

He grinned. "I like that. Tell me, do you think you might be interested in going with me to Africa on my next vacation?"

"That's a big trip," Mia said. "I hope I have a lot of time to get to know you before then."

"Oh, yes. I was definitely speaking of the distant future. You would love it. There are many beautiful women there. But none quite as beautiful as you are tonight."

"Hey, flattery will get you everywhere," she teased. "My son would like Africa. He's wanted to go since the first time he saw a cheetah chase a gazelle."

"Your son?"

"Yes, my son, and my daughter. Don't tell me you didn't know I have children."

"Yes, of course I knew. I did my share of research before taking on this venture."

"Good," Mia said. "For a minute there I thought this was going to turn into an awkward moment."

"I would like to know about your children," he said. "What are their ages?"

"My son's name is TC. He's nine. My daughter is Mica. She's seven. They're very beautiful. And smart. You'd like them."

"I'm sure I would," Mr. Manitou said. "I like children. Your son, why do you call him TC?"

"His name is Tyrone Christopher. I call him TC for short."

"That is nice. Everything gets a nickname in America."

Mia smiled.

"Tell me something," Mr. Manitou said. "Your children, their father is your ex-husband?"

"No," Mia said. "I wasn't married to either of my children's fathers. I've never been married." This news wasn't always a big deal to most of Mia's dates, but the analyst responded like she'd just grown a third eye.

"You have *two* children by *two* different men and you were not married to either of them?"

Oh, God, Mia thought, *He's going to be one of them.* But she had no idea.

"I had my children when I was younger, Mr. Manitou. I was a young girl, a different girl. But after they were born I *still* went to school. I busted my ass and I graduated. I'm doing well for myself. Maybe my children were not conceived under ideal circumstances, but I love them and don't consider them mistakes."

Mr. Manitou still looked confused. "These . . . *men*, they are still around? You see them still?"

Mia was getting a little ticked off by this line of questioning. "My daughter's father is dead, so, no. I don't see him anymore. My son's father just got out of prison a little over a month ago. He's been coming by to see TC. So yeah, I do see *him*. I saw *him* today, as a matter of fact." She was getting more and more heated. Mia knew she was about to redline. What Mr. Manitou said next would determine whether she gave a damn or not.

"This is not good," he said. "I do not believe this will work."

"Why, whatever do you mean?" she asked politely.

"Mia, I will be honest: I am surprised by this information. This is something I was not aware of. You do not seem like the sort of woman who would do these things."

"Do what, Mr. Babatunde? *Have sex?* I don't seem like the kind of woman who would *have sex?* Well, don't worry about it. I sure as hell ain't *having sex* with an asshole like you."

The analyst looked around nervously. "Mia, I will have to ask you to lower your voice. And watch your language."

"*Babatunde*, you don't tell me what to do." She gave him a once-over. "You got *some* nerve, you know that. You ask *me* out, then condemn me for something I did *ten* years ago. You don't know me. You have no idea who I am or what sort of woman I am."

"Yes, I believe I now know *exactly* what type of woman you are," he snapped.

Mia flicked her plate. She did not throw it. She did not swing it. She merely grabbed it with two hands and lifted it from the table with a quick motion, and at a distinct angle. When she stopped the plate's forward progress, the grilled salmon, prepared according to the chef's whim, accompanied with mixed vegetables, continued its route. Most of it landed on Mr. Manitou's face. The rest splashed on his nice white shirt.

A few nearby patrons watched in disdain. An elderly woman gasped. Mr. Manitou let out a startled yelp that was both depressing and satisfying. He wiped sautéed onions from his eyes and stared at Mia with a look of abject horror. She casually picked up her wine glass and downed it in one swallow.

They stared at each other in complete silence for what felt like a whole minute.

A waiter approached their table cautiously with a bundle of white cloths in hand.

"Napkin, sir?"

Mia smiled. That would have been nice, but not too kosher. She already broke a windshield this year. That crazed act would have to last her.

So instead of throwing her poisson du jour, Mia stared at Mr. Manitou defiantly, then took one last sip of her wine.

"Enjoy your meal," she said and then stood graciously, gathered her flowers, and left the restaurant. Mr. Manitou stared after her, as neat and clean as he was when she arrived.

Mia got into the car laughing. By the time she hit the freeway she was crying, but the tears were gone when she got home.

And damned if Tyrone's car wasn't sitting in her driveway.

Mia waited down the street for a few minutes, hoping he would leave and not see her, but his car didn't move. From where she was parked, Mia couldn't see her own front door. She didn't know if Tyrone was in the car or in the house or in the doorway or coming or going. But the longer she sat there, the more frustrated she became. Finally, Mia asked herself why she was avoiding her own house. Men had been making her life miserable as of late, but she'd be damned if they'd make her uncomfortable on her own property.

She drove up to her driveway just as Tyrone was backing out. She waited for him, and then took the spot he vacated. Rather than continue on his way, Tyrone parked next to the curb, just as she knew he would. Mia opened her door, and he was standing there by the time she got out.

"What do you want, Tyrone?"

"Those some nice flowers," he said.

"Okay, thanks. What do you want?"

"What's wrong?" he asked.

She looked into his eyes. They were warm and comforting, as usual. He looked genuinely concerned, which was funny to her for some reason. She chuckled. "You're some piece of work."

"Why you say that?"

"Do you have a curse on me, or what?"

Tyrone shook his head. "Naw, I ain't got no curse on you. Why you think that?"

"'Cause since you've been back, since you gave that declaration of love, I've been having big-time problems with men. You said nothing would work out for me, right? I think you put a hex on me. You know, I haven't had sex since you got out."

"I haven't either," Tyrone said. He still looked serious, not a glint of happiness on his face.

"Yeah, right," Mia said. She felt drunk, though she only had one glass of wine.

"I said I was gon' wait for you, and I am," he said. "You don't have to believe me. *I* know the truth."

But Mia did believe him.

"All right, Tyrone," she said. "Where do you want to take me for our *date*?"

"Oh, you wanna go out with me now?"

"Yes. I want to go out with you. You wore me down."

He shook his head. "I don't want to go out with you 'cause you *wore down*. I want you to go out with me, 'cause you see I'm a good man. A good man who'll love you and never treat you bad."

"Is that what you are?"

"I ain't go' no money," he said. "But *I am* a good man."

Mia smiled. "Well, I could use a hug from a *good man*."

Tyrone closed the distance between them and held her like he'd been waiting on the embrace for six years. He did not grab her butt and he did not kiss her. He simply clung to her for a full five minutes, sometime during which Mia dropped her flowers. They would remain in her driveway until morning.

When she got inside, the kids were ready for bed. Mia read them five chapters of a Scooby Doo mystery and tucked them in tenderly. They were precious, and beautiful, and if she could go back in time and have them all over again, she would.

CHAPTER 14
FIXIN' MIA

Tyrone showed up Sunday afternoon at 3:00 p.m. He wore dark blue denim jeans that were starched and neat. He had on a white Polo golf shirt, and it was actually tucked in. He had on a pair of Polo boots that looked new. He was clean-shaven and had apparently been using a wave cap: a sea of ripples cascaded from the back to the front of his head. Mia answered the door herself, and was very impressed.

"You look nice, Tyrone."

"You look good too, Mia."

She wore white twill shorts, a short-sleeved linen blouse and white low-top sneakers. Her blouse was a beautiful baby blue. She wore it unbuttoned and untucked with a white camisole underneath. She didn't think there was anything special about her outfit, but once again Tyrone looked her up and down like she was dressed to the nines.

"You look like a model," he said.

"It's just shorts, Tyrone."

"I know, but no matter what you got on, you're beautiful. I like how you dress for work, and that dress you had on the other day was the prettiest thing I've ever seen. Even *now*, you're not wearing anything special, but you're awesome, fresh, and vibrant."

"*Fresh and vibrant?*"

"I've been reading Essence," Tyrone admitted.

Mia laughed. "Why are y'all having a family reunion this time of year?" she asked.

"It's really my grandma's birthday," he said. "It's the only birthday the whole family gets together for. We still have a family reunion in the summer."

"What'd you get her?" Mia asked.

"A microwave."

"*A microwave?*"

"Yeah. She's had the same one since before I got locked up. It's not even digital. I'm trying to bring her into the twenty-first century."

"That's a good gift," Mia said. "I didn't know it was going to be a birthday party. We're going to have to stop somewhere so I can get her something, too."

"You cool," Tyrone said. "The microwave's from both of us. I already put your name on the card."

"That's nice," Mia said. "Okay, let me get the kids, and we're ready to go."

"You know she lives in Cleburne, right?"

Mia didn't know that, but decided not to let it ruin her day.

Cleburne, Texas, is about thirty miles south of Overbrook Meadows. It's a quaint little town, but not a place Mia would ever have reason to visit if not for

Tyrone. She couldn't imagine living there. Not only was Cleburne small, but it was borderline desolate. Driving there from the big city, you would see an immediate shift in scenery once you passed Alvarado. The buildings got smaller and smaller and more spread apart. Soon you would see no buildings at all, just rolling hills, dense tree lines, and enough land for all the illegal immigrants in the United States.

When power lines started to pop up again, you knew you were getting close, but you still had to pay attention. If you went too fast you would miss the whole city. Cleburne boasted a population of 29,000. Main Street was only eight blocks long, and that was the whole downtown. There was only one movie theatre in Cleburne, and one bowling alley. The two fancy restaurants there were Chili's and Applebees.

The kids had never seen so many horses and goats in people's front yards, so Mia drove slowly and let them gawk. When Tyrone pointed to a rundown shack with a real, live chicken coop beside it and said, "There it is," Mia thought he was kidding.

He wasn't.

She parked in front of a wooden fence made from knotted tree branches rather than flattened stakes. The kids jumped out of her SUV and ran immediately to the poultry. Mia rushed to get out herself; she was worried part of the house might fall on them, but Tyrone assured her the shanty had sound engineering.

"Everything here is old," he said. "But it still works fine."

He wasn't kidding about the *old* part. Tyrone took her inside to meet his grandma, and Mia became more and more awed with each step. Everything in the house was antique, from the porcelain kitchen sink to the floor-model television in the living room. Tyrone's grandmother had a *real* record player. And it worked! A Tina Turner album was on, and the scratchy quality of the audio gave Mia a bit of nostalgia.

There were priceless figurines in the living room, a completely wooden ironing board folded in one corner, and as Mia passed the bathroom, she saw that the tub had four stubby legs with clawed feet.

"How long has your grandmother lived here?" she whispered to Tyrone.

"I think she was *born* here," he said. "Literally. In that room over there."

There were already dozens of people there, so Tyrone and Mia had to navigate through a massive crowd to get to his grandma. Each person they bumped into wanted to know who the pretty lady on his arm was. Tyrone introduced Mia as, "My baby's mama," but everyone assumed there was more to it than that. Mia didn't mind their curious gazes.

Everyone called Tyrone's grandmother Maw Maw, and she looked pretty much how Mia would have expected a Maw Maw to look. She was dark-skinned, frail, and as old as the dust on her Victorian nightstand. Paw Paw, her husband of seventy-two years, died just three years ago, making her the oldest member of the Story clan.

215

Maw Maw had no teeth, bad eyes, and equally aged ears. She never left her room, which explained the large crowd they had to fight through to get to her.

Grandma didn't look like much of a conversationalist, but Tyrone gave it his all.

"Maw Maw!" he yelled. "How you doing? *Happy birthday!*"

"Oh, thank you," she said. "You Erlinda's baby, ain't you?"

"Yes, ma'am! It's me, Tyrone!"

"Tyrone? Come give me some sugar, boy."

Tyrone leaned forward and hugged the old lady. He planted a kiss on her sunken jaw and then turned and pulled Mia forward.

"This is TC's mother. You remember my son, TC?"

"*Treecie?* Oh, she's pretty," Maw Maw said.

"No, her name's *Mia*, Grandma," Tyrone explained.

"*Mia?* Oh, you're a pretty girl. Come give me some sugar."

Mia approached the fossil. "How you doing, ma'am? Happy birthday," she said and gave her a peck on the cheek.

"The kids are outside playing with the chickens," Tyrone said.

"Chickens?" Maw Maw looked confused. "Naw, baby, I don't eat too much chicken. Unless it's boiled. Doctor said I can't eat it fried no more."

"No, ma'am," Tyrone agreed. "Fried chicken's not good for you."

He smiled at Mia, and then they left the room so other relatives could visit their granny.

Tyrone leaned close to whisper to Mia as they walked. "If we went back in five minutes," he said, "she won't even remember us."

Mia giggled. "How old is she?" she asked.

"Today she's a hundred and one."

Mia didn't think she would have a good time in such a modest environment, but her mood grew more festive by the hour. She met Tyrone's uncles, great-uncles, aunts and great-aunts. She met first, second, and third cousins. Tyrone's mother showed up, and Mia got a chance to hug her for the first time in ten years.

Most of Tyrone's relatives lived in Overbrook Meadows, but a good number of them grew up in Cleburne and never left the town; these were the most countrified people Mia had ever met. When they spoke negatively of someone, they said he was *washed*, or *no 'count*. They wore tube socks with slacks, and a few of them had real-live Jheri curls. They slapped their knee when they laughed, and this was the heartiest laughter Mia had ever heard.

And they all said Mia and Tyrone made a *handsome* couple. They thought Mica and TC were well-behaved, intelligent kids. One of Tyrone's uncles said Mica was *as smart as a monkey*, but Mia didn't really know how to take that one.

The real excitement came when the food was served. Big women with big hands and big, strong arms laid out a spread in the kitchen that put Luby's to shame. There was ham, fried chicken, meatloaf, hotlinks, deviled eggs, macaroni with *real* cheese, biscuits, rolls, potato salad, tuna casserole, green bean casserole, spaghetti, and six different vegetables. There were strawberry cheesecakes, pecan, pumpkin, and sweet potato pies. And there was a huge white cake that measured three feet from end to end.

Tyrone fixed plates for Mica and TC, then made two more for Mia and himself. The four of them ate at a picnic table in Maw Maw's front yard. They wolfed down seconds and had dessert, too. The kids were as happy as a pig in a puddle of mud. Mia leaned back in her seat, as stuffed as a tick.

"These country folk can cook, can't they?" Tyrone asked.

"I like it here," Mica said.

"I want some more cake," TC said.

"If I lived here, I would be *so* fat," Mia said.

"All the women here are fat," Tyrone noted. "It's all good. You'd be the cutest fat girl in town."

As night fell, bottles of alcohol showed up from everywhere. The more they drank, the livelier Tyrone's relatives got, and soon the whole yard was filled with hoots and hollers. Two domino matches started, and a game of Spades kicked off on the kitchen table. Mia heard a rowdy woman call her husband a "jive ass turkey" for overbidding in their card game. She watched a snaggle-toothed bumpkin holler out, "*Three piece, dark meat!*" when he scored fifteen in the domino match.

And not to be outdone by the glamour and glitz of city life, fireflies showed up just as the stars did. TC didn't even know what they were.

"What's that?" he asked Tyrone when one lit up three feet from his nose.

"That's a lightning bug, boy. You ain't never seen one of them?"

"No."

"Want me to catch one for you?"

"You can't catch one of those," TC said.

"Boy, you got a lot to learn about the country."

Tyrone caught the first one in his bare hands, but he went inside and found a mason jar for TC to use. It took him a while, but TC finally nabbed one of his own. Mica tried, too, but the elusive insects managed to zig or zag away from her at the last minute. Mia would have let them play longer, but the fireflies weren't the only winged beasts on the prowl. Maw Maw had country-sized mosquitoes and not one drop of Off in the house. But that was okay. It was already after nine, and the kids had school tomorrow.

It took ten minutes to bid everyone a fond farewell, and when the foursome climbed back into Mia's car, everyone was a little richer from the experience. TC met relatives he never knew existed. Mica touched her first *live* chicken, and Mia spent time with a big family for the first time in almost a decade. With her parents dead and her brothers all the way in New York, there were never any hooplas like this on her side of the family.

It looked like they were going to get home an hour later than expected, but the kids fell asleep as soon as they hit the freeway, so that was okay.

"Did you have fun?" Tyrone asked when they left the city limits.

"I did," Mia said. "When we pulled up to that shack, I thought it was going to end up like the *Texas Chainsaw Massacre,* but it was nice. You have a nice family."

"I knew you'd like them. They all like you, too," he said.

"I think your uncle Ray *really* liked me," she said.

"I know," Tyrone said. "I thought he wasn't never gon' let go of your hand when he shook it."

"I'm just glad he didn't start kissing it."

"I would have hit him if he did that," Tyrone said.

Mia chuckled. "You would have hit your own uncle?"

"Shit, I would have kicked that fake leg right out from under him."

"You're crazy."

Tyrone leaned back in his seat. "So, did you enjoy our first date?" he asked.

"That was a *date?*"

"Yeah. We went somewhere special, ate a good meal. We sat outside and looked at the stars. That wasn't romantic?"

"That was *very* romantic," Mia said.

"Better than your last date?"

"Leagues better," Mia said and smiled.

They drove the rest of the way home in relative silence. Mia played R&B albums on her CD changer, and the mood was nice. When they got to her house, Mia carried Mica's sleeping body inside, and Tyrone hefted TC. Mia put her daughter in bed and took off her shoes and pants before tucking her in. When she checked on TC, she was surprised to see that Tyrone had already done the same for him.

Mia left TC's room looking for her baby's daddy, but Tyrone was nowhere in sight. She thought he left without saying good-bye, but found him in the living room, standing quietly in the darkness.

"What are you doing?" she asked him.

"Waiting on you," he said.

Mia smiled as she stepped forward to embrace him. His body was hard and rigid. She laid her head on his chest and thought his heartbeat was a little quickened.

"Yo sister here?" he asked.

"No," Mia said. She didn't know where Crystal was and didn't know why Tyrone was asking, but he made his intentions clear right away. His hands were on her butt, without permission this time, and Mia couldn't think of a better place for them to be.

They kissed in the living room. It started off softly; he pecked her top lip like before, and then the bottom one. When she kissed him back, Tyrone's grip on her ass intensified. She darted her tongue a couple of times, and he caught it and sucked it like it was candy.

Mia caressed the back of his head, and Tyrone's kisses trailed down her cheek until he was sucking the tender spot under her ear. Mia moaned softly, and Tyrone squeezed her ass tighter and pulled her hips forward. She felt his rigid member poking through his jeans, but it did not scare her. This time it caused a rivulet of moisture to dampen her own panties.

She broke the embrace. Tyrone looked panicked for a second, but her smile let him know everything was all right.

"Come on," she whispered and headed towards her bedroom.

"Quit bullshittin'," Tyrone said.

"Come on," she said again and kept walking.

Tyrone caught up with her quickly. He put a hand on each of her hips and tried to kiss the side of her neck as they walked. The move was awkward, but he could put those red lips anywhere he wanted as far as she was concerned.

When they got to her room, Mia turned to face him and they kissed again, more passionately this time. As their tongues danced, Tyrone reached down and unbuttoned her shorts. He slid them down her hips with the panties still inside and then fondled her bare bottom with increased vigor. His touch excited her so much Mia thought her moisture would begin to drip down her thigh.

She pulled his shirt out of his pants and ran her hands from his belly button up to his massive chest. Tyrone's stomach was chiseled and hard. His chest was like nothing she had ever felt. It was smooth, with no hair. There was clear definition on the bottom and down the middle. His pectorals protruded at least two inches from his torso. His nipples were soft, yet hard. Mia couldn't resist; she ducked her head under his shirt and sucked one of them, and then nibbled it a little.

Tyrone backed her towards the bed and lifted her. Mia wrapped her legs around him and seemed to float in space for a minute before he laid her on her back. Mia looked up to him, and a quiver shot down her belly. Tyrone pulled his shirt over his head and a lump caught in Mia's throat. He was like a painting, definitely a work of art. Tyrone's torso looked like a Batman costume, only that really was his chest. Every knot and bulge was *his* and oh so sexy.

He unbuckled his pants and dropped them to the floor and there it was. His penis was huge, red, and throbbing. It actually pulsated. Mia wanted to touch it. She wanted to kiss it, actually, but the sight of his full physique had her spellbound.

"Scoot back," he said. Mia was obliged to obey. She pushed back with her legs until her whole body was on the bed.

"Take off your shirt," he said, and again Mia did as she was told. Tyrone came forward, and in the split second it took her to get the camisole over her head, something unexpectedly wonderful happened. Tyrone fell between her legs, with his *face*, and began licking and sucking like he was at a pie-eating contest.

Mia wanted to stop him. She wanted to tell him that he didn't have to, that she knew how bad he wanted to be inside her and she was ready, too. But when she put her hands on his head to pull him up, Tyrone sucked a spot that made all arguments null and void. Not only did she want him to keep going, but if he stopped on his own Mia was liable to break his neck.

As the strokes of his tongue increased, Mia's hips became more and more difficult to control. She slipped to the right and left. She bounced, and wiggled, and at one point squeezed her thighs against his face so hard, he had to come up for a breath.

He stared up at her, and she stared back at him with a look that went way past *come hither*.

Tyrone kissed his way up. His tongue dashed in and out of her belly button, then traced up to her chest. Mia's breasts were small. Tyrone grabbed one in each hand and sucked her nipples one at a time.

Mia was so wet he didn't have to reach down to glide himself inside. He entered her like a hand sliding in a glove, and Mia climaxed within seconds. Tyrone did, too, but Vasantha was right about something: He had the stamina of a sixteen-year-old.

For the next few hours, they did things Mia hadn't done since they were in love some ten years ago. She got on top and grinded like a stripper on the pole. When she was spent, Tyrone rolled her over and mounted in his favorite position. But Mia didn't experience any trepidation with doggy style this time. She knew *exactly* what Tyrone was doing back there. He was holding on for dear life and jabbing like Ali in his prime.

When Mia climaxed for a stunning *fourth* time, she could no longer support her body weight on her limbs. She slid slowly until she lay flat on her stomach, but Tyrone didn't stop then like Eric had. Tyrone kept on stabbing for another twenty minutes. Mia thought he would go on forever, and it was just fine with her if he did, but eventually his movements became erratic, and she felt him pulsating inside her.

When he was spent, he rolled off and lay flat on his back. His chest rose and fell like a sprinter nearing the finish. He craned his neck towards her for a kiss, and Mia reached for him, too, but they both fell asleep before the smooch was completed.

Mia woke up at three in the morning. She went to the bathroom, then roused Tyrone and told him he had to leave.

"Why?" he asked.

"I don't want the kids to wake up and see you here."

"But I'm *tired*," he whined.

"It won't be like this all the time," she promised. "Just let me talk to them and tell them what's going on. They need to hear it from me before they see you walking around here at six in the morning."

Tyrone grudgingly complied. They shared a sensual kiss on her porch, and Mia slept like a rock when she got back into bed. When morning came, her body didn't want to get up, but her brain raced like a runaway train. She did not regret the time spent with Tyrone. On the contrary, she was excited and couldn't wait to see him again. Thug love may have led to a lot of sorrow back in the day, but last night, it was everything she needed.

CHAPTER 15

PROVERBS 26:11

Mia always tried to look her best on Mondays. Today she wore a dark chocolate suit with slacks rather than a skirt. She had on a white blouse with a chiffon, leopard-print scarf. She stood before her full-length mirror knowing she looked good, but even better, she *felt* good. The intimacy with Tyrone last night left her radiant and invigorated, even though she only got a few hours sleep.

She went to the dining room to see how breakfast was going. Once again, TC's plate was half empty, while Mica's fork was still sparkling clean.

"What's wrong?" she asked the grumbling grade-schooler.

"I don't like eggs," Mica said.

"Yes, you do," Mia said. "You eat eggs all the time."

"These are nasty."

Mia leaned over to get a look at her plate, but it looked like Crystal did a good job. The scrambled eggs were light and fluffy.

"I'll eat hers," TC offered.

Mia shook her head. "No, she's gonna eat it. And you'd better be halfway through by the time I get back." She gave Mica a hard look, then went to check on her sister.

Crystal's door was closed. Mia walked in and flipped the light switch. Crystal rolled onto her stomach and buried her face in the pillow.

"What'd you do, get back in bed?" Mia asked. "Where were you last night?"

Crystal rolled over groggily. She held a hand over her eyes and squinted through her fingers. "I was with Sydney."

"What time did you get home?"

"I don't know. I know Tyrone's car was still here." Crystal grinned. "I thought you wasn't giving him none."

Mia couldn't help but smile. "I thought I wasn't either."

"Was it *good*?" Crystal asked. "Did he really wait for you?"

Mia didn't have to answer; the glow on her face told the whole story. "I think it was the best ever," she said.

Crystal's eyes lit up. "*Ever*?"

Mia scanned her memory bank, but nothing she experienced in the last decade compared. "Yeah, I think it was . . ."

Crystal shook her head in awe. "That boy loves you more than anything," she said. "You lucky."

Mia considered that for a second and agreed that she was. When she got back to the dining room, Mica surprised her with a half-eaten plate. She looked up at her mom and smiled.

"I like the country, Mama," TC said.

"I do, too, baby."

Mia's day at work was hectic. When Miss Tenery stepped into her office a few minutes before lunchtime and said Mr. Manitou wanted to speak with her, Mia thought she heard the woman wrong.

"*Mr. Manitou?*"

"Yes, ma'am."

Mia looked first to her phone and then back to her secretary's skinny face.

"No, he's *here*," Miss Tenery said. "He didn't say what he wants."

Mia asked the woman to show him in.

She fixed a look of unease on her visitor when he walked into her office. Mr. Manitou wore a blue suit with a black tie today. Mia was disturbed by his visit, and her expression showed it.

"May I close your door?" he asked.

Mia nodded. When he sat down, she asked him, "To what do I owe this pleasure?"

Mr. Manitou took a deep breath and stared into her eyes. "Mia, I would like to talk to you about what happened at the restaurant on Friday."

Mia shook her head. "Mr. Manitou, I don't think—"

He put a hand up. "No, Mia. Please. Let me say what I have to say."

She rolled her eyes and shrugged.

Mr. Manitou clasped his hands together and held them under his chin as if praying.

"Mia, I would like to apologize for what I said to you at the restaurant. I was totally out of line. My words were inexcusable, and for that I am deeply sorry."

Mia didn't say anything.

"I was speaking with some of my American friends," he went on, "and they tell me your situation is not so uncommon in the States. It was *shocking* to me, I cannot lie, but I believe there were cultural differences that led to our misunderstanding. My friends tell me I should not condemn you for what happened so long ago. I am willing to give it another try if you will accept my apology."

Mia couldn't believe what she was hearing. "What?"

"If you will forgive me," he repeated, "I would still like to see you on a romantic level."

Mia shook her head. "I don't think that would be a good idea. You hurt me, Mr. Manitou."

His expression was even more forlorn. "Mia, I am sorry. What I did was totally out of line. You have every right to curse me like a dog, but my apology is sincere." He reached into his breast pocket and came out with a long jewelry box. "Here. I have brought a peace offering."

Mia was hesitant.

"Here. Take it, please."

She took the box and was very surprised by what was inside. He gave her a beautiful pearl necklace. It was exquisite, and Mia didn't have to rub them together to know they were real.

"Mr. Manitou, I can't—"

He put a finger to his lips. "No, Mia. Don't say that. Every man will be an asshole sooner or later. I got my ignorance out of the way early, so there's nothing but good times for us from now on."

He was so hopeful, and cute. Mia smiled. "Okay, Babatunde. I accept your apology."

"Really?" His face lit up. He wiped his brow comically. "Honestly, I did not think you would forgive me. This is great. We should go out again. Are you free tonight?"

"Slow down," Mia said with a giggle. "How about I call you and we go from there."

"That is fine," Mr. Manitou said. "I cannot wait to hear from you." He gave her one last grin and turned to leave the office.

Mia stared at her pearl necklace for a long time after he was gone. He was right: a lot of guys were assholes, but very few made up for it with expensive jewelry. If this was how Mr. Manitou courted his women, she didn't mind. She didn't mind at all.

Miss Tenery stepped in again at noon and asked if she wanted to share a pizza, but Mia told her she was stepping out of the office today.

As a manager, Mia was allowed an hour and a half lunch break, but she rarely took advantage. Usually, she ate at her desk or grabbed a Snickers and soda, but today was a beautiful day.

Mia took the elevators down with no briefcase in hand for the first time in recent memory. She walked through the front doors of the Prospect building, and the sun felt good on her skin. She had pep in her step and a smile on her face as she navigated the streets of downtown Overbrook Meadows. She couldn't remember the last time she actually walked downtown, but there was a Cajun restaurant just a few blocks away. An African guy once told her she should eat whatever she wanted whenever she wanted to.

Across the street from the restaurant, Mia spotted a Zales jewelry store. It reminded her of Mr. Manitou's gift, and that made her think of Tyrone. She thought about his silver necklace and decided to replace it with a gold one. She knew it might be telling to buy him a gift immediately after good sex, but if she was going to fall in love with him, she'd do it however she wanted. She would buy him a gift if she chose to, and she certainly had the means to do so.

Mia walked into the jewelry store and told the salesman she wanted a gold necklace for a certain gentleman. The associate took in her appearance and steered her to a group of beautiful chains ranging from $2,500 to $6,000.

Mia told him, "I don't like him that much."

"Ah, come on. Nothing says love like a big price tag," the guy said.

"And no one loses their commission faster than a pushy salesman," Mia countered.

The jeweler relented, and they settled on a fourteen-karat Figaro necklace for $400. Mia carried her gift in a small bag and wore a big smile when she left the store.

There was something about Tyrone. Ten years ago he had her feeling the same way. He only wanted to please her, and Mia felt guilty for making him jump through so many hoops. She gave him her body, but still felt like she owed him something. The sex might have been fleeting, but the necklace would let him know he was her man now.

At Razzoos Cajun café, Mia had crawfish etouffee and rat toes (stuffed jalapeños). Mr. Manitou was an odd man, but he did know how to enjoy life. Eating by herself did not take away from her mood or the meal. Everything was just fine.

Mia didn't get out of the office until 6:42 p.m.

After such a long day, she ached to be home with her family, but decided to drop off Tyrone's present on the way home. She wanted to see him again. She wanted to see his eyes light up when she gave him the necklace. She wanted to kiss him and feel his arms around her.

She got to his house at a quarter after seven, but Tyrone wasn't home. His mother answered the door.

"Mia! How you doing, baby?"

"I'm fine," Mia said.

"You sho' look sharp in your little suit," the woman said.

Mia smiled. "Thank you, Mrs. Story. Is Tyrone here?"

"Naw, baby. I haven't seen him since three. He's probably around here somewhere. Did you check over at Byron's house?"

"Uh, I don't know who Byron is."

"That's one of his friends since before he got locked up. I thought you might know him."

Mia shook her head.

"Well, why don't you check over there by Sycamore Park," the woman suggested. "He be over there sometime."

Mia wasn't going to search the whole city, but Sycamore Community Center was on the way home, so she decided to ride by and check. It only took her three minutes to get there. The park was big, full of pecan trees. It was also crowded, but Tyrone was the only light-skinned brother there. He stood out like a sore thumb.

Mia expected him to be playing basketball. She thought he might go to the park to run around the track. There were weights inside the center. Maybe he went in there to maintain his physique. But that wasn't it.

When Mia spotted Tyrone, he was standing under a cluster of trees. If she didn't know any better, Mia would swear he was selling drugs.

She parked next to the curb some twenty-five feet away and watched him for a full five minutes. Tyrone wore blue Dickey pants and a black tee shirt. His pants hung off his ass and a toothpick poked out of his mouth. He had two guys with him who looked like they were selling drugs, too. They may not have been, but if they weren't, they certain got their clothes from Dope Boys R Us.

One of Tyrone's friends was short and stocky. He wore Dickies that had been cut off to make long shorts. His pants sagged too, showing off the better half of his boxer shorts. He had no shirt on. The other guy was tall and slinky. He had on a wife-beater and baggy jeans. He had a huge belt buckle, but his pants were still falling down. The trio showed off more underwear than a Victoria's Secret catalogue.

Mia's fingers grew white around the steering wheel as she watched them. Her breath was hot. What she saw was obvious, but she tried to stick up for him. No one had dope in their hands, and no transactions had been made while she was there. Maybe they were just kicking it. Maybe the other two guys *were* drug dealers, but Tyrone just stopped by to say hi.

All those maybes fell through when a junkie approached the group.

But wait.

Mia stopped herself from making rash judgments. Maybe the homeless-looking guy wasn't a dope fiend. Maybe those soiled Levi's weren't the only pants he owned. Maybe he just got off work. Maybe he ripped his T-shirt on the job.

But all of those maybes fell threw when the dope fiend walked up to Tyrone. Not the short one or the scarecrow; the junkie walked right up to *Tyrone*. They had a short conversation, and then the junkie reached into his pocket and produced a handful of crumpled bills.

Mia almost left right then, but she had to know for sure. She had to see it for herself.

Tyrone reached into his pocket.

Mia's heart stopped.

But Tyrone didn't come out with a handful of rocks. He looked around first, for the police probably, and that's when he saw Mia's car parked on the curb. His face registered immediate shock. He brought his hand out of his pocket quickly, and it was empty. The dope fiend looked first to Tyrone's empty hand, and then he followed Tyrone's gaze to Mia's car.

Tyrone fixed his face quickly. He walked to Mia with a fresh smile. The dope fiend tried to follow, but Tyrone turned and said something to make him stay there. By the time Tyrone leaned into Mia's passenger window, she was already crying.

"Hey, uh, what you doing here?"

"I came to bring you that," she said, and shot a thumb at the gift box on her passenger seat. But Tyrone didn't take his eyes off her. His smile slipped, then went away entirely.

"What's wrong?" he asked. A bold, purple hickey stood out on his neck, and Mia hated herself for putting it there.

She took a deep breath and let it out through her nose. "That guy's waiting for you," she said.

Tyrone looked back to the zombie, then faced Mia again. "He's not waiting on me."

"Oh, he's not?" Mia said. "'Cause I was sitting here watching when he walked up, and it looked like you were about to deal drugs. He was about to give you some money. Don't you want it?"

Tyrone didn't look back again. His face washed over with grief and he forced an awkward smile. "He wasn't finna give me no money, Mia. Wh—why you crying?"

"Oh, he wasn't?" Mia leaned forward in her seat until she could see past Tyrone. "Hey!" she yelled at the bum. "He's ready now!"

The addict's face lit up and he started jogging to her car.

Tyrone turned to face him. "Get the hell away from here!"

The junkie stopped in his tracks with a stupid look on his face. He held out his money. "I—I got eight, man. I'ma get you the other two. I told you."

"Get the hell away from me!" Tyrone barked.

The fiend wavered for a second, then one of Tyrone's buddies hollered out to him.

"Say, school, I got you over here." It was the short one with no shirt. The customer turned and staggered off in that direction.

Tyrone turned back to Mia, his face angry and pained. "It's not what you think," he said.

"I think you're a liar," Mia spat.

"Mia—"

"I think I'm *stupid*. How the hell did I let you do that to me again?"

"Wait—"

"I think you're going back to the pen just like I knew you would. I think you played with my head and played with TC's head and you never gave a damn about us!"

"That's not true, Mia. I love you. I love *all* y'all. You know that."

"That's why you selling drugs—trying to leave us again, huh?"

"I'm not—"

"*Stop lying!*"

Tyrone sighed. His whole body seemed to deflate. He was on the verge of tears himself, but he admitted nothing.

"Take the box," Mia said, but Tyrone wouldn't even look at it.

"I don't want it. Can we go somewhere and talk?"

"I don't want to talk to you. Just take the present my *stupid ass* bought you so I can go." The tears streamed down her face now.

"Mia—"

"*Take it or I'm throwing it out on the freeway!*"

"Mia, we—"

"Shut up!" She snatched up the box herself and threw it at Tyrone's chest. It impacted and fell to the ground between him and the Lexus. He tried to open her passenger door, but found it locked. Mia sped away before he could reach inside to push the lever.

In her rearview mirror, she watched Tyrone walk to the middle of the street and look after her. Mia sped up, not caring about the speed limit. The harder she stomped on the gas pedal, the further away she got from his sorry ass. She never saw whether he picked up the necklace or not.

CHAPTER 16
BAD TO WORSE

Mia pulled into her driveway and parked next to Crystal's Tahoe. Her boyfriend Sydney had his sanded Cutlass parked on the street. Mia didn't like the idea of him there at seven-thirty, but at least he had enough sense not to be in her driveway.

Mia sat in her car and cleaned herself up for a few minutes before going inside. If Mica saw her crying again, the girl would think her mother was an emotional train wreck.

Tyrone had already called. Mia didn't answer it on the highway, but he left something on her voice mail. She listened to it now. It was short:

"Mia, give me a call. I know how you is. Don't start trippin'."

Mia erased the message before checking her features one last time in the rearview mirror. Crystal would probably know she'd been crying, but the kids weren't so perceptive.

She went inside, and things quickly went from bad to worse.

From the living room, Mia could hear TC and Mica arguing in her daughter's room. Crystal's room was closer, so Mia went there first.

Crystal's door was closed. Mia didn't like that at all, but she remained calm. She knocked with two knuckles rather than pound with her fist.

"Crystal! You in there?"

"Huh?" Mia heard her sister call from inside.

"What are you doing?" she asked, but Mica started screaming at the same time: "*Stop hittin me!*"

Mia left Crystal's doorway and marched to her daughter's room. She was halfway down the hallway before it occurred to her that Crystal was in her bedroom with her boyfriend *and* the door was *locked*! But if TC put his hands on Mica, that came first. Mia stormed into her daughter's room and found them arguing over the video game. TC had his own controller, but was trying to wrench Mica's from her hands.

"*What are you doing?*"

TC jumped at the sound of his mother's voice, and then immediately pleaded his case.

"Mama, she won't go into that *cave*! We been on this part for *thirty minutes*. I keep trying to do it for her, but she won't let me and she doesn't know how to do it herself!" His face was a mask of frustration.

"You're arguing over a *video game*?" Mia couldn't stand these asinine spats.

"It's *her* fault!" TC wailed. "We would have been done if—"

"Did you hit her?"

TC's face registered confusion as he pondered whether he should lie or not.

"No," he said cautiously.

"*Yes you did!*" Mica shouted. "He *did* hit me!"

"*She wouldn't give me the controller!*"

"Get up!" Mia said, but TC didn't move quickly enough. She closed the distance between them and grabbed his arm roughly. "What did I tell you about hitting your sister?"

TC wailed and threw his hands to his backside to ward off the blow he knew was coming.

"Go to your room," Mia shouted, steering him in that direction. "And don't come out!"

TC let his guard down as he raced past her. Mia grabbed him again and delivered two open-handed smacks before he could react. He stumbled, then fell, but was up quickly. He ran down the hallway screaming, holding his burning buttocks.

Mia looked down at her daughter, who was probably not as innocent as she appeared to be. "Stay in your room," she told her.

"But Mama, I didn't d—"

"Talk back to me again!" Mia dared her, but Mica wanted no part.

Mia made it back into the hallway just in time to see Crystal's boyfriend coming out of her room. The idiot was still buckling his pants. Mia stomped up to him with her tiny fists balled.

"What the hell are you doing in my house?" They faced off like a ball player and an umpire. Sydney was taller and had a good fifty pounds on her, but he took a step back.

"I—I was jus—"

Mia stepped past him, shoving a little on the way by. Crystal sat on her bed wearing jogging pants and a tee shirt, but there was a pair of jeans on the floor. Crystal's makeup was a little messed up, her hair slightly unkempt.

Mia wore a look of supreme confusion. "Are you serious?"

"We was just—"

The voice came from behind her. Mia spun to face him, revolted the idiot was still there.

"What are you doing? Get out of my house!"

Sydney hesitated. He tried to look over Mia's shoulder, as if Crystal had a say in things.

Mia's look now was incredulous. She moved her face to block Sydney's gaze.

"What are you looking for?" she asked. "I said get out of my house!"

Sydney reluctantly complied. Mia followed him out, quick on his heels. The boy was moving so slowly that she wanted to shove him in the back a few times. She locked the door after him, then charged back into Crystal's room. She closed the door behind herself, slamming it so hard the whole house shook.

Crystal was still on her bed. Mia stood over her and ground her teeth. Mia's hand was over her mouth, her face twisted in pain and confusion.

"Are you serious?" she asked again. "You're really doing this guy with my kids at home?"

Crystal lowered her head. She twirled the sheets with her finger.

This was literally the dumbest thing Mia had seen in a good five years, and that included Mica and TC's antics. It was mind-blowing. It was finding out Santa wasn't real, Mama was the Tooth Fairy, and that cute little bunny was really just stealing Easter from Jesus all at the same time.

Mia knew her sister would never study nuclear physics, but this level of stupidity was inexcusable, well past Crystal's known level of ignorance.

"Do you have absolutely *no* control over your hormones?" Mia asked her.

"It just happened," Crystal said softly.

"*Rain* just happens, Crystal! *Getting naked* takes active participation. Why did you have him in your room in the first place?"

"We was just looking at something on the computer, then—".

"You were supposed to be watching the kids!"

"I *was* watching them."

"They were in there arguing!" Mia pointed a finger in her sister's face. "I don't want to see that boy over here *no more.*"

"But I don't never have no time to see him," Crystal whined.

"Don't even start with that."

"You're always working late. I pick the kids up and keep 'em all day. It's almost eight o'clock and you're *just* now getting home. When am I supposed to have *my* life?"

"That's the last time you're going to throw that in my face," Mia said. "I already told you I can get a nanny to do *everything* you're doing. I don't *need* you to pick up the kids! I don't *need* you to bring them home, and I definitely don't need you to be in here *having sex* while my children are home. I bet you nobody I hire will be doing that!"

"I—I don't mind picking the kids up," Crystal pouted.

"Yeah, you don't mind living in my house for free, either. I think it's about time you got on with whatever *life* you've got planned, Crystal."

"Don't start saying that."

"I don't want these dumb-ass niggas in my house! I don't want them around my kids. You ain't got sense enough to keep your damned pants on for a couple of hours . . ." Mia crossed her arms and flared her nostrils.

Crystal looked up with the best puppy dog eyes she could muster. "I'm sorry. I won't do it no more."

"I don't want him in my house," Mia said again. "*Ever.*"

Crystal looked crushed, but she didn't respond.

"Did you hear me?"

"Yeah."

"You let me down," Mia said. "You know that? I took you in, treated you good, bought you a car. You repay me like this?"

Crystal was crying now. "Why you saying that? I said I was sorry. It was just, I didn't mean to do it. I didn't mean to hurt you."

Mia caught herself. Maybe she was going overboard. Every child had sex at their parent's house at least once, didn't they? Crystal was twenty-one, but she was still a kid at heart.

Mia sighed. "I, okay, something happened today. What you did, it's bad, but I guess I shouldn't make it sound like you *betrayed* me. I was already upset when I got home."

Crystal smiled.

Mia rolled her eyes and let the anger go, but the pain still stayed. "The kids were fighting when I came in."

"They was playing video games," Crystal said. "I thought I, we was just gonna kiss for a couple of minutes."

Mia shook her head. "That's crazy, Crystal. You can't control yourself any better than that?"

Crystal leaned forward and grabbed her sister's hand. "I'm sorry."

Mia raised an eyebrow. "You are pretty *sorry*," she agreed, then turned to leave.

"What happened today?" Crystal asked.

Mia stopped, her heart once again breaking with just the memory. "I don't want to talk about it," she said, and left to see if TC was still crying.

TC was not mortally wounded, though you'd never know it by looking at him. He lay on his stomach moaning, his shoulders hitching. It was always the shock of being hit by his mother that shook him up more than anything else. Mia sat on his bed and watched him for a while.

"You okay?"

"You . . . you . . . hit . . . me."

"Stop crying. It didn't even hurt."

"Yes . . . yes it did."

Mia put a hand on his back. "I told you not to hit your sister."

He didn't have a response for that.

"A boy is never supposed to hit a girl," Mia chastised. "Remember?"

"Ye—yes."

"Did you finish your homework?"

TC nodded.

"Let me see it."

He got up to retrieve his lessons, and Mia looked over them. She found four mistakes, and set him up at his desk so he could correct them.

Mia went to check on her daughter and found that Mica was still upset, too, but only because she didn't have anyone to play *Shrek* with.

Mia finally got a chance to take a bath at eight-thirty. Tyrone hadn't left any more messages on her cell phone, and he didn't call the house phone either. That was good, but it only reminded Mia of him even more. She couldn't believe she trusted him. He gave up $400 in one day. She was blind not to see the signs.

After her bath, Mia dressed in shorts and a T-shirt. She herded the kids to the living room and they played a board game before bed. They knew she was upset with Aunt Crystal, but neither knew why. They didn't ask any questions, and Mia didn't volunteer the information.

When she tucked them in that night, Mica made a vow to play the video games fairly and let her big brother help if she got stuck on a difficult part. TC promised to never hit his sister again. Mia promised to get right on his butt again if he did.

Mia went to talk to her sister after that. Crystal was again apologetic for the incident with Sydney, but Mia didn't feel like arguing anymore. She had a story to tell, and Crystal was always a good listener.

"I can't believe I've had so much bad luck with these men," she said. "I'm glad I went over there, though. I almost came straight home."

The two sat on Crystal's bed. Mia looked heartsick and weary. Wore down.

"You would have found out sooner or later," Crystal reckoned. "He wouldn't have been able to hide that."

"What's done in the dark always comes to light," Mia agreed.

"Have you talked to him?"

"No. Why? What's he going to say? I saw it with my own eyes."

"So you not gon' be with him no more?"

"Of course not."

"Why not?"

"What do you mean, *why not*? I don't want that mess around my children. He's no good. I knew he was full of shit."

"You give up on people too quick," Crystal noted.

"I *give up* on people? What am I supposed to do, accept it? I can get another man if I want. I don't have to settle."

"I'm not saying you should settle, but it seems like if anything goes wrong, you through. You did that with *all* of them."

"All of *who*?"

"You said Eric was like, the *perfect* man, but you broke up with him anyway."

"His girlfriend threw a br—"

"I know. I was here. But you didn't try to work it out with him. Maybe y'all could have done something."

"Like what?"

"I don't know. *Something*. You didn't even talk to any different police. You just took those guys' word for it and dropped it. You broke up with Eric, and he didn't even do nothing wrong."

"This has something to do with Tyrone?"

"You kinda doing the same thing to him. If you want him to stop selling drugs, why don't you just tell him? How do you know he won't stop if you tell him to?"

That actually made a little sense. Crystal was right; Mia never even considered talking to Tyrone about it. "Why should I have to tell him to stop doing something that's gonna send him to the penitentiary? If he's not smart enough to know how stupid that is, why should I bother?"

"You can't judge people. Everybody selling drugs isn't stupid. You don't know their circumstances. What they grew up in."

"Why are you defending Tyrone so much?"

"I like Tyrone."

"Why?"

"The same reasons you like him, Mia. You know he's trying to do right."

"I need to talk to someone else. You like *thugs*. This is what you're expected to say."

"I'm not defending *thugs*. I'm talking about the way you do people. One thing wrong, and they're gone. You did the same to that guy from work."

Mia wasn't having that at all. "What? I told you what he said to me."

"But you said he tried to apologize. You kicked him out of your office. He do *one thing* wrong, and you're through with him. Just like Eric, and now with Tyrone. I think you give up on people. You want it all *picture perfect*. Sometimes you have to go through some shit to get what you want."

Mia shook her head. "Tyrone must have gave you some money. Tell the truth. I *know* you're not preaching that *hard work and perseverance* stuff to m—" Mia sneezed into her hands.

"Ewww!" Crystal said.

Mia looked around her sister's room, her hand still over her face. "Where's your Kleenex?"

Crystal looked around, too. "I don't have any."

Mia got up and went into her sister's bathroom. She pulled toilet paper from the roll next to the toilet. Crystal was not a great housekeeper, but she kept her bathroom fairly clean. If not for that, and the fact that the tiles in there were white, Mia might not have seen the small brown capsule on the floor next to the toilet.

She picked it up. It wasn't a brown capsule. It was a clear capsule with brown powder inside, about the size of an allergy pill. It would have meant nothing to Mia if not for the fact that Mica's father had a fondness for those little pills.

Mia blew her nose and stepped out with the dope in hand. She felt like someone had punched her in the stomach.

"I think your boyfriend dropped this boy pill in there," she said nonchalantly.

Crystal didn't know how to respond. She looked baffled for a moment, then came up with, "What are you talking about?"

Mia held the capsule between her thumb and first finger. She walked up to her sister and held it close to her face. "*This*. This right here. This is a ten-dollar pill of *heroin*. In *my house*. The same house where my babies are."

Mia hoped this would be as big a shock to her sister, but Crystal's face gave her away.

"You *knew*?" Mia asked.

"He don't never do it here," Crystal said.

Mia's eyes grew wide. "Crystal, what the hell are you doing? You're going with a dope fiend?"

"He not a dope fiend."

"What the hell do you call this?" Mia wiggled the dope before her nose.

Crystal was close to panic. "I'm sorry. I didn't know he left that. It must have fell out his pocket, Mia. *I swear.* He don't never do it here."

"But Crystal, you don't even seemed worried about him doing it. Do y'all think this is a *recreation* drug or what? This is heroin, just as bad as *crack*."

"A lot of people do it," Crystal said. "Those rappers, at the studio. All of them do it. It's not that bad."

Mia couldn't believe what she was hearing. A horrible thought struck her. "Are *you* doing it, too?"

When Crystal didn't answer right away, Mia almost passed out. "Oh, my God, I don't even know you."

"I just did it a couple of times," Crystal admitted.

"Crystal, why the hell would you do heroin *at all?* You might as well put a gun to your head. *Oh, my God.*" Mia rubbed her temples. "I got a dopehead watching my babies."

"How can you call me that?"

"I can't even believe this."

"Mia, I only did it twice."

"You're *crazy.* Is this, did he leave this for you?"

"No. I didn't even know it was in there."

"Well, do you want it?" Mia held the pill out to her. "Here. You wanna get high *now?*"

"Mia, stop."

"Take it."

"I don't want it."

"Then flush it down the toilet."

Crystal was flustered. "Why don't you do it?"

"It's *your* dope. If you don't want it, flush it."

Crystal stared at her for a second, and then took the pill and did as she was told. Mia was standing in the center of the room waiting on her when she got back.

"Do you need to go to rehab?"

"Mia, I'm not on drugs."

"I'll put you in rehab. You can get some help before this gets worse."

Crystal smiled. "Mia, *I'm not on drugs*. I swear."

"You plan on breaking up with Sydney, or are you still gonna see him behind my back."

"I'll break up with him if you want me to," Crystal said.

"What do you want to do? You want to stay with him?"

"No."

"Crystal, I don't know what to think about you." Mia stared at the girl as if she were a stranger. "You did *two* stupid-ass things back-to-back in the *same day*. Your decision making is flawed, and I don't know if I can trust you around my kids anymore."

Crystal looked like she'd been shot. "Mia, how can you say that?"

"I'm serious. I don't want some dope fiend driving my kids around."

"I'm not a *dope fiend*. You know I'm not a dope fiend."

"Maybe you're in denial. I think you need to go to rehab."

"You don't go to rehab for using a drug *twice*. Didn't you do some drugs when you was growing up? I know you smoked weed."

"Weed was *all* I did, Crystal. You wanna get high, fine. Why can't you get a pothead boyfriend like regular people?"

"I don't want to get high."

"You're a liar."

"Mia, please don't start treating me like that." Crystal's face washed over with anguish. A lone tear snaked down her cheek.

"Do you plan on seeing that boy again?" Mia asked.

"No."

"If I ever see him in my house again, I'm kicking you out with him."

"Okay."

"I mean it, Crystal."

"Okay, Mia. I promise."

Mia left her sister's room with no answers and millions more questions. Her mind was racing, but her mental fatigue was surpassed by her physical exhaustion. She drifted away as soon as her head hit the pillow, and she slept heavily, glad this crazy-ass day was over.

CHAPTER 17
SOUND REASONING

Mia went to work on Tuesday a little skeptical about Crystal and her boyfriend, but she felt powerless. If Crystal really wanted to see the boy, she would do so no matter how Mia felt. All Mia could do was give good advice, but there was a problem with that, too. No matter how sound her arguments were, it was still just big sister advice. Mia knew Crystal wouldn't take things seriously until she bumped her head a few times.

Finding heroin in her own home was something Mia wouldn't have expected in a million years. That Crystal would willingly snort that crap up her nose was almost unimaginable, but the world was changing. People looked at snorting and shooting as two different things nowadays. And it wasn't just heroin: If you used a needle to get your cocaine fix, you were a junkie. But the rich guy at the club snorting cocaine off his fingernail had it going on.

When Mica's father used heroin, Mia remembered it was almost a *cool* thing at the time. He always had money and was a clean and snazzy dresser. He used the drug every day, but no one, not even Mia, considered him a dope fiend.

The fact that Crystal was in love with a rapper made it worse. Within the hip-hop community, there was a subculture of thugs who did hard drugs on a regular basis. They popped pills, snorted white and brown, and sipped on promethazine mixed with cough syrup, calling it syrup.

Mia knew of these things, but she never thought this level of ignorance would come anywhere near her family. She kept them safe in a fairy-tale bubble of protection, but Crystal and her boyfriend popped that bubble. Mia hoped her sister was smart enough to let the boy go, but was it *only* Sydney she had to resist? Mia thought she'd notice it if her sister had sustained cravings, but how can you really know for sure?

When not thinking about Crystal, Mia spent a lot of time with Tyrone on her mind. She expected repeated calls from him throughout the day, but Tyrone did not call at all on Tuesday. He didn't call Wednesday or Thursday, either. He usually saw the kids every weekend, so when Friday came Mia knew she would probably hear from the drug-pedaling ex-con. And he did not disappoint. Tyrone called during her lunch hour, but Mia didn't return the call until the drive home.

"Hello?"

"Tyrone, this is Mia."

"Hey. I thought you weren't gonna call back."

"What do you want?"

"You still mad at me?"

"Tyrone, I don't even want to talk about that. If you want to go to prison, that's your deal."

"I don't want to go to prison."

"Hate to break it to ya, but that's where you're headed."

"What about us?"

"There is no '*us*', Tyrone. You're a liar."

"I'm not a liar, Mia. I'm sorry you saw what you saw, but that don't mean we have to be through. I still want to be with you."

"Tyrone, I manage the securities and loans for an investment firm. You sell crack. What the hell makes you think we should be together?"

"I love you, and I know you love me."

"Well, love *does not* conquer all. I know that sounds good, but it's not true. It's bullshit."

"So you sayin' we can't work it out?"

"Tyrone, I don't even want to talk about it. If that's what you called for, I gotta go."

"I wanna see the kids this weekend," he said. "That's why I called. Is that all right, or I can't see them either?"

"Mica's not your daughter."

"I know, but I want to see her, too. You already know how I feel about that."

As much as she hated him right now, hearing that still made Mia's heart light in her chest. "Where do you want to take them?"

"To Putt Putt. They got a lot of video games there, some go-carts. I never played golf, but we can do that too if they want to."

"When are you talking about?"

"Tomorrow or Sunday. Are you gonna come, too?"

"Tomorrow's fine," Mia said.

"Are you gonna come?"

Up until the moment she saw him selling crack, Mia was actually okay with Tyrone having the kids by himself. "Yeah, I'll go," she said.

"Are we gonna talk, or are you gonna roll your eyes at me all day?"

"What difference does it make?"

"I wanna talk."

"All right, fine. We'll talk," Mia said.

"What time should I be there?"

She told him to come at three and disconnected.

On Saturday morning, Mia went to Claire's to get her hair trimmed. Mama Ernestine was there today. She wore a white blouse with beige pants and a wig she called the Condoleezza. Nancy was there, too, so Mia finally got her much-needed manicure. Everyone thought it was tragic she had to break up with Eric, but Mia had a new love story to tell that was just as juicy and twice as titillating.

Vasantha stood awestruck with her mouth ajar and Mia's hair in hand. She couldn't believe her classy client finally took her advice and gave it up to a thug.

"When he grabbed my booty, I knew it was all over," Mia said.

"Did he grab it with both hands?" Vasantha asked.

"He *always* grabs it with both hands." Mia grinned.

"They *gotta* grab mine with both hands," Gayle said, and the ladies laughed.

"*Sooo*, what happened?" Vasantha asked. She wore denim Capris with a plaid blouse today.

Mia smiled. "Well, I took him back to my room, and . . ." She paused, wondering how much to divulge.

"And what, girl?" Gayle was almost bouncing with anticipation.

"He, um . . ." Just thinking about Tyrone's head between her legs made Mia very excited. A bit of perspiration dotted her forehead.

Vasantha thumped her ear.

"Ouch!"

"Tell us!"

"Did you *thump* me?"

"Aw, shut up and spill it, Mia." Gayle was supposed to be gluing tracks for a loud-mouthed girl named Natiesha, but no tracks had been laid since Mia started talking. Natiesha didn't notice. Everyone stared at Mia, waiting to hear what they already knew: *Thug niggas know how to lay it down.*

"Well, when we got to my room, he took my shorts off," Mia continued. "Then he laid me down on the bed and stood over me. He took his shirt off and I think I passed out for a second."

"What his chest look like?" Gayle asked.

Mia threw her head back. "*Oh, God.* I can't even describe it. With no oils or anything, it was, it was stacked. He's built like Roy Jones Jr., only bigger."

Gayle closed her eyes and smiled.

"Oh, *wow*," Vasantha said.

"You're pulling my hair," Mia told her.

"Sorry."

"So, what happened?" Gayle wanted to know.

"What do you want? A play by play?"

About four women said "Yes!" in unison.

Mia grinned. "Well, he told me to take my shirt off, and I did, and he started doing something I *never expected* from Tyrone."

"What?" Vasantha asked, but Gayle's smile was wicked, like she already knew.

Mia looked up to Mama Ernestine at the register and felt a little embarrassed, although the old woman was just as enthralled as everyone else. "I can't say," Mia said.

Vasantha thumped her ear again. "You better tell us!"

"Girl, you better stop thump—"

"Did he *lick* you?" Gayle asked.

The whole room grew quiet.

Mia took a deep breath and blushed. Her eyes twinkled. She put a hand over her mouth and the salon erupted in laughter and cat calls.

"Was he good?" Vasantha asked when things died down.

"Oh, he was good," Mia mused. "He was like a little dog down there. You know, like if you give a puppy your plate after dinner."

"My God," Gayle said.

"Then he came up and made love to me like he'd been waiting his *whole life*."

"*Aww*," Gayle said. "That's sweet."

"So, was he telling the truth about waiting for you?" Vasantha asked.

"Well, you know how I am," Mia said. "I didn't believe *anything* Tyrone had to say, especially about *that*. But when he laid me down it was like *ecstasy*. He was still going strong thee hours later . . ."

"*Three hours?*" Gayle repeated.

"Yes, *three full hours*," Mia confirmed.

Vasantha shook her head. "That's *beautiful*, girl. It's like a fairy-tale love story: Big, *evil* guy gets out of prison. He falls in love with little, innocent you. And somehow you guys work it out and live happily every after."

"Oh, I haven't told about the *happily ever after* part yet," Mia said. "The next day I go to work all happy and invigorated—"

"Walking pigeon-toed," Gayle said.

"Nose wide-open!" Natiesha offered.

"Yeah, yeah," Mia said. "So, I go out for lunch and there's this jewelry store across the street. I'm still thinking about Tyrone, so I popped in for a second—"

"Don't tell me you bought him something," Gayle said.

"It was just a necklace."

"Uhn, uhn. You ain't never supposed to buy them a gift after good sex," Gayle advised. "They'll think they got you sprung."

"It's okay to buy him something," Vasantha said.

"I do that sometimes," Natiesha said.

"Anyway," Mia went on. "I take him the necklace after work, and you won't believe what I catch this Negro doing."

"He was cheating on you!" Vasantha guessed. "I knew it!"

"You just said we lived happily ever after," Mia reminded.

Gayle looked shocked. "Girl, *was* he cheating on you?"

"No," Mia said. "*Worse*. I catch his dumb ass *on the cut selling dope.*"

"Oh my God," Gayle said.

"What'd you do?" Vasantha asked.

"I threw the necklace at him and drove off," Mia said. "I was so pissed I couldn't see straight."

"Damn, you be havin' some serious man problems," Natiesha noticed.

"Don't I know it."

"What'd you tell him?" Vasantha asked.

"I didn't tell him anything. He tried to call, but I didn't answer. I finally talked to him yesterday. He says he wants to see the kids. I told him he could, but nothing was going on with him and me."

"You broke up with him?" Vasantha couldn't believe it.

Mia couldn't believe she was so shocked. "What'd you expect me to do?"

"I don't know," the Latina said. "But you break up with *everybody.*"

"You're starting to sound like my sister."

"I agree with Vasantha," Gayle said, and that, too, was a shock. "You keep breaking up with these men every time something happens. If they're making you so happy, how come you don't ever try to work it out?"

"Um, he was *selling drugs*," Mia said.

"You right," Natiesha said. "You make too much money to be with some *hood nigga*. What's gonna happen when you have an office party? Tyrone gon' go up there with his Dickies and house shoes on?"

"Thank you," Mia said.

"I don't know," Vasantha said. "If he loves you and your son, and he makes you happy, I think you should try to work it out. He's probably just doing it 'cause he needs the money. You keep looking for this *perfect* man with nothing at all wrong with him."

"Sometimes you gotta work with what you got," Gayle agreed. "See, what you got right now is a *rough-neck*. He's like a piece of rock straight out the ground. You gotta clean him up and *refine him*. Add a little bit of this. Take out the impurities. When you get through, you can have him sparkling like a diamond. Ooh, that's good. I'ma write a poem about that."

Mia thought the whole salon was against her, but Natiesha was shaking her head with her lips poked out. "Girl, don't believe that shit. *You can't fix no man.* What you got now is what you gon' have ten years from now."

And *that* was exactly what Mia was waiting to hear. As confirmation, Mama Ernestine stopped her on the way out and reiterated those fateful words:

"Listen, child. Don't be listening to those hot-tailed gals in there. You're a successful woman, Mia, and you know what kind of man you want in your life. That dope dealer ain't nothing but *bad news*. *You know it*. You gon' make a fool out of yourself following some idiot around trying to change him. *You can't fix no man.* Don't ever forget that."

And Mia wouldn't.

She took solace in the matriarch's words and left the beauty shop, as always, a fresh, vibrant, and confident woman.

CHAPTER 18
THE REPRIEVE

When Mia got home, Crystal had the kids dressed and ready for their day out with Tyrone. Mia had to change clothes, so she gave them carrot sticks and celery to munch on in the interim. Mia put on khaki shorts with a blue camisole and a long-sleeved denim shirt.

She stopped in the bathroom on her way out and marveled at her hairstyle. Vasantha had terrible dating advice, but Mia would go crazy if she quit her job as a stylist.

Back in the living room, Mia found the kids a bit more excited than usual.

"Where's my daddy taking us?" TC wanted to know.

"To a land of fun and adventure," Mia said vaguely. "You're guaranteed to have the time of your life."

TC gave her a big grin.

"Are you and TC's daddy getting married?" Mica asked.

Mia was taken aback. "No. Why would you say that?"

"Do you remember you said you were going to get married and I would have a new daddy?"

"I remember," Mia said.

"You said I could pick him," Mica reminded.

"Oh, I don't remember that."

"I do," Mica said. "You said you wouldn't marry anybody unless *I* liked them."

"Okay. I remember now. Don't tell me you're picking *Tyrone.*"

"I like Tyrone," Mica said. "He's a good daddy."

"Well, I'll take your vote into consideration, honey, but I think *I* have to like the guy, too, if I'm going to marry him."

"But you *do* like him," Mica persisted.

"I think *you* like him," Mia countered.

"You like him, too."

"*You* like him more," Mia said, eager to be through with the conversation.

"If you marry TC's daddy, I'll be good," Mica promised.

"You'll be good *that day*, or you'll be good *forever*?" Mia asked.

"Forever," Mica said, and she was so cute and innocent you almost believed her.

"Wow," Mia said. "How can I turn that down?"

"So, you're gonna do it?"

"I don't think so, but we'll see."

The doorbell rang and TC jumped up to answer it. It was Tyrone, right on time as usual. He scooped up his son for a hug and watched Mia over TC's shoulder. Today Tyrone had on baggy Fubus, but he had them pulled up to his waist. He had on a lime green Hilfiger golf shirt that was tucked in. He wore his Polo boots, and, yep, that was her chain. He wore it under his shirt, but you could still see part of it around his collar. It looked good on him, just as she knew it would. But then again, Tyrone looked good. He always did. He put his son down and embraced Mica with the same fondness.

"Where are we going?" TC asked.

"We're going to Putt Putt," Tyrone announced.

"I've been there," TC said with a slight frown.

"Well, have y'all ever played miniature golf before?" Tyrone asked.

"Yes!"

"*Dang*! Well, uh, they got a batting cage, too. Have y'all ever been in a batting cage?"

"What's a batting cage?" TC asked.

"Yeah! I knew it was *something* y'all ain't did before!" Tyrone looked happier than the kids.

Mia got up and threw her purse over her shoulder. "Where's your toothpick?" she asked Tyrone.

He looked at her with a shocked expression, then nervously down at the kids.

"What toothpick? I don't have no toothpick. C'mon, y'all. Let's go!" he headed for the door.

"What toothpick?" TC asked.

Tyrone looked at Mia again, still smiling. "Ain't no toothpick," he said.

"But I thought you liked to have a toothpick in your mouth," Mia said, grinning now.

Tyrone rolled his eyes. "Naw, Mia. You got me confused with *somebody else*. C'mon, y'all!"

"You don't like to chew on a toothpick and wear your pants on your butt?" Mia asked.

Tyrone blushed. His ears were as red as beets. Mica giggled.

"Mia. I don't do that stuff," Tyrone said. "Now, come on. We're gonna be late."

Mia let him off the hook. "Okay. I guess that *wasn't* you. But if you won't do it in front of the kids, then you shouldn't do it at all, is all I'm saying."

"Do what?" TC asked.

"Never mind," Mia said. "I'll be right back." She went to Crystal's room to see what her sister might be up to today. Crystal was on the computer updating her MySpace page.

"How's it going?" Mia asked from her doorway.

"It's cool. I took the kids to the library and got 'em ready just like you said. Everything went fine."

"Why you being so defensive?"

"I'm not."

"You doing okay?"

"Yes, Mia. Everything's fine."

"What about that boy? You seen him lately?"

"I haven't seen him since you kicked him out of the house. You said you don't want me to be with him, so I'm not."

This was everything Mia wanted to hear, but she still felt uneasy. "What are you doing today?"

"I don't know. I might go to the movies with Keyshia." Keyshia was the only friend from school Crystal still kept up with.

"What's Keyshia been up to?"

"She's still in college. She's engaged now, getting married in March."

"Good," Mia said. "You sure you're doing okay?"

"I'm fine," Crystal said. "Stop looking at me like that. You make me feel funny."

Mia wanted to ask if she had any cravings for the big H, but decided not to. If Crystal really only tried the drug twice, there wouldn't be any lingering effects. Asking about it would reveal how little faith Mia really had in her.

"All right, well, we're gonna be gone most of the day. If you're going to be out late, give me a call."

"I won't be out late," Crystal said and turned back to her computer screen.

Mia went back to the living room still in a good mood, but there was a bundle of fret in the bottom of her stomach. No matter what reassurances were given, that feeling wasn't going anywhere.

"All right," she said. "Let's go."

They piled into her Lexus with Tyrone on the passenger side.

When he buckled his seat belt, he leaned over and said, "I'ma get you," barely loud enough for Mia to hear.

She looked over at him, and he was smiling. Those lips were beautifully kissable, even if they were attached to a no-good liar. Mia smiled back at him.

"If you don't want the kids to know about it, you shouldn't do it at all," she muttered, then put the car in reverse.

Putt Putt Golf and Games was virtual paradise for kids. For twenty dollars you got *eighty* tokens, and all of the games were configured to operate on just one token each. Tyrone, the big spender of ill-gotten gains, parted with forty dollars immediately. With eighty tokens apiece, he thought the kids would be busy enough for him to steal Mia away for a little time alone, but TC wasn't having it. He had it in his head that this was his day to spend with Daddy. He grabbed Tyrone's hand and jerked him away from Mia's side.

"C'mon! Race against me!" He led his dad to a two-player game. Tyrone looked at Mia over his shoulder, and she shrugged and waved good bye. The adults' conversation would have to wait.

A long time.

After TC's race was done, Mica wanted Tyrone to pound the heads of moles as they emerged from their burrows. Then TC wanted to find out who was the better marksman. Then Mica wanted Tyrone to be Patrick as she raced on a virtual track as SpongeBob.

Two hours later Tyrone bought them pizza and sodas and they ate as a family. After lunch he took control of the entertainment.

"Hey, what do y'all wanna do after we eat?"

"You wanna race again?" TC asked through a mouthful of pepperoni.

"Naw. Y'all need to do something *by yourselves* so me and yo mama can talk."

"Y'all gonna kiss?" Mica asked.

"No, we are not going to kiss," Mia said.

"How about the go-carts?" Tyrone said. "You think you can beat your sister around the track?"

TC rolled his eyes. "I *know* I can."

"No, you can't," Mica said, and the feud was on.

The charge for two laps around the track was $5 per rider. Tyrone gave the attendant enough for both kids to ride three times each.

Mia elbowed him. "They're not going to want to ride that much," she murmured. But she was wrong. The kids got strapped into their cars as happy as crackheads on the first of the month. The only time they complained was when their cars stopped between races, but when the attendant told them they still had more rides, their smiles bounced back like springs.

Tyrone sat on a bench next to Mia. He had exactly fifteen minutes to win back his woman.

"You look real pretty today."

She smirked. "You paid $30 just to tell me that? Oh wait, I forgot. It's *dirty money*, so it doesn't count."

Tyrone shook his head. "You really got a problem with that, huh?"

Mia gave him a stupid look. "No. It's my dream to have a boyfriend who sells crack. Didn't you see how excited I was?"

Tyrone grinned. "So, I'm yo boyfriend?"

Mia rolled her eyes. "No. You *were* my boyfriend. But you couldn't even make it twenty-four hours."

"We can't get back together?" he asked.

Mia straightened her face, making sure all traces of a smile were gone. "Tyrone, seriously, I can't believe I even trusted you. It's my fault, but I'm not making that mistake again."

"Don't say that. Why is everything so black and white with you?"

"Tyrone, *you're a liar.* Everything you said to me was a lie."

"I didn't lie to you about wanting to be with you. I didn't lie about treating Mica like my daughter. I didn't lie about waiting for you, either. I been out of jail more than two months, but I only had sex that one time."

"Is that all you think about?"

"No, Mia. I'm just saying how I didn't lie about it."

"What about the five hundred dollars? You told me you got that from your uncle."

"Okay. I lied about that."

"You lied about selling drugs this whole time."

"I didn't lie, baby. You never asked."

Mia shook her head. "Don't give me that bullshit. That's a lie of omission. You lie so much, you don't even have to open your mouth to do it."

"Don't say that about me."

"Why not?"

"'Cause it's not true. You just sayin' that, 'cause you mad."

"You damned right I'm mad, Tyrone! Do you know how stupid you made me look? I bought you that chain, and you're over there selling *dope*. Pants sagging. You're a big *front*. I don't even know who the *real you* is."

"This is the real me. Right here," Tyrone patted his chest.

"So who is that other guy?"

"That's just for the streets," he said. "If I'm on the block with my pants pulled up, nice shirt tucked in, they gon' think I'm a *narc* or some shit."

"Why does it matter what they think about you?"

"It don't, really, but I needed to make some money."

"By selling drugs?"

"What else I'm supposed to do?"

"That doesn't sound at all ignorant to you?"

"Yeah, I know it's stupid, Mia. But what was I supposed to do? I had to take the kids to Six Flags. I wanted to bring 'em here."

"You didn't *have to* take the kids to Six Flags."

"My son asked me to take him. I told him I would, that means I had to do it—no matter what."

"What about your uncle's shop?"

"I don't make that much there. I'm not even on the clock. He just give me twenty, thirty dollars a day. That wasn't enough to do what I had to do."

"Tyrone, the ends do not justify the means."

"How come it don't? You see how happy them two is?"

"What do you think they'll look like when you get locked up?"

"I'm not getting locked up."

"That's the dumbest thing I've ever heard," Mia said.

Tyrone took offense to that. "Well, Mia, what you expect me to do? You got this . . . high-class lifestyle. You wouldn't give me the time of day if I couldn't bring nothin' to the table."

"Don't you dare put that on me."

"Tell the truth. You ain't tryin' to date no broke nigga."

"I'm not dating a drug dealer, either."

"All right. I'll quit sellin drugs," Tyrone said. "Now, are you going to go out with me when I'm broke or not?"

"You're not going to stop selling drugs. That you would sit there and lie to my fac—"

"Mia," Tyrone took her hand. "That look I saw on yo face when you pulled up to the park, I don't *ever* want to see you like that again. It makes me feel bad just to think about it. I'm not gonna be out there on the cut. When I say I'm not gonna sell drugs again, I mean it. I don't ever want to make you cry again."

His words warmed Mia's frigid heart.

"So, we back together," he asked, "or you don't want to be with me now 'cause I'm broke?"

Mia smiled but shook her head. "I don't know, Tyrone."

He nodded. "See. A regular nigga like me ain't got no chance."

"It's not that," she said.

"Then what is it?"

Mia sighed. "Tyrone, we're just on two different levels."

"I can make as much money as you. *Legally.*"

Mia frowned.

"This is America," Tyrone said. "I can do anything I want."

Mia smiled. She wanted detailed information about Tyrone's plan to get rich, but the kids completed their final lap. They came to a squeaky stop back at the terminal. Mia stood and took a few steps to meet them.

"So what about us?" Tyrone asked.

"We're not through talking," Mia said.

Tyrone stood next to her. "I mean for *today.* I need to know if you still my woman *right now.*"

Mia was curious, but decided to throw the dog a bone. "Okay. For now, I guess I'm still your woman."

Tyrone smiled and loosened visibly. Mia still didn't know why he wanted that information so badly, but she found out when she took a couple more steps. She felt the back of her shirt rising.

"*Nice,*" Tyrone called from behind.

Mia raised her eyebrows. "Um, the kids."

"They didn't see nothing," he said.

And he was right. They didn't.

When they got back to Mia's house, Tyrone wanted to come inside, but Mia bid him a fair adieu on the front porch. With his arms around her waist, he kissed her gently.

"Why can't I come in?"

"'Cause the kids are awake and I know what's on your mind."

He grinned. "I can play with them 'til they go to sleep, then come play with you."

"Well," Mia said. "As tempting as that sounds, let's not forget I caught you selling drugs six days ago."

"So what? You punishing me?"

"Somebody's got to do it."

He kissed her again. "I'm sorry I hurt you."

"If it happens again, you're gone," Mia assured him.

"Just like that?"

"Consider yourself lucky. You're the only one who's got a second chance this year."

Tyrone grinned. "All right. I guess I am lucky then."

"We still need to talk about your future," she said.

"What future?"

"You said you could make as much as me if you wanted to."

"Oh yeah. I'm serious about that."

"We'll see." She moved in for a full body hug. Tyrone's hands were on her butt within seconds, but Mia was starting to think she liked that even more than he did.

CHAPTER 19

WHEN IT RAINS SOME MORE

Mia slept like an infant Sunday night.

On Monday morning she dressed to kill, as always, and left for work in a cheery mood. Her day went fine until 3:30, when Miss Tenery wanted to transfer a call.

"Yes?" Mia answered the phone with unmistakable attitude in her voice.

"Mia. There's a call for you."

"I told you to hold them."

"Yes, ma'am. But this is an emergency. It's your children's school."

A hard knot formed in Mia's throat. She swallowed it down. It felt like swallowing a dry marble.

"Okay. Send them through."

There was a slight click.

"Hello? This is Mia Clemmons."

"Mia. Hi. This is Julie at Woodway. I was calling to let you know we have your two kids, Tyrone and Mica, here. They say their Aunt Crystal is supposed to pick them up. They've been waiting since three, but no one ever came."

Mia was immediately pissed, but a cold wave of dread washed over her at the same time. Crystal was rarely tardy in picking the kids up. Ten minutes Mia could under-stand, but a full thirty minutes late went past irrespon-sible and all the way to scary.

"Where are they now?" Mia asked.

"They're here with me, in the office," the woman said. "But we're closing up soon. Any children not picked up by 3:45 have to go to the daycare area."

"Where's that?"

"It's here in the cafeteria. We'll get 'em started on their homework. They have snacks provided, too."

"How late does the daycare stay open?"

"It's open 'til five, but there is a charge if your chil-dren have to be taken there."

"That's fine. I'll have someone there in fifteen minutes."

"If they come after 3:45, your kids will be in the cafeteria."

"Right," Mia said. "I heard you."

"There's a charge fo—"

"*Okay*, ma'am. I'll take care of it. Thank you for your call, seriously." Mia hung up and stared at the receiver. She pursed her lips and quickly punched in the numbers to her home phone. She nibbled her thumbnail as she lis-tened to it ring.

Four . . . five . . . *six* times . . . And then the answering machine came on.

"*Crystal?* Crystal, this is Mia. Are you there? The kids haven't been picked up from school. Pick up if you're there . . ."

But no one answered. Mia hung up and called Crystal's cell phone. She didn't get an answer on that line, either. She removed her own cell phone from her purse and looked up a number she had saved in the contacts. This number was rarely used. In five years, Mia thought she may have called the woman twice. Mrs. Jeffries answered after only two rings.

"Hello?"

"Janice? Hi. This is Mia Clemmons. Um, I know we don't talk much, but I live right across the street from you."

"Mia, I know who you are. I see you every morning, for Christ's sake. How's it going?"

"I'm fine, I—"

"How are the kids?"

"They're fine, too. Thanks for asking. Hey, I don't mean to trouble you, but could you do a favor?"

"Sure, Mia. Anything."

"I just need you to look at my house and tell me if my sister's Tahoe is in the driveway?"

"That's no problem at all," Mrs. Jeffries said. "As a matter of fact, I'm cleaning the blinds in my living room now. And I can tell you that . . . *yep*! Her car's right there where it always is."

Mia sucked air through her nose. She was about to ask her neighbor if she could go and knock on the door for her when Mrs. Jeffries said something that made the blood in Mia's veins burn hot.

"There's another car there, too. It's parked in the street. Looks like a, I don't know. One of those old Cutlasses. It's gray. It has some really big wheels on it."

Mia was so upset her vision blurred. "Um, thank you, Mrs. Jeffries."

"Is there something wrong?"

"No, ma'am. That's what I wanted to know. I appreciate it a lot."

Mia thanked the woman again and disconnected.

"*Shit!*" she spat in the silence of her office. Not only was that *knucklehead* still around, but Crystal had the bastard in her house again. Mia didn't think Crystal could get so lost in sex she forgot something as important as picking up the kids, but how could she know? If Crystal was using drugs, she was already somewhat of a stranger.

Mia thought quickly about how she would handle the situation, and then made another call. Tyrone answered on the third ring.

"Hello?"

"Tyrone, this is Mia. I need your help. Are you busy?"

"Never too busy for you, baby."

"Alright, calm down, *Billy D*. This is serious. It's an emergency."

"What's up? You all right?"

"I'm fine," Mia said. "Crystal's the one you need to be worried about."

"What's going on?"

"She didn't pick up the kids from school," Mia said. "I just got off the phone with one of my neighbors, and she says Crystal's car is at home. *And* her boyfriend's car is there, too."

"So, what you sayin'? She in there *getting busy*?"

"I don't know what she's doing, but she's not even supposed to have that boy over my house anymore. I found some dope he left last week."

"No shit?"

"He snorts heroin," Mia said. "I think he got Crystal on it, too. She told me she used it twice."

"That's messed up," Tyrone said. "You want me to go over there and whoop that nigga's ass for you?"

That's not what Mia had in mind, but it sure sounded good. "No, Tyrone. But we'll keep that on the back burner. What I wanted to know is if you can pick the kids up."

"Where? They go to Woodway, right?"

"Yeah. They've already been out since three. The secretary say's they'll be in the cafeteria."

"I can do that," Tyrone said.

"Can you take them to your house for about an hour?" Mia asked.

"I can keep them as long as you want."

"I'm about to leave work. I'm going home to see what's happening over there. After I get it settled, you can bring them."

"Cool. Just call me when you're ready for me to bring them."

"Thanks, Tyrone. You don't know how much I appreciate this."

"All right. I'm fixing to go now. The cafeteria, right?"

"Yeah. Tell them I'll see them in just a little bit. I'll call you as soon as I know what's going on."

Mia hung up and stared at her phone again. In the six years Crystal had been living with her, she never pulled a no-call, no-show when it came to picking up TC and Mica. Mia called her home phone one more time, but again no one answered.

She grabbed her purse and told her secretary she was gone for the day.

Mia raced down the freeway, cursing her sister for the tramp she was. How dare she have that boy in her house again? And she *lied!* Mia asked her straight out if she planned on seeing Sydney again, and Crystal looked her right in the face and *lied.* Mia didn't know if it was the *dick* or the *dope* that had Crystal stuck on that fool. Either way, Mia was through coddling the girl.

She told her that if she ever caught Sydney in her house again, Crystal would get kicked out with him. And she meant it. Maybe it wouldn't be anything permanent. Mia thought she might take her sister back in after a stint in rehab. But if it wasn't the drugs, Mia didn't know if she could ever trust her again. All credibility was gone. Mia could certainly forgive her, but her faith in Crystal might never be restored.

When she got to her house, Mia saw that her sister's Tahoe was indeed parked in the driveway. Sydney's Cutlass was still there, too. He parked his hoopty on the street, like a good boy, but Mia knew there was nothing good about him. He was a creep, a *wannabe* who should have kept his silly-ass addiction to himself. Mia cursed herself for not putting her foot down the first time she saw him lounging on her couch.

She pulled in next to the Tahoe and got out ready for war. She marched up to her front door with keys in hand, ready to barge in and put a brutal end to whatever sex/drug party they had going on in there, but her front door was already open. Mia paused at the threshold, wondering for the first time if maybe she shouldn't call the police, or at least get a neighbor to go in with her.

But there was no time to contemplate either.

Crystal's boyfriend appeared in the doorway, and Mia glimpsed the essence of evil. Sydney's eyes were wild, almost deranged. He wore light-colored jeans and a white T-shirt. Sweat poured from his face as if he'd just stepped out of the shower. The perspiration matted his shirt to his chest. His lips were ashen, yet they glistened with saliva, mouthing some word or words that never got articulated.

Mia's heart shot up in her throat. Her immediate thought was that this bastard did something foul to her sister. He had the look of a crazed animal. Mia hated that she didn't keep a gun in her purse. She had a small can of pepper spray on her keychain, but this lunatic was only three feet away. She would have to look down at her keys to get the spray ready, and Mia didn't want to take her eyes off him.

"What are you doing in my house?" she asked. Her voice was strong and confident. Mia didn't know where the strength came from, but her words didn't tremble at all.

Sydney stared at her and wavered in the doorway. He looked like he was trying to decide whether to go back inside the house or flee. He took a good look at Mia and chose the latter. Mia blocked his escape, but he had a good fifty pounds on her.

"*Get out my way, lady.*" He lumbered forward and knocked her aside with a swooping forearm to the chest.

Mia stumbled backwards and sideways. The heel of her right pump twisted underneath her, and she found herself falling. Her arms flailed wildly and her keys slipped from her fingers. She landed hard on one of the mushroom bushes that lined her walkway and felt the limbs and twigs poke into the back of her sports coat like stab wounds. Something sharp and rough scraped across her cheek, and a red light flashed before her eyes.

Mia let out a sharp scream that was first from shock, and then from pain. Crystal's boyfriend walked right past her. Mia struggled to free herself, but each movement brought more pain. She felt like she was caught in the jagged mouth of some green beast. The branches scratched, poked, and snagged. With all her might, Mia pushed off with her hands and managed to throw herself forward.

She landed on her hands and knees. To her right Sydney climbed into his car. To the left, her front door stood open. Somewhere inside her sister was either injured or dead. Mia knew it had to be one or the other.

She quickly made it to her feet. There was pain in a lot of places, but three body parts hurt more than others: her backside, her shoulder, and the small of her back. Mia limped to the porch and put a hand on the door-frame to steady herself once she made it. Her breaths came quick. On a subconscious level she noticed that one of her fingernails had broken. Not merely broken, it was ripped off halfway down the nail plate. Blood seeped from the wound, staining the paint next to her doorbell.

Mia looked back to Sydney, but the Cutlass was on the move now, already two houses down. She took a half second to memorize his license plate number, and then she stumbled into her house to see what horrors he left behind.

It was much worse than she thought.

In her room, Crystal lay on her bed completely nude and uncovered. Her breathing was shallow and labored. Crystal's lips were bluish. Her fingertips were, too.

Mia let out a soulful wail and almost collapsed in the doorway.

"*Crystal*." She staggered to her sister's bedside and leaned over the body. She held her sister's head and lifted it from the pillow.

"*Crystal*."

The girl was warm to the touch. Beads of perspiration dotted her forehead. Mia felt for a pulse next to her jugular and found one. It was weak, but it was there. Mia lifted her sister's eyelids and saw that Crystal's sclera was not bloodshot like one would expect with strangulation or other physical trauma. There were no bruises on her neck or face, either. Crystal's pupils were extremely small, almost pinpoints. On a hunch, Mia looked up her sister's nose. There was a small clump of what looked like dirt caught in the thin hairs lining her nostrils. It was the same kind of dirt that was in the pill Mia found last week.

"That son of a bitch," Mia breathed. Her eyes watered and the tears flowed like blood. Her bottom lip quivered.

"It's all right, baby." She brushed her sister's forehead and kissed it. "It's gon' be all right."

Mia looked around the room for Crystal's cordless phone. She found it on the bed next to the girl's foot. She called 911 and told the operator her sister might be having a drug overdose. The operator told Mia to remain calm and stay with Crystal until an ambulance arrived. She said Mia should watch Crystal closely and begin CPR if she stopped breathing.

After Mia hung up, she found a pair of panties and a Nike jumpsuit. She dressed her sister, then held Crystal's hand and whispered encouragement for what felt like an hour. Mia didn't realize she left her front door open until she looked up and two paramedics stood in the doorway. She rose stiffly and stepped aside and let the professionals do their job.

She stood in the corner of the room and watched as they attempted, with no luck, to rouse her sister. They kept asking questions Mia didn't have answers to. *No*, she couldn't tell them what happened. *No*, she couldn't say for sure if Crystal did any heroin today. And *no*, she couldn't say how long she had been in this state.

After a quick assessment, they loaded Crystal onto a stretcher and affixed an oxygen line under her nose. Mia said she would follow them to the hospital in her own car, but when she got to the driveway, she realized she didn't have her keys. One of the EMTs found them in her lawn close to the front door. He handed them to her and then looked Mia up and down.

"Ma'am, are you okay?"

"I'm fine," she said, eager to be on the road.

"You've got a cut on your face," he said. "You look disheveled. Was there a fight?"

"I'm fine," Mia said, then stepped by him and got into her car. *He's already got a hurt girl in the back of his truck*, she thought. *What the hell is he worried about me for?* But when she checked her rearview mirror the answer to that became clear. The cut on her face went from her earlobe to the corner of her right eye. It was thin, but at one point it bled pretty good. The dried blood looked like Halloween makeup. Mia had leaves in her hair, too. She plucked the biggest one, and then another figure appeared in her window. It was a uniformed police officer this time. Mia had no idea when they got there.

"Ma'am, we're gonna need to ask you some questions."

"You'll have to ask me at the hospital," Mia said.

"Was there a sexual assault?"

"I don't know. She was naked when I found her."

"Were there drugs involved?"

"I don't know," Mia said. "All I know is it was her boyfriend. His name is Sydney. I don't know his last name. He drives a gray Cutlass with twenty-inch rims." Mia rattled off the license plate number.

The cop jotted down all of this information.

"Can I go now?" she asked.

"Yeah. We'll meet you at the hospital."

Mia backed out and got behind the ambulance. The ambulance had its sirens on, and that felt like a bad sign. Mia chased it, running every red light and stop sign it did.

She called Tyrone when they got on the freeway.

"Hello?"

"Tyrone, this is Mia." Her voice hitched.

"What's wrong?" he asked, immediately worried.

"It went ba—bad," she said. "*Real* bad, Tyrone."

"Mia, what's wrong? Are you all right? You sister okay?"

"No, she's not," Mia said. "I think she *overdosed*."

"*Oh, shit*."

"She was naked, too. I think he rape—raped her."

"*What?* What the—where are you?"

"I'm right behind the ambulance. We're on our way to the hospital. The police were there. She was . . . *oh, my God* . . ."

"Mia, are you okay? You want me to come up there?"

"No. I don't want the kids up here. Can you . . . can you take them to my house? I left the fr—the front door open."

"All right, Mia. You wan—"

"Stay with them," she said. "I'll call you when I get to the hospital."

"Mia, this is jacked up. Man, I can't believe this. You say she *overdosed*?"

"I don't know. I think that's what it is. Her boyfriend was still there when I got home."

"You *saw* him?"

"Yeah."

"*Rape?* Man, that's crazy. I'ma kick that nigga's ass," Tyrone said.

"I wish you would. He was sweat—sweating bad. He ran out. Pushed me down."

"He *what?*"

"He pushed me. In the bushes. I'm hurt, my back. My face. Bleeding a lit—"

"Man, *what the hell?* That nigga put his hands on you? *I knew* I shoulda went over there. I shouldn—"

"Tyrone, calm down. Don't worry about me. Just take the kids home. If *you* start tripping, they'll start crying. Don't tell them about *me*. Just tell them Aunt Crystal is sick."

"*I'ma kill that ho-ass nigga.*"

"Tyrone . . ."

"Mia, I'm pissed off for real. That punk givin' yo sister that shit. Put his hands—"

"Tyrone, listen, I need you to calm down. I'm doing bad already. You're making it worse."

"Mia, I . . ." He took a breath and was a bit more composed when he spoke again. "So, what you want me to do?"

"Just take the kids home. Let them do their home-work. I've got Hamburger Helper in the fridge. If it's not there, just get something easy out of the freezer, like pizza, corn dogs. I should be back by the time they get ready for bed."

"Where you bleedin' at?" Tyrone asked.

"Are you listening to me?"

"Yeah. I heard you. Tell me where you hurtin' at. I'm worried about you, too."

"I broke a nail," Mia said. "I think halfway off. I have a scratch on my face, but it's not really that big. My back hurts and my shoulder hurts. I got poked a few times when I fell in the bush. I haven't looked at it. I don't know—*I gotta go.* We're getting off the freeway."

"*Ho-ass, coward-ass nigga . . .*"

"Tyrone."

"What hospital you going to?"

"*Jackson*," Mia said.

"Call me as soon as—"

But Mia disconnected the line.

CHAPTER 20

THE BIG H

The time Mia spent at Jackson Memorial was like a long, slow-motion blur.

When they got to the ER, the paramedics rolled Crystal into a triage area, but they directed Mia to another door that led to the waiting room. Once there, a large woman dressed in pink handed her forms and release papers to fill out. The same woman brought Mia individually wrapped alcohol swabs a few minutes later.

"There's some blood on your face," she said, her concern genuine and warm.

Mia took a compact from her purse and wiped the blood from her cheek. The scratch wasn't deep, but it was long. Mia thought it would heal up in a couple of weeks. It was noticeable, but not to the point that anyone would stop and stare; or at least Mia didn't think it was that bad.

While she had a mirror out, she went ahead and plucked the few leaves remaining in her hair. Her suit was soiled, there were *serious* scuffs on her shoes, and blood on her hands, but overall Mia thought she still looked presentable. There were certainly people in the waiting room who looked worse than her. A large woman to Mia's left had bandages wrapped around a foot that was two times bigger than it should be. A homeless guy two chairs down looked like he went a few rounds with one of the local gangs.

Mia checked her watch and it was already after five. She called the office to tell Miss Tenery she wouldn't be in tomorrow.

"Is everything all right?"

"No. My sister is in the hospital. I'm here with her."

"I'm sorry to hear that. Is there anything I can do?"

"No. I'll call you tomorrow."

"Very well."

Mia disconnected. She was about to call Tyrone to see if he made it inside okay, but a nurse summoned her to the front of the room. It was a Caucasian lady with dark hair, a large nose, and large eyes.

"You can come back now."

Mia followed the woman through narrow hallways made even more cramped by stretchers set up along one side. All of the stretchers had patients on them in varying stages of disarray. Some family members had pulled up chairs next to their loved ones.

Mia hoped they had an actual *room* for Crystal, and she was in luck. The nurse led her to a screened-off section where Crystal's unconscious body lay. She had a new oxygen line on her face, a catheter snaking between her legs, and EKG leads attached to her torso and legs. Mia expected *more* machinery.

"Is she okay?" she asked before the nurse could run off.

"Well, her O2 stats are looking good. We didn't have to intubate her. That's good, but she *did* test positive for heroin. She actually has high levels of the drug in her bloodstream. Someone should be by in a minute to get a drug history on her."

"I don't know anything about her drug history," Mia said. "She told me she only used it twice."

"That's fine," the nurse said. "Any information you have is good." She turned to walk away, but Mia put a hand on her shoulder.

"So, what's going on? Are y'all treating her? Does she have a prognosis yet, or what?"

"No, ma'am. Your physician is Dr. Brown. He's already looked at her. He'll be back in a little while to talk with you." Again she tried to leave.

"But is she *all right*?" Mia asked.

"She's stable," the nurse said. She sounded slightly perturbed, but Mia didn't give a damn. Maybe the woman had a stereotype about the kinds of patients who overdosed, but this particular dopehead was important to Mia. She needed to know that Crystal's caregivers felt the same way.

"Listen, this is my sister. This is her first problem with drugs, and this is the first time I've seen an overdose. I need to know what's going on."

The nurse sighed. "Look, she isn't my patient. We're pretty busy, but someone will be in here to talk to you shortly. Without seeing your sister's chart, I can only give you the basics."

"That's fine," Mia said. "Give me the basics."

"Well, she's ingested a large amount of heroin. I don't believe it's fatal, but I really don't know. I think she'd be intubated if she were critical."

"What's intubated?"

"If her O2 stats were low, they would put a tube down her throat to supply air directly to her lungs. But she's breathing okay on her own. We monitor her stats and basically wait for the heroin to wear off. When she wakes up, she gets a stern lecture, and then we send her home. That's pretty much all we can do."

"So, she's not in a coma or anything? She's gonna wake up?"

"We assume she'll wake up," the nurse said. "Heroin is basically a sedative. Take too much, and it'll knock you out, but that's not usually the big problem. *Excessive* amounts of heroin leads to respiratory distress in most patients. If *that* was happening, you'd have a lot of people in there with your sister, but, as you can see, she's all right."

Mia still wasn't convinced. "But I saw this one movie where they gave this girl a shot—*directly in the heart*—when she had . . ." She trailed off because the nurse was chuckling and shaking her head.

"That's *Hollywood*. Your sister's nowhere near that bad. Look at her. She's *asleep*."

Mia thanked the nurse and allowed her to run off to another of many errands. The lady was snippy, and a bit uncompassionate, but the information she gave Mia was dead on. No one else Mia talked to could add very much to that preliminary synopsis.

Mia turned and walked into the room where her sister lay. Crystal had been undressed. She now wore a traditional hospital gown with the opening in the back. She lay on her back, her body perfectly aligned, with her arms down along her sides and her feet meeting at the ankles.

It was a terrible reaction, but Mia thought the girl looked dead. She couldn't get it out of her mind. Crystal looked just as she would on the metal slab in the coroner's office. All she needed was the toe tag.

Mia started to cry again. She found a napkin in her purse and blew her nose. She stood next to the stretcher and watched the erratic lines skating on the monitor above Crystal's head. The readings meant nothing to her, but Mia watched them anyway. She knew what it meant if one of those lines flattened out.

Mia shook her head slowly.

"Why you have to be so stupid?" she asked and stroked the girl's hair. She knew Crystal was going to bump her head at some point, but this went *way* past what Mia had expected. *Way, way* past.

The police showed up before the doctor did. It was the same two officers who came to the house earlier. They told Mia a rape test had been administered, and there *was* semen present, but there were no signs of forced intercourse. Mia told them maybe her sister being totally unconscious might have something to do with that. They said that because Sydney was her boyfriend, they couldn't necessarily assume a rape had taken place. They said they would have to wait until Crystal woke up and simply ask her if the sex was consensual.

Mia told them about the attack on her own person, and the policemen were eager to take down that information.

"We can definitely pick him up for the assault. Maybe he won't make bail for a couple days. By then, hopefully your sister will be awake, and we can talk to her about the sexual assault."

That didn't seem like enough, but as long as it got Sydney off the streets Mia was fine with it.

Crystal's doctor finally came to the room thirty minutes later, but he didn't tell Mia anything she didn't already know. Crystal had a substantial amount of heroin in her system, but apparently it wasn't life threatening. She was already breathing by herself, which was the only big hurdle she had to overcome. There was no antidote for heroin. They would send Crystal up to her own room shortly, and from there all they could do was wait for her to wake up.

Mia asked about a possible coma, but the doctor was positive she would wake up on her own. And since Crystal never stopped breathing, there wasn't expected to be any brain damage, either. Mia was glad to hear all of this, but it did little to calm her nerves. She was left alone with her sister for another fifteen minutes, and then a teenage girl wearing Dickies appeared in the doorway.

"Hi. I'm April. I'll be taking her up to her room."

"*You're* patient transport?" Mia asked. The girl was no more than seventeen and didn't look physically up to the task.

"I know I'm *small*," April said with a smile, "but I only have to push the stretcher. Once we get upstairs, the techs will help me get her in the bed."

Mia nodded and collected the few items she had in the small room. She then followed the teenager halfway across the hospital, or so it seemed. They finally got on an elevator and came out on the fifth floor of the Peterson tower.

"This is a telemetry floor," the transporter said, breathing a little harder because they were on carpet now.

Mia stood outside of room 521 as they transferred Crystal from her stretcher to the bed. Once she was settled, a medical assistant came in and recorded Crystal's vital signs. After that, Mia was left alone with her sister again. She looked around and had to admit the room was comfortable. There was a recliner, a sink, telephone, television, and bathroom—all the amenities of home, except they were so far from home it was nauseating.

Mia caressed her sister's hand for a while and tried to coddle her from this interminable slumber, but nothing she said made those beautiful eyes open. She finally sat back in the recliner and fished her cell phone from her purse. Tyrone hadn't called since the last time she talked to him. Mia appreciated his patience and understanding. Certain guys like *Eric* would have tried to reach her a dozen times by now.

She dialed the numbers to her house phone, and Tyrone answered after only a couple of rings.

"Hello? Mia?"

"Yeah. It's me."

"How's it going over there? Yo sister all right?"

Mia told him what the doctors and nurses told her, and Tyrone was glad Crystal wasn't in ICU. He was not happy to hear that Crystal's boyfriend was still on the loose, however.

"Did you tell them what he did to you?"

"Yeah, and they say they will arrest him for that. Once Crystal wakes up, they might add more charges."

"What you say his name was?" Tyrone asked.

"Why?"

"I just wanna know. I might know him."

"His name is Sydney."

"What he drive?"

"Why, Tyrone?"

"I told you. I want to know if I know him."

"I don't want you getting in trouble behind this. The police are going to get him."

"But just in case they don't," Tyrone said, "what he drive?"

"A gray Cutlass with twenty-inch rims. He's dark-skinned. Wears a lot of fake silver jewelry." Mia felt she was doing something dangerous, but her anger and pain overrode her conscious.

Tyrone didn't say anything.

"How are the kids?" Mia asked.

"They fine. What about you?"

"I cleaned that cut on my face. It looked a lot worse than it was. It's just a little scratch. My shoulder still hurts. And my back. I haven't taken off my coat yet, so I don't know what it looks like back there."

"They didn't look at your injuries?"

"No. I didn't say anything about it."

"Do you want me to bring the kids up there?"

"No. Not tonight. I might bring them tomorrow when she wakes up."

"What time do you want me to put them to bed?"

"They usually go to sleep at about nine-thirty or ten. But I should be home by then."

"Oh, you're coming home?"

"Yeah. I'll probably leave in just a little bit if she doesn't wake up."

"You can stay if you want," Tyrone said. "I can take care of TC and Mica."

"I know you can. It's not that. I want to be there before they go to sleep. I need to talk to them about what's going on."

"All right," Tyrone said. "Well, call me and let me know."

Mia said she would and hung up the phone.

At 7:45 a.m. Crystal's eyelids fluttered a little, but did not open. That was the only movement Mia saw in her for the rest of the night. She gave Crystal's nurses her cell phone number and told them to call at any hour if Crystal woke up.

Mia was on the highway by 9:10 p.m.

Back at home, the children were excited about their mom's arrival. They both ran to the door to greet her, but Tyrone stood off and watched her with a funky look on his face. Mia knew what was wrong with him, but kept a smile on in front of the kids.

"What happened to your cheek?" TC asked.

"It's okay," Mia said. "I slipped and fell, but it's all right."

Mica thought she could kiss it and make it better, and Mia leaned down to let her.

She told them she was going to take a shower and talk to them about their aunt when she got done. Tyrone followed her into her bathroom and closed the door behind him.

Mia looked at herself in the mirror, and watched Tyrone's reflection over her shoulder. The scratch on her face had started to swell, and now looked like a long welt. Tyrone approached from behind and wrapped his arms around her stomach, his face set in unmasked anguish.

"Stop looking like that," Mia said.

"I can't believe that nigga put his hands on you," he said. "You got a scar on yo face."

"It'll heal," she promised.

"But still . . ." Tyrone brought his hands up to her collar and removed her soiled sports coat. He let it fall to the floor and then unbuttoned her blouse, still from behind. Through the mirror Mia studied his features. She rubbed the top of her head on his chin. Once he had the buttons free, Mia slid her arms out of the shirt. Tyrone dropped the garment to the floor. Mia looked after it and saw a few spots of blood on the back, none bigger than a dime.

She had on just her bra now, but Mia didn't feel at all self-conscious about the size of her breasts. Tyrone held her bare sides, and then traced his fingers up her spine. His right hand moved slowly and came to rest on one of Mia's sore spots.

"It hurts right here?" he asked.

She nodded. "What does it look like?"

"It's a bruise. Not that big. It was bleeding, but it stopped."

His hands moved again and stopped on the small of her back. "Right here, too?"

Again, Mia nodded.

"You've got a tear on your pants," he said. His hands went to the front of her body, and he undid the buckle. He slid the slacks past her hips and touched her right buttock more tenderly than he ever had. He slid his finger over her third sore spot.

"You got poked here, too."

"It's starting to feel better already," Mia admitted.

Tyrone's head came back up. He kissed her neck, right under her left ear. He stared at her reflection in the mirror. His eyes were glazed.

"I'll be out there with the kids," he said and left her in the bathroom alone.

Mia took a shower and dressed in shorts and a tee shirt. She cleaned her ragged nail and put a Band-Aid on it. When she got back to the living room, Tyrone had the kids gathered on the couch with him. Mia took a seat on the far end of the sofa, and Tyrone pushed mute on the remote.

"Well, how you guys doing?" she asked.

The kids were innocent. *Sweetly innocent.* They smiled up at her, and that gave her the strength to smile back.

"Is Aunt Crystal coming home tomorrow?" Mica asked.

"She might, but I don't think so. It'll probably be a few days."

"Who's gonna pick us up from school?" TC asked.

"Well, I will tomorrow. Or maybe your dad." She looked over at Tyrone, and he nodded.

"What about Saturday?" TC asked. "Who's going to take us to the library?"

"That's *five days away*," Mia said. "I'm sure your aunt will be okay by then, but if not, I guess you'll have to go with your *grubby old mama*."

Mica grinned. "You're not grubby."

"What about Daddy?" TC said. "He can take us to the library."

"Yeah. I can take you," Tyrone said and palmed his son's head.

"Don't worry about it," Mia said. "We'll make sure you get to everywhere you need to be. Did you guys brush your teeth yet?"

Both children responded in the negative.

"Well, go brush up so you can get in bed. I'll come tuck you in a minute."

The kids got up, and Mica stopped in front of Tyrone. "We get out of school at *three o'clock*," she said. "Not *three-forty*."

He laughed. "Hey, I'm not the one who was late. I got there as soon as I could."

"Well, *now you know*," she said, and ran off as cute and bubbly as could be.

Neither of the kids ever asked exactly what was wrong with Crystal, and that was a blessing. Their aunt was simply sick, and that's all they needed to know.

When Mia returned from sending her little ones to their fields of dreams, Tyrone was still on the living room couch, still watching cartoons, for some reason.

"What are Mickey and Minnie been up to?" Mia asked him.

He looked over at her and smiled. He turned off the TV and stood to meet her.

"You don't like cartoons no more?"

"Sometimes," Mia said and stepped in to embrace him.

Tyrone held her gingerly, as if not sure where he could apply pressure.

"I'm not that fragile," she told him.

"You not a man, either," he said. "A man ain't never supposed to put his hands on a woman."

Mia looked up at him and Tyrone kissed her as softly as he was holding her.

"Do you want me to go home?" he asked.

"No," Mia said. "I want you to stay."

In her bedroom, Tyrone told her to take off her shirt again and lay on the bed. Mia did so. She lay on her side, but Tyrone rolled her onto her stomach. He left the room and returned with medicines from her bathroom. He climbed onto the bed and straddled her, his legs resting on her thighs, just under her butt.

Mia turned her head and laid her cheek on the mattress. "Take your pants off," she murmured.

He dismounted. When he returned, his bare thighs rested on hers.

Mia never remembered Tyrone for having magical hands, but he did that night. He used a cotton swab to wipe alcohol on the three spots where she bled into her blouse. He then applied a dab of Neosporin to the wounds and smoothed it out with his fingertip.

He had a bottle of lotion, too. Mia was tender in a lot of places, and Tyrone seemed to find each one. He rubbed and massaged her back and neck for what felt like *heavenly* hours. By the time he was done, Mia was physically ready for sex, but Tyrone never made an attempt.

He lay down beside her and kissed her shoulder. Mia turned to her side and backed into him. Tyrone wrapped himself around her like a flesh blanket, and Mia began to doze almost immediately.

He kissed the back of her neck and whispered, "I love you."

Mia told him she loved him, too, and slipped into blissful unconscious.

She never felt so safe.

CHAPTER 21
REAL TALK

"Wake up, sleepyhead."

Tyrone rolled over and squinted at the sunrays peeping through Mia's bedroom curtains.

"Hey."

"Hey," Mia said. She wore blue jeans with a white sweater and white tennis shoes. Tyrone wore only his tee shirt and boxers.

"You already been up?" he asked.

Mia grinned. "I've been up and been gone, lazy. I just took the kids to school."

He sat up and wiped the sleep from his eyes. "Why didn't you wake me up?"

"You looked so comfortable. I didn't want to disturb you. I figured since you kept them for me yesterday, I'd let you have an extra hour of sleep. I'm going to the hospital. You wanna go?"

"Did they call yet? Is she awake?"

"No. They didn't call all last night. I called this morning, and they said she's still the same. They said her eyeballs are moving around a lot under her lids, though. That's a good sign. They think she'll come around in a couple of hours."

"Yeah, I wanna go," Tyrone said. "What time is it?"

"It's a quarter 'til eight."

"I don't have anything to wear. Do we have time to stop by my house so I can shower?"

"Yeah. Come on, stinky."

"*You* the one stinky."

"Oh, and they arrested Crystal's boyfriend last night."

"For real?" Tyrone's eyes grew livelier with that news.

"Yeah. He got out last night, too."

"You bullshittin'."

Mia shook her head.

"How the hell he get out so quick?"

"All he did was push me down," Mia said. "That's an assault, but it's basically a ticket. They really didn't have to arrest him."

"So he bailed out?"

"He didn't have to bail out. He got arraigned and they set up a court date, just like with a traffic ticket. They didn't have anything to hold him on."

"That ain't cool," Tyrone said.

Mia agreed that it wasn't.

Mia sat on a love seat in Tyrone's living room as he took a quick shower and put on clean clothes. Tyrone's mother lounged on a nearby sofa, and she was not the great conversationalist Mia remembered her to be.

"Do you think you can get me a loan down at yo job?" the woman asked.

Mia knew she wouldn't, but was curious. "What do you need a loan for?"

"I been thinking about fixing up that back room there. Putting in a pool table and a movie screen for the grandkids when they come to visit."

Mia was pretty sure no room in the woman's house could fit both a pool table *and* a theatre. "I don't handle those kinds of loans," she told her.

"My Aunt Ruby used to have a pool table in her garage. I told her one day I would do her one better."

Mia hummed.

"Do you play pool?" the lady asked.

Mia shook her head. "Not really."

"You should come by and teach me when I get my table put up."

"*You* don't play pool?" Mia asked.

"Oh, no, child. I can't stand it."

Tyrone stepped into the room a few minutes later wearing khaki Dickies with a blue tee shirt. His gold chain glistened like a samurai's sword. Mia had never been so happy to see the thug.

"You ready?" She stood and threw her purse over her shoulder.

"Yeah," Tyrone said. He kissed his mom good bye and followed Mia outside.

"She asked me to get her a loan," Mia told him when they got back into her car.

"Aw, don't tell me she's talking about that pool table again."

"Pool table *and* movie theatre. In the *same* room."

"You gon' give it to her?" Tyrone asked with a wry smile.

"Yeah. I'm faxing the paperwork right over," she said, then, "You smell good."

When they got up to Crystal's room, they found her still sleeping. She had a new IV depositing slow drips from a saline solution, but other than that, there were no changes.

Tyrone stood over her with both hands on the bed. "She look pretty peaceful."

"She does, doesn't she?"

He grinned. "Have you even tried to wake her up?"

"Uh, *yeah.*"

"For real," he said, then pushed Crystal's shoulder. "Hey, girl! Wake up!"

"Stop!" Mia said.

"What?"

"What are you doing?"

Tyrone looked at her like it was pretty obvious. "I'm trying to wake her up."

"I don't think you're supposed to do that."

"See, that's what I'm talking about. I bet nobody's really *trying* to wake her up."

They walked to the nursing station and asked Crystal's current RN for a progress report. She was a light-skinned woman with thick lips and thick hips.

"She's doing fine," the nurse said. "If she's not up by noon, the doctor is gonna come look at her again."

"Is it all right if I try to wake her up?" Tyrone asked.

"What do you mean?" the nurse asked.

"You know, like push on her shoulder a little bit, and say, '*Hey, wake up!*' "

Mia rolled her eyes, and the nurse laughed. "I don't think that's gonna help, but it won't hurt, either."

"See, told you," Tyrone said.

Mia grabbed his arm and led him away. "You wanna get some breakfast?"

"Yeah," he said with a big smile. "But I left my dope money at home."

Mia sent an elbow to his gut.

"*Ow!*"

"Let me find out you have some dope money," she said.

"I *do* got some dope money. What you want me to do with it? Throw it away?"

Mia stopped and stood before him. "Are you still selling drugs, Tyrone?"

"Naw, baby. But I do have money left over."

"You'd better quit playing," she told him, and continued down the hall.

"You need to quit being so serious," he said.

Mia got on an idling elevator and Tyrone glided in with her. They were the only two on, so he slipped in for a hug.

"We have to have a talk," Mia said between kisses.

"About what?"

"You looking at that nurse's ass, for one."

"I wasn't looking at nobody's ass."

"I saw you, Tyrone."

He pulled away and looked into her eyes, but Mia was still smiling.

"You think I want that chunky girl?"

"I think her ass is big and round, just like you like 'em."

"I might have *looked*, but that don't mean I want her."

"I know you," Mia said. "You like a big booty. But are you gonna be happy with my mid-sized one? That's the question."

Tyrone grinned. "Well, let me see." He moved in for another hug. As soon as he wrapped his hands around her lusciousness, the elevator dinged and the doors began to open.

"I like this one a whole lot better," he said.

"You better."

~~~

Tyrone had biscuits drowned in gravy with sausage patties. Mia had a bowl of assorted fruits; mango, cantaloupe, watermelon, and grapes. They both had orange juice.

"Want me to pick the kids up today?" Tyrone asked around a mouthful.

"I can pick them up," Mia said. "You didn't even bring your car."

"You don't want me to take yours?" he asked.

The question reminded Mia of something she told her sister a little while ago, but she couldn't think of what it was. "No. I want to pick them up."

"Oh," Tyrone said. "What about tomorrow? Want me to get them then?"

"When I dropped them off this morning, I got some fliers for after-school programs. There's a center right around the corner from my house. They'll pick them up from school and keep them as late as nine."

"You want them to go to *daycare*?"

"Well, until I get things situated. For now at least."

"Why you don't want me to pick them up?"

"And do what with them?"

"I can take them home, or take them to your house."

"You want to go to *my* house every day after school?"

"Just to keep the kids. So they don't have to change their schedule."

"No. I'd rather have them in daycare."

"Why you want *them people* keeping them instead of me?" Tyrone asked. He sounded a little offended, but Mia was not one to hold her punches, even if she was in love.

"I don't want you to have a key to my house," she said.

"Why? You don't trust me?"

"We need to talk, huh?"

Tyrone sat back in his chair. "Yeah. I guess we do."

"Well," Mia said, "you're my boyfriend, right?"

He nodded.

"But you're not my *husband*, and you're not living with me. You understand that, right?"

Tyrone rolled his eyes. "Course I do."

"We're not going to be able to talk if you get an attitude."

He nodded. "All right. Let's talk."

Mia smiled. "Okay. So I know it looks like I need you right now, but I really don't. I've been doing just fine by myself, and I will continue to do just fine by myself."

Tyrone started to say something, but she put a hand up to stop him. "I wanna be with you," she went on, "but I'm not rushing into anything. You can visit me sometimes, but I don't want you there *every day*. I don't mind if you spend the night, but that's not going to be an everyday thing, either. Once a week is probably too much."

"That's *too* much?"

"I think so," Mia said. "For now. I want to take this slow."

"You don't think this is gonna work, do you?"

Mia shrugged. "I want it to, but you know I have doubts."

"What doubts? Let's get them out in the open right now."

Mia looked at her wristwatch. "You done eating? We'll talk upstairs."

Tyrone shoved one last bite between his choppers. "Let's go."

They got on the elevator a lot less cuddly than they were on the way down.

Back in Crystal's room, they surveyed Sleeping Beauty's features. There were no changes. Tyrone took a seat in the recliner, shaking his head. Mia sat across from him in a far less comfortable wooden chair.

"I'ma kick that nigga's ass," Tyrone said. "Some of my peeps know where he be at."

"I told you to let the police handle it."

"I did," Tyrone said. "You said they let him go."

"It's not over. They still have to talk to Crystal when she wakes up."

"I said I'm kicking that nigga's ass," Tyrone reiterated.

Mia didn't feel like arguing. "We still need to talk about us," she said.

Tyrone threw his head back. "You finna back out again, ain't you? I ain't even did nothing, but you—"

"I'm not backing out," Mia said.

"Then what's the problem?"

"I told you, there are things we need to get straight."

"Well, let's talk," he said. "I ain't got nothin' but time."

Mia smiled. "Okay. Tell me how you plan on making a good living."

He squinted at her. "You serious?"

"Yes, I'm serious, Tyrone. I want to be with you, but if you don't have any plans for the future it's not gonna work. I'm not gonna carry you. If you need help getting to where you want to be, *I'll help you*, but you have to help yourself, too."

"Damn, Mia."

"What? Are you happy being an unemployed convicted felon?"

"You know I'm not. I just didn't know I was gonna have to fill out an application to be with you."

"It's not as hard as you're making it sound. Just tell me what your goals are."

"Right now?"

"Sure."

"Okay." He sat up in the chair. "The only thing I'm really good at is working on cars. I figure I can get a good job at a good garage and work my way up to manager or supervisor one day."

Mia nodded. "Where do you plan on working? Are you talking about working your way up at your uncle's place?"

"Naw. I have to go somewhere else. I don't think the manager makes much at my uncle's shop."

"Can you work on *any* kind of car?"

"Most of them. Well, the American ones, at least."

"Did you get any training or certificates while you were in prison?"

"Naw. They don't do that too much anymore. *They say* they want to rehabilitate us, but they only have the funds to put a one out of every hundred inmates in school."

"Can you get a job at *any* shop, or do they check for your criminal background?"

"I think they check at all the good places."

"Okay," Mia said. "What else you got?"

"Um, I got this homeboy who sells DVDs. He said he could put me down with that."

"I thought you said *legally*."

"What? That is legal."

"Are you talking about selling them out of a store-front or *out of your trunk?*"

"The trunk," Tyrone said. "Oh, wait." He knitted his eyebrows. "That's illegal, ain't it?"

"Big time," Mia said. "What else you got?"

"That's probably the same with CDs, huh?"

Mia nodded, already disappointed with the way this was going.

"I always wanted to open a club," Tyrone said.

Mia raised her eyebrows. "Has someone in your family run a club?"

"No."

"Do you know someone who has?"

"I know a couple of club owners," Tyrone said. "They not my friends or nothing like that."

"What makes you think you'll be good at running a club?"

"I'm good with people," Tyrone said.

"*Okay*," Mia said. "Got any other ideas?"

"I can buff floors," he said. "I can cut grass and plant flowers."

"You want to get into landscaping?" Mia asked.

"I guess."

"That might work," she said with a smile, but Tyrone was frowning.

"Look, you ain't gotta make me look stupid," he said. "If you wanna break up with me, then just do it."

Mia looked into his eyes. "Is that what you think this is about?"

He shrugged.

"Tyrone, *we're together*. You're my man. I'm not trying to break up with you. I just want to figure out what we're going to do with you. I want the best for you."

"But I can't do shit. You said so yourself."

"I didn't say that. Some of your ideas need to be *refined*, but I never said they were no good. Except the bootleg thing, that's no good."

He smiled. "So, how do you plan on *refining* me?"

"Well, it looks like the automotive industry would be your best bet, unless you really want to cut grass . . ."

"Naw, I like working on cars."

"You're pretty good at it?"

"I'm the best," he said.

"All right. We can focus on that. But I don't want you under cars for too long. You have to think bigger."

She had his attention now.

"I want my own shop," Tyrone said.

Mia smiled. "That's what I'm talking about. But you can't just go out and get a shop. You have to put in a lot of work first."

"I need to go to school," Tyrone acknowledged. "I know a lot right now, but I have to know a lot more if I want to run my own shop. I saw this commercial for ATI the other day. You think I should give that a try?"

Mia's heart fluttered. "That would be great, Tyrone."

He nodded. "If I get a degree from ATI, I could work anywhere."

"And then you could save up some money for your shop."

"Your really think I can do that?"

Mia frowned. "You're the one who told me, '*This is America. I can do anything I want.*' "

Tyrone grinned. "You right. But if I'm gonna get my own shop, then I need to know about more than just cars. I think I should go to the community college, learn about running a business."

Mia couldn't have been more pleased. "You want to get an associate's degree?"

"I didn't say all that."

"Come on, Tyrone. You're almost there. You've just about got this worked out."

He sat back and rubbed his chin. "You know that program at ATI takes a long time, right? You want me to do two years in college after that?"

"Tyrone, you're only thirty-two. Plus that'll give you time to save up your money."

"I know, but that's still a long-ass time."

Mia cocked her head. "Tyrone, this was your idea. Why are you trying to back out?"

"I'm just, you know, what if I don't make it?"

"I'll be there for you," Mia said. "If you get a degree from ATI, get a good job, and get your associates, I'll help you get your shop opened."

His smile was puppy dog cute. "No shit?"

"No shit," Mia said. "And speaking of *shit*, we're gonna have to work on your potty mouth, too."

He shook his head, still smiling. "You serious, ain't you?"

"Your vocabulary will change when you get into school, but in the meantime I do want you to make an effort to watch your cursing. Especially the N word. Everything can't be *nigga this* and *nigga that*. TC will start to say whatever you say, and I don't want him talking like that."

Tyrone rolled his eyes. "You're pushing it."

Mia tried a little sensitivity. "Please, baby. Try it for me . . ."

Tyrone melted like butter on a skillet. "Mia, if you're gonna help me through this, I'd be a fool not to want to do it for myself, too. I'ma take care of my business, girl. I told you when I got out, we're meant to be together. I'm not gonna be the one to fuc—I mean, *mess* that up."

Mia was extremely giddy. "*Awww!* Give me a hug!"

Tyrone stood and wrapped his arms around her like Mia was a life preserver.

"Y'all niggas corny," Crystal said, or at least Mia thought it was Crystal. She pushed Tyrone away and rushed to the bed, her heart thumping in her chest.

But Crystal's eyes were still closed. She hadn't moved. Mia looked to Tyrone quizzically.

"Didn't you hear something?"

"I thought I did."

"I said y'all is corny," Crystal said again, and this time Mia saw her lips move.

CHAPTER 22
TOUGH LOVE

Tyrone and Mia left the hospital at two o'clock. They went home to get a few things, and came back with the kids an hour and a half later. Crystal was wide awake by then, already complaining about her substandard living conditions.

"*I don't like this*. What is this supposed to be?" She stared at a spoonful of dressing drenched with white gravy.

"That's turkey and dressing," Mia said. "You sure don't have a problem with it at Thanksgiving."

"That's the problem," Crystal said. "It's *not* Thanksgiving. You not supposed to eat this stuff this time of year. There's no telling how long they've had it sitting around."

"Can I have it?" TC asked. He hung on his aunt's bed like a starving puppy.

Crystal looked a lot better now. Her color was back, along with her sense of humor. She sat up in bed on her own and had already had her catheter removed. She'd been on her feet already and couldn't wait to get back home. The doctor said she would probably be released in a few hours.

The only obvious lingering effects of her slight over-dose were her drowsy, sleepy eyes. She looked like she was still nodding a little. Plus, she had on no makeup at all. She had her hair tied back in a ponytail, and it was nowhere near as dashing as normal.

"Stop begging," Mia told TC. "We're gonna go get something to eat in a minute. Plus, you've still got to do your homework. We've got to get going," she told her sister.

"They're gonna discharge me pretty soon," Crystal said.

Mia shot Tyrone a worried glance, and he returned it. "They said it's gonna be a few hours," Mia said. "I think I'll take Mica and TC to the house and come back to get you by myself."

"Who's gonna watch them?" Crystal asked.

"Daddy watched us yesterday," TC said.

Crystal's eyes registered unease, but she didn't say anything.

"So, we're gonna go now," Mia said, looking at her watch. "I'll make sure I'm back in time. Y'all give your Aunt Crystal a kiss."

The kids did as they were told. Tyrone told Crystal he would see her later, and TC and Mica followed him out of the room. Mia was the last to go.

"Here, put this over there," Crystal said, holding out her lunch tray. "I'm not eating that."

Mia took it and set it on a nearby counter. "How you feeling?"

"I feel all right," Crystal said, rubbing her hair back with her hands. "I can't wait to get out of here, though. You better hurry up."

Mia smiled down at her. It was a warm, caring smile. "I won't be long," she promised and reached out to hold her sister's hand.

Crystal looked up at her queerly. "Why you looking at me like that?"

Mia was on the verge of tears, but she fought them back. "I've just been worried about you, is all. You had us really scared." She leaned down and kissed Crystal on her forehead.

"You'd *better* come back for me," Crystal said. It was a joke, but she looked like she was really worried.

When they got home, Mia sent the kids upstairs to change out of their school clothes. She made a pizza for them and let them bring their homework to the dining room so they could work while they ate.

At six o'clock she got a phone call. Crystal was discharged and ready to be picked up. Mia made a call herself, and then went to the living room where Tyrone lounged on the couch, watching cartoons again. It was the Boondocks this time.

"Don't let the kids watch that," she said. She thought she sounded friendly enough, but Tyrone was immediately offended.

"I know that, Mia. You don't think I know nothing?"

"I'm sorry. I was just . . . what's wrong?"

"I didn't know this *plan* of yours had you correcting me in front of the kids."

On the way home from the hospital Tyrone said Crystal's doctor was a dumb-ass. Mia did ask him to watch his language, but she didn't think it was that big of a deal.

"They didn't notice."

"Yeah? They will if you're doing it all the time."

"You said you were going to make an effort to speak better in front of them," Mia reminded him.

"It ain't gonna happen overnight."

"All it takes is a conscious—"

"*It ain't gonna happen overnight*," Tyrone said again, and this time Mia knew to back down.

"I'm sorry," she said. "I just . . . it's been stressful. When I did that in the car, I wasn't, I mean . . . I wasn't thinking. I can understand how it made you feel, though. I didn't mean to offend you."

Tyrone's eyes softened. "It's all right. I guess I do need to try harder. This is new to me. It's hard."

Mia smiled. "I know it is. I really can't believe you're putting up with me. It's really special."

Tyrone melted some more. He smiled, and Mia had to move in to kiss those lips. She sat on the couch next to him with her hand behind his head.

"I have to go to the hospital. They just called."

"Have you talked to her yet?"

Mia shook her head and looked away. "No."

The biggest problem was that Crystal seemed to be in a state of delusion. She told Mia and Tyrone there had been *no sex*. She said she didn't remember taking off her clothes. But when the police showed up, Crystal said she didn't remember what happened. She told the detective she and Sydney were kissing, and there "might have been" some foreplay.

When asked point-black if the sex was consensual or not, Crystal said it must have been, because Sydney wouldn't have raped her. The detective later told Mia they wouldn't even seek charges for the drug aspect of this would-be crime. Crystal sounded like a willing participant in everything that went on.

Mia kissed Tyrone again. "I'll be back in a little bit."

He nodded and watched her as she stood to go.

"They shouldn't be hungry before I get back, but there's some leftover–"

"I know." Tyrone cut her off. "I've been in your kitchen before."

Mia rolled her eyes. "You think I'm crazy, don't you?"

"No," he said with a grin. "You're like a mama possum. Touch one of her babies, and she'll bite your hand off."

Mia sneered. "You compare me to a *possum*? Not a cuddly mama *bear*, but a *possum*?"

Tyrone laughed. "I ain't seen no bears over at Maw Maw's house. But I seen some possums!"

Mia left the house in a good mood, but she had butterflies in her stomach when she got to the hospital. Her heart felt sick by the time she walked into her sister's room.

Crystal was fully dressed and on her feet. She had on the jumpsuit Mia put on after the sexual assault *that probably wasn't an assault.* She stood in the bathroom with the door ajar. In the mirror, she was putting on red lipstick acquired from God-knew-where. Crystal wasn't particular about her sources during a fashion crisis.

She looked up when Mia walked through the door and started towards her.

"Come on, girl. I gotta hurry up and get outta here. Somebody I know might see me looking like this."

Her excitement withered when she saw the look on her sister's face. Mia was very close to tears. Not only that, but Mia closed the door and sat in the recliner next to Crystal's bed. She motioned for Crystal to take the far less comfortable wooden chair.

"Sit down."

But Crystal didn't want to. "Why? They said I could go. I'm all right."

"I know," Mia said. "But we have to talk. Sit down."

Crystal took the seat uneasily and fixed a look of complete remorse on her big sister. "Mia, I'm sorry. The only reason he was over there is 'cause I told him I couldn't see him anymore. I told him we had to talk, and he came over, and . . ."

Mia wished she hadn't trailed off. She wished Crystal could finish that sentence with something logical, or maybe even something profoundly and totally weird. Mia wasn't picky. Anything even halfway believable would work, but that was the problem. Crystal had nothing—not one ounce of explanation. Mia looked into her eyes and the tears started to fall.

Crystal began to cry too. "Mia. What's . . . what are you . . ."

Mia closed her eyes. She opened them slowly and wiped the tears away with the back of her hand. "I've, uh, I've set it up for you to go to rehab."

Crystal shook her head. "Mia, I don't need to go to *rehab*. I'm all right. I'm not a *junkie*."

"I don't think you're a junkie," Mia said. "I don't think you steal. I don't think you do a lot of other bad things, either. But you *do* have a problem with drugs. If you don't see that, then we have another problem right there."

"I'm all right," Crystal said. She looked like Mia told her she had to go to jail. "It was just an accident. I'm not gonna do it no more."

Mia reached out and held her hand. "I believe you," she said. And she really did. "But what you did, Crystal, it was something, it was, it was *awful*. I can't—"

"Mia, I'm sorry. Just give me one more chance. I promise . . ."

"Crystal, I'm not throwing you out with the garbage. I love you. *I am* giving you a chance. I want you to go to rehab. There's a program in Grapevine. I talked to the people. You have to live there for three months. It won't be that—"

"*Mia, please.*" Crystal was blubbering now. Tears streamed down her face. Mia took a handkerchief from her purse and wiped her sister's cheek with it. Crystal took it and blew her nose. Mia produced another hankie for herself.

"Mia, just give me *one more chance.* Let me come home. I promise I'll—"

"Shhhh." Mia shook her head. "Crystal, I have faith in you. I really do. I know you can pull through this. I believe this was an isolated event. *Honestly.* But the fact is, you got high. In my house. Probably more than once."

"I didn—"

"Crystal, I've already made up my mind. If you don't want to go to rehab, *rehab I'm paying for*, then you have to find somewhere else to live. I've already got your clothes in the trunk. We can either go *right now*, or you can tell me where you want me to drop you and your stuff off. I'm sorry, but those are your only options."

Crystal's mouth dropped. "Mia."

Mia wiped away a fresh batch of tears, but stood firm. "Crystal, it's the best thing for you. *You* know it, and *I* know it. If it was just a freak occurrence, then you can do these three months and have your life back. If you don't want to go, then you make me wonder if it's because you *don't* want to stop using drugs."

"It's not that."

"Then what is it?"

"I just don't want to lose you," Crystal said. Her whole body shuddered. Mia put a hand on her shoulder. "I know I let you down," Crystal said, "and you don't want me around no more."

Mia stood and hugged the girl. "Crystal, I love you. You know we don't have a real close family. I don't plan on losing the little family I still have around. I promise, if you do the three months and get your life back together, you can come home. I just can't have you around my kids like this. You of all people should know that."

And Crystal did know. "Just three months?" she asked, and Mia knew she had her.

Grapevine, Texas, is only twenty minutes east of Overbrook Meadows. When they got in the car, Mia tried to get answers to some poignant questions, but even this late in the game, Crystal was still elusive.

"How many times did you snort? *Seriously.*"

"Just those couple of times."

Mia gave her a sideways glance.

"Not that much . . ."

"How much were you using?"

"I don't know. Not that much."

"What, a *whole* pill?"

"Not that much."

"Why did you have him at the house again, anyway?"

"I don't know. We were just supposed to talk."

"And you ended up using dope again? Crystal, that doesn't make any sense."

Crystal kept her hands in her lap and her eyes on her hands. She nibbled her bottom lip.

"Why can't you admit you wanted it?" Mia asked.

"Maybe I did, a little."

"And you were going to have sex again? In my house?"

"I wasn't, Mia. I swear. But then we got high . . ."

Mia shook her head. "How much did you do?"

"I wasn't getting high at first. I thought I had enough, but I wasn't getting high. So I did some more. But I still wasn't getting high . . ."

For Mia, this was all utterly revolting. She thought she wanted to know all the slimy details, but she really didn't. She dropped the questions and they drove in silence for a while. She played a Jagged Edge CD, surprised she could actually listen to it again.

Crystal had surprisingly few question about what her stay at the facility would be like. She wanted to know if she could have visits and use the phone. She asked if Mia packed her favorite socks and jewelry. She mainly wanted to know that Mia wouldn't forget about her over there. Mia told her to stop being silly.

They got checked in at seven o'clock. Mia met the director, a few residents, and a squirrelly security guard named Rufus who claimed to have an eye on *everything*. Crystal got a room all to herself, and Mia stayed another thirty minutes to help her unpack and get acclimated to her new surroundings.

Crystal broke down again when Mia tried to leave, but that was to be expected. Mia found the strength to look her sister in the eyes, tell her it was for her own good, and walk away. In her recollection, it was the hardest thing she ever had to do.

When she got home Tyrone and the kids were sprawled on the living room floor playing Go Fish with a deck of regular playing cards. The kids greeted their mom briefly and then went immediately back to their cards. Only Tyrone's gaze lingered. Mia forced a smile at him and nodded. He nodded back and then asked Mica if she had a four.

"Go fish."

When the kids were bathed and fast asleep, Mia snuggled with her boyfriend on the couch.

"So she wasn't really tripping?" he asked.

"She was when I tried to leave, but she knew I wasn't changing my mind."

"Did she ever admit to what was going on?"

"Not really. She kept saying it wasn't a big deal. The counselors will help."

"You going to work tomorrow?" he asked.

"Yeah."

"You gonna get those people to pick up the kids from school?"

"Yes. I already talked to them. I'm not going to stay too late, these next few weeks at least. I'll be off at five."

Tyrone nodded. "So how *you* doing?"

Mia subconsciously rubbed the scratch on her face. Tyrone saw the move, and his eyes flashed fire, but then it was gone.

"I'll be all right," Mia said. "It's only three months. When she gets out, I think she'll have a good head on her shoulders. Maybe she'll want to do something better with her life."

Tyrone smiled. "*Like me.*"

Mia smiled too. "Yeah. Like you. How are *you* doing?"

"What you mean?"

"I mean with the kids and your new ambitions. How you handling all of this?"

"Oh, I'm cool," he said. "I told you I wanted to raise Mica like she was mine."

Mia couldn't understand how just a few months ago those exact words made her sick to the stomach. "What about that other stuff?" she asked. "You still think you wanna go through all that?"

Tyrone looked at her like she said the world was flat. "Yeah, I wanna do it. Why wouldn't I?"

"I don't know. You might think it's too hard."

"It's not so hard," he said, and kissed her. "All I have to do is go to school."

"Make good grades," she said.

He put his hand under her shirt and held her side. The hand slid up to her breast.

"I'm gonna make all A's," he said and kissed her again.

Mia closed her eyes. "It's gonna be hard," she whispered.

Tyrone took her hand and placed it in his lap. "It's already hard."

Mia giggled and opened her eyes. "You freak." Then she squeezed it and said, "*Ooh.*"

"I know I'm not supposed to spend the night more than once a week . . ." Tyrone said.

"I see you still remember the rules," Mia noticed.

"I told you, I'm going to make all A's," he said.

Mia didn't know what it was about him, but Tyrone seemed serious about everything. She knew the road ahead was rough, worse than either of them really expected, but she believed they could make it. It was ridiculous, anyone would tell her so, but she had faith in Tyrone.

"Come on," she said. "But don't think I'm a pushover."

"Trust me, I know you're not."

She took him to her bedroom and rocked *his* world this time around. Tyrone wasn't normally a vocal lover, but when she got on top and held his chest, grinding like it was his birthday, Tyrone's ecstasy was too much to contain.

"Mia."

"What?"

"That . . . that feels good."

"*Huh?*"

"That feels . . . that feels good."

"I know."

When he rolled her onto her back, and looked into her eyes, and they were face to face and breast to breast, Mia believed a meshing of souls was occurring as the sweat on their bellies mingled.

CHAPTER 23

FIXIN' TYRONE

"Wake up, sleepyhead."

Tyrone rolled over. He wore only boxing shorts. The lone blanket on the bed was draped over his legs. Staring at his muscular torso and arms made Mia want to slide back between the sheets with him. He shook off the last holds of sleep and smiled at her.

Mia wore a dark-blue skirt suit with a white blouse today.

"You been up already?" he asked.

"I've already taken the kids to school, lazy. I'm on my way to work."

"Why you didn't wake me up?"

Mia sat on the corner of the bed and held his head against her chest. "You looked so peaceful, I didn't want to bother you."

He rubbed his face on her stomach. "You smell good."

"You smell like *sex*," she said.

"It was good. I'm not gonna take a bath. I want to smell like this all day."

"*Eww. Nasty.*"

He sat up and looked around the room. "Where my pants?"

Mia found them on the other side of the bed. "You're just throwing your clothes everywhere."

"I don't even remember taking them off," he said and stood. Even half sleep he was awesomely handsome. Mia stepped to him and put both hands on his chest.

"I like these," she said, rubbing from top to bottom.

Tyrone dropped his pants and grabbed the bulge in the back of Mia's skirt. "I like *these*," he said.

Mia stood eye level with his Adam's apple. She kissed it, then his collarbone, then the side of his neck. Tyrone squeezed harder, and Mia felt him growing against her belly. She backed away and eyed the bulge in his boxers.

"That was quick."

He licked his lips. "You look good, Mia. It took you a long time to put all that stuff on?"

"Yeah," she admitted. "It did."

"So, you probably don't want to take it all off then, huh?"

"Wish I could, baby. I *really* do."

Tyrone reluctantly picked up his britches. "You sure you don't need me to pick the kids up today?"

"No. It's all taken care of. This place they're going to is really good. They're already picking up twelve kids from the school. One of them is in TC's class. I talked to a few parents, too. Everybody likes them. They say it's one of the best day cares in the city—and they should be for what they're charging."

"If you let me watch them, you could save that money."

"It's all right," Mia said. "But we do need to start getting some money saved for *your* schooling. Do you have a bank account?"

Tyrone sat on the corner of the bed, slipping into his shoes. He grinned at her.

"So, we're starting already?"

"*The Plan* officially started at the hospital when you said you were willing to try."

"I'm not just gonna try. I'm gonna succeed. Is that what you're calling it? *The Plan?*"

"Yeah. I like The Plan, you got something better?"

"How bout *Tyrone's Super Sexy Gangstalicious Plan?*"

"Yeah, we'll just roll with The Plan, if that's all right with you."

Tyrone chuckled. "That's fine with me, ma'am. But I don't make a lot with my uncle. I think we'd be better off funding my education with dope money."

Mia tossed his tee shirt at him, hitting him in the face. "I think we'll be okay with what little you can bring in," she said. "How much do you make? Do you get paid by the week or what?"

"You're serious?"

Mia looked him in the eyes. "From now on, when we talk about The Plan, I'm always serious."

Tyrone's wages came out to $25 to $30 a day, which he was paid cash. Some evenings he made more, but they used the $25 as a base salary. With $125 coming in a week, Mia thought he should save $50 of it for his school expenses. Tyrone thought he could save up to $100, but

Mia said he should give his mother some type of rent. Even though it was not requested, it was still necessary if he was to become a responsible adult.

Tyrone agreed. Fifty dollars a week would go to The Plan. That left $75 for the rent and other miscellaneous needs. Tyrone's only objection was that he'd have no money to spend on the kids, but Mia came up with a whole list of activities that were both free and adored by TC and Mica, like the library, the park, and the museum on certain days. She said she'd even get them season passes so they could go to Six Flags. Tyrone said he could also take the kids to Cleburne to visit Maw Maw sometimes.

"They had a lot of fun down there," he noted. "And that's always free."

"Now you're thinking," Mia said.

She dropped him off and went to work a little apprehensive about the new after-school arrangements on that first day, but her worries were totally unfounded. When Mia picked her children up, they were happy and excited. Not only did their caregivers help them with their homework, but they had a copy of Woodway's curriculum for the whole school year. TC and Mica got a head start on topics their teachers wouldn't bring up for a couple of weeks.

Everyone missed Crystal, but Mia was very happy with her alternative plan.

Because he spent the night Monday and Tuesday, Mia didn't expect to see Tyrone again until the weekend, but he called her Thursday night.

"Hello?"

"What's up. It's Tyrone."

"Where are you calling from?"

"I'm with my homeboy. This his cell phone. Can I stop by for a minute?"

"It's late. I'm getting the kids ready for bed. I'm tired, too."

"It won't take that long. I don't want to come in. I just need to see you for a second."

"All right," Mia said. "How long before you're here?"

"I'm on the road now. I'll be there in five minutes."

Tyrone called again a few minutes later and said he was pulling up. Mia turned the porch light off on her way outside, but reached in to flip it back on when she caught a look at her man: Tyrone wore blue jeans and a white tee shirt. His shirt was not only ripped at the collar, but had a bloodstain on the chest area. The source of the blood was quickly traced to Tyrone's face: His bottom lip—*his beautiful bottom lip*—was bruised. Half of it was swollen, and there was a small cut.

Mia turned the light off again, her chest pounding, her eyes wide. "What happened?"

"I got into it with ol' boy, Crystal's boyfriend *Sydney*."

"What do you mean you '*got into it*'?"

"Okay, I went and found him."

Looking at Tyrone's physique, Mia would have never thought he'd lose a fight, but the evidence was clear. "He beat you up?"

Tyrone looked incredulous. He knitted his eyebrows and smiled. His wonderful smile was marred by that fat lip. "Naw, he didn't beat me up. He only hit me one time."

Mia reached up and touched the wound. "It looks bad."

Tyrone rubbed it too. "Yeah. I didn't think he had nothing in him. I walked up to him, talking shit, you know, asking about him getting Crystal high and raping her. He started apologizing right off, so I figured he was a punk. I slapped him a couple of times, still talking shit. I'm *playing with him* really, but he ducked under one of my punches and came up with his fists raised. He caught me in the mouth that one time."

"He hit you?"

"Yeah, but it was my fault. I was the one goofing around. I thought he was weak, but that ugly nigga had a little something."

Mia couldn't help but chuckle. "What happened after that?"

"Shit, I beat his monkey ass. Once I saw he had some skills, I stopped playing. I messed him up pretty good. Made him tell the truth about what happened."

"What'd he say?"

"He said *Crystal* was the one who called him over. He said she'd been calling him every since you caught him in the house. He said *she* was the one wanted to get high, *and* he said she was the one who kept snorting even after he told her she had enough. He said she stole two pills from him. Oh, and he said she was still woke when they started, you know."

"You believe him?" Mia asked.

"Yeah. I had that fool in a choke hold. He wasn't lying."

Mia shook her head. She looked past Tyrone and saw an old-school Fleetwood idling on the street. "Who is that? Y'all jumped him?"

"That's my homeboy Kody," Tyrone said. "And, naw, we didn't jump him. I don't need no help fighting."

Mia stepped forward and wrapped her arms around him. Tyrone did the same. "I told you violence doesn't solve anything," she said.

"I had to stand up for your honor. He said he's sorry for pushing you, by the way."

Mia pulled back and looked into his eyes. "He said that?"

"I ain't gonna lie to you."

"*My hero*," she said and kissed him. Bubble-lip and all, it was still a good kiss.

The following Saturday Mia went to Claire's. As gung-ho as the girls were about Tyrone a couple weeks ago, Mia thought she'd get support for The Plan, but no such luck.

"Girl, you can't change no man. School? A savings account? Mia, you need to quit playing. All that stuff's gonna take forever. You expect Tyrone to do right for that long? I told you to give him some and then go on about your business."

And that came from Gayle. Mia couldn't believe it.

"You're the one who told me to work it out with him!"

"I don't remember that."

"He just wants your money," Vasantha said.

Mia's mouth fell open as she stared at her hairstylist in the mirror. "Vasantha, I know for a fact you told me to get with Tyrone."

"I said get with him, I didn't say try to turn him into Mr. Right. He's a *thug*, girl!"

Mia was dumbfounded. She looked around the room in awe. "So, no one here remembers telling me Tyrone could make a good man?"

"Uhn-uhn."

"Naw."

"*Hell*, naw."

"I didn't say that."

"I didn't, either."

"Nope, nope, nope."

Mia laughed. "I'm gonna start wearing a tape recorder in here. You two-faced heifers don't even remember your own advice half the time."

"If *I* said you should go with Tyrone, I would remember that," Gayle said. "I told you thugs know how to *lay pipe real good*, but I never said to *be with him*, like in a regular relationship."

"Well, I am with him," Mia said. "And we're gonna make it work. Everything I told you about is going to happen."

"You'll probably get him to enroll in school, but that's gonna be the end of it," Gayle predicted.

"Once he sees how hard it is, he won't stay," Vasantha agreed.

Mia didn't expect anything different from Mama Ernestine on the way out, and the matriarch did not disappoint.

Today she wore blue jeans with a denim blouse and a wig she called the Lady Sings the Blues. "Mia, you're a smart woman. Don't let that boy mess up your head. You go offering him his own business, and yeah, he'll say anything to get that. But it's not going to work. You can't fix no man. You should know better than that."

Despite every woman she knew being against The Plan, Mia still left the beauty shop, as always, a fresh, vibrant, and confident woman.

She took the kids to see Crystal on Sunday. It may have been different during the week, but on the weekends Crystal's center was a lively place. Relatives from all over the state came to support and bring a bit of cheer to their addict sons and daughters, sisters and brothers, and moms and dads, too.

After just one week at the facility, Mia thought Crystal looked a lot better already. She gained a little weight, her makeup was neat and stylish, and Crystal's face and hair had a glow to it.

"Well, look who's getting all pretty and healthy again," Mia told her. Crystal rolled her eyes. The kids still didn't know what brand of sickness kept their aunt at this *odd* hospital.

"She looks fine. Can she come home today, Mommy?" Mica asked.

"Yeah," Crystal said. "I feel fine, *Mommy*. Can I come home?"

Mia frowned at her. "She has to stay here for three more months," she told Mica.

"*Two months and twenty-four days*," Crystal corrected.

"Seems like you know *exactly* how long you have to be here," Mia noticed. "So quit asking to leave until that time is up."

Crystal sat back in her chair and pouted. That was all she had in her power to do, so she took full advantage. She refined, tweaked, and sported that pout eleven weekends straight. The only time Crystal had a smile on her face was the last time Mia drove to Grapevine to take her home.

"You don't know how much I *hated* that place," Crystal said on the drive home.

"What was so bad about it?" Mia wanted to know.

"*Everything*. All the boys there are *ugly*. They only let you use the phone once a week, and you only get thirty minutes. The food *sucks*, you can't go *nowhere*. And they make you go to all these stupid meetings. *And* they make you work, *every* day, but you don't get the money."

Mia listened, her heart sinking with each word. It sounded like the whole three months had been in vain. "So, you didn't learn anything?" she finally asked.

"Yes, I did," Crystal said immediately. "I learned to stop blaming everyone else and take responsibility for what I did. I learned to admit I have a problem with drugs. And I learned how to avoid those situations that lead me to my drug abuse."

Mia was surprised. "So, you *do* have a problem with drugs? That's news to me."

Crystal smiled. "Yes, Mia. I do. I used heroin and I abused it. And I lied about how much I used, and I lied about how much I wanted it. I'm sorry."

"Wow. Is this the new and improved Crystal? You sound more mature."

"I am," she said. "I met a lot of people who *really* had drug problems. I'm not saying I didn't, I'm just saying theirs was *worse*. Some of them lost their kids, houses, businesses. I don't ever want to end up like them."

"That's good," Mia said. "What about your *next* boyfriend?"

"He's going to be a nerd," Crystal predicted. "I'm not messing with no more rappers. No more thugs."

Mia smiled.

"And how's everything's going with *your* thug boyfriend?" Crystal asked.

"It's going fine," Mia said. The more she thought about it, the bigger her smile grew. "Every day we're getting a little more *thug* out of him. You know he started school last month?"

"Quit lying."

"For real."

"What *kind* of school?"

"He's going to ATI. It's a twelve-month program. He's going to know how to work on *any* car when he finishes."

"You got Tyrone in school?"

"*He* filled out the application himself, Crystal, and he wakes up for classes on his own. I merely *suggested* it."

"I don't believe it."

"No one does."

"But ain't he still gonna be a *mechanic* when he gets out?"

"That's just phase one," Mia said. "I didn't tell you about The Plan?"

"What plan?"

"When Tyrone finishes at ATI, he's going to get a good job at one of the bigger auto shops. While he's working there, he's going to go to the community college and get an associate's degree in business."

"Please."

"*And then* he's going to open his own shop."

"Tyrone's gonna do *all that*?"

"You've been gone a long time. A lot has changed."

"Tyrone's not going to do all that."

"He's already started," Mia said. "And he's doing just fine. He sees the kids every Saturday, and he takes them to the library and the museum sometimes."

"*I'm* supposed to keep them while you're at the beauty shop."

"Like I said, Crystal, a lot of things have changed. They've been going to daycare after school, and I want them to keep going there."

"Why?" Crystal asked. "You don't trust me?"

"If I didn't trust you, I wouldn't be picking you up. I actually think the daycare's good for them. They get a lot of work done. They don't have as many distractions. TC's teacher says he's doing better in class."

"TC was already doing good."

"Yeah, but she says he's more focused. He talks less and doesn't seem bored like he used to be."

"Sounds like everything's going great with me out of the way," Crystal said.

"You're not going to start crying, are you?" Mia asked with a wry smile.

"I might," Crystal said. She crossed her arms and stared out of the window.

"Tell you what, I've been leaving at five to pick the kids up from daycare, but maybe if I have to work late, you can get them instead."

"I can pick them up from *school*."

"No. I want them at daycare until *five*. I don't want it to be like it was, Crystal. I want you to work on your own life more. I've had the kids for the past three months, *all by myself*, and nobody lost a finger. I'm glad you're coming home, but I'm not going to use you like I did. Tyrone gets the kids on Saturdays, and they stay in daycare after school. I want you to go to school and do something with *your* life. Tyrone says he's going to get his associates before you."

"Yeah, right."

"You shouldn't underestimate my man," Mia said. "We wouldn't even be trying this if I didn't think he could do it. He beat Sydney up for me."

"He what?"

Mia laughed. She knew that would get her attention. She told Crystal the whole sordid story, even about the one lick Tyrone took during the fight, and they laughed about it the rest of the way home.

THE FINAL CHAPTER
A DIAMOND IN THE ROUGH

The Plan was going according to schedule, but Mia didn't tell her sister about a problem that nearly did them in when they first enrolled at ATI. Tyrone was definitely a skilled mechanic, but many of his automotive techniques were of the shade tree variety. Mia would never forget the day he brought his first textbook home. He flipped through it, growing more perplexed by the page.

"This some bullshit," he said finally.

"What's wrong?" Mia asked. They were in her living room on a warm Wednesday night.

"This is too much stuff. Nobody does it like this. I don't even know what some of these parts are."

"They'll teach you," Mia comforted.

"Yeah, they'll teach me the *wrong* way," Tyrone mused. "Like right here," he pointed to a complicated diagram. "You don't have to do all this to change out a fuel pump. A lot of this is unnecessary."

"I had to learn a lot of unnecessary stuff when I went to school," Mia said. "I memorized the periodic table of elements. No one cares about that. And I'm still waiting for someone to ask what a *pronoun* is."

"That's different. They taught you stuff you don't need. These people are trying to teach me the *wrong way* to do something.

"How do you know it's wrong? Maybe it's just different."

"It's a lot of extra steps."

"Oh," Mia said, finally getting it. "So you know a *better* way to do it?"

"A *whole lot* better."

"That just means you're *better* than the average mechanic, Tyrone. The next time your teacher shows you something that doesn't look right, tell him how it could be done easier. But be polite about it. The other students might appreciate it."

And she was right. Tyrone told her so three weeks later.

"You remember what you said about how I should tell my teacher if I know a better way to do something?"

"Yeah," Mia said.

"The guy teaching our class, I think he just got out of school hisself. He showed us how to change brakes today. Took him thirty minutes."

"You're faster than that," Mia guessed.

"For real. When he got finished, I told him I knew a *different way* to do it, and he let me try."

Mia smiled.

"And I did them brakes in like ten minutes," Tyrone said. "Everybody was trippin'. The teacher said he was going to do it like I showed him when he taught his next class."

Tyrone was very excited. He gave her a big hug. Unfortunately Mia had to cut the embrace short when her cell phone rang. She dug it from her purse and got a little fretful when she saw the number in the caller ID.

"Hello?"

"Hi, Mia." It was Mr. Manitou. "I thought you were going to call me. I gave you time to do so on your own, but it's been so long . . ."

Mia looked into Tyrone's eyes, and he waited patiently.

"I'm sorry," she said. "I have a boyfriend now."

Mr. Manitou sighed. "But I thought would get an opportunity when you said you were single."

Mia knew she was making a choice between a hard-working millionaire and a thug who might not make it in the long run, but she had to follow her heart.

"I'm sorry, Mr. Manitou. I can't talk to you anymore."

He sighed again. "Fine, Mia. I will not attempt again."

"That's cool," she said and hung up. She looked back to Tyrone, and he wasn't jealous at all.

"*Anyway*, I think I'm going to be at the top of my class when I graduate," he said.

"I knew you could do it."

"Nobody ever had this much faith in me. I wanted to thank you, so I got you this." He let go of her and pulled a jewelry box from his front pocket.

Mia was surprised, but not necessarily pleased with the gift. "I thought you were supposed to be saving money. They're going to send you bills when you graduate."

"I know. Don't worry. It didn't cost that much."

Mia reluctantly accepted the box. Inside was a gold necklace. It was thin, and of too little quality to garnish any real praise for the item alone, but it was the thought that counted. Her eyes watered.

"Tyrone, I don't expect you to get me any gifts. It's gonna be hard for a while. I already know that."

"I know," Tyrone said, "but I found a way to get the money. I used to eat at Wendy's every day for lunch. But I took a sandwich from home for the last three weeks and saved up the money. I'm still putting $50 in the bank every Friday. I'm not messing with that at all."

"You ate bologna just so you could give me this?"

"I'd eat bologna the rest of my life to make you happy," he said, and Mia gave him some real good loving that evening. She even let him spend the night.

The first year of The Plan went well. Tyrone went to school five days a week. He got out at noon and went straight to his uncle's shop, where he replaced alternators and rotated tires until six. He went home and studied every night. At school he was always fresh and excited, eager to wow his peers with his superior automotive skills. He didn't make all A's as promised, but he did remain at the top of his class. And he remained the teacher's favorite.

When bragging about his schooling, Mia once made the mistake of calling Tyrone a teacher's pet one day. His face wrinkled up like she called him a *punk*.

"I ain't no *teacher's pet*. I just help sometimes. The teacher says I'm his *special helper*."

Mia thought that *still* sounded like he was a teacher's pet, even more so, but she didn't say anything else.

The only downside to Tyrone's growth was that he couldn't get a better job while in school. He averaged two applications a week for a while, but whenever it came time for the interview, that same question was always his downfall.

Have you ever been convicted of a felony? If so, explain.

But Mia didn't see this as a serious problem. "Once you get your license from ATI, you'll find a garage that will hire you despite your felony. If they know how good you are, and know you've made serious changes since getting out, things will be different."

Tyrone didn't like it much, but at least his uncle's shop was steady work. He put his $50 in every Friday and resolved to bide his time until graduation.

And even with school and his job, Tyrone still came by to kick it with the kids every weekend. On Saturday afternoons, Tyrone took TC and Mica to free venues like the library and the park. He saved $15 from his pay so they could go to McDonald's afterwards.

Sunday nights was usually time for Tyrone and Mia to be alone. Tyrone couldn't afford to take her very many places, but just being in each other's company was usually enough. Mia paid the few times they went out to eat or to the movies, but Tyrone didn't like that. So they went to the arboretum a lot, and romantic walks through the park became a mainstay. More than anything else, they rented movies and cuddled on the sofa.

And not to be outdone by Tyrone's achievements, Crystal signed up for five classes her first fall back from rehab. She eventually dropped two and got a D in one of the remaining three, but Mia was still proud of her.

"Rome wasn't built in a day," she told her one afternoon.

"You corny," Crystal said.

Two months before Tyrone's graduation, Mia got the shock of her life when she decided to surprise her man with a visit after work. The situation was pretty similar to the first time she left the office in search of him: At lunch she bought him a pair of diamond earrings, but when she got to his house, Tyrone's mother said he wasn't home.

"I think he at the rec," the old woman said, causing a solid knot to form in Mia's stomach. Something told her to just go home, but they were too far in the game for that nonsense. She headed to Sycamore Park doing sixty mph. When she got there and saw Tyrone standing under a tree with three other hoodlums, Mia didn't sit behind the wheel and cry like last time. She got out and stomped up to him with a taste for war. But when Tyrone turned and saw her, he didn't appear frightful at all. He actually started laughing.

"Mia, I already know what you're thinking."

"You damned right you know what I'm thinking! What the hell are you doing over here?" Mia was quite a sight, standing there with her little fists balled up, wearing a sport coat and slacks.

"I'm just kicking it with my friends," Tyrone said, still laughing. "Say, y'all, she thinks I'm still selling dope. Tell her the truth."

"Oh, is this yo woman?" one of the thugs asked. "Hey, ma'am, Tyrone has told us a lot about you. You a good woman. You got some friends like you?"

"Watch out," Tyrone said, when he saw that Mia was still upset. "For real, y'all. Tell her I'm not selling dope. She not gonna believe me."

A skinny creep with too many teeth stepped forward. "Miss, ma'am, my name is Beenie." He put a hand over his chest. "I can tell you, with all honesty, yo man is not selling dope. He just came by to visit. I been knowing Tyrone since the fifth grade. He a good dude."

"For real, Mia," Tyrone said, still smiling. He pulled his pockets completely out. There was no dope, money, or even lint. "I just came to say what's up to my niggas. I ain't selling dope. You should see the look on your face."

Mia felt her body physically cooling as the rage wafted from her. "You were about to get beat up," she said.

"I know." Tyrone put an arm around her and they walked back to her car. "You came running up like the laws."

Mia shook her head. "Tyrone, I'm serious. If I had seen you selling drugs . . ."

"Mia," he grabbed her shoulders and turned her towards him, "I don't sell drugs no more. That day you told me to stop, I stopped. I'm not gonna lie to you. Don't ever think I'm lying to you."

"I believe you," she said. "I'm sorry I accused you."

"It's cool."

"I came to bring you this," she said, producing a jewelry box she'd almost crushed in her fist.

Tyrone took the gift, opened it, and suddenly he was the one with emotional trauma. He looked like he was witnessing the birth of his son. "Mia, these . . . these look *real.*"

"Of course they're real."

He shook his head. "I can't . . . I don't deserve this."

"Why not?"

"'Cause I ain't got no money. I can't buy you nothing nice."

"It's okay," Mia said. "You'll get there."

But he still almost didn't take them. Mia had to tell him they were an early graduation gift to get him to accept. He sat in her car and put them on, and they somehow made him more handsome than ever.

Tyrone's graduation for ATI was a happening event. Many of the students at the trade school had no greater ambitions past their automotive certificate, so the commencement exercises resembled that of a very small high school. They wore gowns, hats with tassels, slacks and slippery shoes, the whole nine yards.

When Tyrone marched across the stage, Mia, TC, and Mica stood up and cheered like he was being presented with the Nobel Prize. Mia frowned when Crystal rose slowly and clapped lethargically. She gave her sister an elbow.

"What's wrong? *Jealous?*"

"I'm not jealous. It's just a trade school."

"Yeah, but he did it in *one year*," Mia said. "How long have you been in school? You'd better clap for my man."

So Crystal did.

After the celebration, they took Tyrone out for a nice dinner. Dressed in slacks and a button-down, Mia thought Tyrone had never looked better. She'd never been so proud, but they still had another graduation to look forward to in a couple of years. Mia knew this was just the beginning of the praise Tyrone would garner.

After the dinner, Mia took him to his mother's house where one of two graduation surprises awaited him. When Tyrone saw the 2003 Impala sitting in his mother's driveway, he thought a relative was visiting. Mia pulled to a stop on the curb and beamed at her man.

"I'm proud of you," she said.

He grinned like the Cheshire cat.

"I'm proud of you, too, Daddy," TC called from the back seat.

"Me, too," Mica said.

Mia turned and gave Crystal a look, and suddenly lil' sis had a little praise as well.

"Yeah. We're all proud of you, *Tyrone.*"

He laughed. "All right. Thanks. All of y'all. I guess I'll see you later," he said to Mia, but she put a hand on his arm and stopped him from leaving.

"I've got something to confess," she said. "Do you remember those earrings I bought you?"

Tyrone was wearing them. "Of course I do."

"Well, that wasn't really your gift," she said. "Look in the glove compartment."

Mia's glove compartment was notoriously neat. There was only one thing in there out of place. Tyron removed a set of keys with a red ribbon on them, but he didn't get it. He looked up at Mia rather than the car in his mother's driveway.

"What's this for?"

She nodded towards the Impala.

Tyrone looked at it, then back to Mia, then he looked at the car again. When his gaze fell on Mia a second time, his mouth was open and his eyes were big like half dollars.

"Quit playin'."

"It's yours, baby."

"Mia. I know you didn't."

She shrugged. "Come on. Let's take a look at it." They got out of her Lexus, and Tyrone went directly to his woman, wrapping her up in the biggest bear hug she'd ever experienced. He lifted her into the air and twirled.

"Mia! I can't believe you did this. Oh, my God! I love you!"

"Please don't drop me!"

"I'm not." He put her down and stared into her eyes. "I can't believe this. How did you, why?" He shook his head. "Mia, I don't deserve this."

"There's another surprise," she said.

He was stupefied. He couldn't even fix his mouth to ask what it was.

"Look at your keychain," she said.

He did. There were three keys on the ring. Two were for the car. One was a house key. When he looked up at Mia again, she was smiling.

"Yes. That's *my* house key. I've been thinking that maybe it's time for us to take it a step forward." She thought this would usher at least as much excitement as the car, but Tyrone looked like he was being deflated. His arms fell to his sides and his face went slack.

"Mia," was all he could get out.

"Don't tell me you don't want to come."

"Of course I want to come."

"So, what's the problem?"

He shook his head. "I don't think I deserve any of this. I feel like I'm gonna let you down."

"You just graduated, Tyrone. You make me more proud every day."

"But what if I can't—"

"You will," she said.

"But what if they don't—"

"They will," Mia promised.

He came forward and held her close. "I'ma make you proud of me," he said.

"You already have, Tyrone. You already have."

Tyrone moving in was not as big an adjustment as Mia thought it would be. The kids already loved him and were excited about the new venture. No one even had to change their schedules very much. Tyrone still got off work at six o'clock, and everyone was already home by then.

Mia had to learn how to come home and fix dinner for a man, but that task actually thrilled her. Tyrone eagerly devoured anything she put on his plate and wanted seconds most of the time. TC used to be the one with the voracious appetite, and everyone finally saw where he got it from.

Mia had to give up half the space in her bedroom, but she would have eagerly given up more to be with Tyrone. She came home from work, showered, and waited for her man now. When Tyrone got home dirty and stinky, she loved his messy clothes and adored his funky smell. She loved how motor oil would stay under his nails for days at a time, and how he needed help scrubbing the middle part of his back when he showered. Mia would scrub that back for the next fifty years if she could.

She admired Tyrone's handyman qualities, too. One of the kitchen drawers had been hard to manipulate for ten years, but Tyrone had it sliding smoothly in five minutes. He fixed the leak in Crystal's bathroom, too, and renovated Mia's backyard. The reason she didn't want to get the kids a dog was because her picket fence didn't come flush to the ground all the way around. Even a big dog could have burrowed under it. But Tyrone brought in wood, bricks, and dirt to solve the problem.

Three days later he brought home a two-month-old Labrador retriever. The kids were so excited, they nearly peed their pants. Mia thought it was the most precious thing she'd ever seen, and even Crystal couldn't stop cuddling the chocolate lab. As a group, they settled on the name Queenie, and thanks to Tyrone, they had their first family pet.

Mia loved a lot of things about their new living arrangements, but the in-house sex was close to the top of the list. Even a year and a half out of prison, Tyrone still laid pipe like a Viagra-popping porn star. They made love in the closet. They made love in the shower. They made love in the evening, and they made love at daybreak before Mia woke the kids.

One such morning, Tyrone rolled over to suckle Mia's breasts.

"I've got some bad news," he said between licks.

"You're making my nipple hard."

"I know," he said, then sucked the other for uniformity. "But I got some bad news."

"What's wrong?"

Tyrone moved downward and ducked his head between Mia's legs. He kissed the outer lips, then licked down the middle. "I got rejected for another job," he said, and licked again.

Mia squirmed. "Where at?"

"Auto Boys."

"The one with those stupid commercials?" Mia asked, and then bit her bottom lip. "*Oh.*"

Tyrone sucked and kissed some more. "They start their mechanics off at $25 an hour."

"You'll make th—*thirty*," she said, and moaned.

"You sure?" he asked, and his lips latched on to her clitoris.

Mia's legs clamped closed on his head. "*Stop.*"

"Why?"

"'Cause we don't have time."

"We got plenty time," he said, and mounted like he was trying to make a baby.

Even with his certificate from ATI, it was still five months before Tyrone found a good job. By then he was already enrolled in community college, taking four core courses and one remedial class; math was never Tyrone's strong point. When he came home from work one day clean and neat, Mia expected the worst.

"You got fired?"

"From my uncle's shop? Why would they fire me?"

"Why you so clean?" she asked.

"'Cause I quit," Tyrone said with a smirk.

Mia thought she knew her man better than that. "Why would you quit your only job?"

"It wasn't my only job," he informed. "I had *two* jobs for a while today, so I had to quit one."

Mia smiled. "You got a job?"

"I got a damned good job," he said. "I got a job at Auto Boys."

"I thought you said they told you *no*."

"They did. I went back up there and tried again."

That was bold, even for Tyrone. "Why would you do that?"

"I got a homeboy who works there. He told me they have *two* supervisors. One's a bitch. The other one's cool. Turns out I interviewed with the *bitch* the first time. I went back on his day off."

Mia laughed. "What about your criminal record?"

"This other guy still asked about it, but when I told him I just got out of ATI, he *really* wanted me. And since I didn't get locked up for stealing or for shooting somebody, he said he could work with my felony."

Mia didn't think she'd ever been happier. "What happens when the first supervisor sees you?"

"I told the other supervisor about that. He says I shouldn't care what Mr. Dickerson says because Mr. Dickerson ain't running nothing."

Mia jumped up and threw her arms around him. "We've got to go out for dinner."

"It's not a big deal."

She gave him a dumb look. "What do you mean? This is damned-sure a big deal. How much do you make?"

Tyrone smiled. "I told you they start off at $25 an hour, right?"

"Yeah."

"Well, since I went to ATI, they're giving me $30."

Mia shook her head slowly, her eyes filling with moisture. "I knew you could do it."

"You're the *only* one who did," he said. "That's why I got you this."

Tyrone's jewelry box was felt this time, and the gold-plated, diamond teardrop earrings were exquisite.

"Tyrone."

"It's okay."

"How can you afford this?"

"I had the money."

"How?"

"In the bank."

"You're not supposed to spend that. You need that for your shop."

"That's two years away."

"But you're going to need as much as possible."

"I'll put it back. I make thirty dollars an hour now."

"How much did these cost?"

"Don't do that."

"Tell me."

"No."

"*Tyrone.*"

"It's the best gift I've ever given you," he said. "I want you to have them."

"The best gift you've given me is getting a good job. You graduated from ATI and you're doing good in college. I don't need this."

"I want you to have them."

"Take 'em back."

"Mia."

"Take them back," she said.

But he wouldn't.

The next two years were difficult, but everyone was ready for that. Tyrone's new job at Auto Boys paid well, but the hours were hard on his school schedule. Technically, he made enough to forget the rest of The Plan, but he never even thought about quitting, even when his remedial math had him bogged down in fractions and decimals. He did his homework late into the night, usually in the dining room so Mia could still get her sleep. She found him passed out on the table at three o'clock one morning.

"Tyrone."

He lifted his head and immediately began to write.

"Tyrone, come to bed."

"I can't. I didn't do well on my last test. The teacher says I need to study more."

"What'd you get on your last test?"

"A sixty-five."

"Isn't that still passing?"

"It is in college, but it wasn't in high school. I don't know why, but when I see *sixty-five*, I still think I'm failing."

Mia stood behind him and wrapped her arms around his neck. Each time she thought she could be no more proud of him, Tyrone proved her wrong.

He ended up making a B in his remedial math class, but got an A in College Algebra six months later. After his first year at community college, Tyrone showed Mia his transcript. The B in remedial math was his lowest grade.

"I *almost* made straight A's," he said.

Mia smiled. "Tyrone, you don't have to make straight A's. That you've done this much makes me happy. Everyone's proud of you."

He shook his head. "Uhn-uhn. I told you I was going to make straight A's, and I meant it."

And he wasn't lying.

Halfway into his second year of college, Tyrone brought home a certificate from the administration office. Mia stared at it, then pulled him down to the couch.

Tyrone sat next to her, nodding and grinning like a pedophile at day camp.

"You made the dean's list?" Mia asked.

"That's what that paper says."

Mia was awed. "Tyrone, how is it possible that you barely squeaked by in high school, failed a couple of your *electives*, as a matter of fact, but now you're rolling through college with straight A's?"

"It's not *me*. It's *you*," he said.

"No, it's not. You're the one staying up all night to do this stuff."

"Yeah, but I wouldn't have done it if not for you. I would have been on the block selling dope. You know it."

Mia did know it.

"I want you to let me take some money out of my account so I can buy you a ring," Tyrone said. "I want us to get married."

That was not the proposal Mia had dreamed of. It wasn't even as romantic as Eric's blubbering declaration of love, but it made Mia very happy just the same.

"We don't have to get a diamond right now," she said. "We just need the wedding bands. I'll get them."

Tyrone lit up. "When?"

"Soon," she said, and they kissed like newlyweds.

Mia took her man's certificate to the beauty shop with her the following Sunday, but the women at Claire's pulled another swift one on her.

"I knew he was gonna do good," Gayle said.

"That is not what you said!" Mia was starting to think she'd gone crazy, but Vasantha had her back.

"Yeah, you said Tyrone wouldn't never be shit. I remember."

"I never said that," Gayle said.

"Yes, you did," Vasantha said. "You said it after Mia left."

"What?" Mia said.

Vasantha leaned in for a conspiratorial whisper. "Don't worry about these bitches, I got your back."

"*You* said Tyrone was going to take all her money," Gayle reminded the golden-skinned girl.

"I didn't say that," Vasantha said.

"Yes, you did," Mia said. "You said that while I was sitting right here. But both of y'all were wrong. Tyrone's doing great. If he stayed in school two more years and got a bachelors, he could get any job wanted."

"All right," Gayle said, "so you're a miracle worker. Tell me how you did it, 'cause this lazy nigga I got at my house is about two minutes from getting evicted."

"You just have to encourage them," Mia said sheepishly.

"Yeah, right. You must have diamonds between your legs," Gayle guessed.

"Tyrone says it's *platinum*," Mia said, and the room erupted in laughter. "We're getting married," she said when the noise died down, and that brought a fresh round of questioning. But *no one* had anything bad to say about Tyrone this time.

Tyrone got his associates degree in business on a warm July afternoon.

Later that day, he and Mia were married at a private ceremony in Mia's back yard. She would have married him *after* they got his business going, but Tyrone wanted to go into the venture as husband and wife.

TC was the ring bearer and Mica was the flower girl. Vasantha was Mia's maid of honor, and a tall, skinny man with too many teeth was Tyrone's best man. Mia didn't really know the guy, but nothing could spoil that day for her. Not even when Queenie, a full-grown dog now, barked as they read their vows.

After three years of saving, Tyrone had an astounding $18,000 in his bank account. Mia couldn't believe it, but he showed her his statement. And there it was, in black and white.

Eighteen thousand dollars.

"How'd you save this much money?"

"What do you mean?"

"This is a lot of money."

"I've been saving religiously," he said.

"Fifty dollars a week?"

Tyrone gave her a silly look. "I've been putting in three hundred a week since I started at Auto Boys."

Mia squinted at the digits again. "You had enough to buy me a ring then."

"I told you I did."

"Let's get your shop *first* and see how much we have left," she said with a smile.

Tyrone went out and bought an old-timey filling station with the outdated gas pumps still planted. The first time he rode by and pointed it out to Mia and the kids, TC didn't hold any punches.

"That's ugly."

"We have to clean it up," Tyrone said.

"That will take forever."

"That's why we're starting *now*," Tyrone said. He pulled up to the building, got out, and popped the trunk. Inside, he had trash bags, mops, brooms, buckets, and a lot of soap. Mia stood beside him and surveyed his equipment.

"I hope you've got someone else coming to help," she said. "With just us four, this *will* take forever."

Tyrone laughed. "Yeah. I got some of my homeys coming. They'll be here in a minute."

True to his word, two carloads of the roughest looking thugs you'd ever want to meet converged on the property. Between pulling their pants up, washing paint off of their rings, and talking on their cell phones, Mia didn't think any work would ever get done, but once again her husband knew what he was talking about. In just two weeks TC's Automotive was spic-and-span, freshly painted, and ready for business. Tyrone had his grand opening on a balmy Monday morning.

He came home that first day not in the best of moods.

"We're already in the red," he told his wife over dinner.

"What's wrong?" Mia asked.

"I only had *five* customers all day."

"*Five?* That's a lot," Mia said.

"Not if we're gonna pay off that building."

"You should put ads in the paper," Crystal suggested. "You need to put up fliers, too, at the mall and beauty shops, and at the auto part stores. You can put them anywhere, really, just ask the owner of whatever business you're at."

Tyrone and Mia stopped eating and stared at her with big smiles. "I didn't know Crystal could do all that," he said.

"I didn't either," Mia said. "Wow, Crystal, you'd do all that for us?"

"I love you, sister-in-law," Tyrone said.

"Y'all is corny," Crystal said, but she became their advertising executive anyway. And the fruits of her labors became evident in the very next quarter.

Tyrone went from five cars a day, to ten, to having so many he had to turn away business. His marketing strategy was genius, based on a wonderfully simple motto: *We'll do the work of Auto Boys for half the price.*

Crystal actually printed that on some of the early fliers before Mia made her stop, fearing they would get sued.

"How can you do the same work as Auto Boys and only charge half of what they do?" Crystal asked him one day.

"Simple," Tyrone said, "Auto Boys *overcharges* for everything. It's all a scam. I'm gonna be the only honest mechanic out there."

It sounded too legitimate to work, but Tyrone's strategy of bringing integrity to the auto repair business was effective. Six months in, and TC's Automotive got out of the red. Two months later, Tyrone hired his first employee, a mechanic he knew from ATI. Eleven months into the venture, and Tyrone was able to pay off his building.

He bought another one eight months later.

They didn't purchase the third building for another two years, but it was worth the wait. This one was erected from the ground up. It had a large office and an even larger waiting room. Tyrone had enough bays and parking lot space to work on a dozen cars at the same time.

With three shops in the city, Tyrone was definitely a force to be reckoned with. He had twenty-three employees, serviced over a hundred vehicles a day, and never had to get under any of them, just as Mia said it would one day be. Tyrone bought Mia the biggest rock they had in the jewelry store on the day he went, and even paid for a very, very late honeymoon to the Caribbean Islands. They stayed five wonderful days and four beautiful nights, returning more in love than before they left.

They never teased her, but Crystal never managed to reach the same level of success. Even while witnessing the power of education firsthand, she still dropped out of most of her courses and ended up taking one class a semester again. By the time Tyrone's third shop was being built, Crystal still didn't have enough credits for a two-year degree.

She did manage to find a nerdy boyfriend, however. Crystal swore she would never marry Chad, but she eventually moved into his apartment. Mia was so happy to see her go, she toted three trips worth of Crystal's belongings personally.

Mia went to Claire's one stormy Saturday afternoon. She walked in talking on her cell phone. When she hung up, she sat down in Vasantha's chair with a loud sigh.

"What's wrong?" the stylist asked her.

"I got a flat," Mia said. "Right when I was pulling up."

"That's messed up," Gayle said. "You gonna get out there in that rain, or wait 'til it stops?"

"*I'm* not changing that tire," Mia said.

"Oh, that's right. Your husband owns all those repair shops. Is he gonna come fix it?"

"No. I just talked to him," Mia said. "He said he'd probably send someone."

"Ooh, *big time*," Vasantha said. "He's not going to fix it *hisself,* y'all. He's going to *send someone* over to do it for him."

"You hear that, everybody?" Gayle announced. "We have been blessed by the rich and famous!"

Everyone laughed, but they weren't laughing ten minutes later when a brand new Ford F-350 pulled up behind Mia's Navigator. A brawny, light-skinned gentleman stepped out into the environment as if wasn't even raining and kneeled next to Mia's flat tire. He then went to the back of his truck and hefted a hundred-pound hydraulic jack like it was a bag of potatoes.

"Girl, who is that?" Gayle asked, doing a whole 360 so she could stare out of the front window.

"I don't know," Mia said without looking back.

"He's changing your tire," Gayle said.

"Tyrone's got twenty-five employees," Mia said. "I don't know which one that is."

"But this one is *fine*," Gayle said, causing Vasantha and a few more stylists to turn and look.

"*Ooh*, he is fine," Vasantha said.

Natiesha left her seat in the waiting room to see, and soon there were a dozen or more women at the window.

"Look, girl, he bending," Gayle said to no one in particular. A second later the girls squealed as the mechanic did whatever he was doing back there. Mia was happy with her man, so she was the only one who didn't turn to gawk.

"Look at his *arms*," one woman said.

"Look at his *chest*," said another.

"It's still raining, Mia. You'd better check this out. His shirt is sticking, *ooh*, it's sticking to his body. His pants, too. Look at that ass, y'all."

"Damn, he do got a nice ass," Vasantha said.

Mia did turn to look then. What she saw made a silly grin spread across her face. She turned back in her seat like it was no big deal and listened to the girls ogle her man for another ten minutes, and then Gayle announced, "Okay, y'all, he coming inside!"

Everyone scrambled to their places and almost looked normal by the time Tyrone walked through the front door. He wore blue Dickey pants and a short-sleeved collar shirt that was tucked in. He was completely drenched, which, as Gayle pointed out, made his shirt stick to his body like a second skin. Tyrone had no under-shirt, and Mia could see his nipples clearly through the fabric.

The slight workout had his muscles pumped up to competition level. His chest was like a silverback's. His biceps were like two cantaloupe halves. Fresh rain glis-tened on the waves in his hair like a mystical black beach. His lips were full, and his eyes were the color of a flowing field of wheat.

He scanned the room until his eyes found his bride.

"Baby, you had a nail in there, but I got you taken care of."

"Thanks, Tyrone," Mia said. "You're the best."

Tyrone looked around nervously. "Uh, how you ladies doing?"

"*Heeey*," they all said, almost in unison.

Mia rolled her eyes at them.

"I'll see you later," Tyrone said and turned to leave.

"All right. Be careful out there," Mia said.

When he was gone, all the ladies turned and stared at Mia as if her outfit was made of solid gold.

Mia leaned back in her chair with a smug grin. "Yeah, that's *Tyrone*," she said finally. "And you bitches need to quit eyeballing my husband. Go fix your own man!" The ladies laughed and returned to what they were doing, but a few of them went back to the window anyway to see if Tyrone looked as good going as he did coming.

THE END
BY KEITH WALKER

ABOUT THE AUTHOR

Keith Walker is a graduate of Texas Wesleyan University, where he earned a bachelor's degree in English. He enjoys reading, poetry and music of all genres. He lives in Fort Worth, Texas, with his wife and two children and currently works in administration at one of the city's largest hospitals.

2009 Reprint Mass Market Titles

January

I'm Gonna Make You Love Me
Gwyneth Bolton
ISBN-13: 978-1-58571-294-6
$6.99

Shades of Desire
Monica White
ISBN-13: 978-1-58571-292-2
$6.99

February

A Love of Her Own
Cheris Hodges
ISBN-13: 978-1-58571-293-9
$6.99

Color of Trouble
Dyanne Davis
ISBN-13: 978-1-58571-294-6
$6.99

March

Twist of Fate
Beverly Clark
ISBN-13: 978-1-58571-295-3
$6.99

Chances
Pamela Leigh Starr
ISBN-13: 978-1-58571-296-0
$6.99

April

Sinful Intentions
Crystal Rhodes
ISBN-13: 978-1-585712-297-7
$6.99

Rock Star
Roslyn Hardy Holcomb
ISBN-13: 978-1-58571-298-4
$6.99

May

Paths of Fire
T.T. Henderson
ISBN-13: 978-1-58571-343-1
$6.99

Caught Up in the Rapture
Lisa Riley
ISBN-13: 978-1-58571-344-8
$6.99

June

Reckless Surrender
Rochelle Alers
ISBN-13: 978-1-58571-345-5
$6.99

No Ordinary Love
Angela Weaver
ISBN-13: 978-1-58571-346-2
$6.99

2009 Reprint Mass Market Titles (continued)

July

Intentional Mistakes
Michele Sudler
ISBN-13: 978-1-58571-347-9
$6.99

It's In His Kiss
Reon Carter
ISBN-13: 978-1-58571-348-6
$6.99

August

Unfinished Love Affair
Barbara Keaton
ISBN-13: 978-1-58571-349-3
$6.99

A Perfect Place to Pray
I.L Goodwin
ISBN-13: 978-1-58571-299-1
$6.99

September

Love in High Gear
Charlotte Roy
ISBN-13: 978-1-58571-355-4
$6.99

Ebony Eyes
Kei Swanson
ISBN-13: 978-1-58571-356-1
$6.99

October

Midnight Clear, Part I
Leslie Esdale/Carmen Green
ISBN-13: 978-1-58571-357-8
$6.99

Midnight Clear, Part II
Gwynne Forster/Monica
  Jackson
ISBN-13: 978-1-58571-358-5
$6.99

November

Midnight Peril
Vicki Andrews
ISBN-13: 978-1-58571-359-2
$6.99

One Day At A Time
Bella McFarland
ISBN-13: 978-1-58571-360-8
$6.99

December

Just An Affair
Eugenia O'Neal
ISBN-13: 978-1-58571-361-5
$6.99

Shades of Brown
Denise Becker
ISBN-13: 978-1-58571-362-2
$6.99

2009 New Mass Market Titles

January

Singing A Song...
Crystal Rhodes
ISBN-13: 978-1-58571-283-0
$6.99

Look Both Ways
Joan Early
ISBN-13: 978-1-58571-284-7
$6.99

February

Six O'Clock
Katrina Spencer
ISBN-13: 978-1-58571-285-4
$6.99

Red Sky
Renee Alexis
ISBN-13: 978-1-58571-286-1
$6.99

March

Anything But Love
Celya Bowers
ISBN-13: 978-1-58571-287-8
$6.99

Tempting Faith
Crystal Hubbard
ISBN-13: 978-1-58571-288-5
$6.99

April

If I Were Your Woman
La Connie Taylor-Jones
ISBN-13: 978-1-58571-289-2
$6.99

Best Of Luck Elsewhere
Trisha Haddad
ISBN-13: 978-1-58571-290-8
$6.99

May

All I'll Ever Need
Mildred Riley
ISBN-13: 978-1-58571-335-6
$6.99

A Place Like Home
Alicia Wiggins
ISBN-13: 978-1-58571-336-3
$6.99

June

Best Foot Forward
Michele Sudler
ISBN-13: 978-1-58571-337-0
$6.99

It's In the Rhythm
Sammie Ward
ISBN-13: 978-1-58571-338-7
$6.99

2009 New Mass Market Titles (continued)

July

Checks and Balances
Elaine Sims
ISBN-13: 978-1-58571-339-4
$6.99

Save Me
Africa Fine
ISBN-13: 978-1-58571-340-0
$6.99

August

When Lightening Strikes
Michele Cameron
ISBN-13: 978-1-58571-369-1
$6.99

Blindsided
Tammy Williams
ISBN-13: 978-1-58571-342-4
$6.99

September

2 Good
Celya Bowers
ISBN-13: 978-1-58571-350-9
$6.99

Waiting for Mr. Darcy
Chamein Canton
ISBN-13: 978-1-58571-351-6
$6.99

October

Fireflies
Joan Early
ISBN-13: 978-1-58571-352-3
$6.99

Frost On My Window
Angela Weaver
ISBN-13: 978-1-58571-353-0
$6.99

November

Waiting in the Shadows
Michele Sudler
ISBN-13: 978-1-58571-364-6
$6.99

Fixin' Tyrone
Keith Walker
ISBN-13: 978-1-58571-365-3
$6.99

December

Dream Keeper
Gail McFarland
ISBN-13: 978-1-58571-366-0
$6.99

Another Memory
Pamela Ridley
ISBN-13: 978-1-58571-367-7
$6.99

Other Genesis Press, Inc. Titles

Other Genesis Press, Inc. Titles (continued)

Other Genesis Press, Inc. Titles (continued)

Ebony Angel	Deatri King-Bey	$9.95
Ebony Butterfly II	Delilah Dawson	$14.95
Echoes of Yesterday	Beverly Clark	$9.95
Eden's Garden	Elizabeth Rose	$8.95
Eve's Prescription	Edwina Martin Arnold	$8.95
Everlastin' Love	Gay G. Gunn	$8.95
Everlasting Moments	Dorothy Elizabeth Love	$8.95
Everything and More	Sinclair Lebeau	$8.95
Everything but Love	Natalie Dunbar	$8.95
Falling	Natalie Dunbar	$9.95
Fate	Pamela Leigh Starr	$8.95
Finding Isabella	A.J. Garrotto	$8.95
Forbidden Quest	Dar Tomlinson	$10.95
Forever Love	Wanda Y. Thomas	$8.95
From the Ashes	Kathleen Suzanne	$8.95
	Jeanne Sumerix	
Gentle Yearning	Rochelle Alers	$10.95
Glory of Love	Sinclair LeBeau	$10.95
Go Gentle into that Good Night	Malcom Boyd	$12.95
Goldengroove	Mary Beth Craft	$16.95
Groove, Bang, and Jive	Steve Cannon	$8.99
Hand in Glove	Andrea Jackson	$9.95
Hard to Love	Kimberley White	$9.95
Hart & Soul	Angie Daniels	$8.95
Heart of the Phoenix	A.C. Arthur	$9.95
Heartbeat	Stephanie Bedwell-Grime	$8.95
Hearts Remember	M. Loui Quezada	$8.95
Hidden Memories	Robin Allen	$10.95
Higher Ground	Leah Latimer	$19.95
Hitler, the War, and the Pope	Ronald Rychiak	$26.95
How to Write a Romance	Kathryn Falk	$18.95
I Married a Reclining Chair	Lisa M. Fuhs	$8.95
I'll Be Your Shelter	Giselle Carmichael	$8.95
I'll Paint a Sun	A.J. Garrotto	$9.95

Other Genesis Press, Inc. Titles (continued)

Icie	Pamela Leigh Starr	$8.95
Illusions	Pamela Leigh Starr	$8.95
Indigo After Dark Vol. I	Nia Dixon/Angelique	$10.95
Indigo After Dark Vol. II	Dolores Bundy/ Cole Riley	$10.95
Indigo After Dark Vol. III	Montana Blue/ Coco Morena	$10.95
Indigo After Dark Vol. IV	Cassandra Colt/	$14.95
Indigo After Dark Vol. V	Delilah Dawson	$14.95
Indiscretions	Donna Hill	$8.95
Intentional Mistakes	Michele Sudler	$9.95
Interlude	Donna Hill	$8.95
Intimate Intentions	Angie Daniels	$8.95
It's Not Over Yet	J.J. Michael	$9.95
Jolie's Surrender	Edwina Martin-Arnold	$8.95
Kiss or Keep	Debra Phillips	$8.95
Lace	Giselle Carmichael	$9.95
Lady Preacher	K.T. Richey	$6.99
Last Train to Memphis	Elsa Cook	$12.95
Lasting Valor	Ken Olsen	$24.95
Let Us Prey	Hunter Lundy	$25.95
Lies Too Long	Pamela Ridley	$13.95
Life Is Never As It Seems	J.J. Michael	$12.95
Lighter Shade of Brown	Vicki Andrews	$8.95
Looking for Lily	Africa Fine	$6.99
Love Always	Mildred E. Riley	$10.95
Love Doesn't Come Easy	Charlyne Dickerson	$8.95
Love Unveiled	Gloria Greene	$10.95
Love's Deception	Charlene Berry	$10.95
Love's Destiny	M. Loui Quezada	$8.95
Love's Secrets	Yolanda McVey	$6.99
Mae's Promise	Melody Walcott	$8.95
Magnolia Sunset	Giselle Carmichael	$8.95
Many Shades of Gray	Dyanne Davis	$6.99
Matters of Life and Death	Lesego Malepe, Ph.D.	$15.95

Other Genesis Press, Inc. Titles (continued)

Other Genesis Press, Inc. Titles (continued)

Peace Be Still	Colette Haywood	$12.95
Picture Perfect	Reon Carter	$8.95
Playing for Keeps	Stephanie Salinas	$8.95
Pride & Joi	Gay G. Gunn	$8.95
Promises Made	Bernice Layton	$6.99
Promises to Keep	Alicia Wiggins	$8.95
Quiet Storm	Donna Hill	$10.95
Reckless Surrender	Rochelle Alers	$6.95
Red Polka Dot in a World of Plaid	Varian Johnson	$12.95
Reluctant Captive	Joyce Jackson	$8.95
Rendezvous with Fate	Jeanne Sumerix	$8.95
Revelations	Cheris F. Hodges	$8.95
Rivers of the Soul	Leslie Esdaile	$8.95
Rocky Mountain Romance	Kathleen Suzanne	$8.95
Rooms of the Heart	Donna Hill	$8.95
Rough on Rats and Tough on Cats	Chris Parker	$12.95
Secret Library Vol. 1	Nina Sheridan	$18.95
Secret Library Vol. 2	Cassandra Colt	$8.95
Secret Thunder	Annetta P. Lee	$9.95
Shades of Brown	Denise Becker	$8.95
Shades of Desire	Monica White	$8.95
Shadows in the Moonlight	Jeanne Sumerix	$8.95
Sin	Crystal Rhodes	$8.95
Small Whispers	Annetta P. Lee	$6.99
So Amazing	Sinclair LeBeau	$8.95
Somebody's Someone	Sinclair LeBeau	$8.95
Someone to Love	Alicia Wiggins	$8.95
Song in the Park	Martin Brant	$15.95
Soul Eyes	Wayne L. Wilson	$12.95
Soul to Soul	Donna Hill	$8.95
Southern Comfort	J.M. Jeffries	$8.95
Southern Fried Standards	S.R. Maddox	$6.99
Still the Storm	Sharon Robinson	$8.95

Other Genesis Press, Inc. Titles (continued)

Other Genesis Press, Inc. Titles (continued)

Tiger Woods	Libby Hughes	$5.95
Time is of the Essence	Angie Daniels	$9.95
Timeless Devotion	Bella McFarland	$9.95
Tomorrow's Promise	Leslie Esdaile	$8.95
Truly Inseparable	Wanda Y. Thomas	$8.95
Two Sides to Every Story	Dyanne Davis	$9.95
Unbreak My Heart	Dar Tomlinson	$8.95
Uncommon Prayer	Kenneth Swanson	$9.95
Unconditional Love	Alicia Wiggins	$8.95
Unconditional	A.C. Arthur	$9.95
Undying Love	Renee Alexis	$6.99
Until Death Do Us Part	Susan Paul	$8.95
Vows of Passion	Bella McFarland	$9.95
Wedding Gown	Dyanne Davis	$8.95
What's Under Benjamin's Bed	Sandra Schaffer	$8.95
When A Man Loves A Woman	La Connie Taylor-Jones	$6.99
When Dreams Float	Dorothy Elizabeth Love	$8.95
When I'm With You	LaConnie Taylor-Jones	$6.99
Where I Want To Be	Maryam Diaab	$6.99
Whispers in the Night	Dorothy Elizabeth Love	$8.95
Whispers in the Sand	LaFlorya Gauthier	$10.95
Who's That Lady?	Andrea Jackson	$9.95
Wild Ravens	Altonya Washington	$9.95
Yesterday Is Gone	Beverly Clark	$10.95
Yesterday's Dreams, Tomorrow's Promises	Reon Laudat	$8.95
Your Precious Love	Sinclair LeBeau	$8.95

Order Form

Mail to: Genesis Press, Inc.
P.O. Box 101
Columbus, MS 39703

Name _____
Address _____
City/State _____ Zip _____
Telephone _____

Ship to (if different from above)
Name _____
Address _____
City/State _____ Zip _____
Telephone _____

Credit Card Information
Credit Card # _____ ☐ Visa ☐ Mastercard
Expiration Date (mm/yy) _____ ☐ AmEx ☐ Discover

Qty.	Author	Title	Price	Total

Use this order form, or call
1-888-INDIGO-1

Total for books _____
Shipping and handling:
  $5 first two books,
  $1 each additional book _____
Total S & H _____
Total amount enclosed _____
Mississippi residents add 7% sales tax